VALLEY OF PROGRESS

GORAKA

2

Cory Sheldon

GORAKA
VALLEY OF PROGRESS
BOOK 2

Copyright © 2022 by Cory Sheldon

Published by Ooi Iro

Illustrations by Cory Sheldon
Edited by Lauren Folk
Layout by Melissa Olson

Library of Congress Control Number: 2022907197

ISBN 978-0-9975692-6-1

www.valleyofprogress.com
twitter @valleyprogress
www.corysheldoncreative.com

FIRST EDITION

In Memory of Rob Lucas

Friend
Dreamer
Thinker
Believer

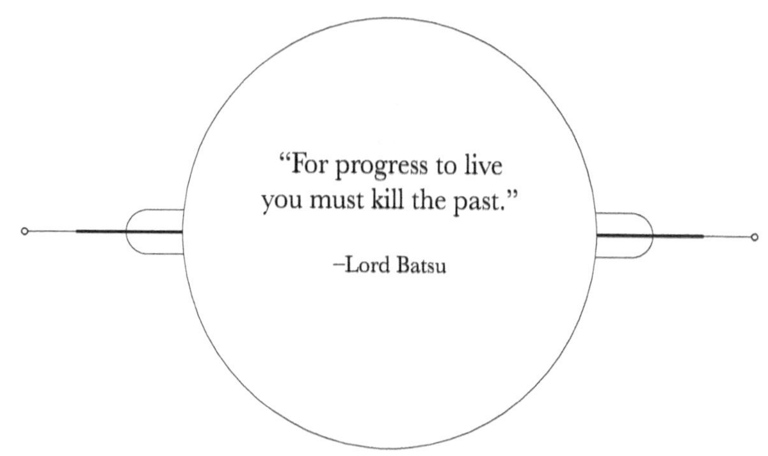

"For progress to live
you must kill the past."

–Lord Batsu

1
PEST

Dark silhouettes floated through the warm sun as it shimmered off the water. Boats sat on the perfectly symmetrical lake, supporting the people that had created them both. Families laughed the day away, their voices bouncing across liquid glass. The destination had become a haven away from the bustling downtown, a place where briefcases were swapped for picnic baskets. The vista perfectly resembled countless paintings one would see in cafés—fitting, as there were at least six artists with their easels up on the dam wall. A single young Lady wearing all black sat on the edge. The entire scene made her want to vomit.

The beauty of placid leisure didn't disgust her, and although she acted indifferently, jealousy smoldered deep within. Her nausea came from the grotesque obstruction she sat on—a river-plug collecting all the pollution that floated down from Primichi. The water, with its fleshy, fancily dressed bugs, sat behind five million tons of concrete that her parents had died trying to prevent. The patrons enjoyed their fabricated reservoir posing as something natural as the sludge conveniently hid below the surface.

Suzu made a habit of visiting the Long Frost Dam, always by herself and never telling anyone. She'd sit at the edge and imagine her lost parents there next to her. Looking into the water, she'd convince herself their reflection was just out of sight. Her father, Carmin, would talk about how much energy his design produced, while her mother, Kiara, would go on and on about the toxic mass growing below their feet. Then she'd say something like, *I hate to admit it, but it does look beautiful at sunset. Maybe we should get a little boat, I'll bake some pastries, and then we can paint protest art on the inlet pipe.*

The sound of cheap shoes then dragged behind her. Suzu then heard a mess of metal and wood tumble to the concrete. She didn't bother to look—probably another sloppy artist or lazy fisherman. The noise stopped, and she could feel the invader's stare interrupt her afternoon of natural beauty and industrial abominations. Her head lowered a few degrees, allowing angled bangs to shield her eyes.

"I'd bet you must be the saddest person at the dam." The voice begged for attention.

Suzu'd bet he was a creep.

The voice continued, "What's the matter? Doesn't this giant fake lake just make you want to fake smile all day?"

The cynicism intrigued her. She turned her head just enough to allow her eyes to appear. A messy beard nearly hid what certainly looked like the smile of a creep, making the young man appear deceptively old. Likewise, his outfit looked proudly jumbled together. Suzu noticed a fishing pole dangling a fat weight. "Isn't that ball a little big for that stick?"

"You know a lot about fishing?" the man asked.

"No, but I can tell it looks funny," Suzu countered before looking back at the perfect, floating families.

The man continued assembling his disproportioned angler's rig before lowering it down the dam and into the water. "So, did you look that depressed when you came here, or is the place *where progress finds peace* having the opposite effect on you?"

An image sprang into Suzu's mind, a painfully pleasant advertisement luring families towards the relatively new recreation area. A stoic father smiled down on his flawless family while cruising in a small, steam-powered Aya-Precision personal watercraft. The company name made her think of Jin, which made her think of Nia and death and how unfair life was. The advertisement also showed a statuesque mother—whose hair somehow seemed impervious to the wind—gazing at two kids with jaw-breaking circus smiles. Above it, bold and colorful type proclaimed the biggest lie she had ever read: *Long Frost Reservoir, Where Progress Finds Peace.*

"I wouldn't eat any fish near this dam if I were you. This thing is collecting all the industrial junk Primichi pukes into the river," Suzu offered.

"Well, well. Looks like we have a little Soran princess keeping guard at the lake. How lucky we are to have you."

Suzu turned her head, whipping back the veil of hair. "People have died trying to stop the destruction of this land. You shouldn't use that word if you don't value it."

"Hey, little girl, I know more about being a Soran than—" and with that, a mutual realization hit them. The fog of an idea started to coalesce—a memory that one had nearly forgotten while the other painfully refused to let go. "Hey... no, wait, it can't be."

Suzu gave her attention back to the little boats. She could sense the man lose all interest in fishing, instead leaning down to get a better look at her. She leaned away.

"I must say, I certainly never thought I'd see you again. You look... different, but it's you. I don't forget a face easily, especially not the daughter of Kiara Komou."

Despite having no interest in discussing her family history, Suzu remembered the man and the name: Mouba. Her parents had mentioned him more than once in arguments over ideology and risks. By the time she finally met him, he already stood for the worst parts of what people called *Sorans*—environmentalists so extreme in their views they completely forgot, or detested, that humans were also a part of nature.

Mouba kept staring until even an imbecile would have realized Suzu had no interest in discussing the matter. "Man oh man. Well, I can't blame you for not wanting to talk about it. Glad to see you're carrying on the family spirit though... not turning into a Tasi."

Being short and an orphan, Suzu typically stood on guard against names and patronizing remarks. She cast Mouba a hard glare at the vaguely familiar word. "What's a Tasi?"

"You don't know?" Mouba said smugly. "I thought you would have heard the story of Lord Boro, the great founding farmer of The Valley. Came here with Lord Batsu, founded Primichi...

spark an engine for you there?"

"Yes," Suzu spit out. "My mom was a teacher and my dad was an engineer. You think I didn't learn Valley History?"

"Okay, Lady Suzu." Mouba took a step back, went back to fishing, and began to whistle.

"I'm just not good with names." Suzu found the off-key melody decidedly worse than the story. "So... who or what is a Tasi?"

"It's okay to be forgetful. Tasi was this young dandy from Meijune who visited with some fancy food he wanted to impress Boro with. Problem was, the food had parasites that caused an infection on the farm. It spread fast and nearly wiped out all of Primichi's crops."

"Yes, yes, I remember," Suzu cut in. "Thanks for thinking I don't spread parasites around. You're so sweet."

"Don't mention it," Mouba said, getting back to fishing. "Raka Nusan is coming up too, but certainly you'd remember a day that important."

Having heard of Raka Nusan from her parents, Suzu got up and abandoned the unsolicited history lesson. She managed two steps when Mouba flung one last thought.

"Hey, Lady Suzu."

Slowing down but not stopping, Suzu offered half a glance. "What?"

"Sorry about your mom. She was a real believer, a real fighter."

Suzu finally stopped, meditating on the spoken truth few people seemed to know, but his thought was incomplete.

"They *both* were."

Long Frost
Reservoir
Where Progress Finds Peace

2
CAMPER

The endless tunnel of green and brown blurred by. His lungs ached from the uphill sprint that stretched into a marathon; he couldn't remember where it had begun. Every stride felt desperate, heavy with the burden of sensing tragedy nearby. He knew he had to continue, and that his body would eventually fail.

His heart revved towards cardiac arrest as the red blur shot past him. He heard only the infinite pummeling of branches and his dying breaths. The crimson ghost circled him. How could something as large as himself move that quickly in near silence? Muscles ached as he reached behind his back, grasping for his Masu, but the retractable sword was gone. Desperation consumed him. Burning fatigue proclaimed his imminent death.

A burst of light burned his eyes, complementing his scorched throat. The trees had cleared away as the hill turned into a field of wild grass. Upwards, a fog hid the remaining mountain. His focus then dropped onto a darker shape—a pair sitting with their backs to him, stealing attention away from the crimson predator.

Dire determination dragged his numb body up the hill. The couple slid into focus, revealing gray hair and clothes older than him. Wrinkled hands were held together below hanging heads.

Suddenly, a wind charged in. The tall grass bent forward as he felt the air sucking everything in towards the couple. A dissonant whine emerged through the torrent. Slowly, its volume grew into a horrible cry. He tried to cover his ears but needed his arms to balance. The volume erupted as their faces finally turned, "Jin, why did you let our daughter die? Jin, why did you let our daughter die…"

"Jin!"

Bright eyes flew open as the young man shot up. Jin grabbed onto the door handle, gasping for twice the air his lungs would allow.

"You okay?" Gozen asked doubtfully.

"Yes, Lord Gozen. Of course. Just a bewildering daydream is all."

Considering their destination, Gozen felt more than a little concerned about his partner's unsettled state. He eased up on Neko's throttle, quieting the truck's cabin. "Seemed more nightmare than bewildering daydream."

Jin aligned his white scarf and dark gray vest. "Oh, well, yes. Perhaps a bit eldritch, especially for one so far from childhood," he confessed, "but I assure you, I am steadfast."

"Because I don't want you to feel forced to do this if you're not ready, for whatever reason."

Pedestrians glanced up to Gozen's massive truck as Jin leaned his head on the window. "I have committed to this course, and I am fully prepared to continue towards its conclusion, whatever that may be."

Jin had confidence like gold chain on a jeweler's spool—simple, gilded, and endless. Gozen didn't understand it, but he had come to accept it.

"Alright," he answered, putting weight back on the pedal. The truck sped up towards west IQ, a nearly forgotten part of Industrial Quarter—perfectly suited for the kind of operation their tipoff suggested. Subtly, Jin reached behind his back, checking to make sure his Masu still sat firmly on his belt.

The glimmer of downtown eventually shifted into the dark, soot-stained walls of southern Chigou. It still felt foreign to the Aya heir. If any black-hand saw him, they would assume him to be either lost or searching for something illegal, but such was the plan that day.

To Gozen, the neighborhood felt both familiar and painful— the center of his jurisdiction as a Lord Enforcer—and their current task felt like old business. He hoped the information proved good, and that they'd go in smart and get out fast. He should have taken the intel straight to a CE Depot, but he liked to chomp before things got cold.

Gozen slowed down, identifying the decrepit sign pretending to offer Primichi-style noodles and cheap smoked coffee. The dirty, rusted storefront looked as if it hadn't housed a business transaction in a decade. Everything matched up. Gozen knew what they sold inside, and it wasn't lunch.

He glanced over to Jin, who looked focused, or bored; he could never tell the difference. "Remember, you need to see them in person; a promise is worthless. And if you can get a photo, even better, but don't push it."

"Gozen," Jin said, shifting the tone, "did you ever take civilians on missions when you were a Lord Enforcer?"

"Absolutely not," Gozen responded. "Well, good luck, and if I don't see you in ten, I'm coming in."

With that, Jin stepped out of Neko and walked up to the door. He wondered why the proprietors wouldn't appropriately service the primary entrance to their establishment. Not a very convincing false front. He grabbed the rotted door handle and entered.

Inside, his eyes needed to adjust. A few lights, some of them working, were scattered around the room and he wondered how a bulb could glow so dimly. The interior design stood between cozy-futurist and derelict. A man, paying him no attention, sat at a counter across from who Jin assumed to be the cook. Jin approached the counter looking like a misplaced dandy.

"We don't serve Shumé or Sanamée here, Lord, so don't ask," the cook suggested, eliciting a snicker from the other customer. Sanamée was lightly smoked and salted fish eggs, considered an impractical delicacy by any commoner.

"I didn't assume this establishment would have achieved certification to serve such an item, but I appreciate the information," Jin stated.

The cook dropped his smirk and stepped over. "You're lost. If you don't want to stay that way, I suggest you turn back towards the shimmer and walk."

"I don't believe I am misplaced…"

Another, much larger man appeared from a doorway. A long greasy beard revealed teeth like overripe corn. With arms crossed over a puffed chest, the man stared straight at Jin, who finished, "… not misplaced at all. I am looking for resources. Small, versatile, and easy to manage."

The bearded man looked over Jin's shoulder to see the front of Neko's cab through the window. "That's a pretty big vehicle. Just how much are you looking for?"

Jin responded without hesitation. "All that you have available."

The cook's hands slid below the stained counter. The request sounded too big, too vague. "And you have that kind of money?"

Reaching into a vest so finely crafted it nearly answered the question, Jin pulled out a tightly bundled stack of new currency. "I have much more money than time."

Everyone looked at it like a hot steak, even Snicker down at the end of the bar.

"Or am I simply lost?" Jin asked, channeling bravado from his favorite character in the crime series *Dark Nights, Bright City.*

The cook finally stood upright and gave a nod to the larger man. "Show him what we got."

Jin followed the bearded hulk down a hallway. It stretched on and on like the architect had forgotten to end it. A buzzing light accompanied their hike. Eventually, they reached a stairway, and the guide had to turn his body to squeeze down. As they descended deeper into darkness, an acrid musk made Jin cough. The guide glared back at his delicate customer. They passed a door, cracked open with yellow light pouring out, but they did not pause.

The journey dead-ended at a single, heavy door; Jin noticed an oversized lock peculiarly placed on the outside. Standing to the side as much as his thick torso would allow, the bearded man opened the door. Somehow even dirtier than upstairs, the floor faded into blackness.

"Stand up," he ordered into the dark room while keeping his gaze on Jin. Fidgeting with his scarf, Jin felt sweat soaking through his clothes. His eyes finally adjusted to the darkness and realized the man waited not for his action, but his reaction.

Scattered amongst mattresses and random dishes, twenty-five children struggled to get onto their stained feet.

Jin had underestimated the sight and his poker face cracked. Small, sallow faces silently begged for hope. He tried to act discerning, appearing to evaluate merchandise, but even fabricating such a thought made it worse. Filth filled every crack of the decaying, concrete room and he wondered how the children hadn't died from disease. A few tattered toys filled out the dungeon masquerading as a bedroom. He thought of his childhood home—a Bokai-wood playroom built just for him.

"Well, you still want all of 'em?" The deep voice slithered out from behind him.

Jin's calculated response emerged as a squeak, feebly hidden with a cough. "Certainly," he finally mustered.

Guiding him back out, Jin's escort shut the door. The lock's heavy clang hit Jin in the gut. The bearded man walked him back to the cracked door they'd passed earlier. He stayed behind while pushing Jin through. The room looked bright only relative to the surrounding gloom. A portable copper heater buzzed in the back next to a cheap wood desk. It obscured a man wearing wireframe glasses set under greasy, combed hair. The man's eyes, enlarged through thick lenses, jumped around, scanning the suspiciously dapper guest.

"Who's this?" he asked the bearded guard by the door.

"He wants to buy 'em. Dien sent him through."

The man's chair released an awful creak as he leaned back. For an instant, Jin pondered which lubricant would best recondition the joint. Finally, the man spoke to him. "Okay, so I assume you have the funds. How many do you want?"

"I will take all of them." Jin settled back into the roleplay.

With an ambiguous expression, the man responded, "*All* of them?"

"Yes. I could not state my request with any less complexity."

The man peered longer as if trying to decipher something. "Okay. That's twenty-five little worker bees in there. You're going to pay up and walk out with all of them, right now? And then... do what with them, exactly?"

Gozen had discussed with him the idea of a rescue but had concluded such an action was too risky and legally complex. The mission had been to identify and retrieve evidence… just evidence.

"I had hoped to take a photo so I could make final arrangements, but I can pay now." Jin began to find his own words dubious.

"A photo." The man's voice dropped. Again, another check with the Sentinel by the door. "You don't look like our usual clientele."

Jin looked down at his vest with its eight-hundred thread count. "You shouldn't be bothered by my wealth."

"Oh, I'm not." The man sat back. "But even a delusional rich boy—whatever-the-hell he had in mind—wouldn't come in here asking for a basement full of children, pay in full, and then gladly walk away with only a photograph. So, I'm going to need a little more. Who are you and what do you need all of *those* for," he said with a gesture down the hall.

Having failed to do so prior, Jin silently formulated a more detailed alias. Heavy footsteps approached from behind in a failed attempt at stealth. Jin's muscles tightened. He looked back. The guard reached for something in a jacket pocket, perfectly playing the oaf in a self-defense class. Ready to excise his odium towards these predators, Jin allowed honed instinct to take over.

The guard flinched as Jin grabbed his wrist. The brute had ample strength to pull away, but Jin's speed made the factor irrelevant. A flash of clenched fingers struck the man's thick throat, causing his entire body to lock up. On the next beat, Jin swung his foot up and kicked the guard squarely in the jaw, promptly dropping him to the ground.

Jin spun around as the other man fumbled inside a desk drawer—for a weapon no doubt. Jin reached back, extended his razor-sharp Masu, and threw it straight at the man. It stuck dead center into the desktop as if rehearsed for a circus show.

The man jumped back, shocked at the sight of a sword plunged into the spot his writing hand typically sat. Below it, his gun sat in the now-open drawer. He lunged for it right as Jin pulled on a thin, high-tensile wire attached to the sword, causing the desk to flip back. With a sharp clank, the gun landed by Jin's feet. The bearded guard moaned on the ground.

With a calmness that suddenly seemed far more terrifying than confusing, Jin walked up to the overturned desk. The accountant awkwardly tried to step back where his hand sizzled against the cheap space heater. Jin's fingers gripped the Masu like a steel claw and yanked it out of the desk. "Come here."

The man stayed put, cradling a burnt fist.

"Come over here," Jin again requested, "and put your hand on the desk."

With giant eyes now flooding with terror, the man cowered against the wall, shaking his head. Wanting to get things over with as soon as possible, Jin leaned into the red glow of the floor heater.

"You understand that I could kill you right now if I so choose. So, I'm going to request one last time that you put your hand on the desk."

o o o

A line of Civil Enforcer Voikatsues were parked outside the dilapidated facade. Flashing red light filled the street. The cook remained handcuffed to a broken streetlight while two CEs grilled him.

Gozen watched the scene shrink away in the rearview mirror. "There should have been more kids."

Jin came up from the trailer, drying his clean hands. "Excuse me, Lord Gozen?"

Gozen tucked the nagging thought away. "How are they?"

"I'm having trouble evaluating their body language as a whole, but they seem to be acclimating. Three of them are asleep on your bed," Jin reported, referring to the small cabin Gozen had built between Neko's cab and trailer.

"You know, Jin, the reason I sent you in there instead of me was so money would persuade them instead of brute force."

"Things..." Jin struggled to make a conclusive evaluation. "...I'm not sure what precisely happened, if I may be wholly transparent. I had assumed a more focused state going in, but my physiological composure started to wane at some point. I need to meditate on that."

"Nothing like a good meditation after a raid."

"What was that?"

"You handled yourself well," Gozen offered, still not entirely sure why the young man wasn't spending nights with actresses in his private palace. It made little sense, but he had developed a fondness for their odd dynamic.

"And did you say you put that guy's hand on a desk and threatened to cut it off?"

"No," Jin corrected. "Rather, his hand was pinned between the desk and my retracted Masu, like this"—he pantomimed the action—"and I simply threatened to remove one of his fingers."

"Jin, that's ghastly," Gozen winced. "Do you train like that for ma..." He could never remember the word.

"Maiishi? Certainly not. Maiishi is discerning and noble. *That* scenario derived from a play I performed in at Primichi First Academy, a rather unsavory crime drama that jolted my mother, but my sister seemed rather entertained by my dastardly portrayal. I calculated such roleplay to be appropriate, given the environment."

"Hmm," Gozen mumbled to himself. "Civilians on a raid."

Driving north, they both noticed how every child along the sidewalk looked up to Neko as it passed by. No matter which corner of Chigou they came from, children became enamored by the massive, uniquely designed truck. The wearied children inside remained quiet as they traveled north, finally stopping at the Tree House orphanage. Gozen knew it didn't have the room, but Lady Kyoumére seemed capable of conjuring miracles for lost children.

At the sight of Neko, Lady Kyoumére promptly glided to the front porch. She looked like a painting, glowing and beautiful. Whenever she and Gozen met, their hearts would warm, anticipating a brief sanctuary of smoked coffee and grown-up conversation.

"Brief the little ones back there, would you?" Gozen called back to Jin.

Gozen got out and Suzu's voice materialized out of nowhere. He turned and saw her running down the drive—the first time he'd seen her in weeks. She slid to a stop, kicking up a cloud of dust.

"Hey, big guy. Looks like I made it just in time."

Gozen waved his hands towards the porch; sanctuary would need to wait a minute. "Thanks for helping tonight. This is too many kids for the Tree House."

"Yeah, I saw the wire at Lucette's. How many little pistons did you find?" Suzu then noticed a Charban coffee flask on the dash, fancier than even the one her father had owned. "Ugh, is Jin here?"

"He lives here. Remember?" Gozen skipped the invitation for drama. "I brought some extra fruit from Kora. We can store it in the pantry; they'll need it."

Suzu jumped down and emphatically crossed her arms. "Why are you hanging out with him? You know he told Kits I was looking for him."

"I certainly hope you're not blaming him for that night, which I'm not in a mood to discuss." He hadn't had that nightmare— watching Suzu murdered in an alley the moment before he arrived—in a month.

"He just makes everything worse. Isn't it tiring dealing with the rich-boy-adventure-fantasy he tries to get everyone—"

Gozen cut off her rant. "I'm sorry, Suzu. Are you offended that I don't hate him?"

A variety of responses stuck in her mouth.

"You and me and Jin are not currently important," Gozen began, pointing around. "Now, can you please go grab that crate of nutritious fruit and help with the twenty-five starving children I just dumped on Lady Kyoumére?"

"If I run into Jin, I'm not talking to him."

"I'm not concerned either way," Gozen answered while shutting the door. "And see if any of the kids know their home address."

Suzu grabbed the fruit and went into the kitchen where she found Lady Kyoumére making coffee for Jin. "I guess his butler never showed him how to smoke coffee," she muttered before escaping to the upstairs pantry.

After pouring the grounds and water in, Lady Kyoumére struggled to get the smoker started. "I apologize, Lord Jin, this thing seems to be slipping out of order recently."

"No apology necessary, Lady Kyoumére. I'm sure you have

more pressing responsibilities at the moment," Jin responded.

"Not a problem whatsoever. The other children do well with new guests. It is a commission I maintain here. Also, I'm rather in the mood for a cup myself." She walked back to the stove. "I suppose a pot and strainer will have to do."

Just then, one of the older children came into the kitchen with a crooked lip. "Lady Kyoumére?"

"Yes, dear," she responded, transferring the coffee ingredients to more humble equipment.

"We're out of beds." The child sounded apologetic. "And mattresses."

With a sigh, Lady K looked around, searching for an answer. She saw the semi-functioning pantry that Jin had been sleeping in ever since he had returned from his fateful trip to Goraka. Her look lasted long enough for Jin to anticipate the suggestion.

"Lord Jin, I hate to ask this of you—"

"No, of course. It would be imprudent for me not to…" As Jin relinquished his pantry bedroom, Darou stepped into the kitchen.

"Oh, *you're* here," Darou offered coldly. Despite living across the street from each other, differing schedules prevented nearly all interactions.

"Darou?" Lady Kyoumére prompted Darou to correct his etiquette.

Interested in neither arguing nor apologizing, he turned and walked back out of the kitchen.

"We will see to it, thank you, Olette." Lady K finally responded to the child messenger. "And Jin, I apologize for Darou's manners."

"Oh, Lady Kyoumére, you certainly owe me no such thing. Your unending grace is a gift I count myself favored to…" Jin nearly fell as the edge of the kitchen island he leaned on snapped right off.

"Oh dear," Lady K gasped out, rather embarrassed. "Let us convene to the dining room, shall we?"

Jin looked down at the broken wood, splintered across cracked floorboards. He recalled how rarely he had spent any time in kitchens back home, or with those tasked with feeding his family.

After Lady K turned off the stove, Jin helped transport the improvised coffee to the dining room.

As it was the only room in the orphanage that looked impervious to its horde of children, Lady Kyoumére considered it as an oasis of refinement. The wooden floor had a luxurious softness, surrounded by impressive, heavy wood panels and molding.

High on the wall, a pair of wooden training Masus hung next to an oil painting. Jin walked up, captivated by both. "I am surprised I never asked before, but do you practice Maiishi?"

"You flatter my faint athleticism," Lady K responded. "The previous owner seemed rather devoted, however. I asked if he wanted the swords, but he insisted on leaving them behind, along with almost everything else. Strange but fascinating man. On the day he handed over the keys, I saw him staring into that painting, just like you are now."

In the painting, sunlight shined down across a colossal funnel of ice, creating a striking wedge of illumination. It collected into a blinding pool of light next to a small island of green, set like an emerald in the mountain.

"It appears to be Kuitsu," Jin observed. "A rather precious place to those who study Maiishi."

"Quite a… dramatically beautiful place," Lady Kyoumére added. "Where is it?"

Jin smiled for a moment. "Its value as folklore probably outweighs the collective faith in its existence. Some obscure location is generally suggested, up in the western mountains…" Jin's voice trailed off.

"Well, rather impressive if Lord Shirér made it there," Lady K suggested. "Not the youngest of men when he left."

As the ambient bustle of little feet faded away, Jin's thoughts became lost in the painting. Two rescued children limped behind Olette into the pantry.

"Thank you again, Lord Jin, for giving us more space. Your decorum is a blessing."

"Oh… yes," Jin slipped out of his trance. "The timing is serendipitous, actually. I am planning a move into the poured stone and glass building just down the street."

"So close! That is wonderful. An apartment, I assume?" Lady K smiled, folding her hands.

"Somewhat. I thought having a proper workspace in the city would be practical, so I purchased the building," Jin revealed placidly.

"Oh, OH… yes, I see. Of course." Lady K's eyes froze wide open, having no set congratulations for one who revealed he had just purchased a building. "I'm sure that'll be quite nice for you." A thud came from upstairs. "Oh, sounds as though I am needed."

As the Lady gracefully decamped, Jin grabbed his one bag from the pantry. With little interference, he managed his way out of the house and onto the sidewalk. Goodbyes felt unnecessary, perhaps even disruptive, he decided. The sounds of youth tapered off in the distance as he walked away.

A chill breeze followed Jin to his building, which greeted him with silence. A package sat tucked behind a bush, looking like a rudimentary cardboard wing. Gently working it onto the block porch, he checked the address. A curious sound slid out of his mouth, followed by an unexpected warmth in his neck. The address was immediately familiar.

"Well, big sister, this is rather peculiar."

o o o

Young Noma stood between Gozen and Suzu at what she'd reported at the Tree House was her family's address. She had whispered to Suzu that she remembered where she lived, and it had turned out the Tree House was one bed short anyway, so Gozen and Suzu packed up the small girl and headed for a far corner of the city. Tucked tightly between similar buildings in various states of wear, the street looked more like a back alley than a neighborhood. It was only a few blocks from where Suzu lived— she vaguely recognized the street.

"What are you going to say to the dad? Are you doing the talking?" Suzu struggled to hide her keyed-up voice from Noma. "Because I do *not* have nice things to say to a guy who loses—or sells—his daughter."

"Yes, please let me do the talking," Gozen begged. Noma's frail hand hung onto Suzu's small but calloused fingers. Suzu looked at the welcome mat that said *HELL*, the *O* having been mostly worn off, and knocked at the door again with her shoe.

"I think he might be hiding," Suzu speculated to Gozen. "I mean, one look at you through a window probably sent the guy screaming out the back."

Gozen cleared his throat while motioning down towards Noma.

Suzu shrugged. "Hey, it's not my fault you look like a shaved bear."

Making her first noise in twenty minutes, Noma squeaked out a giggle.

"Just hold her hand… *quietly*." Gozen rubbed his temples, then put his hands on the girls' backs and nudged them forward. "Maybe you two should stand in front."

Just then, corroded locks squeaked on the other side of the door, which finally cracked open. Two suspicious eyes peered out, immediately running up the full height of Gozen.

"What do you want?"

Gesturing downward, Gozen's voice channeled his old profession. "We are looking for the family of young Lady Noma."

Hit with realization, the man opened the door a little more, finally noticing the group of humans ending in his tiny, delicate daughter. "Noma" is all he managed to get out before swinging open the door and kneeling. Stunned from a swell of emotion, the man waited for the small child to react. Slowly, her face began to wrinkle as tears welled up. With hands folded together, she finally settled into her father's arm.

Gozen and Suzu watched silently, their hearts starting to churn. Loss had become an ongoing occurrence, and survival an ongoing practice, for both of them. Eventually, courtesy stepped aside, making way for the inquisition.

"There are some matters we need to discuss," Gozen stated flatly.

Suddenly, Noma's mother appeared holding a baby. The father told his wife to take their children away from the imminent conversation. Flushed with gratitude and anxiety, the mother agreed.

"Do you know where your daughter was?" Gozen asked.

The man looked like a worm had crawled up his back. "I... enrolled her in a camp... group. It was paid for... two weeks. I don't know..."

"She was living in a basement south of here, with two dozen other kids waiting to be sold," Gozen continued.

Covering his mouth, the man held back a sour mixture of sadness and guilt. He searched for words while his face confessed plenty.

It wasn't enough for Gozen. "Who was it that you handed your daughter off to?"

"It was a couple, middle-aged. They just knocked on our door one day. I didn't know them."

"And you just handed her over? How stupid are you?" Suzu interjected.

Gozen coughed into his hand. "What else can you tell me about them?"

Suddenly, the man looked at them differently, as if a light had been turned on. "Who *are* you two?"

"We're the ones that saved your daughter. So, why don't you answer the big man's questions?" Suzu demanded.

"Look, I appreciate ya brought her here, but I don't really have much I can tell you."

"A Civil Enforcer will be here later in the week with a case worker. Being cold to us isn't going to put them into a good mood."

"I..." the man struggled. "They seemed trustworthy—camping at the foot of the mountains with other kids. Why would they lie about that?"

"That's it? Any stranger comes to your door once and you hand off your kid?" Suzu leaned in.

"No, it was a couple of times. We packed her some clothes."

"How long ago was that, and you never reported it?" Gozen asked.

"Well... yeah, we were about to. They were only a couple of days late."

Disappointed, Gozen took stock and settled. "Someone will check up with you, very soon."

Relieved, Noma's father quickly shut the door. Suzu turned around, confounded. "What? You're satisfied with that joke of an answer?"

Gozen considered the question, along with many others. "This guy doesn't know anything."

"And you accept that?"

"I acknowledge it," Gozen volleyed back. "I'll check in with the CE next week." His feet felt swollen in his heavy boots. "Come on, I'll take you home."

3
ORIENTATION

Lights buzzed incessantly above Darou's head as he sat. He hated sitting—standing or laying down felt far more natural. Being in a room filled with nothing but chairs gave him more anxiety than he cared to admit. Time crept unnaturally as the electronic ticker counted numbers. His hand sweat as it gripped a token stamped with the number 78.

Across from him, someone's recently shined shoes led his eyes up to an almost-convincing knock-off suit. The owner slid out a brass Toki from his jacket pocket. The flat, palm-sized clock opened up to reveal a collapsible pen and mechanical notepad. He scrolled the paper up, scribbled down some thoughts, and smugly laughed at his annotation. Darou assumed they weren't applying for the same job. Above, an overbearing sign flickered *Noutess - Leaders In Dark Spark.*

Shaking with impatience, Darou grabbed his Toki and checked the time. He called it a Toki, although Tokis typically had a secondary function. Darou wondered if the minute-hand counted as a bonus feature. Checking against the wall clock, he realized his Toki ran slow.

"Young Lord," shouted the receptionist. Darou got up and scuttled forward before seeing someone else's number on the ticker. Flushing with stupidity, he turned back, hoping no one would notice, but instead walked straight into the faux-designer suit, snagging the coat pocket. Its owner paused with an obnoxious scowl, expecting reparations from the junior black-hand. Darou stood, unconcerned, before noticing a sudden prismatic flash.

Appearing lost, or a bit sugar-drunk, Lucette bobbed in the

doorway holding a large bag. Against the canvas of gray brick and dull faces, her display of braids, accessories, and complementary colors looked like a children's book illustration come to life. She gazed around the room with energetic confusion until discovering Darou. She hurried over and sat, pulling him down into the adjacent seat.

"Hello, Sparky. Looks like we're both pretending to be grownups today," Lucette said, casing the waiting room.

"Pretending?" Darou groaned. "I've been a proper black-hand since thirteen. I've probably had more jobs than the head of this fuel plant."

"Well, old-timer, this is my first job—hopefully, but let's keep that classified," Lucette said, waving a rainbow-colored pen.

Darou smirked. "Best to keep a low profile."

Stored energy rocked Lucette in her seat. "So, I thought you were on disability from getting blown up at Etecid. What are you doing here?"

"I was, but that won't last forever. Besides, I can't stand sitting around all day." Darou's mouth yawned before going crooked. "And what are you doing here? Aren't you in school or something?"

"So kind of you to ask." Lucette adjusted her intricately braided up-do. "I'm here for an internship with—you guessed it—Upper Academy West. So, not a *job* per se, although I do get paid. Actually, I'm not sure… *do* I get paid?"

Darou shrugged as if all academia existed a thousand miles away.

"Either way." Lucette gave a delicate cough. "I'll be with their industrial biochemistry division."

Darou furrowed his brow. "Don't you need to be super smart for that?"

"Yes," she stated confidently. "Which is why I am perfect for it, Lord Darou."

"Right. So, I saw Suzu for a split-second yesterday. Isn't she living with you?"

"Oh, yes, I love her dearly…" Lucette searched for the words. "But with her trying to be a super-spy or something…

NOUTESS
LEADERS
IN
DARK SPARK

there are challenges."

"Really?" Darou tried to picture Suzu roaming the streets at night. "Is she being serious?"

"Yes, very serious. You should ask her about it sometime."

"Okay." Darou always had trouble deciphering Lucette's words. "So, what… is she looking for Kits or something?"

"Oh, sweet river, I hope not. Looking *at* Kits isn't so bad, to be honest, but everything else about him… horrible."

"You can't be serious. Kits?"

"Evil people are often very snappy dressers," Lucette asserted. "You, on the other hand, Lord Darou, are the salt of the valley."

"Thanks. That's just the kind of confidence boost I need."

The receptionist interrupted. "Young Lord…"

They both leaned forward. "She's looking at you, young Lord," Lucette winked. "And remember, you survived an explosion at your last job. Very rare. I'd emphasize that."

Darou walked to the receptionist, holding in his laugh. Behind glass soiled from fine layers of dust and breath, the receptionist's voice melded with the buzzing lights and hissing radiators. She offered the same pre-interview briefing he'd heard at every new job. His eyes drifted to a window behind her, revealing a private parking lot for the executive's luxury cars.

Darou always thought such cars looked odd, sitting amongst the grime of industrial plants. His eyes then narrowed on a specific car, something unique but familiar. Thoughts of Kora and the Tree House shuffled in. After a moment, the memory struck clear. The car was a Móstique, and he knew only a single person who drove one.

o o o

Wanting to burn off some frustration, Suzu skipped the elevator. The day had proven to be another fruitless effort to track down the home of Victou Despré. Chichimou Despré's father currently assisted Pirou Naizen, an entitled fuel researcher swimming in nepotism.

She had met Pirou through Remi, an engineer and former colleague of her father's at Kasic. Suzu wondered why Remi had helped her. Perhaps Remi, smothered by his job and family, was feeding a repressed desire for adventure. Maybe he saw her as tragic and endangered, and sought to learn how his own child could avoid such a fate. Remi had revealed to Suzu that Pirou suspected someone was trying to steal his new Dark Spark research. Pirou's current suspect was his assistant, Victou. Suzu wanted a path to get back to Kits, and eventually Daimó, the author of her parents' death. Victou seemed to be a link between them somehow. She had been tracking him after work, on and off for weeks, but Victou had proven surprisingly slippery.

She reached the door and cycled through her mechanical key case to Lucette's apartment—currently *their* apartment. Inside, Lucette stood in the middle of their small living room, offering an unrelenting smile. Suzu sneaked to the kitchen for some water.

"*My dear Lucette,*" began Lucette, "*didn't you start your new internship today at Noutess? Why, yes I did! Thank you for asking.*"

Suzu took gulps by the sink and then gruffly used her sleeve as a napkin. "Noutess… isn't that the new Dark Spark plant?"

Having heard countless comments about the sins of Dark Spark, Lucette quickly deciphered Suzu's layered tone. "Yes… well, yes, but I'm interning there for Upper Academy West. But don't worry, I only *sound* like an adult."

Suzu, face thoroughly soured, leaned against the doorframe. "A Dark Spark plant? Lucette. You *know* my parents died trying to stop that disgusting technology."

Lucette felt the shiny bubble deflate within. "I… I know, but I'll be working in their Biochemistry division. So…" she emphasized, "…I'll be able to keep an eye on things, making sure everything is clean and proper."

"Clean… Dark Spark? So, I guess that means you'll be shutting down the plant," Suzu chuckled sardonically.

Lucette put fists to hips. "You know, I've been busting my little butt for a long time trying to get out of that orphanage and into a school so I can get a real job and do something important. Can't you—at the very least—fake some indifference?"

Suzu took a long drink of water, headed into the kitchen and filled up again. Lucette waited for the answer. "Okay, I think it's great you're in school, really," Suzu offered. "But just because *you're* working at a Dark Spark plant doesn't mean *I'll* forget it's poisoning the valley."

Lucette nodded vigorously. "Well, thank you for that gracious compromise. So, how was your afternoon doing… whatever it is that you do?"

"Not good… but I can't talk about it."

Lucette squinted. "You better not be trying to find Kits. I don't even want to know what Gozen would do if he found out, and we both know Gozen is the iron overlord of figuring things out."

"I'm sorry it bothers you, Lucette, but I can't tell you. That's it."

Lucette's eyes nearly rolled out of her head.

"Hey, look," Suzu warned. "Don't get all upset just because I don't tell you *everything*."

"Or *anything*."

"Whatever. Maybe it's hard to understand, but what I'm doing is important—*actually* important, Lucette."

In a rare moment, despite having had an entire childhood to build up resilience, Lucette felt a few tears poking through. She did her best to choke them down.

"Well, if we're all about doing the world's most important things now, I'm going to go color-coordinate my sock drawer." She escaped to her room and shut the door.

Under her breath, Suzu muttered, "Whatever, as if your socks aren't already color-coordinated."

○ ○ ○

Gozen had offered Darou a ride after the interview. The offer felt a bit nosy, but Neko proved more comfortable than the Hotrail at rush hour.

"I bet the two of you looked quite the couple in that place," Gozen smirked, having just been told about Darou's run-in with Lucette.

"Me and the walking rainbow? Right—when I'm next to her, I bet most people mistake me for her shadow."

"I wish some of that sunshine would rub off on Suzu." Gozen braked hard at a yellow light. Society chattered outside and Gozen's eyes seemed to drift.

"So, that was a load of kids the other night. Crazy someone stashed them in a basement."

Gozen leaned over, still hazy. "Yeah… not enough."

Darou squinted. "Enough what?"

"Just that the tip put a lot more kids down there."

"So, the tip was off?"

"Or late," Gozen suggested, watching the light turn green. "So, how are you feeling about this new place? You sure you want to go back to a fuel plant?"

Darou looked out the window. Hats and hairdos floated above bumping shoulders while briefcases and shopping bags bounced off knees. "Well, you know, I just got that one job skill. Besides, what do I have to worry about? It's not like the place will suddenly blow up."

They shared a laugh which was neither joyful nor cathartic. The explosion at Etecid had destroyed jobs and taken lives, including, very nearly, both of theirs.

"How did that investigation end up? They're not blaming you for anything, are they?"

The investigation had lasted a while. Trying to protect those around him, Gozen had spent months pulling favors with Enforcer buddies and making court visits.

"I'm okay. They decided that the worker who spiked the Tulúki with Akyulose must have been some radical Soran whack-job. He's gone, so I guess that's over."

"Yeah... maybe a Soran makes sense."

Gozen hesitated a moment but figured ignorance wouldn't make Darou any safer. "Kits knew him. Pretty sure he sent him there."

"Kits? The *anti*-Soran?"

"Coerce a Soran into doing something dangerous? Sure, if it suited him."

Darou picked at a hangnail. "I wasn't gonna bring this up— don't want to sound paranoid—but I saw a black Móstique parked in the executive lot out back."

The two shared plenty of bad memories involving that car.

"You didn't see *him*, did you?" Gozen's voice was sharp.

"Kits? No."

Thoughts of espionage and precautions fluttered into Gozen's mind. "Are you worried?"

Darou shrugged. "Eh, he probably thinks I'm dead."

4

CLANDESTINE

"Finally."

Suzu strangled her excitement into a whisper. After more nights than she cared to admit, the amateur snoop had finally tracked a single man from Kasic headquarters to his home. Victou Despré predictably left his office and took Hotrail-C to a junction station east. As the rush-hour crowd spilled out, Suzu had scrambled unsuccessfully to acquire him, until finally realizing that the men's room had a second exit.

Across the street from the main Hotrail exit, Suzu saw Victou slip out of a door so poorly marked it looked decommissioned. Excellent signage had been such a big initiative when Opaji had started Chigou that poorly marked structures had practically become invisible. Victou crossed down the opposite side of a narrow street, hopping between shadows.

Likewise, Suzu stayed away from streetlights, following behind. She wondered if somehow this man that Pirou had described as "incompetent" had actually detected her efforts.

Rounding a corner, Victou finally stopped in front of an unexceptional Family-stack. Simple but stable structures, Family-stacks provided cheap housing that faded into the background without becoming an embarrassment for the city. Climbing the half flight of steps, Victou went inside. Suzu waited for a light to come on before climbing a fire escape across the street and perching on top.

Dark ambiance accompanied her for the next two hours. Her feet developed an ache from the stillness. Internally, she went back and forth, debating her plan or what she was even waiting for. She skipped dinner and began to feel it as two headlights approached down the quiet street. Few people owned cars in that part of town. She held her breath as the vehicle slowed down. Finally, the headlights turned off and two black silhouettes got out.

Suzu blinked to clear the sting of cold air. The two shapes— one short, one tall—went straight up to Victou's door. She heard the cheap doorbell clang. Victou's face peeked out from behind a curtain. Once the door opened, light hit their faces and Suzu clawed at the iron railing. She'd never forget those two monsters from the alley, promising her pain and death. A discrepancy then rattled her memory: one of the men seemed to be missing an arm.

Below, words were exchanged, along with a small portfolio. The scene seemed to corroborate Pirou's suspicions. The short stranger snarled something indecipherable and then they both left. Suzu's stomach growled and she checked a cheap Toki bought from a Fast-gadget. It mocked the masterpiece her father had made for her, but she had lost it, just like the cherished DaiLansu she had borrowed—stolen—from Nia. Suzu wondered why she was so good at losing precious things.

∘ ∘ ∘

The Steam Roller bustled with its usual mix of professionals and upper academy students. The dense crowd satisfied social cravings while providing enough noise to protect private conversations. When Pirou first suggested a meeting—paranoid that someone wanted to steal his precious research—Remi had recommended the popular eatery. Pirou found the beloved diner asphyxiating, much to Remi's amusement.

He perused the menu for something to accompany his extra-rich coffee while Pirou squirmed.

"Is this necessary?" Pirou muttered. "My wife scowled rather dubiously when I got a wire-type from 'Lady S' to meet here after dark."

Remi grinned over the pastry selections.

"Hey, aren't you married?" Pirou questioned.

"Yeah, but *my* wife trusts me. These chocolate blashu butter rolls look about right. You want some?"

Pirou checked his Toki, twice. "What I want is to meet at normal hours, in a place where stimulated singles aren't sucking up all the air. And your clandestine little Lady Scout better have something useful. This research is getting ready to pop, and I can't afford someone jumping in line for the patent."

Remi finally put down the menu. "Hey, Pirou, just relax. I don't think she'd want to meet unless she had something."

"She damn well better, Remi. You hear me?"

Remi tilted his head. "Or what, you going to *fire* me? Of course, you'd have to rehire me to do that."

"I feel like I hired academy students," Pirou picked up a cloth napkin and wiped his sweating face. "I am ruined if this goes bad, Remi. Do you understand that? I am finished, okay? *Decommissioned*."

Remi checked his Toki. "Order some cake or something, would you? I think your blood sugar is low."

Just then, Suzu's small frame squeezed in from below two cocktails held by a pair of stimulated singles. She slid into the seat next to Remi. They exchanged warm greetings as Pirou tapped the table. "Heartwarming. Now can we get on with this?"

Remi leaned over to Suzu. "You hungry?"

"*Lord of industry*, are you serious?" Pirou squealed.

"I'll give you some of mine," offered Remi before niceties were finally tucked away.

"Your assistant Victou is trickier than he leads on," Suzu confessed.

Pirou leaned forward, his hands raised like puppets. "Yeah, little one, I told you that the day we met, and so far, you haven't been much help."

"Well, you can track people fast or you can track people *right*," Suzu said with implied wisdom.

In disbelief, Pirou looked between the two young faces across from him. "Did your grandpa teach you that out on the job? Can I hire him instead?"

"Too late. I caught him."

"What's wrong with me?" Pirou looked lost. "I hired a little

Lady Scout for protection. I've lost my mind."

"Hey," Suzu interrupted, "I *was* a scout, and it's just Lady Scouts, not *little* Lady Scouts… and I said I caught him."

Pirou's focus realigned. "What does that mean, you *caught* him?"

"Well, I didn't grab him or anything, but I finally found where he lives."

Although this was good news, Pirou remained far from relieved. "So, what… his address? That doesn't help me."

Suzu cautiously looked over her shoulder, then leaned in. "I waited a couple of hours. Two guys showed up—nasty couple of screws I've definitely run into before, and they went straight to Victou's door. A minute or two later, he handed them some folder, and they left."

Remi wanted everyone to leave happy. "Well, that's good. That's *something*. Pirou, maybe you could figure out what he's taking from the office and—"

"What do you mean, *what*?" Pirou shouted through his teeth, the sound still covered by the enlivened crowd. "You think Victou is in a men's only, midnight book exchange? He's selling my *research*, children!"

Pirou looked as if he could suddenly smell his house burning from across town. Remi tried to offer some rational encouragement, but Pirou heard only the voices in his head. "I can't… I can't wait anymore. He… they could fire the boiler any day."

Remi and Suzu turned to one another, confirming how crazed the pair of eyes across the table looked.

"Hey, Pirou," Remi said slowly. "Are you alright?"

Pirou stood up as if possessed. "I need to go now. We don't need to meet anymore." And then he vanished like a ghost into the social swarm.

A despondent Suzu turned back to Remi. "That's it?"

"I guess… I guess this is our last meeting. I don't know. I never really understood him."

"But what about Victou? We finally have a lead to whoever set him up. I can't stop now."

Remi thought of Carmin, and Suzu before she was ripped from

childhood. "I don't know, those guys could be properly dangerous. Maybe it's a good time to stop."

She leaned back, clearly offended. "Remi, what are you talking about? I'm not scared. I'm not stopping because that nitwit is done. This Victou guy could be working for the man who blew up the Etecid plant."

"Yeah, I know, that's why…"

"The man who *killed* my *parents*, Remi." Her chest heaved, ready to explode.

A much younger girl entered Remi's mind, his daughter whom he worried about all the time. He thought of his wife, who had always trusted him. "Suzu, I didn't know your dad all that well, and I barely knew your mother… but it was pretty easy to see they cared about fighting for what they believed in. I remember seeing your mom protest at Kasic one day. You were there, too… maybe you don't remember that."

Suzu stayed still, certain she remembered the day much better than Remi.

His thought carried on. "It seemed crazy to me, but Carmin didn't look mad, just… concerned. I always thought your parents were so impressive, pushing for these big things they believed in, not afraid of anyone." Finally, with a soft voice, he looked right at Suzu. "You're a fighter like them. And as much as I want to honor that… I don't know. I mean, I'm no first-class father—I honestly don't know what I'm doing most of the time—but Suzu, I don't think your parents would want you to be in danger, not like this… not even if it meant finding who… you know."

Suzu looked like a swollen boiler, slowly bleeding pressure off. "Okay. Thanks."

Remi felt like saying something, but his mind hummed, blank. Suzu got out of the booth just as a waitress brought over a tray with coffee and chocolate blashu rolls. In a web of awkwardness, Remi tried to thank the woman while asking Suzu to stay and eat, but it all got caught in his throat. Suzu just stole two rolls and disappeared.

Laughs and smiles surrounded him as he sat alone with his plate of pastries—minus a pair. He then waved the waitress back for a take-home bag.

◦ ◦ ◦

Slowly, the lock turned, and the door cracked open, allowing streetlights to shine across the polished Bokai-wood floor. Immediately, he took off his shoes and shut the door as if it were made of paper-thin glass.

He thanked the floorboards for not creaking as he went towards his den—although they shouldn't have creaked anyway, they cost so damn much. Pirou had heard the proclamation a hundred times from his uncle, the man who had paid for them. Having incorrectly memorized the floor plan, Pirou choked on a scream after his socked toe caught some floor trim.

A light then blinded him as a blurry silhouette slowly came into focus. "Pirou! What in the name of industry are you doing?"

Pirou managed to partially stand up while rubbing his sore foot. "I didn't want to wake you or the boy."

"Well, there's no need to stumble around in the dark. I don't want to call Uncle again, needing to replace another cabinet."

"You didn't need to the first time," Pirou mumbled under his breath.

"What was that?" Jané asked.

"Just... my toe. I'm sorry I woke you." He lumbered over.

"Sincerely. Well, since I'm awake, would you like some ice?" she asked.

"I'm fine."

"And your meeting went well, I hope? And how is... what was her name, Lady S?" Jané asked in a tone that felt like a finger jabbing in his ear.

"Obnoxiously unconcerned."

"I'm sorry, what?" Her arms crossed.

"I... I'll probably not be meeting with her again. I was more there to see Remi, my old assistant, but... that doesn't matter. I need to wire something out before bed. I'll be quiet."

Jané only managed a slight mumble in retort as Pirou disappeared into the darkness. Five doors down, he fumbled into his office and onto a custom desk chair, another gift from his wife. But, like half the things they "owned," it had come from her favorite uncle and Pirou's boss, Bardin. Tired shoulders dropped for a moment.

He could never fully relax in that borrowed house. Despite having a large family himself, nearly every frame in the house contained images of Jané's relatives. At least half of them were paintings. Pirou found them pretentious and archaic. He had wanted Jané as badly as he had wanted a grand position at Kasic, and Bardin offered him both. The house felt like a prison of debt.

Pirou pulled out a drawer and reached down deep to a hidden folder. Inside, crisp documents finalized the down payment for a house across town. A similar document below it applied to a townhouse on the east coast in Meijune, a single bedroom. Both promised financial commitment and personal freedom; his wife knew of neither.

Seeming as though it would never materialize, his plan finally stood at a critical juncture. Pirou resolved to fully reveal his research, demand Kasic file patents, and finally be elevated to the position he deserved. If Jané's patronizing uncle refused, all work would be sold to Jinaru Fuel Co., far out east in Meijune. That part of the plan felt complicated—taking airships between there and Chigou, hiding things from Bardin—but it mattered not. By the time anyone discovered his position out east, he'd already be standing on bedrock.

A bottle of Shumé sat on the thick wood desk, unopened and well-aged. Pirou had never much cared for liquor, but the occasion, and whatever it would become, seemed appropriate. He nearly cut his finger removing the foil cap. He poured into a dusty glass and took a hesitant sip. The second one tasted better.

Setting the glass down, Pirou pulled the wire-type over and punched in a corporate Meijune number. His fingers nervously rapped on the keys, as if preparing to confess intentions to some secret infatuation.

With a hit of the *open transmission* lever, his future shifted.

◦ ◦ ◦

Miles away, Daimó sat reading an original copy of Primichi's first printed novel when the wire-type's incoming bell chimed. Kits glanced over from a far corner, thumbing through a picture book of airship blueprints. Without putting his book down, Daimó reached over and grabbed the printout. He immediately recognized the address from Meijune: Jinaru, an energy plant he had owned a third of since before Pirou was alive. He had hidden the fact from nearly every associate in Chigou, especially Opaji, who obsessed over his city's exclusive greatness.

The print read:

CONFIDENTIAL
Lord Daimó,

Pirou Naizen has just sent us a message carrying much urgency. He presses greatly the need to close off the state of his Dark Spark research for patent submission. Per usual, he desires strict discretion, emphasizing the longest possible delay in notifying any entities in the Naifin Valley, especially Kasic. He notified us of his intentions to visit the plant in the next few days and begin official partnership and conjoined development, under an ancillary identifier.

We have been collecting the duplicates you sent via your associate Kits Bodu. We will not finalize any deals until explicit consent is received directly from yourself.

Request action.
Renni Ocano

Amongst the silence, Kits noticed a faint murmur from his boss. Daimó was void of nearly any charm or quirk, so even the slightest anomalous emotion seemed relatively dramatic.

"I need you to dictate a request."

Kits stood up, simultaneously obeying and assessing. "Do... you just want a copy, or am I wire-typing this somewhere?"

"The situation in Chigou has reached a transitional point," Daimó responded.

Kits scrambled to pull the wire-type away from Daimó, set it to record, and began typing. He hated asking Daimó to repeat himself. "The situation in Chigou..."

"Immediate announcement concerning the Noutess-Jinaru partnership in the development of next-generation Dark Spark technology. Patent filing submission finalized, with a full, detailed announcement soon to follow."

Kits stretched out his fingers, fighting off an oncoming cramp. "Patent filing submission..."

Daimó kept his tempo. "We are... delighted, to give a full presentation soon. End of transmission."

Kits's fingers paused at typing *delighted*. Daimó spoke the word strangely, like a child ignorantly repeating a word they had heard from an adult. Suddenly noticing the silence, Kits finished the record. "Who is this for?"

Daimó slid the original message from Jinaru over, tapping the return address. "Also, send an appropriate release to the *Beacon of Knowledge*."

Kits grabbed a pen and hurried. "I'll try. What day would you prefer?"

"Tomorrow's edition will do." Daimó, in the occasional way that arrested Kits's nerves, looked him straight in the eye. "Front page."

"Yes... well..." Kits endured his overseer's gaze, "...it's just... late. They're probably sending it to press any minute."

Daimó got out of his chair and walked to the small wet bar by the window. Knowing such a last-minute request would never be fulfilled with a wire-type, Kits clenched his jaw, grabbed his coat and headed for the door—the *Beacon of Knowledge* building stood on the opposite side of downtown, so he would need to hurry.

5
DISCLOSE

Never before had Pirou experienced such a cocktail of emotions. Leaving his house felt finite, bringing him to whisper goodbye. Fear and empowerment tangled within him like teenage siblings. Kasic would get the first chance at Pirou's new technology. Far to the east, Meijune offered a valuable backup; he waited on the Jinaru fuel plant's response. With his options laid out, Pirou sensed his due success in the air.

The thirteenth floor of Kasic HQ ran as it did every weekday. More than a few heads turned as a second-term intern ran down the hall and collided with a bemused co-worker.

"Pirou!"

The engineer choked on his gasp. He vaguely recognized the young employee from his department. "Geeze, kid! Keep some distance, would you?"

"Right, sorry." The intern apologized while Pirou pushed him back. "I guess the new partnership just got me worked up. But Lord Bardin... yikes!" The intern nervously laughed until noticing Pirou did not. "Wait, did you know about it?

Pirou felt like a student being awakened in the middle of class. "The partnership..."

"Yeah, the one between Noutess and Jinuru..."

"Jinaru," Pirou corrected automatically, his mind weaving doom-filled visions.

"Jinaru, right. So, you did know, because isn't this your project?" the intern asked.

Something horrible had happened, but Pirou couldn't process what. An instinctive flight response bloomed as a vocal harpoon stabbed him in the back.

"Pirou!"

He slowly turned around as if before a firing squad. Bardin stood at the end of the hall, jabbing his finger towards an empty conference room like a knife. Pirou obeyed, trawling his feet across the floor, finally following his boss—his wife's favorite uncle—into the heavily insulated room. The entire floor heard the door shut.

"You insolent little *parasite*."

Pirou assumed that Jané's uncle had always wanted to say those words to his face. The executive's left hand strangled a newspaper. "After everything I've done for you! And did you think I wouldn't notice?"

Instead of nods and apologies, Pirou froze like a corpse. This infuriated Bardin even more.

"I don't know how someone smart enough to create fuel this efficient could be stupid enough to develop it at one company and sell it to another... *two* others!" He slammed the paper into Pirou's chest.

Bardin paced around, steam practically pouring through his teeth. Pirou unfurled the front page of the business section, but it felt like staring at the obituaries. Between his fingers, the nightmare explained itself in bold, black ink.

MEIJUNE COMPANY JINARU PARTNERS WITH NOUTESS BY DEVELOPING GROUNDBREAKING NEW FUEL – Is Kasic developing complacency?

The plan had worked, but someone had beat him to it. "Victou."

"What?" Bardin spun back around, ready to bite.

"My... my assistant. I suspected him of stealing my research and giving it to someone else."

"Lords on fire, Pirou, don't trade in one pitiful course for another."

"No, I just started to notice, but now I'm sure of what he did."

Bardin squinted. "And you have proof of this betrayal?"

Pirou remembered his girl-spy-for-hire describe catching

Victou in the act. He couldn't use the evidence, he just needed to know it existed. Even if he raided Victou's apartment, anything that incriminated Victou would simultaneously provide evidence that Pirou had tried to betray Kasic. Proof... yes, but of his innocence? "No."

Bardin poured a glass of Pats liquor. "No? Well, that's not too good for you. Even if you are telling the truth, that means Kasic needs to admit its research isn't secure and we hired a traitor, and then we'd need to pursue criminal cases against two major energy companies."

Pirou stood like a mannequin.

"At least right now, we just look slow... and like we wasted a few years on you." Bardin's fury settled into a simmer, his voiced deepened. "Did you tell anyone about your... suspicions?"

Pirou cowered. "No."

Bardin jabbed his old, hardened finger into Pirou's sternum. "If you've done anything to jeopardize my Jané in any way, you will regret that you two ever met." He pushed Pirou back. "I always have."

Neurons started to settle in Pirou's head. There's a lot to think about on the edge, but less when the floor has already dropped out from under you.

"Go lock down your office. I don't want anyone going in or out of that room." Bardin swallowed his fiery glass in one gulp. "I'll figure out what to do with *you* later."

o o o

The bright light surprised him. The oppressively familiar sensation of panic felt far away. The usual clanging of metal, promptly demanding he rise for work, remained charitably absent. Slowly, as his brain entered consciousness, a word burst out.

"Chichi!" Victou shot out of bed and onto the floor, his feet caught in a snare of sheets. He kicked his cotton bonds off like a panicked woodland mammal.

Chichimou stood in the doorway. "Yeah, dad?"

"I'm late for work. Why didn't you wake me up?" Frenzied, Victou searched for appropriate clothing.

"Why didn't you set your alarm?" Chichi asked through a yawn that morphed into a giggle as Victou juggled his clothes. He finally got dressed and ran to the door.

"Dad."

"What?" Victou said, grabbing his coat.

"Why did you do it crooked?"

Looking down, Victou saw he had misaligned his button-down shirt, by two holes. He screeched like an owl, clawing apart the tiny fasteners. "I know he's suspicious. Being late isn't going to help."

Chichimou scooted down the short hall. "Who's suspicious?"

"Uhm, nobody, Chichi. Are you hungry? You know how to work the hotplate, right?" Victou, triple checking, buttoned back up. Chichi didn't answer.

"Good," Victou grabbed keys and swung open the door. "Have a good day," and with a wink, he was gone.

o o o

Tension wove through the crowd of workers but Victou didn't notice. He wiped his sweating face off one more time with his shirt sleeve before hiding it back in his coat.

Unlike most jobs he had attempted before, the current one carried a risk of double elimination. Being fired from any job had its own set of hassles, nothing new there, but Kits and the nameless lackeys who had visited him presented a complex problem. His value to them relied solely on the research he was able to steal. Being fired would require a quick retreat on all fronts. At least for the time, it paid well.

Finally at the door, Victou stopped, quieted his breathing, and listened in. He heard only ambient office sounds. Slowly turning the door handle, he took an impulsive look down the hall and noticed a curious number of eyes staring at him. Feeling more concerned with the other side of the door, he ignored them and stepped in.

The room effectively disappeared when the two men noticed one another. Pirou lacked his typical, agitated facade, instead wearing an unsettling, boiler-struck gaze. The term described the traumatic shock one experienced being near a boiler explosion: Pirou just lacked the bruises and bleeding ears.

He then began to drift towards Victou who saw the newspaper crushed in his hand. Victou backed up and ran into his desk, knocking over a cup of pens. Ready for a volley of spit-laced damnation, the newspaper suddenly dropped to the floor and Pirou looked as if he might cry or vomit. He opened his lips, but no sound escaped.

Pirou then turned and walked out into the hallway, moving like the undead. Victou leaned out carefully and watched him retreat. A concerned Kasic employee approached Pirou and began to speak, but Pirou drifted away, a body without a soul.

Victou scooted to the discarded paper and picked it up. A single headline emerged from the pile of words. Pirou's and Victou's separate schemes had been hijacked in one deft maneuver, eliminating what little value he held with Kits.

Victou looked around the space for anything he could still use as leverage. He gathered up drawings and small record books and threw them into his bag. Ready to run out, he then noticed some drawings he had never seen before, suddenly uncovered. Fuzzy with dust, the drawings displayed some kind of probe going into the ground. The title read *Core-thermic*; the designer, *Carmin Komou*.

He barely understood them, but desperation fuels a particular type of greed. Not wanting to waste time thinking about it, he packed them up and hurried out.

o o o

Suzu counted the bouncing coins in her hand. Little West Café in Chacier sold their pastries half-off right before they closed. They didn't taste as good later in the day—were atrocities compared to morning bakes with her mother—but she could afford them. Luckily, hunger proved a powerful spice.

Crossing the street, she slowed, seeing a familiar face. Pacing back and forth like a smoked coffee addict, Remi wobbled when he saw Suzu.

"Why are you at my apartment?" she asked.

"Sorry, I know, but with what happened I didn't want to wait,"

Remi said, clearly unsettled.

"Okay, well, hurry. I'm famished." Suzu looked over Remi's shoulder to a sign reading *Today's Special – Bollo Butter Tarts*.

"You read about the Noutess-Jinaru announcement, right?" Remi asked.

"Uhm… I don't… what's Jinaru?"

"It was all over the paper yesterday! How did you not read that?"

Suzu dropped her shoulders. "I'm not an old man who lusts for my daily paper. Just spit it out."

Remi moaned with anxiety. "Noutess made a partnership with Jinaru—a fuel plant back in Meijune. They announced this new, incredibly efficient fuel that would be massive for Dark Spark development."

"Okay, that's partially interesting. Kind of sounds like what Pirou—"

"Suzu, Pirou is dead," Remi burst out, unable to contain the news any longer.

"What?"

Remi rubbed his tight jaw muscles. "Pirou is… well, he's dead. Suicide… I think. If not… oh, I don't even *want* to think about that."

Suzu's hunger vanished. "Are you sure? I mean, he was crazy uptight."

"Suzu, he was *right*. Clearly someone was after what he was working on."

"Yeah, I finally busted Victou, remember? Isn't that what Pirou wanted?" she blurted out before shrugging. "Seems stupid to kill himself."

"Yes, I remember. I'm talking about the next day's paper, Suzu. Kasic—world's greatest energy company—is humiliated by Noutess, this brand-new fuel company that just so happens to announce an identical new fuel to what Pirou was developing. Even if you got that evidence—whatever Victou slipped to those guys—it was too late. At best, Pirou would only be blamed for letting his lackey snatch-and-sell his top-secret research for months, ending his career."

Remi paced in tiny laps, comprehending their place amongst

a massive gambit now involving multiple industrial titans. "Look, Suzu, I got to be honest. I wasn't always sure this was a great idea. I don't know… I just felt like you deserved to know what happened to your parents, but this… this is *bad*. We know things that very powerful people—whoever they might be—are currently not aware of, and I think it would be very dangerous to let that change." Remi thought of his family and how nothing would justify putting them in danger.

Suzu thought of her parents—their bodies buried—and how she wouldn't let anything destroy their spirit. "I have a pretty good idea who *they* are," she said, "and our pal Victou seems to have a standing invitation with them."

Her face held a steely determination that shook Remi.

"Suzu, I think more than anything, your parents would want you to live a long life, pursuing what you believe in. They wouldn't want you to *risk* your life."

She looked up. "You were right the other day, Remi. You didn't know my parents that well."

○ ○ ○

With his back to the counter, the store owner looked over the diverse, curated offerings aligned on brass hooks or spinning on mechanized display carousels. He took pride in having the finest Comeback shop in west Chigou, even if some failed to recognize it as such. A few customers found his fastidious nature alienating, but nobody paid him to cure ignorance.

The door chimed and the store owner spoke. "Welcome to Meiru Comeback. What fine item can I…"

Turning around, he cut off his well-practiced preamble and instead offered, "This isn't a cold creamery."

"I need a tool," Suzu informed him.

Knowing curious children had shallow pockets, the store owner sighed. "Young Lady, I doubt you would require anything quite like what I have."

Having lived in the world of adults far longer than the clerk would believe, Suzu ignored the patronizing remark and scanned the wall. Her search ended high up behind him. "Is that all you have?"

Having memorized his inventory, the man felt a little amused by her suggestion. "I assure you, child, that nothing up there is for you. Now, this is a serious shop for serious buyers. Why don't you go find a slide somewhere."

Suzu pulled out a thick cylinder of money, craftily rolled to look like twice its value. It hit the polished wood counter with a thud.

The store owner's eyes doubled in size. "Where did you get that?"

"What, you don't want it?"

"I'm not in the business of stolen commodities."

Suzu laughed. "This is a Comeback shop, and I'm not as innocent as I look."

"I'm sure I'd rather not know. However, I'm certain you're not old enough for anything out of the armory," the shop owner said, looking down his nose at Suzu.

Among an almost endless array of lightly used gadgetry, ranging from Tokis to kitchen tools to musical instruments, Comeback shops were also known to carry items of self-defense. Since labeling anything explicitly for assault would deem it felonious, shopkeepers often developed creative marketing to give softer images to barbarous tools.

"That Toki next to the retractable alloy baton, what's the little pressure tank for? Something pneumatic?"

She had found an opening, as this shop owner—like all of them—savored any chance to describe the mysteries of his fine Tokis. "Alright, little Lady, how did you know it was a gas chamber?"

Suzu crossed her arms. "Because I'm smart. Now, what's its special?"

As if preparing to take a newborn baby out of a crib, the man grabbed a clean cloth and gently removed the Toki from its brass nest. He set it down on the counter, giving it a corrective polish. "The two-millimeter chamber wall holds a five-second burst of itoú gas."

Suzu thought she had heard the vaguely familiar term from Gozen once before. "In case I wanted someone to take a step back?"

"In case you wanted them to collapse in a fit of blind coughing for several minutes."

Suzu slowly reached for the Toki. Disarmed by her sincerity, the shop owner let her engage the well-crafted apparatus. After years of having her father demonstrate one gadget after another, handling intricate tools felt second nature. Before the clerk could instruct her, Suzu flipped open the face of the clock and found the trigger. Showing adept dexterity, she managed to avoid spraying the owner in the face.

"What kind of a discount does a young Lady get for simply wanting to defend herself out on the streets?"

The older man stood upright. "Oh, are we going with innocent *now*?"

6
REUNION

No plants would grow in the sunless world of Oubli Street. The tight corridor stood as a fracture in Chigou's gleaming facade. Suzu's eyelids hung low from fatigue as she waited for Victou and a couple of shadowy men. Cool air constantly swirled over the stoop she perched on. Her bones began to ache.

"Ugh, enough of this."

Suzu navigated around back into an alleyway nearly squeezed out of existence. Fire escapes almost touched, floating over a forgotten terrain of junk. Above, the dusky sky peeked through a narrow slit of rooftops, left over from what the rest of Chigou hadn't sucked up.

After spotting narrow exits at either end, Suzu climbed up one floor and checked the rear door. She had badgered Gozen into teaching her how to lockpick, but the latch hid behind so much rust she wondered if even a proper key would open it.

After at least fifteen minutes of picking, racking, and cleaning, the fused lock barrel snapped loose with a loud clang.

As the sound echoed away, she put her ear to the door. No sound, no lights. She held her breath and slowly pried it open. Disappearing into shadow, she shut the door behind her.

One floor below, Victou tripped on the second stair, causing a stumble up the broken stoop. His briefcase burst open as it hit the step and he scrambled to catch a small paper, crumpling it in his hand.

"Idiot," he cursed.

When he heard that Pirou had died, Victou wanted nothing more than to leave Kasic forever. Realizing his biweekly paycheck had just been posted, however, he detoured to the payroll office and cashed it on the way home.

He rattled the latch open, his nerves still humming. Inside, he set his briefcase down in the dark, then groped for a small lamp. On the third try, it sparked on, barely lighting the corner. He contorted his neck into a sickening crack; it felt great. Curious if his little girl had made any food, he headed down the hall.

Victou's finger switched another light on, and a pale-faced creature materialized out of the darkness. Black hair cast a dramatic shadow down her face, hiding her eyes.

"Victou Despré?" Her voice was tempered, calm.

"What do you want?" Victou's finger remained on the switch.

"You work for Kasic," Suzu stated.

"Yeah… well… yeah." Victou had long since practiced the art of need-to-know.

"But they're not the only people you work for."

Victou, finally noticing his size advantage, dropped his hand to his side. A breath later, he noticed a black metal rod held in the girl's white-knuckled grip.

"What is that?"

Her voice became more direct. "Very bad for your health. Now, since we haven't disagreed upon your employment situation, I have a few questions."

"I probably know a lot less than you think." Victou offered sincerely.

"Those leeches who collected that folder from you the other night—what do you know about them?"

Victou rationed what little he had to offer. "The squatty one just breaths heavy through his mouth. The lanky fella—the one who is missing an arm—hisses when he talks. I suppose of the two, you'd call him the brains."

"And the stolen research you handed over, who did they give it to?"

Victou was startled by the ease with which the girl rattled off supposed secrets. "Look, I don't have anything meaningful to tell you. You sound like you know more than me."

Victou heard her knuckles crack as she squeezed the unhealthy thing in her hand. "The guy they work for has tried to kill me—twice. You're going to have to give me something."

"Then you know him better than me. I saw him once. Applied to Kasic, lied on my resume, and then this young guy blackmails me into stealing research. Those two come to pick it up when they feel like it."

"That guy also killed my parents. So, you see, I need a way to see him one last time," Suzu said.

Victou saw her fiddle with some kind of trigger on the device. "I don't... look, okay. The short one said the young guy's name once, I think, because the tall guy hit him when he said it. I think it was... I don't know... Cats?"

"Kits. Yeah, him. Now, how do I find him?"

"I don't know."

"Then you should start thinking." She began to raise her self-defense weapon. "Because I'm not leaving until—"

"Hello," a young girl quietly interrupted, stepping into the small kitchen doorway. "I'm Chichi."

"Who is this?" Suzu demanded, looking at Victou.

Victou looked down at his daughter, who bent her eyebrow and replied to Suzu, "I *said* I'm Chichi. Chichimou if you want my long name."

Suzu was silent, her mind sputtering, and the girl politely continued.

"What's *your*—"

A loud knock pulsed through the front door. Everyone but Chichi jumped.

"Dammit," Victou muttered.

"Is that them?" Suzu promptly asked.

Victou nodded, tense.

Vengeance flooded into Suzu's veins, and she pointed at Chichi. "Get *her* away from them."

Happy to exit, Victou grabbed his daughter.

"Chichi, get your go-pack." She ran off.

He snatched his briefcase and a pre-packed bag, paying

no attention to the few items on the counter. Chichi returned quickly. The two left as if they had always planned to move out that very minute.

Suzu suddenly realized Victou wasn't a conspirator, he was a nomad. She followed him as he led his daughter onto the fire escape. A louder knock thumped behind them, followed by muffled arguing. Victou scooted little Chichimou down the ladder as her bag snagged a rusty corner.

Before following them, Suzu stopped to look over her shoulder at the door. She imagined kicking it open right into their greasy faces.

By the time she turned back around, Victou and Chichi had already reached the ground level and were running towards an adjacent alley. A second before they disappeared around the corner, Victou looked back. Suzu wanted something badly but wasn't going to sacrifice Chichi, or even him, to get it. She watched one opportunity escape and decided to focus on another.

Grabbing her Lansu, Suzu smashed a foggy light illuminating the back door. Gas and electrons popped with the shattered glass and the alley slipped into deeper darkness. She jumped off the fire escape and braced herself by the side alley leading to the front. Pressing her cheek against the grimy corner, she leaned around, waiting for the thugs to investigate the noise.

Faint conversation came from around the corner. Suzu wiped the sweat off her hand, getting a better grip on the metal staff. Her breathing steadied.

A stocky silhouette leaned out further down the alley. Suzu slipped back behind cover. Her ears caught footsteps beginning to approach and she waited for a long shadow to reveal her target. Water dripped off a steam pipe. She heard breathing through a spit-filled mouth and her vision tinted red.

A face peeked around the corner, and in an instant of recognition, she thrust her weapon straight into it. Bones cracked as his body was flung backwards and landed on wet trash. Blinded by blood, he moaned on the ground, hands shaking near his broken nose.

Suzu dashed at him and raised the Toki filled with itoú gas. The face triggered a name—Guso, and she wanted to stomp it out of existence. An inner rage begged her to take a foot and crush his windpipe. She then noticed his quivering mouth covered in blood, which bubbled out from where a tooth had sat seconds earlier. She had fantasized about killing the man more times than she could count, but as he lay at her feet, the fantasy suddenly felt grotesque.

So riled with emotion, she nearly missed the lankier man appear down the alley, fumbling into his jacket with the one arm. Suzu dove down just as a bullet smashed into the wall right where she'd been standing. Her memory suddenly replayed Remi's plea to her to stay alive, and she decided not to run down a narrow alley towards a man with a gun. Instead, she spun around the corner and ran deeper into the back alley, away from where little Chichimou had escaped with her father.

Suzu heard footsteps and curses chase her down the side alley. She vaulted over a wood fence just as the man emerged around the corner. Another shot ricocheted into the dark clutter behind her.

Her arms grabbed steam-slicked railings as she drilled through an alley so cramped it felt like it was trying to crush her. Her focus narrowed onto a sliver of streetlight ahead. The image of Guso's bloodied face flashed in her mind. She heard the echo of his threats from their first meeting, promising a young girl pain and death.

Finally, she emerged onto a proper street and the pressure lifted. Nausea came out of nowhere and she suddenly wanted to vomit her rage onto the sidewalk. An old lady clutched her shoulder bag and scurried quickly past.

Suzu wanted to go back and fight, but she didn't want to see their heinous faces ever again. *Maybe,* she thought, *Gozen will find them and do what he promised, right after he found them pinning me to the ground.*

She spat bile onto the sidewalk, "or maybe I can get Kola to snack on their eyeballs."

7
EXPLORER

When Jin was four years old, he had received a book from his mother, entitled *Sacred Guide - Places and Practices for One Dedicated to Maiishi*. Between the covers, it provided a cornucopia of locations, exercises, philosophies, and even recipes long revered in the martial art. Over the years he had found its images increasingly captivating, but none had grabbed his attention more than the brilliant landscape called *Kuitsu*.

At first glance, the image had boldly presented an alpine peak, engulfed in a lacework of angelic light that funneled down into a blinding bloom. On his twenty-third reread, Jin had finally noticed a diminutive lawn and small pool existing inside that luminescent cradle. The discovery had made its accompanying text seem more concrete, as it had described a setting for the purest mediation one could hope for. Whenever Jin had asked about it, however, his Maiishi instructors would always regard it metaphorically, suggesting each student *find their own Kuitsu*.

After he and Lady Kyoumére had discussed the large Kuitsu painting at the Tree House, Jin had decided to pursue the obscure path of the painting's former owner. The *Sacred Guide* gave only one clue as to Kuitsu's location: *With late-sun to its back, the mountain reaches up, cradling the light onto its lap*. Jin assumed this meant Kuitsu was positioned on a western peak facing east, one of the few parts of the Naifin Valley that remained largely unexplored.

A few days later, Jin had examined the mountain using a high-powered telescope gifted from his sister. In their adolescence, she had used it to spy on academy mates. He recognized that she had brought him along as an ear for gossip or to provide a patsy if Mother ever caught them. Despite her motivations, Jin had welcomed any attention from his typically preoccupied big sister.

The mountain inspection had concluded with a camera he then coupled to the telescope. Comparing an array of photographic exposures, he had discovered a subtle glow one stop above the surrounding area—a gathering of light nearly hidden behind an isolated peak. Jin had thought of his great-grandfather Poel Jastoú, who had even less to go on when he had helped to discover the Valley. Having been born at high altitude, Jin assumed himself to be even better equipped than his ancestor to explore the soaring unknown.

As the sun began its escape on the first day of his journey, the temperature dropped ruthlessly fast. Jin decided to make camp and establish a small perimeter of temperate protection. Jin's proactive tinkering had reworked his complex assortment of gear into an impressively manageable load that he anchored to the slope.

His compressed tent slid out of a narrow sleeve. Pulling the release-line triggered an organized explosion of fabric and alloy, culminating in a fully assembled shelter. Two adjustable legs hoisted the bottom to a near-level position. He then took off his boots and unrolled his sleep-sack stuffed with Chitori underwing feathers.

Buzzing with adventure, Jin kept the sleep-sack unzipped to vent his heavy pulse. He hung an electric torch and a pocket steam heater and began reading *Sacred Guide*. The story most closely associated with Kuitsu involved two pioneering newlyweds starting their careers in a burgeoning colony.

The couple, both devoted to Maiishi, led a successful life as a baker and woodworker until an accident cost the husband his life. Tormented by grief, the young bride could not cope in a society roaring on at a relentless pace. Needing sanctuary, the lady went on a trek to purge her darkness and find peace.

After weeks of wandering the forest, unable to cure her suffering soul, she decided to ascend the mountain. There, she hoped to fulfill one of Maiishi's most crucial tenets: eliminating distractions to achieve one's true purpose. If she couldn't find favor on the mountain, she resolved it would consume the remainder of her fading life. The story concluded with her finding Kuitsu and living amongst uncorrupted beauty.

Despite being able to read, Jin had often requested it read to him as a young child. He quickly deciphered his mother's regard and father's disdain for the story, which both seemed to have an impact on him. Jin had long since considered himself a romantic pragmatist.

◦ ◦ ◦

As the glow of early sun hit his tent, Jin awoke, happily rejuvenated. He went to scratch his scalp but observed that only his right hand obeyed. Lifting his head, Jin noticed he hadn't fully secured the tent, allowing his left hand to slip into the elements. It didn't feel cold. It didn't feel like anything at all.

Grabbing the stiff hand with the other, he managed to slip the bluish digits behind his back. The jarring sting of cold caused him to yelp like a cat being stepped on. His mind cycled through family research, documenting the often catastrophic results of black, cold-burnt skin. *Not black*, he told himself, *just blue, you lucky fool.*

His shoulder eventually cramped, so Jin sat up and peeked out of the tent, inviting an assault by frozen particulate. He immediately zipped the tent back up and dug out his coffee flask. After loading the canister with melted snow and coffee grounds, Jin fired the fuel cell and impatiently waited for smoke and steam while examining his now red and puffy hand. A frozen wind stormed up the mountain face, penetrating his tiny shelter and causing his head to ache. Unable to wait any longer, he took a sip of the under-brewed beverage. The warm liquid tasted better than any beverage he could recall.

Jin nursed the heated stimulant as best he could, but the second day went slower. His back sweat while the dry air cracked his skin. He occasionally looked back to Chigou, noting how harmonious it appeared from so far away. It reminded him of a model of the city he had built at age seven.

Darkness came more quickly. Wind blew in like a frozen wraith, sucking the life right out of his body. He hastily set up camp and ate a dinner of dried meats and blashu rolls packed with herbs. He decided not to read afterward. Before sleeping, he meticulously checked every seam in his womb of feathers and fabric.

∘ ∘ ∘

Waking up to darkness, Jin strained to recall details from a dream. His sister had guided him through the family's prize-winning garden, but everything was oversized and misshapen. She told him to fetch a small toy glider which she threw around the hedges and flower bushes; she had always had a fascination with flight. Eventually tossing it into a tree, she ordered Jin to retrieve her cherished plaything, perched a solid fifteen meters up. Jin went right up, unbothered by climbing or heights. After achieving the glider's altitude, he found himself unable to reach it. Encouraged—*or was it taunted?*—by his sister, Jin stretched out as far as he could until he clenched the model and promptly fell straight towards the ground.

He couldn't remember if his sister had caught him or if he had died in the dream, but his stomach demanded breakfast, so he got up. Coffee went down hot, mixing well with spiced nuts and fruit. The sun ascended and he felt motivated for an early start.

The wind settled and things went smoothly until the strength in his legs began to wane. Jin knew himself to be in excellent condition, but fatigue had found him nonetheless. The thin, cold air took more away from him than he had expected. His vision grew strained, and he found himself blinking and squinting more. Cold burrowed below his skin, seeping into bone. Perhaps the immunity of being an alpine native had its limits.

High Altitude and the Human Body, written by his great-grandfather Poel, had become a popular read even outside the medical community. Individuals new to mountain living soaked in the potential dangers surrounding their climate controlled rooms. Jin had nearly memorized it. The book presented injury and death through an assortment of avenues involving thin atmosphere and sub-zero temperatures. On the third day, Jin found himself recalling them often.

The sound of snow crunching under his feet initially offered a satisfying, youthful delight but had transposed into a vexatious reminder of his sluggish progress. Early morning hours drifted by with little notice. The end goal faded from his mind, replaced with the biting of endless snow.

Having kept his head down for so long, the peak surprised Jin when he finally reached it. His fatigue disappeared when he discovered a second, narrow peak just behind, with a glowing fog sitting right between them. His feet picked up and stomped through thick snow. The steep slope began to level off, as if he was cresting over into a chasm. The cloud looked like a fallen remnant of the heavens, trapped between two frozen peaks, but as he got closer, he saw that the mist actually floated upward. A faint hum of falling water came from somewhere within. The bottom was hidden below, but it sounded deep.

He noticed a bare spine of black rock running down the back of the peak. Although steep, the notched facade offered a precarious stairway into the unknown. He was heading straight for the single route when something stole his breath.

Splayed out in the endless white, remnants of bone and blood formed a circle of death. *High Altitude and the Human Body*, chapter seven: a single Shiroku had maimed and even killed a few of Batsu's troupe, including their seasoned mountain guide. Having remembered to bring his compact Masu, Jin questioned whether it would defend him against a colossal ice cat.

His eyes jumped around, searching for the apex predator. Each breath froze in his throat. His stiff fingers reached back for the sword. *High Altitude* described the group walking right into the massive cat, unaware of its presence until claws lunged out. The wind blew hard enough to hide any sound of movement.

Tiny antlers then shot out of the grotesque pile. Jin jumped backwards, the weight of his pack pulling him down flat. He flailed in the frozen powder, trying to right himself. Ice stuck to his eyelids and light shimmered around his vision like a migraine. Raising his sword, readying for the attack, he saw a set of tiny black eyes blinking back at him. Thick white fur framed a stained beard dripping with blood on a creature no larger than his leg. Unbothered, the snow-fox proceeded to nibble on its meal.

Jin brushed himself off and decided to approach, sword ready at his side. A horn identified the victim as a large mountain ram—a Memorin, if he recalled the classification correctly. The snow-fox continued to munch on what Jin assumed to be leftovers of a kill made by some larger predator and preserved in ice. Jin stopped four meters short of petting distance. The snow-fox let out a satisfied yawn, its belly full of breakfast. Jin admired the small creature, who seemed unbothered by the harsh setting as it licked its chops. With bloodstained antlers, the fox then scampered straight towards the luminous mist. Jin stood and observed the frisky creature before recognizing an opportunity.

With high knees, Jin ran through the snow that now sloped downward. Upon entering the glow, his skin felt… warmth? He paused, watching as the agile fox pranced down the thin ridge of black rock and disappeared into the mist. Jin stepped up to the first ledge, looking and listening. He poked his sword at the ground below, blindly trying to assess the path. The roar of water became louder. Jin then decided to take the snow-fox's confidence for himself.

Time became vague in the fog, measured only by one craggy step after another, the beginning and end out of sight. The tepid air felt relatively tropical, but Jin reminded himself to stay sharp. He couldn't see more than five meters below, nor did he care to dishonor his great-grandfather's precedent; the old Lord had traveled three times the distance at nearly twice the age.

Jin squinted as the light somehow seemed to intensify deeper within. As he relied more on his hands to feel out his path, Jin realized that the ice surrounding his thin track of black rock actually felt warm to the touch. He pulled off a glove and scraped some of the glassy surface with his fingernail. His head spun around as he realized the ice had given way to a wall almost entirely composed of crystal, bouncing light down below. Motivated to see more, he climbed down a mere ten meters when the veil of mist finally opened. Although he had expected to see it, Jin still gasped at his first sight of Kuitsu.

Across the ravine, snowmelt converged to form a waterfall that reflected against a million crystal facets. The ice-cold liquid collected into a pool, barely visible as a blue smudge at the bottom, which was adjacent to a tiny patch of green as lush as the central valley. Jin pulled out a Toki telescope and saw a cabin on the grass, plainly visible and undeniably man-made.

His attention shifted onto the snow-fox, which continued its descent towards the pool. *Are you a pet? Will you transform into a person?* Jin wondered, feeling the return of an unbridled imagination he had shared with his sister in childhood. He then recalled the note she had written, attached to an unexpected package sent from their home in Primichi.

Dear Baby Brother,

I sincerely hope this note finds you well. I received your postcard and shared it with Mother, who nearly shed a tear. Apparently, even a mere change-of-address notice is enough to have Mother loudly lament the absence of her dearest baby Jin nonstop for a full week. Jealousy and whatnot aside, I have always found her pudding-soft love for you rather endearing. I told her you'd come back sometime, handsomely grown and nearly unidentifiable from the innocent, smooth-faced boy who left. I thought that'd pick up her spirits, but she drifted off with yet another tear.

But, on to business. As I'm sure you remember, I was accepted into Sky Academy before you left. Considering the unmitigated joy I experience there, it is no surprise that my time has been almost perfectly successful. Yes, only almost, as I'm beginning to find that the lumbering pace of airship travel reflects its gas-bloated grandeur. I'm a thriving young woman and my time for progress is present, wouldn't you agree?

So, I bestow upon you an airfoil of my design, one perfectly produced for personal, low-profile gliding. The wing, of course, works flawlessly, but I've decided a retractable version would simply be sublime, for portability. I know well your prowess for modifying gadgetry into compact variations, so here you have it. I leave my precious work in your tinkering, talented hands, baby brother.

With unfeigned approval,
Pepa

ALPINE FOX | F33

UPPER MURDES

LORD ROU KADELA

After performing crude tests against an industrial-sized fan, Jin had assessed Pepa's grasp of aeronautics as spectacular. It had proven no surprise, as he had always admired her aptitude for anything she attempted. After a few days, he had successfully modified the wing to transform in and out of a collapsed formation, allowing it to be mounted into a harness which he now strapped to his back. He teetered a bit, as the robust device altered his center of gravity.

Staring down into the deep descent before him, Jin thought the setting perfectly suited a field test. He eyed the pool as a suitable landing zone should things go awry. Having studied his sister's flying tips, Jin felt confident with a maiden flight.

Jin reached back and felt for the glider's release lever. Alloy wings shot out into their flight configuration. He clutched the wired flight control and toggled the joystick with his thumb as ailerons squeaked on the wing's trailing edge. Working backwards from the small plot of grass, he charted a course. With one final tightening of the straps, Jin jumped.

Immediately, he noticed an initial lack of lift which caused him to careen towards the black, jagged rock. With little time to calculate, Jin yanked the thumb-stick back, protecting his face with the opposite hand. The wings jerked and vaulted him instead towards the icy falls. He yanked the stick aft and felt the sting of snow melt against his eyes, cursing his lack of adequate eye protection.

With a dripping, ice-cold face, Jin felt the glider ease into a downward spiral as the controls began to meld with his hand. Blinking hard, the lush sight beneath him clarified, as if he had suddenly jumped into the painting he had admired since childhood. The astonishing multitude of crystal stretched nearly to the pool before folding into black rock. It enveloped him in a halo of light that shimmered like a thousand prisms. The water seemed gentle as it fell, and as Jin circled towards the bottom, he imagined his great-grandfather flying next to him.

The dream melted away as Jin noticed how quickly the ground was approaching. Recalling the diagram his sister had drawn, he remembered a periphery doodle titled *Theories on Landing*. The foil had flaps to drag air while increasing lift at lower speeds. Only seconds from the ground, instinct took over.

He aimed for a last-second lift, stalling to soften his speed at touchdown. With a delicate touch, the maneuver worked well but he was still at a questionable altitude. Attempting to avoid a knee injury on solid ground, he pushed forward as far as he could, just making the edge of the pool. Water sprayed in all directions as he splashed forward up to the shore. Soaked and frozen, he assessed himself for broken bones before releasing a smile.

Jin dragged his gear onto the shore, struggling in his waterlogged clothes. Remembering something from his great-grandfather's book about being soaked and cold—something involving dying— he decided to strip down to a minimally civilized layer. Steam billowed off his torso as if he had stepped out of a sauna. He gazed around at lush grass, a turquoise pool, and cascading falls. Above him, the luminous walls disappeared into a glorious canopy of light. He gulped in the purest air he had ever tasted, sweet and rich with minerals. The natural splendor captivated him for a full five minutes before he remembered the cabin.

Although primarily built with loose stones, the cabin contained more wood than what seemed plausible; he could not see a single tree in the ravine. Set into the mountain, the cabin's earthen roof sprouted upward with a variety of plants. *Someone has planted a garden*, Jin ruminated. Other, larger plants grew along the sides in a natural layout. The scene reminded Jin of a flower growing in the fissure of a hefty boulder, lush and isolated.

Despite the stories, not once did he consider someone actually *living* in Kuitsu. The banality of daily life in such a fantastical, inaccessible place seemed improbable. Wicking the moisture off his face and leaving his gear behind, Jin set his assumptions aside and approached the cabin.

He looked for signs of life, wondering if the proprietor had long since left or passed away. Perhaps a corpse lay inside on a bed. Recalling the pile of bones that the snow-fox had jumped out of and wondering where the little antlered fellow had gone, Jin watched as the door creaked open and a small man with a flowing white beard sauntered out. They paused, each silently evaluating the other until the elder glanced over towards the landing site. "You crashed your thing."

"Uhm… yes, Lord. I'd argue it was a reasonable landing, considering the brief acclimation period I had with the controls in any practical, real-world…"

Jin's excessive explanation was cut short as the small man suddenly threw a rock at his face. Caught entirely off guard, Jin reacted just quickly enough to take the small stone on the shoulder instead of the nose.

"You're too slow," the old man accused.

"Excuse me?"

"That's why ya crashed. Ya gotta be quicker than the mountain." His wrinkled finger pointed around.

Jin had never thought of a mountain as quick—or as moving in any capacity. The old man waddled closer until they nearly touched. He rubbed his belly and asked, "Ya got any candy in those sacks?"

8
EXPEDITION

Darou glanced out the porthole window next to his locker. After just a few days on the job at Noutess, his initial curiosity had been swapped with tedium. His manager treated him as if he had never held a job before; he had enough experience to know not to argue. Fingernails still got stained, back still ached. Walks home felt long and lonely, so he appreciated Gozen offering to pick him up that day.

A billow of ground steam cleared and Darou saw the unmistakable shape of his friend through a window; after nearly dying together, he felt okay thinking of them as friends. Darou shut his locker and scurried down the steps. He kept his head low, ready to ignore any patronizing remarks from older black-hands too miserable to just let a young employee leave peacefully.

Gozen looked around the place like the old Lord Enforcer in him had never really retired.

Darou wasn't sure if the huge man had noticed him walk up. "Hey, Gozen. I'm here."

Gozen offered only a slight nod in return. Darou walked past him, more than happy to leave his shift a minute early. He jumped up to Neko's passenger door but halted on the step, facing a woman he had never dared cross. "La... Lady Kyoumére?"

"Lord Darou," she said, looking to Darou like a porcelain vase sitting on a mechanic's bench.

"Uhm, I'll get in the back," he offered, already retreating.

In the cab, Lady Kyoumére watched Gozen continue his obscure examination of the space. She enjoyed seeing her old friend utilize the impressive investigative abilities that once drove his life. Although he no longer wore the uniform, Gozen still donned all the honor of a Lord Enforcer in her eyes.

The husky sleuth's focus zeroed in on an unusual sound. It was similar to rolling tires, but the tone didn't match. Gozen spotted a cargo truck with a giant *E* painted on the side. It looked more nimble than most fuel transporters. The sound disappeared as it braked to a stop.

He walked over as the driver left the cab to report in. The truck looked wet in some of the corners; odd, as it had not rained for a week. Trying to keep a low profile as best he could, Gozen drifted towards the rear double set of tires; a mounted industrial lamp revealed the answer straight away. Small, metal studs sparkled in a fixed pattern across the thicker part of the tread. Knowing that not a single Dark-spark mine had been approved above the snow line, he found the snow tires peculiar.

Lady Kyoumére heard Darou shimmy into the back of the cab. She glanced back, hands lightly folded in her lap, waiting for him to speak.

"Uhm, Lady K… I mean Lady Kyoumére," he finally let out.

"Yes, young Lord."

"I'm… I'm sorry about the other day in the kitchen. I didn't mean to be so…" he struggled to find the right balance of confession and deflection.

"Spontaneously coarse?"

"Yes," Darou humbly said before picking up the volume. "It's just… Jin comes from all this money and the way he talks… it just makes me feel…"

"Your feelings require no apology," Lady K said. "And how was your day at work?"

Just then, the truck shifted as Gozen stepped up and into the cab. He paused, seeing Darou's head sticking between the seats. They exchanged looks before Gozen glanced over to Lady Kyoumére, and then back to Darou. "What?"

Darou simply slipped back into the rear cabin.

o o o

Blonde hair bounced in the wind while a single-cylinder

engine hummed underneath the roar of freighters and executive sedans. Jealous of the breezy streets in quaint neighborhoods up North, Lucette found driving her scooter across downtown a bit unnerving. Even heading back out to the Tree House—halfway between downtown and Doulan—she noticed her knuckles looked bleached.

Lucette pulled into the orphanage's drive with a long exhale, anticipating someone scampering out to see her impressive new ride. As the tiny engine revved down, she took off her bright red helmet, ready to talk all about it. She saw only one boy who picked his nose by a tree and an unusually large pile of trash by the house. With a disappointed groan, she then saw Suzu sitting up on the roof, looking like a compact ball of angst ready to pop. Lucette put her helmet back on.

Foam swirled in a whirlpool down near the shore, hypnotizing Suzu with its dance of toxic scum. She hated the entirety of Primichi, a pristine city sending its bile downriver, collecting at the feet of Chigou's children.

A bright red sphere poked around the roof's edge. The rest of Lucette followed, cautiously balancing around, plodding up shingles.

"If you think you need to wear a helmet, maybe you just shouldn't climb on roofs," Suzu suggested.

Lucette playfully grunted her way up to the peak. She pretended to be flabbergasted, eyes emphatically staring at the driveway. "Oh, young Lady, do you see that Aya Motors Puchi scooter, only *slightly* used, with a *scarcely* legal fifty-cc super engine, and glistening cherry-red body accented with extremely appropriate chrome racing stripes?" She waited for reciprocating glee, but her audience remained silent. "Of course, you can't see it, you're not even looking… or acknowledging my existence in any manner."

Suzu squinted up. "Hey, Lucette."

Lucette dropped her expression. "Is the river so captivating that you can't even *pretend* to be completely jealous of my exquisite, previously owned scooter?"

Suzu tilted a glance. "Where did you get the money to buy that?"

"I robbed the city's teeniest bank. Just the right amount." Lucette took a seat, careful to not slip down shingles that needed replacing. "Truth be told, I bought it from an old man who told me his daughter snored at anything with a motor, whereas I couldn't shut up about the lil' mechanical guy. Instead of adopting *me*, he just gave me a superb deal."

Suzu nodded dully. "So, what are you doing here?"

Remembering their last conversation about the subject, Lucette hesitated to even bring it up. "I need a letter from Lady K."

"For what?"

"I like looking at her pretty handwriting."

"What?"

"I still need a recommendation for this internship at Noutess. Not sure why they don't trust me. *Me*, right? Oh, what a world of suspicion these adults have welcomed me into."

"Well, it *is* a Dark-spark plant."

"And now I have stained my soul by entering the cathedral of all things evil?"

"Just a little."

"Hmm, yes, well, sometimes you gotta get a little dirty to clean things up. My first job is testing water samples from their drainage. They probably think it's a perfectly useless job, hence giving it to me—just some joint project with the academy to look… environmental. So, anyways, what are *you* doing up here?"

Suzu looked south, past downtown. "Kola flew down there a while ago, towards Goraka."

"Such a brave little owl."

Suzu prickled. "It's not a *joke*, Lucette."

Lucette's voice slanted towards a mumble. "I'm not joking. I think he's a very brave owl."

"Also, the prince of the company that made your scooter left Nia there to die there, you know that?" Suzu asked.

"I miss her too, you know." Lucette stared down at the whirlpool, as toxic as their conversation.

Suzu's mind suddenly switched gears. "How often do you work at Noutess?"

"I haven't, quite yet, but three days a week, or so I'm told."

Suzu, having lost her previous connection to Kits, now sensed another possibility. "I think Noutess might be linked to Etilé."

Lucette was hesitant to ask. "What's Etilé?"

Suzu leaned in. "The company that's everywhere but doesn't exist? *Daimó's* company?"

"I'm not aware of many things that don't exist."

Suzu was irritated. "It's the guy Kits works for, the guy who killed my parents."

"Okay… what do you want me to do about it?"

"I need to find out for sure. Maybe you could ask around, see if anyone recognizes the name." Suzu felt progress, planning.

"Oh, Suzu, I don't know." Lucette's voice dimmed.

"Have you ever seen Kits there? Maybe you could sneak me in. I could dress up, just look around until I find something."

"Suzu, I just got this internship. I *just* got it. If my school publishes the results of the water study, I could get my name on that. For once, a document with my name on it that isn't about being an orphan. Why are you asking me this? They'd fire me… they'd kick me out of the school!"

"So, you don't want to help me find the people that killed my parents?"

Of course she wanted to, but a salvo of comebacks piled up in her brain, making her so tense she wanted to cry. Begging for something to change the subject, she spotted the white owl flying in from the south. "Thank you."

"What?" Suzu asked.

Lucette stood up, ready to get off the roof. "Here, why don't you ask Lord Kola to spy for you. He appears unburdened by the shackles of academic responsibility."

While Kola flew down to perch on Suzu's shoulder, Lucette made her way out the back, hearing the rumble of Neko as it pulled in. She slipped around the side and ran into Darou near the front corner.

"Hey, did you see Lady K?"

Darou, distracted by a large pile of trash off towards the

opposite side of the house, took a second to reply. "Uh... what? I mean, she's in the truck with Gozen, just the two of them."

Lucette's eyes lit up. "Together? Out in public? But that's practically admitting to *mutual fondness*." She skipped on, eager to get her paper signed and catch the two adults in an awkward moment. Leaving Darou, she offered, "If you want to see a grumpy girl solicit favors from a predatory bird, Suzu's on the roof."

Too confused to even ask for clarity, Darou roamed to the back.

Inside Neko's cabin, Lady Kyoumére stretched out her goodbye. The truck offered a quiet view of the grand Laizou tree by the river, dancing in the breeze. She slid her thin fingers over to Gozen's strong hand and gently took hold.

A red flash then materialized in the passenger window. "Yes, Lady Lucette?"

"Hey you two," Lucette winked, glancing back at the apartment on wheels.

"Is this a *constructive* intrusion?"

"Yes, a million pardons." Lucette straightened her back. "I require a signed letter explaining how I am mature, responsible, and focused deeply into my bright academic future."

"Brighter than your helmet? Because it's making my eye twitch," Gozen offered.

"You like it, Lord Gozen?" Lucette displayed her bollo-red helmet like a model. "And I know you've been eyeing my fiery chariot over there, but I regret to inform you that it is not for sale."

"I'd pop those tiny tires the second I sat on it," Gozen warned.

"I will be in the house momentarily, Lucette," Lady K said, "and I will help you with whatever recommendation you need."

"Thank you." Lucette curtsied while balancing on the doorstep. "I'll just be over there, tuning up the little beast." She skipped away.

From opposite heights, Darou and Suzu met on the second-floor back porch. He jumped at the sight of a stark-white owl that screeched ten inches from his face. No matter how many times he saw it, Kola and Suzu's relationship mystified him.

"Careful, he smells fear," Suzu smirked.

"Oh, I think we've mutually understood that for a long time."

"Says the guy who survived being exploded out of a window."

Darou leaned on the railing, looking out to the river as the wood creaked. "Desperation and luck are not the same as bravery."

"Got some free paychecks out of it though, right?"

"Yeah," Darou murmured, "but that's over."

"You working again?"

"Yeah." He stretched his neck until a joint cracked. "This new Dark-spark plant down south—don't hate me."

Suzu likewise leaned over the railing. "Noutess?"

"Yeah, did Lucette tell you?"

Suzu nodded. Her pool of opportunities was growing. "So, what do you do there?"

"Same black-hand busy work I always do." Darou scratched at some soot embedded in the cracks of his fingers.

"How'd you like to make work more interesting?" Her voice was grave.

"What, you going to recommend me for a promotion?" Darou laughed.

"I need you to keep an eye on something for me."

"Hmm, keeping an eye on something doesn't sound that much more interesting—"

"I need to know if Kits ever goes there. I think he might," Suzu said as Kola began to clean his feathers.

Darou straightened up a bit. "Oh, I already got that one for ya. I saw Kits, well… Kits's car… actually, what I'm pretty sure was Kits's car, back in the executive lot my first day."

Suzu grabbed the rail, forcing the old wood to lean. "Has he been back since?"

"Like I said, I didn't exactly see him the first time, but if you want me to tell you when I do, I'm up for a little cloak-and-dagger." Darou recalled the unpleasant occasion of meeting Kits at the Tree House. "What exactly do you plan on doing if I see him?"

Releasing her grip from the rail, Suzu looked up to the sky for answers. She didn't have an explicit, comprehensive plan for what she'd do to Kits or even Daimó if she found them again; killing them seemed reasonable. Maybe that was fantasy, maybe not.

She leaned towards Darou, her voice low. "He works for this guy named Daimó, under the company name of Etilé. You ever hear or see those words, I'd be equally interested."

"Alright." Darou shrugged. One of the orphans' toys swirled in a foaming greenish whirlpool below.

"If you say you're doing this, Darou, I need to know you'll do it."

"Rat out the patronizing ass who tried to kill me in an industrial explosion? Don't let my bored face fool you. I'm *motivated*."

From Neko's cab, the two adults watched Kola fly over to the Laizou tree and grip a branch. Lady Kyoumére took in a final breath of stillness. "Thank you again for the extended outing. It was truly rejuvenating."

The sweet, recent memory came and went, replaced in Gozen's mind with a darker fixation. "Regretfully, I feel there is something I need to look into up in the mountains, past the snow line. Might take a few days."

"I never knew you to be concerned with climbing, Lord Gozen. Whatever would you be looking for up there?"

He didn't practice theorizing out loud, but he wanted to at least give the orphanage's Lady a heads up. "The rest of the children I expected to find down south, the ones I didn't overload your sanctuary with—at least not yet."

Lady Kyoumére clenched her hands, ever furious at this progressive society's willingness to abandon children. "I'll never understand how someone could treat them in such a way."

"But hope is not lost when someone like you exists."

She choked back a tear. "Like *us*, dear, like *us*. Now, please do try to stay warm up there." She tried her best to look encouraging. "Thankfully, I am patient, and you always come back."

Lady Kyoumére finally conceded to awaiting children and meal schedules. "Perhaps I should finally relieve Lady Suzu. I'm sure she is quite ready."

Gozen got out of the cab and assisted Lady Kyoumére down to the ground. As they walked to the front door, the sight seized Lady K in her tracks. "*Mother of invention*, what is all of this?"

Looking up, Gozen finally noticed the rather large pile of

building materials ripped up and discarded by the side of the Tree House. Not sure whether to protect Suzu or offer to clean it up himself, Gozen waited for the Lady to react.

Lady K walked briskly up to the pile, appalled at the chaos. "Is that one of my cabinets?"

Without missing a beat, she marched straight into the house. Gozen followed behind at a safe distance, hands in pockets. The two went straight into the kitchen where a stranger stood, holding tools.

"Oh my," Lady Kyoumére breathed out.

Before them, a sanctuary of food preparation gleamed in untarnished glory. Sloped counters and bent nails had been replaced with perfection. A polished mountain-stone counter sat between Bokai-wood cabinets, edged with fine details and finished with dark oil. A new icebox stood next to a clean stove on an unstained tile floor.

Lady Kyoumére then saw the face of glory. In the middle of the counter stood a Charban, Sugo Mark Three coffee smoker, trimmed with albino brass and fitted with a steam wand.

"But we have no steam line," she murmured faintly.

The man in the kitchen, who only then noticed the couple, took off his hat and bowed.

"Oh, you must be the Lady of the house. I do apologize about the mess outside—rubbish-hauler is running late." He moved to reveal the nearly finished steam-wand line running out of the wall. "But yes, no need to worry. I'll have you hooked up to city steam in a few days, but I installed a small boiler for the time being. Sorry about the delay."

Lady K was struggling to find the words. "Sorry? Delay?"

Gozen leaned over to Lady Kyoumére, who appeared entranced. "I take it *you* didn't order this." He then turned to the craftsman. "Who paid for this?"

"I just go where I'm told," the builder said humbly. "Boss seemed real motivated for this one though. Had two full crews here, you just missed them."

A jolt of recognition came across Lady Kyoumére. "Is it… *no…*

is Lord Jin behind this?"

"Ohhh, that would make sense," Gozen said, remembering the standing relationship between Jin, vast sums of money, and the unexpected. "But he didn't tell you about this?"

"No." She thought back to the last time she had seen him, walking away to his new apartment. "Oh *sweet river*, I asked him to leave—to make more room for the new children. I made him this embarrassingly meager cup of coffee, and—"

"And he paid to have your entire kitchen remodeled. Yeah, I guess that would seem reasonable to him."

The two looked at each other, wide-eyed, like kids who had accidentally gotten an extra scoop of cold cream at Michelou's.

"Oh, Gozen. I'm going to spend all night figuring this beautiful apparatus out, and as soon as you're back from your alpine expedition, I'll serve you the finest cup of smoked coffee that has ever been."

Gozen enjoyed witnessing this rare display of unbridled joy from his friend. He desperately wanted to share in her enthusiasm, arm-in-arm, but dreadful suspicions lurked in a frozen mountain, waiting for him.

9
MOUNTAIN

Well-worn pencil-lead pressed hard over the faint lines. Having run out of pages in her sketchbook, Chichimou had resorted to tracing older drawings. Even at such a young age, she had learned how to treasure old or forgotten things. Currently, a small bag contained everything she owned.

Her stomach sounded funny, but not in a fun way. When her father had them traveling from place to place—a familiar activity—they often resorted to eating the food her mother had called *industrial-filler*. Chichi remembered the food her mom had cooked. It had tasted like a tree smelled, but at least it had made her feel good.

Footsteps sounded outside the door—her dad's, and they sounded tired. Lock tumblers clicked and Victou flopped into the hotel room like a sack of wheat tossed into a truck.

"Hey, Chichi. How was your day?"

She shrugged.

"Right, well, you hungry? I could use some food."

Chichimou put down her pencil. "My stomach's gurgling."

"Uh oh." Victou sat on the lone chair in the room. He ran his fingers through his hair, trying to brush out the day. "You getting sick?"

"I don't know," Chichi murmured, glancing to a small pile of junk food wrappers. "I think I need some of Mom's food."

Back in Primichi, Victou had gladly let Meilu tend to their daughter's dietary needs. At age seven, Chichi had yet to develop her full culinary potential, but Victou still considered her the dietitian in their small family.

"You're probably right. I saw Varis opened a new market down here. Not as big as the one up north, but I think your mother would have approved."

Chichi looked unsure. "But aren't there are a lot of people there?"

Victou knew what his daughter meant. "Yeah, but… you probably need—we *both* probably need it. We'll just blend in, ya know, hiding out in the open."

Chichi didn't understand, but she agreed. "Should I get my go-bag?"

∘ ∘ ∘

He swam through a sea of faces that ranged from euphoric to shrewd. Fresh produce was slung back and forth between handfuls of money, making the scene look like a Soran casino where dealers dressed like farmers. He held his daughter's hand more firmly than usual, afraid to lose her in the churning current of bodies.

Farmer's markets always made Victou think of his wife. The first day of every week would include a late morning smoked coffee and a trip to the market where he'd stick next to her like a nervous child. He could never focus beyond the chaos, but loved seeing Meilu's eyes as they hunted delightedly through the stalls.

"Hey dad, it's Kora," Chichi said, pointing to the screen-printed logo on a crate of mimi fruit.

"What's a Kora?" Victou asked, accepting his vast ignorance of produce and agriculture.

"No," Chichi giggled. "It's the farm place. They had those boxes up at the Tree House."

"What treehouse?"

"Dad, nooo." Chichi's voice tweaked into frustration. "*The* Tree House. The orphanage I stayed in with Jin before he found you. Remember?"

Victou wished he could forget and erase all of those people from his life. Blackmail and blood, hiding and lying: it ate him from the inside. He still had nightmares about Ansel getting his arm cut off and feared the insecure sicko would take it out on him one day. Escaping that goon had brought some relief, but the city only had so many streets.

"Can't I have some? You should have some, they smell like flowers."

"Sure, Chichi. Uh, we'll take… I don't know, a bag, I guess." Victou clumsily suggested a shape with his hands. The fruit vendor, an older man with squinty eyes and a permanent grin, nodded. His wrinkled but nimble fingers grabbed a large bunch of the bright orange fruit and put it into a paper bag. Victou fanned out some money and the vendor plucked his fair share.

"Thank you," Victou offered, handing the bag to his daughter. She grabbed it with both hands and strained to get her nose over the top. Chichi breathed in the sweet bouquet with delight. The vendor bent down and waved as the small family walked off.

Victou tried a few mimis, wincing at the sour jab that slid into botanical sweetness. Between each bite, he found himself anxiously scanning the crowd. Being on the run had become an exhausting and inescapable lifestyle. He barely allowed himself to process what it did to his daughter.

He then felt a tug on his hand. Chichi's gaze had frozen, either from terror or overwhelming delight—Victou often had trouble telling the difference. He looked out and saw a vibrant poster advertising *Michelou's Cold Cream Drops, Now At The Market, Take Some Home Today!* The frozen, bite-sized treats came entombed within layers of chocolate, toasted nuts, toasted blashu, caramel, crunch, jam, salt, rock-sugar, rainbow-crystals, and sour-powder. Chichi examined the sweet strata like a geologist.

"I thought you wanted healthy food?"

"*Both* foods," Chichi reasoned.

Meilu had a sweet tooth, too, not that she ever admitted it. "Sure, we can take some home."

"Where's our home tonight?"

A woman walked by with two children about Chichimou's age. Her face twisted upon hearing the odd question from daughter to father. Victou pretended not to notice, uninterested in explaining to anyone how his mediocre parenting was working out. "We'll get some on the way out."

"What if we forget?" Chichimou frowned.

"We don't want it to melt."

Chichimou reluctantly agreed—another tough life lesson.

Victou continued to walk her around, listening for a whisper from his wife about what to feed their daughter. "Maybe I should just ask someone what's good. I think we can trust people here—" His musing was cut off as he saw a man in the distance—a man with one arm.

"Ow," Chichi whimpered as Victou clenched her small fingers too tightly. She hadn't yet noticed the fear in his eyes.

He started to pull her back, away from the man who had yet to see them.

"Chichi, it's time to go."

"We're getting cold cream drops now?"

"Not now," Victou whispered, weaving them through the crowd, back towards the street.

Legs flashed past Chichimou's face, occasionally interrupted by another child; they'd stare at each other for a brief moment as their adults pulled them apart. A thousand sounds fought their way into her ears. She nearly tripped trying to keep up until she face-planted into her father's hip.

Chichi looked up to see her father's stunned face. He stared down a giant ice cat just half a meter away, baring its fangs, frozen in time. Sculpted, forced-perspective mountains stood in the background as coats floated in the air, missing the bodies they were intended to keep warm. Ceramic food circled a fire made of glass. Above the large diorama, a sign read *Nesa Camping Co.*

With one more glance behind, Victou pulled his daughter into the store where a forest of camping gear and floor signage bewildered them. Camouflaged browns and greens were framed by bright colors and shiny metal fasteners. With enough money and the right brands of products, it suggested, one could permanently live in the great outdoors.

"Are we going camping?" Chichi asked.

An answer sprouted in Victou's head, simple and perfect; he couldn't believe he had come up with it. With no plan, he had dragged his daughter down from Primichi and through every alley of Chigou. She deserved peace, away from the real monsters of the world, even if that meant being with the ones from legends instead. "Would you like that, Chichimou?"

She reached down and picked up a picture book from a shelf; on the cover was an illustration of two people gazing into idyllic wilderness. Chichi began to flip through one incredible vista after another. The idea of being inside any one of them made her heart tingle.

Next to the stack of books sat a small, collapsible camera. Victou had never before wished to buy a camera, although his wife had always wanted one. Out of nowhere, he finally understood the desire to take photos of their daughter. The moderately expensive device offered no pragmatic benefit, nor had he ever used one, but he picked it up. Relief washed over him when he noticed a label: *Instructions and Film Included.*

"How do you camp?" Chichi asked, not looking up from a page in the book showing tiny fabric houses and food cooking over an actual fire.

"That's a good question." Victou checked out the window again and moved towards the back of the store. He brought Chichi to a clerk near the rear register. The young man had a well-trimmed beard and wore clothes that looked very clean, but were meant to be dirty.

Victou coughed into his hand. "Excuse me there, young Lord. I have a question."

The clerk folded a pair of thick, synthetic fiber socks. "Yes, Lord, how can I assist?"

He knew no other way to put it. "How… do you camp?"

The young man stopped folding and turned to give the young father his full attention. "What do you mean, exactly?"

"Well…" Victou looked down at his daughter, who shrugged. "Maybe we would start camping a few days at a time, then… you know, start doing it regularly."

"Excellent, I think that's exactly the right attitude to have. You'll get the most out of it that way. Even if it's just for one day to start, you really need to get completely out of the city."

"That is our current goal."

The clerk crossed his arms, ready to diagnose. "So, what kind of terrain are we thinking about here? Up in the plains? Maybe a rim forest, or… maybe even up the mountain base a little?"

He grinned down at Chichi, but she didn't reciprocate. Her last trip to the mountain had involved hard labor and rude men.

"I was thinking of going south… Noa," Victou proposed confidently, reading the young clerk's nametag.

Noa's grin disappeared. "South?"

"We like a warmer climate."

"Right." Noa searched for words. "But certainly you don't mean… not that I'm overly concerned about haunted forests, but… not *Goraka*, right?"

"Oh, of course not," Victou said, shaking his head emphatically. "But, let's say, someplace very similar to the Red Valley."

"Right, right. It's just sometimes we get these impulsive steam-heads sprinting towards disaster… Anyways. What equipment do you have already?"

The small family glanced at each other before Victou said, "You're lookin' at it."

"Okay," the young man said, grin returning. "One of everything then."

o o o

Kits had been standing at the door for at least three minutes, questioning whether he should apologize first thing or just let Daimó control the conversation. Of course, Daimó would control the conversation either way. He imagined his superior sensing him through the wall.

Kits advanced quietly into the office, remembering to keep his chin up. He forced his eyes to focus on Daimó, who sat behind a desk, reading something. Ready to take any accusation or vague query, Kits settled on getting it over with.

"I just got back from Kasic. Pirou's office is buttoned up, no problems there. Our contact, though, Victou Despré, took off with his kid when Guso and Ansel arrived, but Ansel is looking for him…"

The last words trailed off as Kits suddenly noticed another person in the room, a figure he'd originally taken to be a new statue. Kits's eyes jumped between Daimó and this new person. In the entire time Kits had worked for Daimó, he had only seen three other human beings in Daimó's office, two of whom had died the next day.

"Not both of them?" Daimó asked, now clearly reading the day's *Beacon of Knowledge*.

Expecting an explanation of the silent presence, Kits ran the question through his mind three times before absorbing it. "Guso lost a tooth. Ansel is picking him up from the clinic today."

In what felt like a full minute to Kits, Daimó finally answered. "Where did he misplace it?"

A condescending chuckle came from the statue.

Kits felt his voice tighten. "It got knocked out. Someone jumped him in the alley."

"Your accomplices are incompetent. You should replace them," Daimó said.

The stranger didn't disagree.

"Right. So, also today, I went down to see the shepherd who got his operation cracked a while back. Says some young guy came in, wanted every kid he had—even had the money—but then he went crazy. Said some big guy was there too—really big. Then a bunch of CEs showed up and closed the show."

Daimó finally looked up from his paper. "Lord Z. He certainly is a constant."

"I can deal with him if needed," Kits said, eyeing the trespasser.

"I want you to head west, past our primary Jinsper mine, to the new facility. Production seems good, but I have yet to receive reports on the exhaust system," Daimó ordered.

"You also mentioned getting the reservoir tested by the dam. Do you still want me—"

"The dam is being looked after. You needn't concern yourself with it." Kits heard the same patronizing tone in his voice that adults always used when talking to children.

Daimó's eyes dropped back down to his newspaper. He had been planning something with the dam but had yet to reveal any meaningful details to Kits, who never knew what to do Daimó's ambiguous offerings of information. It could have been a test, but it felt like a betrayal.

"Right," Kits agreed. He always agreed. "I've also seen Gozen at Noutess, picking up that Darou kid. Saw him checking out one of our alpine trucks. He might still be on the trail of our little miners. I could get lucky and see him up in the mountains."

Daimó turned a page to the obituary. "You'll only be lucky if you see him first."

∘ ∘ ∘

Away from the gloom of its basements and back alleys, Gozen found the distant view of Chigou quite immaculate, like a garden of light shrinking behind him. Many viewed the city as a utopia; he saw it as an incomplete dream worth pursuing.

Looking forward, he saw the ever-present Murde Mountains. A column of smoke marked his destination: the sole Kurokinojinsper mine in the western range. It sat above the mountain's base but short of the snowline. Fitting a transport vehicle with ice-studs was expensive, and industrialists weren't known for overspending on safety. Something lay hidden deeper in the mountains, and the more difficult it proved to locate, the more he needed to find it.

Gozen had followed the suspicious transport from Noutess—Darou had slipped him the truck schedule. Avoiding detection had proven conveniently straightforward, as the road leading west was long and unobstructed and narrowed into few possible destinations.

Wide plains of grass dissolved into tall, needled trees. Gozen sat up in his seat as the path became more precarious, fighting against the slanted terrain. Neko's engine roared louder with each increasing degree of incline. Before any signs of industry emerged, the road split into a fork.

Gozen lowered the window and felt cold air blow over the back of his neck. It hid any distant sound of heavy machines. Both routes looked used, but the left path had shallow tracks from sporty pedestrian vehicles—nothing that he was looking for.

After Neko had crested over the next two hills, the road ended into a large, deforested perimeter. A fortress of steel sat in the middle, churning with its promise of power. The facility's gate remained open, a lax decision that reflected how isolated the plant was positioned. Gozen blended Neko into a line of parked freelance transport rigs, and shut off the engine. Beyond the trucks, a single set of doors allowed the passage of just one or two large vehicles at a time.

With no other path available, Gozen felt the answer lay somewhere far ahead—despite an energy plant and mountain suggesting a rather certain dead end. He had to investigate the plant's interior, taking one of a few options. Gozen's sheer size had made stealth ineffectual since age twelve. He had kept his Enforcer badge, which only *Lord* Enforcers were allowed to retire with. He didn't like to exploit that asset too often, but he valued it more for its practical benefit than as a sentimental charm.

Gozen grabbed his impressive credential from the rear cabin and headed towards the opening. He kept the incoming truck between him and the door attendant, walking with a confidence that kept most people from asking questions. He threw the attendant a hard glance, nodded, and proceeded inside without waiting for permission. Black-hands and heavy machinery bustled throughout the cavernous complex. Gozen found such places rather familiar, but he wasn't in a mood to waste time. Instead of touring the entire complex for answers, he decided to fetch a guide.

Finding the first employee who looked the right combination of bored yet obedient, he led straight ahead with his badge. "Do you have any vehicles that go farther up into the mountain?"

"I don't know," the young man said as his body froze still.

"I'm looking for one with big *E* painted on the side—smaller transport that came in within the hour." Gozen's shoulders blocked any potential distraction.

"Oh, that one. It always parks in bay *C-1*," the black-hand spoke, relieved to have an answer.

"Take me there now."

The young man leaned off the rail and walked deeper into the space. He looked around, wondering if anyone noticed them. One bearded man gave the pair a long glance, but Gozen didn't offer him a gram of acknowledgement. Finally, the young man stopped by a large garage door labeled *C-1*.

"This is where the…"

"Okay, open it," Gozen ordered.

With his eyes still wide open, the black-hand let them in through a side door. Inside, the small transport stood alone in the otherwise empty bay.

"Thank you. I'll let you know if I need anything else." Gozen went straight up to the cab as he heard his escort leave, the mechanical door shutting behind him. With the cab empty, Gozen knelt and saw the tire spikes reflect against the dry, black rubber. He then noticed a set of wet tire tracks, but instead of coming from the garage door, they ran straight into the back wall.

Gozen spotted some conduit leading to a small breaker box in the corner. He opened it up, hit the only switch, and a low-frequency rumble emerged. Scraping steel echoed around the large space before the rear wall crept downward. Gozen checked the front door, making sure the noise hadn't attracted any curious employees. Once the massive wall completed its descent he saw a row of electric lights taper off into darkness. Drops of ice-melt echoed through the cavernous chamber, a tunnel that bored straight through the mountain.

Gozen stepped back to the cab and searched for keys.

10
SCOUTS

Victou gripped the bottom of a brand-new camping pack and heaved it onto the Hotrail. It easily outweighed his daughter, who watched the struggle along with twenty other passengers. Her eyes hid behind pink sunglasses that looked like they'd fit better in a few years.

Once in, Chichi claimed a seat, and the automated doors shut behind her. She set her reasonably sized bag in the adjacent seat as Victou slid his stuff across the floor and plopped down in surrender. "Whew. That was a lot harder than it looked, huh?"

Chichimou shrugged, feeling the effort had matched her expectations.

"So," Victou paused to catch his breath, "what are you most excited about…" another breath, "with camping?"

Chichi knew of camping conceptually but had never imagined she'd ever do it. "Can I say… everything?"

The train started to move. The outside went dark as a tunnel engulfed them. Chichi sat on her feet and turned her nose to the window, wondering which exhibit of the famed Hotrail Museum would reveal itself along the route. Victou smiled, watching her breath steam up the glass.

"Good thinking." He wiped the sweat off his forehead with a brand-new, durable, mold-resistant towel. "Let's just catch our breath and enjoy the show."

A red glow rose against the outer tunnel wall. Neon lights emerged, flowing in gentle waves. Suddenly, a vein of purple joined in and Chichi's eyes grew even wider. The colored lines continued to meander as blue and green joined the dance. Seconds later, an entire rainbow stretched out across from her, following the train like a school of electric eels. Chichi gripped the strap of her camping pack and wondered if she would finally see a real fish.

The display then transferred to a series of posters showing a girl in a pretty dress. The lights flickered in perfect sync like a virtual shutter, causing the model to come alive right on the paper. She danced and twirled around and around while southern Chigou passed overhead. Chichi always liked to watch dancing, which somehow merged athletics and beauty together. She wondered where little girls went to learn how to dance. She had asked her father once before, but Victou dismissed the activity as a hobby for rich people. Chichimou figured that "rich people" didn't mean *them*. The electric parade continued until they reached the last stop on the southbound line.

Victou emerged on the surface with his pack like a deep-sea hunter carrying a giant squid. Finally, with some space, he took five minutes to wrangle his gear into a comfortable state. Downtown peeked through smoke and cooling towers that filled the bulk of southern Chigou, thinning to an edge of small homes and starter warehouses. Longfrost Road continued south as the concrete tributaries feeding into it disappeared, marking the edge of civilization.

Tree cover was miles out of reach and he was getting tired. Victou pulled aside a random pedestrian. "Excuse me, which bus goes farther south?"

After a moment of processing the spontaneous question, the older woman's blank face grew a smile. "Into the Red Valley? Oh, you! Does he tease you like that all the time?" Her wrinkled eyes squinted at Chichimou.

"My dad is serious."

"Oh, you two!" The woman left, warm with amusement.

Victou looked south down the only road, thinning far out into a pinstripe of trees. Like most of Chigou's citizens, he knew the road went to Goraka and abruptly ended somewhere within. After abandoning the project, Opaji had created a gated checkpoint preventing curious fools from disembarking the ship of society and wandering into dangerous waters. Victou planned to hike well wide of that station.

"We might need to just walk. You up for it?" Victou asked while stretching his back.

Chichi replied, "Do you want me to carry your stuff for a while?"

He did. "Uhm... I think I better keep the big stuff. How about we stay on the road a little longer?"

Chichimou looked down the valley at their distant destination. Victou waited for her to confess her fears, heeding the warning of tales and folklore.

"Okay, sounds good."

Victou knew the stories as well as anyone else in Chigou: missing people, fateful expeditions, and red ghosts. They seemed no worse than their current set of nightmares: industrial conspiracies, violent thugs, and adolescent vigilantes. He patted his daughter on the back and the two started their journey into the unknown.

o o o

Their feet brushed along the tall grass in rhythm, producing a theme song for their journey. Having spent so much time running from apartment to street to alley to hotel, the wholly organic environment felt exotic. Neither could vividly remember being so far from the man-made world.

Victou checked his Toki eight times in the first hour. The Murde Mountains stared down at them from all around, too colossal and distant to give their efforts a sense of progress. Naifin Valley citizens saw the Murdes as the end of their world, although few gave the mountains much thought—the city's towers of steel and glass typically made the citizens nearsighted. Seeing the entire rim of mountains in one unobstructed panorama made Victou feel small; it made all of Chigou feel small.

A simple, sweet beauty followed them through the southern plain; it was amazing how much Chigou could keep out. Chichimou giggled every time a butterfly emerged from the grass or a bird flew overhead. The air invigorated them—purified them. *Are health and peace so easily attainable?* Victou wondered. At some point, he heard a whisper from his wife float down from the heavens: *I told you so.*

With dusk settling in, Victou decided to make camp while the world still offered light. Chichimou helped assemble the tent—the first time for either of them.

"This is fun," she said, face aglow.

Victou looked over the waves of grass—their portable island floating away from any concern. "Yeah, it is," he said, surprised at his sincerity. "This feels like the morning of Lemikou, opening all this new stuff."

Chichimou looked up with a blank face. She slowly recalled the posters and advertisements depicting families during the holiday, sitting at a mound of colorful presents. "Maybe if we live out here, we can have Lemikou too."

"Maybe," Victou muttered, feeling foolish for mentioning the experience he'd never properly given his daughter.

"Should I make the kitchen?" Chichimou asked, holding the collapsible culinary set.

Victou walked over; he'd forgotten what exactly they had bought. Tightly packed food, much of it dehydrated for endurance, presented a three-dimensional grid of culinary choices. Victou grabbed a top cube and read, "Chitori stew with root vegetables and mountain herbs." He looked down for Chichi's affirmation.

She responded, "I think it's lying."

Victou took the extruded square and shook it. "The guy at the store explained how it works. It's dehydrated, so when we cook it, the shape will be less... boxy. I'm sure it'll taste fine."

Committed to adventure, the pair attempted to reconstitute the meal cube. Victou found a stream coming in from the mountains. He made the jaunt in twenty minutes without thinking of his pursuers once. At the stream, he knelt down and cupped a handful of chilled spring water and snowmelt. It ran down his chin as he gave a satisfied sigh. *How can* water *be delicious?*

Back at the growing camp, Chichi had already assembled most of the portable stove. The lack of trees meant using a fuel cell—not a problem, as lumber would be abundant in a day or two. Trees only naturally sprouted along the rim of the Naifin Valley, so its two cities had embroidered their roads with them.

After a cooking process full of suspicious glares and laughter-inducing mistakes, the deconstructed geometry—as promised—proved to taste better than it looked. Their full bellies lulled them into silence as they stared at the brightest stars they had ever witnessed. Finally, the pair collapsed into their cozy tent and dreamed of life in a proper forest.

○ ○ ○

Panic shot through his chest as he awoke. The ache slowly burned out as his eyes focused. He opened the tent to reveal unbridled, scenic magnificence, free of goons and grit. His stomach gave a growl.

They ate a simple breakfast consisting of dried fruit and nuts. Victou attempted to activate the portable coffee smoker but found the device perplexing, and instead decided that he drank too much coffee. Fully rejuvenated, they packed up camp and headed south. Only a single day out of the city and Victou already felt acclimated to the outdoors. He joked with Chichi about building a treehouse, accessorized with swings and rope bridges. The conversation played on as they walked through endless wildflowers. Their fantasized home became so detailed they nearly expected it to be there when they arrived.

When the small family finally reached the edge of Goraka, their daydream evaporated into the same thought that everyone had upon their first arrival.

"Should we knock?" Chichi asked.

It should have sounded like a joke, but Victou knew what his daughter meant. The Red Valley presented such an abrupt border, its tree line looked more like a gated fence than any natural edge. Victou saw nothing man made or obviously manicured; the jungle simply stopped.

"It's smells spicy," Chichimou stated while smacking her tongue, sampling the humid air seeping out between the trees.

Victou took in a deep breath of the botanical essence through his mouth. "Yeah, you can taste it."

While Chichimou continued to lick the air, Victou looked back, seeing Chigou as a smoking dot across the long plain of grass. The open field felt tranquil, but they couldn't hide in such an exposed stretch of land. The path ahead offered countless places to make camp—as if anyone would dare to go in after them.

"I think it's okay. We don't need to go in too far."

Each waiting for the other to take the first step, the pair finally grabbed hands and entered the forest like a whisper. Their slow pace proved wise as the ground became soft and dense with vegetation. Fog crept around in disconnected patches. Sounds changed as the clean breeze from a minute earlier died into a heavy stillness. A stream could be heard somewhere. Animal sounds doubled, although the location of any single creature proved a mystery—an orchestra of nature attempting to tune their instruments.

"It's dark in here," Chichimou stated.

Thin beams of light stabbed through the fog and leaves. Deeper in, thicker clouds drifted along the ground. "Pretty different, huh?" Victou said.

"Yeah," Chichi responded, looking nervous.

Victou had underestimated how challenging the transition would be. She had spent the last few years cramped in small apartments down narrow alleys, not to mention a stay doing forced labor in a mine. Victou hadn't even come close to forgiving himself for that and didn't bother to ask if his daughter had. "You okay?" he asked. She didn't answer.

A large, spiked fruit fell from a tree twenty meters ahead and landed with a bone-crushing thud. Farther down, a feathered creature screeched and wove through the treetops, the biggest bird either of them had ever seen.

Victou stopped. "This seems far enough. Let's camp here."

Finding the closest thing to a clearing, they began to assemble camp. Victou clumsily hacked at some vegetation so their tent wouldn't be sitting half on a bush. He then remembered the hammock—they finally had a few thousand trees to anchor it on. Chichi graciously volunteered to test it out, even while he continued to tighten it in place.

The humid air made sweating almost effortless, so Victou joined his daughter for a quick rest in what felt like a fishing net. Their minds and muscles settled as fainter sounds of the Red Valley became clear. All of Chigou felt a million miles away.

His growling stomach woke both of them. Snacks."

Chichi rolled out of the hammock first, nearly flipping her father in the process. He laughed before checking his Toki. An hour of sleep had felt like three minutes. "Oh, wow. I guess we were tired."

Chichi rummaged through the bag of right-angled dinner options, reading them as she went. "Fish chowder?" Chichi asked, holding the cube of soup.

Victou suddenly realized that if they stayed long enough to be forgotten, foraging and food collection would need to happen, but the pocket food pantry would give them some time. He wandered out, looking for the stream he'd heard, while Chichi extended the portable pot into its working position. She cleared an area to make a fire and thought to get some rocks. She had never made a campfire before, but she remembered an illustration at the camping store of a flame, surrounded by rocks and smiling people. She didn't understand what the rocks did, but they looked nice in a circle.

Eventually, Victou made it back, his shirt once again patched with sweat. "I just touched more trees than I have in my entire life." He checked a few scrapes on his forearms. "Oh, that looks nice. Have you built a campfire before?"

"No."

Of course; when would that have happened? Victou filled the pot with water and put pieces of a fallen tree below, snugged into Chichi's fire ring. She stared at the smokey puffs that her dad tried to encourage into a proper fire. After twenty minutes of mumbling, sweating and starting over, a reasonable flame finally took hold.

"It's all this damp wood."

"If you say so, Dad." Chichi yawned.

"How is it so humid in this place?" Victou attempted to aerate his shirt before releasing the block of soup into its pool of rehydration.

They laughed as it plopped in, looking like surrealist food sculpture. Chichi liked how weird camping was. They patiently watched the shape dissolve into an edible, recognizable state. Deciding they didn't need to wait the full twenty minutes, the hungry family started to eat.

Partially recovered with their nap, the pair stayed up longer than they expected, adjusting their makeshift home and chatting. The conversation felt good and Victou pledged to do it more. They considered sleeping overnight in the hammock, but after a joke about blood-sucking insects descending from above, they decided to sleep in the tent.

NESA CAMPING CO.
GEAR
CLOTHING
FOOD
COOKWARE

11
LEVERAGE

Victou awoke from a nightmare while his daughter peacefully slept with her bottom in the air. The outside world had shifted dramatically, but their morning routine seemed no different. Cheap windows and crowded buildings had been exchanged with thick tree-cover and fog, blocking most of the early sun. Birds chirped in the distance, along with a few other creatures he didn't recognize. The neighborhood sounded alive and relaxed.

"The Red Valley... what's all the fuss about? I wouldn't be surprised if a garden club walked by this afternoon."

"What?" Chichimou mumbled while rubbing her eyes.

"Good morning, little one."

Chichi crawled up and met her dad at the entrance of the tent. Keeping their feet on the clean interior, they looked out over the wilderness.

"This place isn't so scary, huh?"

Chichi looked downslope where the darkness of Goraka grew thick. "Is that where the ghosts are?"

"I'm starting to think the stories about this place are just... stories. The only creature worrying me is that bird that won't stop yipping—might annoy us to death." Victou grinned.

"Jin saw one." She spoke with the dry confidence children have when repeating an adult.

Victou remembered Jin—the cordial young man who walked around with a sword and chopped off arms. "What did he see?"

"Jin came down here. He saw the ghost." Chichi put on her socks.

"Oh, okay." Victou went along with it. "What was Jin doing

down here?"

"He went with his friend. They were hiding, like us."

"I see. And did his friend see the ghost?"

"I don't know. She didn't come back." Chichimou put on her shoes and strolled around camp. Victou looked down into the unknown and wondered how deep it went. It did seem odd that the founders of progress had stopped just short of Goraka—the founders were from a breed of man not known for letting resources go unclaimed.

It took just a few days to sample the variety of symmetrical meal units they'd bought. He preferred the beef and forest mushroom stew, while Chichi favored the red Chitori soup because she loved spicy food. Victou again counted their disappearing cubes and decided to face the inevitable. The associate back at Nesa Camping Co. had suggested a field guide to forest edibles, written by the grandson of Lord Boro, Primichi's first patron of agriculture. He pulled the book out of its finely crafted leather sleeve. "Very nice," he murmured.

It offered meticulous illustrations and descriptions, occasionally followed by methods of preparation. One could search by region or genus, and there were many; Victou wondered how any single person could identify so many plant types. After reading for twenty minutes, he discovered a problem with the guide: it covered little of his and Chichi's current environment. Despite generous descriptions spanning most of the valley, only a single page spoke about the fascinating life inside Goraka, ending with a stern warning against any and all exploration of the infamous woodland. Victou stuffed it back into its pristine leather jacket.

"Chichi, are you hungry? This one has a spice-level warning—no wonder you liked it." Getting only forest noise in return, he called out louder, "Chichi?"

Victou got up and looked around. He called again, then checked inside the tent—empty. Although they hadn't seen another human in two days, he felt hesitant to yell; they were hiding, after all. "Chichi," he called out again with tapering volume. "How can you be gone that quickly?"

Victou thought over how long he had been reading the book and how lightly his daughter stepped. With camp marked by their blazing yellow tent, it seemed pointless to wait. He grabbed a vest covered in survival gadgets and left. Having only briefly looked them over, he figured each tool's usefulness would reveal itself in the moment.

Just before he left sight of camp, Victou checked his ability to find the way back. He patted himself down until he found a Toki with a built-in compass. Leave straight south, return straight north; it seemed logical. Keeping his weight back, the young father and amateur explorer began to head down the hill.

"Chichimou," he called out, getting closer to a proper shout. Now traveling with an urgency he had lacked while entering Goraka, Victou swiftly found the thick foliage combative. Branches pushed back and the ground threw off his balance. Every ten meters looked like the last, sans the occasional boulder. He tried to search ahead but the density of the trees made it impossible.

Twelve minutes went by before he checked his Toki. Victou figured he would have caught up to Chichi by then. Sweat dripped into his squinting eyes as he looked around. He then caught a flash of red through the trees and fell over. He spun around on his rear, blinking hard, trying to decipher what he saw. Stories began to knock on the back of his mind and suddenly he felt like a child.

Trying to reclaim his breathing, he watched as red again flashed through the trees. It moved quickly, but it looked much smaller than it had at first glance. Sitting in a bed of moss, Victou managed a clear look at two red birds, no bigger than his hand, fluttering down just past a curtain of vines. He crept up and pulled the vines apart.

Sitting in a small circle as if conducting class, Chichimou held the audience of at least twenty-five petite birds. The crimson spheres bounced on tiny stick legs, while bright yellow beaks pulsed in anticipation of food. One by one, Chichi tossed them bits from a bag of mixed nuts, lightly salted.

She eventually noticed her father and revealed a rare, full-toothed smile. Anxiety evaporated off his shoulder before he silently basked in his daughter's joy. Victou imagined his wife there with them in the enchanted forest. *I wish you were here... it feels like you are.*

With bellies and cheeks full of goodness, the birds assembled into a line and bounced away. The two humans watched quietly, then Victou sighed.

"How did you get them to do that?"

Chichi pursed her lips, slightly confused by the question. "I didn't. I got hungry and it's just nice to share."

Her simple sweetness pierced through his chest. He wiped his eyes again, unsure if it was tears or sweat. "So, how is that thing working out?"

He pointed to the headgear his daughter had put on—officially called an Ata-lamp, it had multiple swappable lenses, plus a tracking reflector and micro storage pouch. Chichi had forgotten it sat, almost too big, on her head. "It's a gadget hat for explorers."

"One begets the other."

"Huh?"

"Just give me some notice next time before running off."

∘ ∘ ∘

According to the calendar, they had just finished up their second week, but their food supply suggested otherwise. Victou wondered if he had missed a few days—not that he could tell any of them apart. The only change seemed to be the patina that had started to form all over them, comprised of humidity, sweat, and bits of nature. It surprised the father how little their increasingly feral appearance bothered him.

Chichimou found a new stream to the east, not particularly big, but the water ran crystal clear. They developed a routine of collecting drinking water, cooking water, and washing up.

Victou had managed to identify one fruit that looked identical to something in the field guide. Taking a chance on looks alone, the fist-sized fruit had reddish skin and a white interior. The texture took some getting used to, but the taste proved delightful. He assumed that fruit alone wouldn't sustain them, but at least it stretched out their packaged meals.

With time for his mind to wander, Victou found himself thinking more and more of Chichimou's mother. He ached to have her there with them, living in the beating heart of nature.

He told Chichi she reminded him of her mother. Her face took on a subtle, complicated expression. He waited for her to say something but instead, she just let him continue. Victou spoke of old memories, most of them missed or forgotten by little Chichimou. She went to bed without saying another word, imagining what she couldn't remember.

° ° °

By the third week, Victou spoke less of camping and more of surviving. Thankfully, water ran in ample supply, but food had thinned out, along with their faces. He counted their remaining boxed meals over and over, but the number never grew over three. At some point they would need to leave, he knew that, but it seemed too soon. Putting one last meal aside, he tried to run the math in his head, knowing that an upward hike back to Chigou burned a lot more calories than lying in a hammock. *Dammit, I really need to find out what we can eat here.*

Another thought oscillated in and out of his mind, one he needed to consider but didn't want to. He had to decide exactly *how* they would go back. Meijune seemed like a good escape, far away on the east coast, but getting there had costs and complications. Victou had long decided upon never going back to Primichi, which really only left Chigou as an option. He would need leverage if he ever saw Kits again, something to make him more valuable alive than dead. Nothing came to mind.

Victou grabbed his vest and got up, causing his knees to crack. "Chichi, let's go forage for food. Do you want to grab your helmet thing and… oh."

Chichimou had been wearing her Ata-lamp for over an hour. Top-heavy, she wobbled a bit as she stood up. "How do you know if something is poisonous?"

"We'll just eat a little at a time—kind of test it out. See if it tastes poisonous." The plan sounded increasingly stupid as each word came out, but his laziness had created a calorie-desperate situation. He then remembered a warning from the field guide, suggesting illness was more costly than skipping a meal. Victou considered himself a split-the-difference kind of guy.

While they hiked down, a newfound recognition gave Victou a spark of confidence. Homogeneous jungle noise had turned into a patchwork of subtle signs. At the edge of their established perimeter, Victou decided to take them deeper into Goraka.

The jungle grew darker with each step. Victou looked up to the thick foliage that choked out the sun. His eyes squinted at a sliver of sunlight just before grabbing his daughter's shoulders and yanking her back. Another giant spiked fruit crashed down like a tropical artillery shell, sending up an explosion of decaying plant life. Victou then saw a small mammal high above them, screeching from where the ordnance must have fallen. Chichimou then heard her father say something she'd only heard back at that nasty mine.

"Dad, what is an evil little bas… ?"

"Never mind." Victou cut her off. "Just… nearly murdered by a squirrel."

They looked down to inspect the spikey green mortar. Its exterior had a thick but soft feel. "Goodness, is this a fruit?" Mutually ignorant, their eyes lit up.

Finding no way to easily open it, Victou decided to get out his modest retractable ax. He gently pushed Chichi back before taking a vengeful swing. The colossal fruit seemed rather unconcerned with the ax poking out of its hide. Victou pushed his daughter back a bit more and took a few more swings, feeling the savagery of the jungle course through his veins. Finally, it cracked open. Inside they saw a radial array of small fruits forming a ring, incomparable to anything they had ever eaten.

"It's pregnant. That's why it's so big," Chichimou declared.

The smell then emerged like a wet slap in the face. "Good Lords," Victou winced. "It's like warm spice cake sitting on a pile of old laundry."

They looked at each other, equally unsure of what to do with it. "Should I scoop out a baby?" Chichi asked.

The combined scent and phrasing triggered Victou's gag reflex.

He watched as Chichi stuck out her tongue out, extracted the spoon from her multi-tool and began to work the pocket of fruit.

"Hey, Chichi," Victou said, putting the back of his hand to his mouth. "I'm going to go look around real quick. You want to stay here and try to get a few of those in a container? A sealed container?"

He sprung up and marched away from the pungent odor before stopping fast. "And no spontaneous adventures. You stay here."

"Yup."

"Got it?"

"Got it."

Checking his compass regularly, Victou walked just far enough to feel responsibly distant. His body had formed a routine: getting sore, adapting, then getting sore somewhere else. He looked around, poking things with his axe, looking up for more deadly produce. While preparing himself to explore the idea of eating a thick leaf, Victou spotted the most attractive fruit he'd ever seen. A bright red cluster of berries hung elegantly on thin vines, anchored to a delicate bouquet of pink and white flowers. The sapling—or perhaps a bush—wielded an impressive number of thorns, but with a little care, he managed to break the tempting fruit loose.

The vibrant color caused his stomach to ache as he held up the berries. He imagined them hiding under a layer of blashu flake pastry, bubbling and buttery. Victou had loved his wife's baking; he'd never eaten pastries much prior to meeting her, but she'd turned him on to all things baked and sweet. Closing his eyes, Victou squeezed one of the berries off with his teeth, letting his imagination do the rest.

He wiped his chin, smearing the small red drops that shot out. Their taste sat nicely between sour and sweet, with not a single wrong note. Plucking one more with his mouth, Victou put the rest away in a utility container. A singular ray of light hit his hand and he suddenly noticed how different his fingers looked. They didn't exactly appear dirty, but rather stained from the constant contact with moss, dirt, and bark. It gave him a feeling of ruggedness, complementing his successful foraging. The sunbeam vanished and Victou decided to head back.

Minding the compass, he walked until the distance felt right. Chichi didn't appear, so he assumed he'd misjudged his trajectory. "Chichi?"

Getting no response, his pulse quickened. After so many days in the woods, Victou still found the place inspired fear in him; three minutes running in any direction and he'd be completely lost. He hated losing her. His eyes cast around the area and finally found the giant fruit, hacked in half.

He jogged over but his daughter was gone. She was curious, for sure, but rarely did she disobey. Certainly, if an animal or somehow a man had taken her, she would have screamed.

Surprised at his perception, Victou then noticed scuff marks on a rock just downhill from the fruit. The moss had been rubbed off. Then he noticed another. The underlying rock looked completely clean and he reasoned it must have just happened. His pulse quickened further and he headed off into the unknown.

All his senses funneled in. The lush forest blurred by as he moved far swifter than he had on arrival. The ground softened as he went deeper into the forest. Moss metastasized onto every surface. Heat rose and the humidity pressed down. The forest seemed to be actively consuming itself.

An anomaly then appeared in the matrix of dark green. He slowed down, trying to see what fruit or bird he ran towards, but nothing fit into what he saw. When it finally came into focus, his muscles locked. Past a row of trees, standing in a small clearing, fiction materialized into reality.

Chichi had told the truth, as had Jin. The world seemed to turn upside down as Victou stared at what he could only describe as a red ghost. Starkly simple in shape, the homogeneous red form floated on the forest floor. Fear and fascination seized him. He tried to explain it, wondering if the strangest plant in existence swayed in front of him until it turned and revealed its face.

Two black sloping eyes shifted towards him and Victou dove behind an adjacent tree, clenching into a ball. Did it see him? What did he even see? He felt too baffled to be terrified and required a better look.

Holding his breath, he rolled over and saw the thing facing away—could he even call that a face? His eyes persisted in their stare, but his brain proved incapable of processing anything. The phantom then slid sideways, revealing Chichimou standing just past it in the clearing. Victou's fingernails clawed into the tree and he wanted to run over, but something told him to do nothing. His daughter looked at the creature with calm curiosity, as if it were any other woodland creature. He wanted her to be afraid and run away but the two species just observed one another. The creature slid again and revealed something far different, but equally perplexing.

A thin object stuck straight out of the ground, emitting a glow around the base of its bulbous top. It looked vaguely mechanical, yet unlike anything Victou had ever seen, like engineering made from living tissue. Tiny components moved and pulsed like machined organs.

A stark black stem then emerged from the phantom's smooth, scarlet exterior. It reached out to the device like a limb, dividing into sharp, spiked fingers.

The glow flared brighter before a burst of steam shot up. Chichi seemed amused, enjoying the curious display. A minute passed, offering Victou time to accept that ghosts existed and were capable engineers as well. It was easily the most incredible thing he had ever seen, and Victou knew not a single person would ever believe it—just one more fairytale from the dark forest.

As Chichimou continued to be amused, a thought struck Victou out of nowhere. He felt all over his vest until recognizing a small, mechanical box. He opened up the pocket and carefully pulled out what had seemed like his most frivolous purchase of camping gear. It instantly became the most precious object he owned.

Muffling the action with his palms, Victou shifted the collapsible camera into position. His fingers trembled as he thought of the moment's significance, capturing proof of a discovery more incredible than the valley itself. Reaching into another pocket, he pulled out a small towel and wrapped it around the untested device while trying to identify the shutter.

A second before making history, Victou's finger locked still as he again looked at his daughter's beaming face. Would this somehow protect her or bring forth even more danger—more chaos in an already fractured life? He thought of protection, of the power to negotiate with powerful men back in town. It would only take a moment.

Victou leaned out further and put the foggy viewfinder to his eyes. His sweaty finger slipped around on the shutter button as he wiped the glass. The creature finally came into view, along with his daughter and whatever technology sat between them. Holding his breath, Victou activated the shutter.

The sound made both of the humans jump. Victou's eyes bulged as a chain of clicks began to ring out, but he realized they didn't come from the camera. He put it down and saw a bizarre snake of metal—or was it tissue?—begin to construct itself away from the probe, racing down the hill. Victou's sweating fingers gripped the camera as he checked the film advance; his mind buzzed with the impossible. He then thought of men who had always talked down to him, thinking he was naive and simpleminded. But they were the ignorant ones, for they certainly had no idea just how ancient yet advanced something could be.

When Victou looked back, the creature had vanished, and his daughter stood alone with the mysterious device. She looked calm, defying every story he had ever heard of Goraka's deadly phantoms. Victou realized he held the most valuable photo in existence and decided to cash it in as soon as possible.

12
PROMISE

Water cascaded down into the turquoise pool, swirling a heavy mist back up into the canopy of soft light. The mild, humid air smelled of purity and minerals, pitying the efforts of any spa Jin had ever visited. The allure wrapped around him as he stood on his hands, feeling more at peace than he usually did on two feet.

The old Lord looked on from shore with wrinkled eyes, focusing on the young visitor perfectly inverted on a floating platform. It carried him around the immaculate pool, constantly churning from the water falling out of the heavens. Leaning on a cane, the old man twirled a rock in his other hand.

"Good morning, Lord Shirér," Jin carefully spoke, trying to keep centered.

"Is doing nothing more interesting when yer upside down?"

Jin found the statement confusing, as they seemed to be in an oasis of eternal solitude. "I do think I have regained my balance. I could pick something from the garden..."

Before he could finish his offer, the old man squinted, cocked back his hand, and threw the rock in Jin's direction.

"Hey," Jin muttered as he tried to avoid the flying stone, causing the entire platform to wobble. Lord Shirér grinned, squinted, and unleashed another payload.

Finding the incoming object rather hard to anticipate while inverted, Jin frantically tried to flip right-side up. The unstable surface flipped Jin into the icy pool like a spatula. With a dainty plop, the stone splashed down two meters short. Jin's head popped up and water drained from his ears, replaced with the sound of yucks and chuckles.

"Good Lord! Is such a thing truly necessary?" Jin sternly asked while spitting out water.

"Tumbling into that ice water? No," the old man laughed. "Not when dodging a rock that wasn't ever going to hit ya."

"You most certainly threw it right at me while I sat in a vulnerable…"

"Ya took that ice bath over a rock to the chin when ya didn't need to choose either one. Your fear acts faster than your perception. Your reflexes are… eh, they're okay though."

Jin bit his tongue, partly from the cold. He swam towards shore, allowing his temper to cool off.

"I'm hungry. Get me food," the old man commanded, pointing to the rooftop garden before heading back inside.

While swimming, Jin considered various possibilities for his host's self-induced alienation. He hoped the old Lord engaged in a beautiful, meditative epilogue to a life full of work and accomplishments. Not wanting to breed naivety, Jin also accepted the possibility that Lord Shirér had just come to the scenic habitat to quietly lose his mind.

Jin dried off in the side room Lord Shirér had allocated to him. Roughly the size of the Tree House's pantry, it had an earthen coziness Jin appreciated. Everything had been built with wood or stone, simply styled but skillfully constructed. The old host sat surrounded by dark wood bowls and boards, with only a few metal utensils that stood out as expensive and machined. As Jin walked into the common space, clothes neatly assembled and hair perfectly combed, the host grunted.

"What time's your date?"

"I've simply readied myself for our afternoon meal. I thought this ensemble met an appropriate level of formality."

"Mmm-hmm." Lord Shirér chopped up a mixture of root vegetables and savory vine fruit. "Interesting assortment of items ya plucked. Ya one of those avant-gardener types?"

Eyeing the intimate cabin that had ages of wear layered through it, Jin thought of his culinary experiences. "Regretfully, I never spent as much time in the kitchen as I should have. Our senior cook, Lady Lason, prepared the meals I enjoyed most—moderately seasoned but interesting ingredients, wonderfully paired. She influenced my tastes substantially."

"So can ya cook?"

"I can, but I would not proclaim deftness."

The old Lord picked up a piece of red fruit. "Ya really like to dress up your yes and no's, don't ya?"

A fox hopped up on the open windowsill from the outside. Waiting for his host to react, Jin held completely still, confused at the combination of tight proximity and casual poise. "A fox is sitting in your window, Lord Shirér."

The old Lord looked up at the fox and then back down. "And?"

"Umm, does it belong to you? I believe that might be the same creature that led me here. Is it a male?"

They both looked up to see the white animal lick traces of blood off of its fangs. "I've never bothered to check but help yourself." Lord Shirér added the chopped produce to a shallow pan of boiling broth. "And among the few things I still possess, that fox is not one of them."

"Curious. It appears you have managed to tame it to some degree. Was that intentionally or inadvertently?" Jin took a few steps closer, fascinated by an animal he had never seen outside of a curated exhibition, and behind glass.

"Hah, tamed? I don't see this freeloader setting the table." Lord Shirér set down some bowls. Jin stepped up and offered his hands, which the host plainly ignored. "Sit down, would ya? Yer making my shoulders tense, standing there with that unnaturally erect posture."

Jin sat down at the simple wooden table, back straight.

"So, what do ya do to unwind, engineering?"

"Certainly, if I've kept up with my Maiishi training."

"Ah yes." The old Lord moved the pot over to the table and placed it in a concave wooden plate, richly colored from years of holding hot iron. "I was wondering what brought ya here."

"I've been an avid student for most of my life and I've always longed to engage Kuitsu with my own eyes…"

"Oh, don't give me that. Every grandma in the valley *wants* to visit this painting-come-to-life. But ya believed it existed and risked a journey to find out." Lord Shirér poured them both lunch, producing a cloud of savory vapor. "So, ya already got more money than you'd ever need while everyone else is chasing it down. Ya get bored and desperate?"

Jin hesitated. "Why would that be your initial guess?"

Without pausing, Lord Shirér shoved a spoonful in his mouth, getting nearly as much in his beard. "Oh, Lord Jin. I know how much that kind of posture costs, but I knew your *name* the moment ya opened your silver spout." He took another big slurp before gesturing around.

Jin didn't understand. "I don't believe I…"

"Aya?" Lord Shirér worked on a piece of meat. "As in the dynasty? I've been away a while, but not so long to forget that name. Along with all the shiny bits fastening your belongings, it's evident you've never experienced a day worrying about it."

"Well, Lord, I would not wholly disagree with that assessment, but I did make a point to travel here with simple accommodations and…" Jin wanted his journey to feel sincere.

Lord Shirér choked as he laughed soup into his lungs. "Simple accommodations? Do ya mean that… what was that? The crazy mechanical vulture ya had strapped to your back, trimmed so finely in albino brass?" Lord Shirér flapped his hands like a bird. "Yeah, I bet every black-hand in Chigou is getting one of those this Leimikou."

Jin felt the sting. Although aware of his unique status growing up, he had often sensed disdain from others, invariably rooted in jealousy or misunderstanding. "I built it with my own hands. Actually, my sister provided the base structure to which I designed a retractable, body-mounted configuration."

Lord Shirér offered a sarcastic grin. "In what, your own private factory?"

Tempted to argue on a technicality, Jin knew the assertion to be essentially accurate. He whispered into his soup spoon, "Maybe."

The host continued to gobble up the soup. "I will give ya one thing, this combination is better than I assumed it'd be. I think that cook of yours rubbed off on ya the right way."

Slurping began to fill the space as their voices quieted for a few minutes. The fox had slyly slipped onto the kitchen counter and helped itself to garden scraps; the homeowner either didn't notice or didn't object. Jin again assessed the fine cutlery. It looked out of place within the relatively humble accommodations. A flash of recognition then ignited, and Jin remembered seeing similar ones before, back at his family estate; they were always behind glass.

"So, ya left Chigou not wanting—at least, not financially—as we were discussing the topic. I am thoughtfully curious: what is it that ya sought in coming here?" Jin asked.

Taking another spoonful of the now-tepid soup Lord Shirér stared off for a moment. "I wasn't searching for anything. I was leaving everything."

Expecting Jin to release another wordy question, the old Lord instead received a sincere, patient gaze. He had no interest in discussing intimacies, but Jin looked as mute as a stone statue. "I don't suppose your shiny frock is flying out of here until I tell ya all the insightful revelations as to why and how I got here."

Jin cleared his throat. "I had hoped to discover a contentment untethered to fiscal assets when I left Chigou, although honestly, my expectations rested more on logic than hope. Considering my current situation and the state of this enchanted place—a sight I'm still processing as reality—I must divulge that a myriad of queries have been continually building and only my conditioned etiquette, largely a product of my cultivated mother, Lady Aya, has been keeping me from releasing a volley of..."

"Oh for the..." Lord Shirér dropped his spoon, patience depleted. "I had what any man wanted: health, money, a family. My wife died giving birth to our youngest son; she was probably too old and... my son thinks I'm rotten, spent too much time making a fortune processing refuse. He wants nothing to do with me... Garbage and money gave me all they had to offer. End of story."

The confession rested on Jin's chest. Lord Shirér went back to his soup, but soon set it aside.

Jin fidgeted with his fingers. "The last thing I ever said to my mother was that I promised to return home. Lord Shirér, do you miss your son?"

The old Lord gave the faintest of nods. He and Jin heard the fox nibbling away in the kitchen, its tiny antlers occasionally tapping against the plate. They gazed as its small fangs and claws worked in steady unison.

Jin continued. "I have personally not experienced much family loss, but in more recent seasons I have known a number of individuals who have. Do you sense your son's distancing resulted from associated pain regarding the loss of your wife, and thusly your traveling to such a remote location?"

Lord Shirér silently picked his teeth.

"Have you felt that your time here has allowed you to focus and transcend beyond the stagnation of grief? Has a clarity developed, one that could even provide peace between you and your offspring?"

Gray hair flared as Lord Shirér's eyebrow bent up. "Geesh, did my son's wife send ya here?" He took his bowl back to the kitchen. Jin watched as wrinkled hands stayed busy, as they had for years. The white fox nonchalantly leapt back onto the windowsill.

"I do not believe I have met any of your relatives, although as I mentioned earlier, Lady Kyoumére notified me of your final goals in Chigou. Now that you have achieved them, I speculate your relationship would improve, if so desired."

Grunting stumbled into a laugh. His hands scrubbed, long enough to divert the conversation. "So, Prince Aya, have ya found what yer looking for?"

Jin answered with a long, contemplative silence.

"Ya dress plenty fancy, so ya don't hate all the money that raised ya. Don't talk about it much, so yer not concerned, except you've never lived without it to really know. Something wasn't there, so ya went looking, but still don't know what for."

As his hands settled, the old Lord put the bowl aside. Water drizzled, then slowly dripped to a near pause. The fox examined him, watching for dropped food or whatever things interest such an animal. "I know why I left. I wanted to... share in my son's life. Maybe I didn't do that well, but I wanted it and he didn't."

Jin nodded.

Lord Shirér pointed to the fox, which started to clean its paw. "That critter shows up one day. Doesn't bother me much, nor I it. Hooligan steals my food sometimes, listens to me mutter, ramble... maybe for a bit, then..." He gestured with his fingers running away. After a long sigh, his shoulders dropped, submitting to something. "Couple times it brought me fish, which was nice." His voice picked up. "Ya see, that's it, that's our relationship. No category, no perfection because there isn't perfection. We choose to share..." He pointed around, to the walls and beyond, up the mountain. "...I can't explain it, not in a way that matters, but *it is* because we *decide* it is."

Jin bobbed his head with greater certainty. He thought about when he had left his home in Primichi. No one had ignored him, not literally, but he had felt alone. "The fear in going back is that you can't choose. Make yourself a part of your son's life. There is hope, and in that, a risk."

As Jin pondered, the old host reached down for a small berry. Without hesitation, he threw it directly at Jin's face. Late to react, Jin shifted, only to catch a red smear on the side of his eyebrow. "Good Lord, I do question your perpetual desire to propel items at me."

"I'm certain ya do."

"I prefer not to overstep my bounds as a guest, but I am strongly tempted to request an explanation."

For the first time, Lord Shirér felt heat in Jin's tone. "Yer too slow."

"I possess no desire to reciprocate your behavior, and while I am certain you have managed more time to focus and meditate than myself, I'm equally confident I would best you in a proper duel of strike and dodge."

"So certain?" Lord Shirér crossed his arm over a puffed up chest. "Then how do I manage to keep pelting you?"

Jin had an insecure habit of comparing himself to others in

imagined physical trials; he had never told anyone about them. In the brief period he spent with Lord Shirér in that idyllic cove, Jin had already fantasized about the two of them competing in swords or sprints, or even competing with the Lord at a younger age. "I do not consider it a matter of ability, but it is poor etiquette to assume one's host…"

"So, ya like being hit with stones and berries."

"Of course I do not, nor would anyone."

"So why?"

Frustration colored Jin's face. "Like… like I said, it is poor etiquette…"

"So yer a victim of insurmountable etiquette?"

"I'm…" Jin felt like punching something, then taking a nap. He stared at the ground, waiting for a word to jump in his mouth.

"Ya lack empathy."

"Excuse me?" Jin looked up.

"I know yer young and fit and all of that. What I'm asking is, *why do ya keep getting pelted?*"

Jin exercised a therapeutic exhale. "Fine, how does this empathy you assume I lack prevent me from avoiding your indiscriminate assaults with tiny, dense objects?"

Lord Shirér coughed through a bout of personal amusement. "Sorry. It's funny when ya say it out loud."

Exasperated, Jin sat up, ready to leave. Lord Shirér gained control of his breathing. "Oh, have a seat, young man."

With a single thread of his tolerance left, Jin clenched his lips and stayed put.

"Ya came up here expecting to find some kind of experience, something that would teach you, show ya what yer searching for." Lord Shirér tapped his temple. "Ya found me and decided I should give ya some Maiishi wisdom, like it's the duty of all mystical mountain men. If instead ya truly wanted to know who I am, you'd see I'm really just an ornery old man that talks to a fox."

Jin scratched the back of his head. "But why did you call me slow?"

"Hah," the old man smacked his knee and leaned forward.

"What was the very first thing I said to ya—the first thing I said to any human in years?"

"You said I was too slow."

"No, I said ya crashed your thing… the flying thing. *Then,* I said you were slow."

Jin threw up his arms.

"Ya didn't listen to the mountain, listen to what that updraft was trying to tell you. Ya fought with it, tried to make it do what you'd expect, ya didn't let it tell ya what it was going to do."

"Right… right…"

"And then this old man came up, pricked ya about it, and told ya to give him your food. Now, is that what a Maiishi monk would say to someone who just traveled all that way to be here?"

Jin thought for a minute. "Now that you ask, I don't imagine…"

"See, I told ya I was ornery right then and there."

The men shared a sudden smile. Lord Shirér continued, "And when I walked up there with that rock in my hand, what did ya think?"

"I…"

"Ya probably thought I was trying to rub a poem out of it or something."

Jin looked guilty. "Maybe just a limerick."

"Ornery old men throw rocks at smug rich kids who trespass on their property. Ya should have known I was going to throw it the second ya saw me with it. Ya were slow because ya didn't *listen.* Humility clears one's vision. Ya listen to someone—*really* listen—you'll know what they'll do even before they do it."

Bewildered by the coherent point that had managed to emerge from Lord Shirér's swirling moralism, Jin took a moment to reflect. The old Lord basked in the glow of a long conversation—a forgotten and cherished part of life. He noticed Jin's face begin to sag as if a weight had clung to him.

"Eh, but don't beat yourself up over it. Yer rich, and being rich doesn't make ya a good listener. Pride and expectation get in the way of your humility, and I know the difference because I wasn't born that way… sure ended up that way though. Considering how much albino brass is shoved up your haunches, I'm surprised ya even care to know the difference."

Jin gave a nod, understanding but unresolved.

"Stay awhile. You'll figure something out." The old Lord went over to the fox, offering his old fingers to the curious creature. With calloused flesh and sharp fangs close, the two explored simple trust. The fox began to rub its snout against the old, wrinkled fingers. A purr squeaked out before the feisty mammal took a quick nibble. Lord Shirér pulled back, wincing into a frown, but playful and familiar. Checking his finger for blood, the bearded grin came back.

Jin's slipping posture straightened back up. "I sincerely appreciate your offer, accepting me into this precious realm you have made your—"

"But I hope ya can figure out how to fish." Lord Shirér pointed to the pool outside, and then the fox. "This freeloader is getting lazy."

o o o

During Jin's childhood, his family had practiced a sparse routine of interaction, but he had never experienced true solitude. When he'd cared to be alone, a valet or maid always waited around the corner, if not in the room. On his fourth day in Kuitsu, Jin did not speak or hear a single word, but he caught nature's voice more clearly than ever before as meditation became an almost inescapable state.

Void of any proper fishing gear, Jin decided to apply his Masu as a fishing spear. He planned to use the retractable sword's vacuum spring mechanism for its speed and silence. Lord Shirér found the entire spectacle amusing but seemed to appreciate the effort that almost caught a fish on seven separate attempts.

Late on the second day of mechanically intricate spearfishing, Jin found his knees beginning to tighten up. Skeptical of this new technique, the white fox sat beside him for the first time, a plump pink fish in its jaws. Jin found himself admiring the creature, so content with its simple existence, so balanced with nature.

Eventually, the fox dropped its fish in front of Jin before

stretching its long body into a downward arch. Jin managed a single pet across its back before the frisky mammal jaunted off towards the house. Jin looked down and explicitly acknowledged the first gift an animal had ever given him. Growing up, he had always seen nature as something to master, or, in a romantic moment, lust over for its beauty below a clear sky.

o o o

Thin wisps of smoke crawled out between dark stained wooden boards. Below, Lord Shirér taught Jin how to smoke fish. Although not strictly necessary with the icy pool's bounty and only one mouth to feed, the old man had never lost his taste for the old preservation method.

Jin had offered his host coffee on his first day there, but the old man had decided it would only make him miss it. Resolving to save the rest for a return trip home, Jin discovered how addicted he had become to the savory stimulant. The scent of smoke triggered his habitual and chemical appetite, resulting in three days of lip-smacking torture.

He hovered, mouth agape, while Lord Shirér pulled a rack of fish out of the smoker. "Ya look like an abandoned cat staring through a restaurant window."

Jin tightened up his shirt. "Apologies for my gluttonous demeanor. I have a powerful affection regarding smoked edibles." He cleared his throat. "And it's been a while."

Lord Shirér shut the small door, clamping off the peppery cloud swirling above. "I suppose she's ready. How about we get some sour peppers and that herb Lidi?"

Jin didn't speak again until only a few bites of fish remained.

"I probably don't need to ask if ya like it," the old host assumed with a smirk.

Jin belched accidentally. "Never before have I eaten a fillet of fish that quickly."

Lord Shirér limped over to the table, evidently feeling the time he had spent on his feet that day. Landing with a grunt, he sat down and patiently ate at a pace which made Jin self-conscious. The room quieted down to chewing and the ting of cutlery, leading

Jin to think of the unconventional garden that sat above them.

"If I may inquire, how did you manage such variety in that garden? I assume you brought an assortment of well-researched seeds, as it appears successfully lush."

Lord Shiér chewed a bit. "Yeah, I brought a few. The Kilarn grows around the back end of the pool, I just planted extra. I get the Red Mimi from a bush just up the cliff by the falls."

"I see. Also, there seems to be no tree here beyond what I would classify as a robust shrub. Were there more when you first arrived?"

Appearing more interested in his sauté of garden finds, the old Lord casually shook his head.

"I am sure the answer is either more obvious or more incredible than I currently imagine, but how did you get so much lumber down—up—here?" Jin still had trouble describing the incredibly deep ravine seated much higher than the mountain valley he had grown up in.

After savoring the final piece of fish, Lord Shirér wiped his mouth. "This place, ya mean?"

"Yes, of course."

"How'd I build it?"

"If you don't mind discussing the experience."

Shrugging it off, Shirér answered, "Oh, I didn't."

Jin's mind scrambled. "Someone... someone else built this?"

The old Lord looked about his abode. "As someone who worked for all he had—even built part of my last house—it brings me no pride, but I'll admit... I'm squatting here, just like you."

Jin considered it for the first time. "So... all of this was already..."

"I mean, sure, I built some of it... modifications more than anything."

Jin's well-fed contentment began to fade. "And the founder? Did you..."

"Nope, nobody, just a little house, a garden-gone-wild, and some bowls. There was a glove with two fingers sewn shut—not sure what that was all about."

After days of processing the fabled destination and its esoteric resident, Jin felt his wonderment dissolve in under a minute. He prepared to ask what common sense would demand, but the old Lord jumped ahead.

"I had the same questions at first, but I don't know how this got here—who built it, or how." He got up and grabbed their bowls stained with smoke and oil. "Ya accept what ya see and accept that there are things ya can't see."

Something transpired in Jin's mind, and for the first time since he had glided into Kuitsu, he thought of leaving.

Before the thought developed any details, Jin's host returned to the table. "So, what were ya doing?"

Void of any context, the statement held Jin in place.

"I mean, before ya came here," Lord Shirér offered bluntly. "Aya, yer all up in Primichi, right? This is quite far from home."

Jin thought it over; he was tired of figuring out the complete answer to that question, so he offered none. Lord Shirér groaned. "Alright, tell me the last time ya used that fancy sword. Bet that's a story."

An arm sitting in a pool of its own blood: Jin's first and least favorite thought regarding the cleverly built Masu. Lord Shirér pressed the young man even after a prolonged silence. Jin mentioned Kora and the Tree House and how his life had been flooded with children who were growing up in a world the opposite of his own.

Jin skipped over Goraka, feeling thoroughly incapable of describing those events without projecting lunacy. He then skipped ahead to Gozen and their nebulous mission regarding child slavers. He mentioned the devious scheme that had burnt a fuel plant to the ground along with a quarter of its employees. Children had been sold, forced to work in mines and dropped down narrow shafts to probe for Kurokinojinsper. The story finally ended with the sword, the guard, and a cell full of children he had helped rescue; it sounded heroic, but it didn't feel that way. Jin remembered himself as a child, thinking that good deeds always produced good feelings.

The explanation had gotten long, and the old Lord stood up. He paced around, looked out the window, and washed the two bowls clean before stacking them neatly on a shelf he hadn't built. "Yer ready to leave, aren't ya?"

The question caught Jin off guard, despite having reflected on it earlier. "I planned on only staying for a brief time, but I had no explicit expectations."

Lord Shirér stroked his wild beard. "I haven't done it since you've been here, but I climb up to the ridge a fair amount."

Jin had trouble picturing the old man anywhere but his isolated sanctuary. Shirér continued. "I look over everything. Up and down the Naifin Valley, that shiny little cluster of dots I used to live in. I'm drawn to the view, to just looking at it, but that world is so far away."

"Are you thinking of returning?"

"Oh, no... no." The old Lord hunkered down. "But one day—maybe a year ago—I saw this tower of smoke rising out of the mountain. Just north." He gestured.

Jin was curious. "Was it a campfire?"

"Hardly. No, this was thick, heavy... industrial."

"So, down at the snow-line?" Jin asked, knowing the elevation of most mining operations.

"No again. This was way up the ridge. Not quite as high as me, but its source sat behind the fog... strange. One day the smoke rose up, and I never saw it again."

Jin asked for more details, but the old Lord's response dwindled to monosyllables. Finally, Jin asked, "So, why are you telling me this?"

The old Lord leaned in. "Why did ya leave your home? Why did ya spend all that time at an orphanage, go hunting for lost kids with your Enforcer friend, and then decide to make the mad trek up to this place? Well, I imagine it's the same reason yer going to head over there and find out the answer to your question."

∘ ∘ ∘

Disenchanted, Jin climbed, remembering the awe he'd felt floating down into a heavenly realization. With all of his gear, including the repacked glider, Jin clambered up a narrow path that offered just enough footing to avoid needing any extra equipment.

Lord Shirér watched from the shore of his pond. Near the canopy of illuminated fog, Jin looked down and gave one final wave goodbye. The weathered host turned and went back to his hut, as impassive while saying farewell as he had been when greeting his only visitor.

When he stepped into the fog, Jin noticed the fox had followed him. He worried the frisky creature would throw off his footing, but the creature passed him in a matter of seconds, scampering up the crystal. The ascension felt long, and Jin appreciated the clear sky once he made it out. Waiting just past the rim and hopping in a circle, the fox escorted him back to the known world. Jin looked back at the glowing cloud and thought of what hid below. He figured some airships must have caught view of the spot but never thought anything of it—never imagined the incredible setting within. A warmth came back into his spirit.

"It is real," he whispered with a growing smile.

The fox had stopped and Jin half expected it to speak a formal goodbye, capping off his journey into fantasy. Instead, it stared across the mountain, fixated on true north. Jin figured it would run off after some lunch. He looked back down into the valley. Chigou looked like the model of a city, idealized in its superficial realization. With the sky clear, he gazed further north and managed the faintest glimpse of his home city, barely more than a sparkle and a shadow. He had trouble remembering the feeling of Primichi, and for a moment, he considered what it would be like to stay in Kuitsu.

The moment passed, and he looked down at his companion. He smiled at the creature's stoic indifference and began his way down. Jin managed only five steps when it hit him. The fox did not stare at prey or fawn over a majestic vista—its snout pointed right towards the direction Lord Shirér had revealed. Jin returned to the fox. "Is there something out there for me to find?"

The fox looked at Jin, licked its teeth, then gazed north again.

"Farewell, my feral friend. You have been an invaluable guide through the unknown."

Hiking laterally across the mountain felt effortless relative to his climb out of Kuitsu. Jin eventually pitched camp, but only due to darkness. The tent felt and even smelled synthetic, and Jin wondered if Lord Shirér had ever tried to return to the industrial paradise of Chigou but turned around the moment he gulped the stench of progress.

Morning froze Jin's bones. After days of temperate perfection, the exposed mountain face tasted bitter. Fog rolled in and blocked much of the morning sun, denying him his only source of heat. Jin then fired up the last bit of coffee he had saved. *I did miss you, old friend.*

With limited visibility, Jin checked his Toki and headed north. Progress felt slow without the anticipation of a hidden paradise. Rock and ice passed under his feet, guiding his march through limbo. He started to count his remaining rations and the time it would take to get back to civilization.

Jin questioned the reasoning for his mission and felt his spirit become anemic. His toes had quickly transformed from spry, to sore, to numb.

The endless drudgery of uneven ground and tedious fog wore on him. He longed for a small, secure space with crafted furniture. Away from the enchanting peace from days earlier, Jin remembered his desire for comfort and design. His fingers restlessly clenched, hungry for detailed work on a clean desk. These thoughts oscillated for hours, whittling down the vague promise he had made to Lord Shirér. His determination eventually waned enough for a change in course and he allowed his weak momentum to turn him east, back towards Chigou.

A dark shape appeared in the corner of his eye, and he halted. After seeing countless gray rocks standing against a crooked field of snow, Jin had trouble deciding what stood out about this one. He squinted, the cold forcing tears from his eyes. He stepped closer. The object didn't move but it somehow looked softer than the array of craggy boulders.

A different chill then cut through him as he recognized what he was seeing. A curled-up child sat frozen in a small cleft. Unable to move, Jin stared at the eerie shape until a macabre curiosity began to lift his feet. He stepped closer and bent down, finally able to see the face of a young boy.

The white skin glistened with a dusting of ice. His long eyelashes were flecked with bits of snow, all forming a hauntingly beautiful image that ached in his heart. The child looked like a prop, perfectly crafted and lifeless. Jin took off his glove and eased forward to touch the child's face. When his fingers made contact, Jin jerked away. The boy felt no different than the frozen rock he had used for shelter.

Alone with the little stranger, a deep sorrow filled Jin. Tears traced lines of ice down his cheeks. An innocent child—someone's *son*—had died, and only he knew about it. Feeling inadequate, he held the frozen arms curling over tiny knees and attempted a prayer. Having only been to two funerals in his life, Jin tried to think of something appropriate. As words formed, the pain of sorrow soon gave birth to anger.

A child could never have made it to that location alone. He turned north, his ears seeking what his eyes failed to detect outside the alpine cloud. A low rumble echoed across the mountain face. Jin knew the sound—not specifically, but it was certainly something industrial. He put his glove back on and got up, tightening the straps of his bags.

The monotonous noise continued like a cursed chant. Jin thought of what it had taken for a child to run into a frozen wasteland instead of staying where he was. Unsure of what he would find, Jin sharpened his focus to a razor's edge. He gave one last bow to the nameless child and promised retribution.

13
DOWNHILL

The chatter of a thousand spikes rattled through the tunnel as Gozen drove towards the glowing pinhole. The roar of his truck ricocheted between rock walls. Sunlight clawed its way in from the entrance, prying open a hole in the mountain and forcing Gozen to squint.

As the cacophony finally escaped into open wilderness, Gozen leaned forward to see the road snake further up through jagged rock. He checked the mirror and saw no signage, no gate or lights that typically—legally—accompanied all commercial access tunnels. For the incredible resources it must have taken to bore a tunnel that size, it seemed suspicious to skimp on some paint and a design intern.

Every major industrial facility had some type of exhaust marking its existence, but Gozen saw nothing ahead. The road's surface proved smooth but lacked guardrails—all speed and no safety. Before long, a layer of snow covered the road, packed down into sludge and ice. His fingers tightened as the incline bent higher, requiring more speed to avoid stalling. With no option to turn around or even stop, a gray fog engulfed him and the world disappeared.

Gozen eyed the dials as he dropped into a lower gear. He stuck his head fully out of the window, trying to listen for what hid ahead. Tires, spikes and ice crunched below. Wind all but vanished in the frozen limbo, but he knew something had to emerge.

Looking up from the preexisting ruts, Gozen finally saw a thick iron sign just before it cleaved off his head. He swung back into the cabin as the post nicked the side mirror. Momentum be damned;

he hit the brakes, remembered to breathe, and killed the engine. After setting every brake, he got out and plodded through the snow, back towards the sign. Rounding the front, he read what had nearly decapitated him: *MINE*, in heavy-set type.

"Answers one question," Gozen muttered, rubbing his neck.

A rhythm of industrial machines seeped into the soundscape, mixed with the low roar of churning water. Gozen walked back up past the truck and noticed a light deep inside the haze. Set ten meters off the ground, it appeared brighter as he walked forward but never grew beyond a dull glow. As the fog thinned out, he saw a massive concrete wall in the distance, ending high above in a sharp, flat edge. Its northern end went straight under a heavy, natural waterfall that disappeared into a ravine, each competing with the magnitude of the other. Gozen had never seen such a large structure so successfully hidden.

Unlike the lower factory, which was only impersonating a final destination, the current operation looked like a fortress; he didn't see a single entrance. Walking forward, he then noticed a line of dark glass running below the top edge like an ominous observation deck, allowing unobstructed views into an endless gray vista.

The success of discovery had transformed into a precarious stillness. With the way home behind him, Gozen faced a million tons of seamless, sinister concrete.

∘ ∘ ∘

The metal chair squeaked as the junior monitor leaned back, glancing at the clock. He cross-referenced a transit chart and scratched his chin. The radiation-green light glowed, signaling an arrival at the front entrance. He double-checked the time, confirming the vehicle had arrived two hours early.

Tempted to replace his stale coffee, he got up to find a supervisor on his way to the kitchenette. Instead, he recognized someone he'd never officially met, who looked younger than him but moved like he owned the entire operation.

"Excuse me, Lord."

The sharply dressed young man slowed his steady pace; the monitor tried to make it quick. "Pardon the interruption, but are you aware of any off-schedule transports?"

Kits rarely had conversations at Daimó's operations, and they only went one way. "Do you know who I am?"

"I… I asked someone what your job was, he said you took care of people who didn't do theirs."

Kits didn't budge.

The monitor gulped. "Unscheduled arrivals are quite unusual at this particular facility, and as I currently understand, you are someone who deals with unusual things here."

Skipping any further inquiry, Kits walked straight into the monitoring room. He stopped opposite the signal board and lowered an eyepiece slotted into a brass housing. Letting his eyes focus through a series of mirrors and lens elements, Kits zeroed in on the truck idling at the entrance, partially obscured by fog.

The monitor crept in behind, just loud enough to be noticed. Kits watched the familiar brand of unmarked transport. "Are you sure this is off schedule?"

"Yes, I double-checked the time," the monitor said as he fumbled over the schedule. "Two hours early."

Kits watched the driver, who seemed content waiting back at the gate. "How many drivers have shown up this far off their time?"

"He'd be the first." The monitor answered, watching Kits fiddle with the focus ring before noticing a handgun poke below the bottom of his jacket.

Suddenly, he saw the secretive Lord tighten his grip on the scope's handles. His face pressed into the eyecup, turning his skin red. He mumbled under his breath in a tone of intense revelation. Kits reached behind into his jacket and jumped off the scope. The monitor watched as Kits pulled components out of hidden pockets, attaching them to the gun as he darted out of the room.

With the gun and its owner gone, the junior monitor peeked into the eyepiece. "Wow, that's one *big* delivery man."

o o o

Staring at the placid gray scene before him, Gozen finally noticed a feature hiding in the shadow of the falls. He expected to see exhaust stacks, but these had been built sideways. It looked comical until the reasoning hit him upside the head. "Of course," he grumbled out as he pictured the thick byproduct of industrialization pumping into the falls, which dragged it down below instead of letting it plume high above for all to see.

No feature of the pipes resembled an entrance, but it appeared more penetrable than the flat wall of poured rock. He surveyed a steep slope of snow leading up towards the pipes, but it ended a good ten meters short of the wall's top edge. He leaned off the truck and walked up, looking for some passage on the corner where man-made mountain met the real thing. High up on the wall a silhouette appeared.

Gozen took cover behind the truck door, squinting just over the window as the blurred silhouette stood still as mist flowed past it. The thin, dark shape then stepped towards the edge and abruptly dropped, sliding down the wall until it tumbled into the ascending snowdrift, which erupted in a cloud of frozen water. Gozen watched the figure ride down the hill until finally rolling out to a stop. It stood up and brushed off the snow.

"What?" is all Gozen managed to get out. Emerging through the mountain haze, the creature—*a little girl!*—looked like a ghost, pale and gaunt. Ignoring any grander mystery, Gozen finally ran forward to meet the incoming child. Before he reached her, he watched as another silhouette dropped off the wall.

He knelt down and gently held the girl's shoulders. "It's okay. I'm going to get you away from here."

Within seconds, more kids had emerged from the mass of fog and pipes above, forming a line of at least ten deep, waiting to take their plunge down the icy slope. In that moment, Gozen realized he would first be filling his truck with escaping children and then racing them straight down the mountain. He took the first one into the cabin and opened up the truck's rear door. The engine fired up and he began the laborious process of turning the truck around.

With the truck finally facing the right way and a group of children approaching, Gozen spotted another, taller figure emerge at the top of the slope. Straight out of a children's dark fable, the larger human sprouted wings and a vortex of fog swirled around them. The figure leapt off the wall and swooped towards the truck like a giant owl, gliding in a circle over the little escaping horde.

Gozen ran back, kicking up snow, waving frantically for the next child. His gaze was fixed on the mythical creature, which managed a parabolic descent onto the ground. In one arm it held the tiniest of the children as the other reached back, collapsing the wings in one brief motion. In a gust of realization, Gozen finally deciphered the strange puzzle that had descended upon him.

"Jin."

High above the massive main door, Kits walked across the flat roof, holding the pistol he'd transformed into a modular rifle. He spotted Gozen, who corralled their entire stock of little mine probes straight into the back of a getaway truck he'd obviously stolen from them. "Dammit!"

Below, Gozen and Jin acknowledged their mutual surprise and hoisted the last child into the truck. Gozen jumped to the cab as Jin climbed in through the back, carefully setting down his small passenger. He scooted the exhausted kids up towards the cabin and turned to close the door.

"Gotcha, prince," Kits said, and he squeezed his trigger finger.

Gozen heard a snap by the floorboard. He looked down to see white snow gleaming up from a finger-sized hole. His young partner's body crashed through the small mob of kids. Gozen jumped back, grabbing the top of the large rolling door and slamming it shut. A sharp dent popped in the makeshift barrier, its sound rattling through the metal box. The kids covered their heads as Gozen hurled himself back into the driver's seat.

Steam whistled out as the tires dug into ice and gravel. He drove straight into the fog, hopefully right back to where he started. Another ping ricocheted off the roof as the covert foundry vanished behind them.

"I got shot in the head" came up from the cabin floor.

Gozen, well-conditioned to trauma, simultaneously assessed the road and his colleague's condition. Jin looked unsure of his state, either in shock or merely shocked. Gozen saw blood on Jin's ear, speckled up through groomed, angel-blond hair. "You feel okay?"

Jin looked around. "I think so. Is that correct?"

"It caught you on the side."

Jin dabbed his finger onto his temple. He winced at the sting before seeing the transfer of blood. A heavy pain throbbed around his left eye. His already fair skin was bleached to a sickly white. "That bullet came dreadfully close to entering my skull."

Gozen agreed, hoping Jin would manage to keep it together. Time to change the subject. "So, Jin…"

Still contemplating death and its proximity, Jin took a moment to respond. "Yes?"

"How did you just manage… what you just did?" Gozen fought the temptation to ask something more complex, as he drove like mad down a mountain in a truck full of children.

"Yes, quite a fascinating turn of events, actually." Jin continued to dab his wound. "The children were being held in an upper level. A vent shaft from the outside nearly led me straight into their room. I discovered it near a small child I found in the mountains who… well… Security proved conveniently light above the main transport entry. I promptly gathered the young ones I had found. Planning to hike back, I then saw a truck. I contemplated hijacking it, but as providence would have it, I recognized you through a scope I fitted with a magnification doubler. I had been planning to hike back to old Lord Shirér who lives by the waterfall in the mountains whose pet fox—actually, he emphatically denied ownership of the animal—had kindly escorted me…"

"Jin, why don't you just tell me how the kids are," Gozen recommended.

Still fidgeting with his wound, the young Lord got up and looked into the back. A flock of white eyes peered up at him. Aside from general malnutrition, none of them appeared any worse for wear. "It appears only I was shot."

He crawled between Gozen and the passenger seat. Rock and ice blurred by along with the occasional tree, too quickly for him to successfully identify the species. "You are maintaining a rather sporty pace." He could feel the tires shift on the uneven path.

"Well, we need to hurry."

Jin looked in the rearview mirror. "I do not believe we are being pursued. We at least got a generous lead if…"

"We're not faster than a wire-type."

Jin agreed, as wire-type messages traveled at 300,000 kilometers per second, but he questioned the timing of such a comparison. "What's the relevance?"

"The installation is going to know we're coming," Gozen pointed ahead, eyes firmly fixed on the careening path.

Jin stopped touching his head. "Which installation?"

The truck hit a bump, sending children bouncing up off the floor. "Sorry," Gozen apologized before answering Jin. "You didn't… how did you get up there?"

"The Kurokinojinsper mine? Like I said earlier, I traveled from Lord Shirér's cabin. *He* didn't build it, as it turned out, but did maintain the garden on the roof rather adeptly. There is a book I read as a child…"

"Jin," Gozen silenced his partner. "You'll want to put your seatbelt on. Kids, brace yourselves against the wall and hold on."

Jin and the kids all did as instructed. Ahead, a mountain face approached through the ground fog. The pace seemed unreasonable to Jin, but an opening emerged, tunneling deep into the ancient mound. The seasoned driver did not slow down.

Inside the dock manager's office at the mining operation downhill, an assistant read a rather confusing wire-type written in all caps. It mentioned a stolen truck heading towards the tunnel from further up the mountain. Most industrial facilities had a risk of truck theft, but not that one.

"Who would steal a truck just to trap yourself in the tunnel?" he mumbled.

Tempted to return to the floor and close his shift, the assistant figured avoiding any potential reprimand would be worth one minute. He walked over to the private tunnel garage, expecting nothing more than a quiet, closed space with a single, empty truck.

Once inside, the sight caused him to immediately read the

wire-type again. Not only was the truck missing, but the tunnel door had been left open. He cursed under his breath and ran up to the tunnel entrance. The garage's bright lights made seeing deep into the tunnel impossible, but once the echo of his footsteps had faded out, he caught the hiss of an engine. He held his breath; the sound got louder.

Checking the order a third time, he ran towards the door control to raise the massive metal barrier back up, where it belonged. He opened the panel and tripped the switch with his sweating fingers. A red light began to blink on the roof. He heard the rumble of gears as the door motor engaged.

In the same breath, blinding headlights popped on and an air horn blared a deafening scream down the tunnel. The assistant covered his ears as the trapped sound swarmed through the garage. Boilers and pistons joined the mad chorus. He looked out into the tunnel just as the thick door began to budge, and he knew the truck wouldn't stop.

Panicked, he ran out the side door and yelled madly into the dock. "Clear out!"

His hands frantically waved at the few workers strolling across the open floor, blocking the exit to the facility with their tiny, fleshy bodies. The assistant yelled again as the hellish shriek of a runaway truck came from the side door.

Inside, the tunnel entrance had raised just above flush with the floor as Gozen crushed the accelerator. He braced himself against the steering wheel as thick rubber slammed into the top of the door, which offered more of a jarring ramp than the speed bump he had hoped for. The truck's front end shot up, teetering with the rear as it passed over. Just before the back wheels finally came down, the truck slammed into the inner bay door.

On the other side, workers dove wildly away from the explosion of metal. Gozen managed to gain control and forced the truck into a tactical, horizontal slide. Perfectly aligned, the transport slammed into the facility's main entry frame, completely blocking any passage through.

"Neko's just down the hill. Let's move!"

His deep, booming voice managed to rouse his rattled passengers. Gozen pulled them out through the driver's door as Jin looked out through his window. Sentinels approached them in a mad dash. Jin locked the door and grabbed the final two children, one in each arm.

The group scurried down towards Neko, right where Gozen had left her. The few workers and drivers outside stood dumbfounded, far too confused to react. They watched the small platoon of scrawny children follow the largest man any of them had ever seen. The sound of clanging metal and breaking glass rattled from the other side of the stolen transport.

Security eventually managed to get through the cabin doors, but Neko had already fled towards Chigou. One Sentinel raised his firearm but held off firing, realizing its futility. The scattered workforce looked over each other, waiting for instructions or an explanation.

Back at the tunnel, another vehicle roared through the darkness. Kits slammed on the brakes, realizing the door had shut, but not after letting the truck through. He thought of banging on the door and shooting the first person he saw, but the thought of Daimó turned his rage into dread. Kits knew he'd need to explain the day's events and wondered what this new failure would cost him.

14
CONFESSION

Small, heavy heads bobbed up and down with the bumps in the road. Two kids lay sound asleep, having succumbed to Neko's hypnotic, mechanical song. Jin stared at the green sprawl through tired eyes that twinkled with reflected light.

Planning occupied Gozen's mind—counting kids, beds, and room dimensions. He knew some of the children would end up at the still-overbooked Tree House. Lady Kyoumére would take them—she'd die caring for them, if needed—but Gozen knew everyone had a breaking point. He didn't want to think of what would happen to those children if she broke down.

Neko drove over Kora's drawbridge as silos appeared in the distance, a welcome sign of abundant food for the famished children. Kora didn't have nearly enough space, but considering how many kids were sleeping in the rumbling truck trailer, he knew any soft and dry surface under caring eyes would make a welcome bed.

As they got out of the truck, the air wrapped them in a warm embrace, and they finally felt delivered from the life-sapping mountain chill. Clora gracefully required no explanation for the large and unexpected intrusion, asking her husband to help with any need. Kojo looked grumpy but dutifully took his wife's suggestion.

Jin helped the children leave the truck but stayed inside, finally dressing his head wound and avoiding the couple whose daughter he had failed to return. Clora had always proven compassionate, but Kojo had yet to offer him a single word since Nia's death. Desiring a quiet space to sleep off his headache, Jin commandeered

Gozen's cabin bed.

Gozen felt unusually cold as he stayed up with Clora in the kitchen. She smoked some coffee and got a quilt to wrap around him. His strong torso heaved in slow breaths, causing the pattern of the blanket to bloom. "There's a new children's clinic in Doulan that just opened. I think because of how beat-up and malnourished these kids are, they'll probably keep them, for a while. I can take them tomorrow."

"No rush. They—and you—can rest here a while," Clora said.

He smiled. "No matter how many dark corners this city shows me, hearing you speak always reignites my hope."

"I may be too old to blush, but I'm glad you don't think I'm too old for flattery." She took a sip of her much smaller cup. "So, how is your lovely friend Lady Kyoumére? Getting crowded over there, isn't it?"

"Yeah..." Gozen answered, fixing his blanket up higher, "there are too many kids. And now, all of these." He gestured around with his eyes, blowing out his frustration in a loud puff of air.

"I don't know Lady K as well as you, but I know she's got hands of silk and a backbone of steel."

Gozen laughed at the admirable truth. Kojo, a few tussled silver hairs hanging over his eyes, floated into the kitchen for a glass of water, and then went back outside.

"Is he okay with Jin being here?" Gozen asked, discrete with his volume.

Clora clenched a fist under the table and fought for composure. "Yes, it's fine. You don't need to worry." She brought her hands up and rubbed them together, "I think he... I think he's accepted what happened. I don't know if he'll ever be able to talk about it. He... he'd never talk to Jin, but it's okay that he's here. I think they both know how to keep that space."

Faint, mournful recollections swam around their heads. Gozen wasn't sure if he'd accepted the loss of Nia. A vacuum still existed from the vibrant lifeforce that no longer existed. The silence ran long enough for Gozen's mind to wander further, and a laugh suddenly popped out.

Clora cocked an eyebrow. "You okay?"

"Yes, sorry." Clearing his throat, he let out another laugh, too weak to stop it.

Clora crossed her arms. "Okay, big fella, what is it?"

"Oh, just… Jin." Gozen's mind wandered back to the mountain. "When I got to that factory in the mountains, those kids came out of the fog—out of nowhere—like magic."

The laugh came right from his belly. "And then Jin just sprouts these wings—metal wings—and flies down the hill like some aristocratic owl."

Clora started to understand and cracked a smile as Gozen tried to keep his voice down. "I was shocked to even see him up there, and with that perfect posture he always has—*whoosh*." He gestured his fingers out like feathers. "I cannot fathom why anyone would hike up in the mountains with metal wings strapped to his back. Or… even own them, for any reason. I mean, I don't think he made them for this purpose, he just happened to have them."

The pair eventually let their giggles simmer out. Gozen's throat felt sore from being up too late. "He got shot up there though." Gozen waved his hand, as to keep Clora from worrying. "He's fine, but he came close to dying for those kids." His voice shifted, humor and empathy mixing into dissonance. "I still don't understand him, truly, but he *did* that. He did that and I bet he'd do it again."

Clora leaned forward and rubbed his cold hands. "Then I'm glad he's here. I know I can't do all that running around nonsense."

Gozen prayed thanks for Kora and all of its beauty. He felt no exaggeration in calling it sacred; as long it survived, the valley still had its heart.

o o o

Darou had become so accustomed to his new workplace that his feet moved out of habit. Faces melded together and despite making an acquaintance or two, he wouldn't call any a friend. He even had the time to choose a favorite toilet in the factory bathroom—the second-to-last stall, because it always seemed the cleanest. Something about having a favorite toilet made him depressed.

Hydraulic pistons hummed off to the side. Giant metal arms hoisted a container of dark Jinsper, dumping it onto a belt for processing. The orchestra of giant machines banged away, drowning out any voice or footstep—a perfect job for the deaf. Darou wore earplugs, which older black-hands scoffed at. He found their mockery—generally impossible to hear—quite easy to ignore. Silence offered boredom, but the accompanying peace made an adequate package.

Despite having held a qualified position at Etecid before it was burnt to the ground, Darou avoided any new supervisor position here at Noutess. He ignored the herd of gruff men who all reminded him of his father, preferring the bright-eyed children and courteous house Lady where he lived. He specifically avoided telling anyone he lived at an orphanage.

A child then appeared and twinkled like a butterfly against the colossal machines. Her small, flushed face nested in a colorful scarf, appearing like a captivating hallucination. The girl's eyes danced around while every passerby ignored her. Forgetting whatever common task he was in the middle of, Darou began to approach when a different face snared his attention.

Looking frustrated, Kits appeared from behind a support beam. He paced around, trading between folded arms and sharp hand gestures. Another man appeared, following Kits around with humbled posture. Darou slipped half behind a steam-lift.

The young girl ignored whatever tense conversations were happening behind her, mesmerized by the circus of men and machines. Occasionally, the unknown man gestured down to her— maybe a daughter—although Kits didn't acknowledge her once. Darou half-expected Kits to pistol-whip the father and demand the family be removed from the site.

Darou found vengeful satisfaction in Kits's frustration. The moment Nia had introduced them, Darou had detested Kits's very presence. He missed her more than he had ever admitted, even to himself, and knew her blood stained Kits's hands.

The scene promptly grew into an amateur soap opera. The child began to spin in a circle under a work-safety poster, trying to make herself dizzy, while Kits rubbed his own neck red. How this sheepish man and wee child held his attention in an industrial operation, for all eyes to see, Darou couldn't explain. He knew Suzu would eat the story up, as her eyes burst into flame at any mention of Kits. Ready for such entertainment, Darou went straight towards the office to announce his sudden case of eruptive bowels, or maybe a highly contagious ear infection.

◦ ◦ ◦

She felt a pebble push against the thinning sole of her shoe. It had worn past the point that her mother would have ever allowed. Suzu had some spare money left over from Pirou—the last of a fountain of espionage cash that had died along with him. Suzu had never developed much of a tolerance for shopping but had always fancied new shoes, having grown up in a family charmed by design and small gadgets. Plus, Nia had always preached the virtue of quality footwear. Suzu thought of getting some new jumpers too. Nia had made a rather big deal gifting Suzu her first pair of proper Soultai jumpers, which still fit. *Hurray for staying short.* She didn't want to throw them away, but they had faded like a memory, comfortable and loose at the seams.

Suzu approached the Tree House and jogged the final stretch around back. As she ran in, Lady Kyoumére entered through the kitchen door, looking flushed and holding a pail and towel. Suzu attempted to slip past the orphanage mother.

"Lady Suzu, back again for the fourth time this week." Lady Kyoumére fixed a thin whisp of hair, sticking from forehead sweat.

Lady K sees everything, stupid. "Oh hey, Lady Kyoumére. Just thought of stopping by." Suzu turned in place and grabbed some mimis out of a bowl.

Lady Kyoumére stood her ground, detecting suspicious nonchalance. "Waiting for your brother?"

Suzu halted. "My what?"

Lady Kyoumére squared up to her questioner. "If Darou is not your newly adopted brother, I'd question why you've been having so many meetings with him."

Suzu processed the nuance of words and tone, feeling like a

master interrogator had just baked her cookies. "Lady K, how do you know everything?"

"The *how* is not so important. If you'd like coffee, it's gone tepid, but our steam wand works now." She walked to the stairs just as Darou flung through the front door. Lady K paused at the top step, looking down at the young man, who resembled a startled cat.

"Fine evening, young Lord. And how are we?"

"Good," he blurted out.

"Lady Suzu is in the dining room."

Darou jumped one foot into a sprint before hammering the brakes. "Thank you, Lady Kyoumére." She walked up to the bustling, overcrowded bedrooms, her rogue lock of hair falling down again.

Suzu saw Darou who, to her surprise, appeared eager to start a conversation. He scanned the quiet space for lurking children before slicking his own disheveled hair back in place.

"You alright?" Suzu asked with a mouth full of mimi fruit.

"Would you like to hear about my day at work?" Darou asked, for the first time in his life.

Suzu's back locked straight. Her eyes turned intense. "Kits? You finally saw him?"

Darou nodded, his pulse running hot. "And I didn't just see him. He met with this guy... well, some limp-hose and a girl—which I don't understand—but he did not look happy."

Brain gears cranked. "Where is he now?"

"Kits?" Darou shrugged. "I don't know. I didn't see him leave."

Suzu grunted like a gambler who had just lost. "Alright, well, who were these people? Were they wearing suits?"

"No, I mean, I don't think he was an industrialist or anything."

"What about her? Was she an upper academy student?"

"Oh... no, no. She looked about... ten, maybe five?" Darou glanced around "I don't know. You think I'd be better at telling kids' ages after being here so long."

Something started to click. "So... like, a father and daughter?"

Darou shrugged. "Could have been, sure. That'd make sense. They seemed anxious, maybe. Well, the girl was like... making herself dizzy, but neither grownup seemed too happy."

"And that's it?" She needed something to act on.

"Well, then I followed them home."

"*Nuts and bolts*, Darou. You could have led with that."

"Sorry." He was new to reconnaissance.

"Was their place on Oubli Street?"

"No, it's just east of IQ… Wait, do you know these people?"

"What's the address?" Just as Suzu spoke, they both heard the roll of Neko's engine approaching from outside. She looked at him urgently. "Hey, don't tell Gozen."

"Okay." Darou wrote the address on the slip of paper Suzu held out, then turned and began walking away.

"Where are you going?" Suzu demanded.

"To see if Gozen needs help. Is that not allowed?" He saw her eyes jumping around, at ideas more than what she saw.

"He'll try to stop me."

"From doing what?" Then, realizing she had no intention of answering, Darou left the kitchen and found Lady Kyoumére standing at the front door. "Darou, could you help Lord Gozen? He just arrived and has a few children who will need to stay here for a while."

"Are some kids leaving, because…" His voice trailed off.

Lady Kyoumére paused, noticeably. "No, no one is leaving. We're making some more room upstairs."

Darou knew they didn't have any, but he didn't question the Lady. He nodded and went outside to meet the new arrivals.

Back in the kitchen, Suzu heard the mumble of conversation through the old, wooden walls of the orphanage. Feet scurried above her, older kids running to windows to see yet more arrivals. Young ones in the back kept playing, concerned only with their imagined worlds. Suzu thought back to when she had arrived, newly orphaned by force. Those responsible still moved freely, destroying more families whose children were escaping to the overcrowded sanctuary on the river. Her stomach growled, still hungry, but she didn't notice.

The muffled sounds sharpened as people entered the hallway,

led by Darou, who looked sheepish.

Suzu's eyes widened and she hissed, "*What did you do?*"

"Like I'm going to lie to *him*," Darou whispered, gesturing to the hulking man following behind.

As the new children made their way upstairs, Suzu heard Lady Kyoumére down the hall, thanking Lord Jin for graciously providing them with such a magnificent kitchen. "Ugh, what is *he* doing here?" Suzu asked Gozen, wrinkling her nose from an imagined stench.

"Jin helped me recover some kids from a clandestine Dark-spark mine up in the mountains."

Suzu rolled her eyes. "Oh, I bet that just made him feel so *fulfilled*."

Gozen folded his arms. "Actually, it was more like I helped him, as it turned out."

Suzu brushed the comment aside with an irritated shrug.

"So, Darou says he saw Kits today," Gozen said calmly, nodding towards Darou, who had the grace to look embarrassed.

"Yeah, how about that," Suzu returned, glaring at both of them.

"And that you asked him to…"

Her head jerked. "Kits, that… greasy, industrialist *errand boy*, killed my parents. And yes! Yes, I *am* looking for him. And no, I'm not going to stop."

Darou imitated a statue. Gozen took a step closer. "I'm not telling you to stop, Suzu, but you need to think about what'll happen when you find him… again."

"Oh, don't worry. I have." Her voice floated out like air from a freezer.

Gozen felt trapped. The only two ways he knew how to support her—stop her or ignore her—both felt wrong.

"Well, maybe *we* should go find him then."

Prepared for more arguing, Suzu's tongue tripped up. She and Darou locked eyes, finding fear and excitement dancing behind a layer of shock. They felt like children who had been given permission to drive the family car.

"Did you mean to say that?" Darou asked.

Gozen turned to him. "Outside, you said Kits met with a guy and his kid."

"You *are* being serious," Suzu said slowly. "Okay. Well, this guy was working for Kasic, but really working for Kits—giving him research on this new fuel project."

"Little Chichimou's father?" Gozen hypothesized.

"I'd hardly call him a father, but yeah—that's him."

"And how do you know that?" Gozen asked.

"Victou took Remi's old job, Remi told me because his old boss was suspicious. Boss is dead now, Victou and his daughter ran off to hide, but something made him think it was worth coming back to Kits... apparently. Like I said, real father-of-the-year winner."

"Excuse me, did I overhear young Lady Chichimou's name?" Jin's face popped into the kitchen.

"This is a private conversation, Jin." Suzu spoke in a strong monotone.

"Oh, did I not hear her name correctly? I certainly have been curious about her status since our last encounter. Has someone heard from..."

"Yes, but like I said, not really your concern."

"Suzu." Gozen lifted his hand. "It's fine."

Suzu threw out her arms. "So, what, we're telling *everyone* now? Gee, why don't we just grab all the kids for story time?"

"Jin has sacrificed more than you'd think for Lady Chichimou... *if* it's really her."

Suzu's eyes narrowed, "The rich never sacrifice, Gozen, they just *invest*."

Jin clarified, "I did have an unfortunate encounter when I last escorted young Chichimou to her father some time ago. A pair of unsavory young Lords, and I hesitate to even give them that title, incited a rather violent situation. Also unfortunate, it resulted in me removing one of their arms."

Suzu, silently gagging through the entire story, froze at the last line. The tall, repulsive silhouette in the alley reappeared in her mind—a sickeningly memorable man who had lost half an arm along the way. "Wait... YOU did that?" As if Jin hadn't been born with enough, now he was even taking her vengeance away from her.

Jin retained an odd expression of polite horror. "I… yes, defending myself did result in that outcome, as grisly as it sounds."

Checking an impulse to thank him for dismembering that thug, Suzu instead offered a curt nod of recognition. She still hated him for Nia, and just being a smug outsider who got in the way. Her attention went back to the table.

Darou finally joined in. "You guys sure keep a lot of secrets from each other. Sorry I don't have anything interesting to confess."

"How about Victou and Chichi's address?" Gozen asked.

Darou pulled out an old notebook that was falling apart. He noticed Jin drawn to the shabby item, ever ready to give patronizing advice on his low-income lifestyle. Just as Jin opened his mouth, Suzu cut him off.

"Already got it." She nodded at Darou and showed Gozen the paper with the address. "So, we actually doing this, big guy?"

Gozen put the address in his pocket. "And who is in charge when we go?"

It took a few seconds for Suzu to push her pride down. "You. Now, can we go?"

"May I join the company? It would be gratifying to see Lady Chichimou again," Jin added.

"We aren't going for blashu rolls and smoked coffee, Jin." Suzu got up and straightened her clothes. "Alright, let's go."

Holding up his hand, Gozen interrupted. "Let's make sure Lady Kyoumére is settled in. We just dropped quite a few kids into an already crowded house."

"You kidding? She's a pro. Come on, we don't know how long they're going to be…"

As Suzu tried to push Gozen's large hand away, Lucette entered into the dining room, bouncing to a stop. "I see someone planned a party and decided not to invite me. I am wholly offended."

Suzu covered her face. "*Sweet Valley*, we're never going to leave."

"*Two* parties I wasn't invited to?" Lucette feigned distress.

Jin leaned towards Gozen. "Lord Gozen, would you prefer my

company on this pursuit?"

Suzu snorted. "No, Jin. Now let's go." She pushed for the door.

"You know, Jin," Gozen said, leaning down, "it may actually be better if you don't come, just to keep things calm. We don't want Victou getting startled, and the last thing he saw you do was cut a guy's arm in half."

"Excuse me, what?" Lucette said, mouth agape.

"Darou, would you mind helping Lady Kyoumére with the boys? She may need help moving some things around," Gozen asked.

Darou nodded and looked over to Suzu. "Good luck." Avoiding Jin, Darou stepped out to find Lady K.

"This place is on the far northeast side. Shouldn't be too long. Meet you at the truck," Gozen announced as he left, leaving Suzu stuck between Jin, Lucette and a countertop.

Lucette attempted a silent *hello*, but Suzu offered her little more than a glance. Suzu mimicked Gozen's momentum, and Lucette watched her roommate—she *thought* they were still roommates—march away.

Jin nodded with ingrained civility, the kind of behavior Lucette wouldn't ordinarily have associated with someone who dismembered others.

"So, that was some kind of metaphor, right?" She mimed sawing her left arm off with her right index finger.

"It wasn't a reciprocating motion—quite sudden and direct, actually."

"Wow. That is… something." Lucette found herself feeling strangely protective rather than frightened. "I wouldn't have pegged such an affluent, educated chap as yourself to be so…" She made claws with her fingers. "Although you do have that lil' bandage by your left eye. Tough guy get into it with a cat?"

"No, I was shot. It only partially contacted my skull though."

Lucette had no response.

"I seem to have lost my color response in this eye, however. Asymmetrical color blindness is an odd sensation. I do hope it is not permanent."

"Wow, asymmetrical color blindness, I hear ya." She cleared her throat. "So… where is the fine Lady of the House? I need a letter of referral from a real adult. Just some fancy academy stuff, nothing to get hot over."

Jin kept his hands behind his back. "I do believe she is attending to some new children Gozen and I delivered from a surreptitious mining operation in the west mountains. She looked quite preoccupied."

"I guess I'll put on the ol' coffee smoker then."

"Yes, I am now noticing a proliferating hunger," Jin replied.

"Well, better go take care of that." Lucette winked.

"Yes," Jin agreed. He leaned awkwardly, as if meaning to walk but forgetting how. "Actually, since we appear to have some downtime… Lady Kyoumére and the children, Lord Gozen and that quest—I would offer to join you for a moderate meal, if you have time for such."

"Oh…" She looked over Jin's attire, everything meticulously crafted. "Thanks, but I'm not so sure we eat near the same bank." She winked again.

"Do you have rather particular tastes?" Jin asked, unsure.

"Nope. I mean, I'm a student-orphan type of gal and I'm guessing you eat with *forks* I couldn't afford."

"I certainly would not invite anyone, especially a fair Lady such as yourself, to dine and expect *you* to pay. That would be entirely uncouth."

Lucette paused to imagine what a proper dinner for someone of the Aya family would be like. "You're right Jin. I would be insane not to accept your fine offer."

15
DISBELIEF

Soft light strobed into Neko's cabin as the sun cut between small buildings. Surfaces had less shimmer in northern neighborhoods, and were less likely to blind someone with hot, reflected sun.

Suzu rested with her soft chin wedged between calloused fingers. Gozen recalled their first trip north, when a much younger Suzu had looked ready to shatter into delicate pieces. She had barely spoken a word—*how that had changed*—and her eyes had floated in shallow pools of sadness. Deep inside, he knew some of that fragility remained behind the determined gaze of a tenacious young Lady. He watched her from the corner of his eye, her black hair fluttering in the wind

"Before we get there, I want to go over a few questions," Gozen stated.

"Just wait for you."

Gozen paused. "Just wait for me?"

"I assume you're going to ask me a bunch of safety questions, and the answer to all of them is just to wait for you… and I will follow."

Gozen didn't argue. "You can keep an eye out and provide a much younger and less threatening presence."

The rumbling road quieted underneath. Suzu sat up in the seat, adjusting her collapsed Lansu. "People find me more threatening than you think. I'm not that little girl anymore."

"You're not that young, but you're still little." Gozen turned onto the final street.

Suzu smiled. "Well, everyone's little to *you*."

Neko stopped one address away from their destination and her passengers stepped out. Gozen eyed doors and open windows as they approached while Suzu glanced behind them. The buildings looked like a hundred cheap rentals jammed together, where few residents bothered to decorate their utilitarian facades. Although a thousand inhabitants could have squeezed onto that street, it looked dead.

Gozen stepped up to the door and put his ear close. After a few seconds he looked down, checking on Suzu.

"I'm still here."

He knocked on the door, sending a heavy thump into the walls. He listened again for someone approaching, or maybe leaving. After one more knock, he reached into his coat pocket.

"Did you convince Darou to follow them out here?"

"I asked if he wanted to collaborate based on our mutual hatred of Kits. I didn't get too specific with how." Suzu kept her eyes on shadows poking around the endless row of dwellings.

While she spoke, Gozen pulled his lock pick gun out. He carefully slipped the needle under the tumblers, shielding the activity with his wide torso. "Did Darou say how Chichimou looked when he saw her?"

"Tired of her father's stupidity."

Gozen gave her a raised eyebrow as his fingers continued to work the lock.

"Well, that's the impression I got when *I* last saw her."

The rumbling of the tumblers finally jumped to a *click*. Gozen quietly cracked the door open. Suzu watched him, seeing the Lord Enforcer take over, emerging from its dormant state. He stepped in, checking corners, analyzing the space.

He blocked the doorway until clearing the small room with his eyes and ears. Suzu impatiently slipped in after him. The space sat silent. Suspecting the wrong address or that Victou and his daughter had simply squatted in there for a few days, Gozen kept his focus towards the back. He cleared the cramped kitchen and saw the back door locked from the inside.

"Doesn't look like anyone lives here."

"Their last place was pretty empty," Suzu added, looking at

what little the room offered. "They didn't take much when they ran, either. I don't think this is the type of father to hang up posters of pink airships."

Suzu checked a few cupboards. They creaked and didn't quite square up when shut. "Darou just saw them here. Maybe they're a proper family on the run."

Gozen looked down the sink and then through the trash. Some crumpled wax paper, probably from a cheap dinner, sat alone in the bin. He picked it up, then saw a smaller paper underneath, stamped with an ornate logo. In his hand, it felt finer than anything else in the space.

"Citadel Station," Gozen spoke, holding the receipt.

"What?" Suzu asked, having only half heard him.

The memory was still clear. Nia had entered the Telakai building with an inextinguishable smile, dreaming of majestic views aboard a wondrous, private machine. Hours later, he saw her run out as if death itself chased her. "They have a ticket for an Unyo-class airship."

Flying machines had been a regular point of discussion between Suzu and her father. "But those aren't passenger ships. Isn't that what Opaji himself flies around in? Why would Victou... *how* would Victou even get on one of those fancy birds?"

"Nia rode on one once—Kits invited her. She was so excited... until Kits and Daimó threw some poor soul off over the mountains."

Suzu straightened up. "You think... but that seems like an expensive way to get rid of someone who's a nobody."

"Expensive is relative, but you can't get more private than thousands of feet above the ground." Gozen pocketed the ticket receipt. "If you have access to it, which Daimó certainly does, I can't think of a cleaner place for interrogation and disposal."

"But Chichimou?" The idea burnt like fuel inside Suzu, who knew better than anyone, what sinister depths those men could plunge.

Gozen shot up. "This ticket is for tomorrow morning."

"Perfect," Suzu said. "Citadel is a public station. We just need to spot them in the lobby before they load."

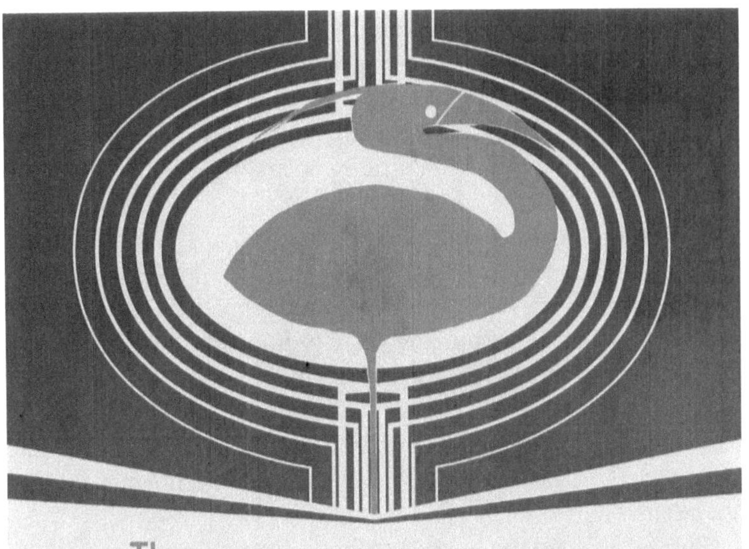

The
Copper Torlúng

"The private lobby is separated," Gozen replied. "It's smaller, and VIP ships often bring a few private Sentinels, on top of the CEs patrolling around."

"Ugh... well, isn't that just washed and waxed. I guess all we need to do is jump off the central mast and float onto the stupid deck."

Gozen didn't disagree and Suzu noticed the pause. "Should that have been a serious suggestion?"

Being thousands of feet above ground severely narrowed their options. "I can't sneak into anywhere unnoticed, and I don't want you up there alone. We should go get Jin."

"No," she argued. "Nia knew Mr. Fragile-and-Fancy would just bail when things stopped entertaining his curiosity. The moment she decided to trust him, when she really *needed* someone, he just abandoned her."

But Gozen had made up his mind. "Jin's got more spine than you think."

o o o

After perusing the sweet wines, Jin became intrigued by a northern blend just kissed with Hotberry blossoms—it promised to pair well with a light blashu grain salad. Having endured so much fish up in the mountains, his palette desired something more like the braised Chitori and field vegetables baked in a delicate pastry shell.

"Do any of the wines appeal to you? I'm not sure what you typically prefer with an evening meal," Jin asked Lucette.

Jin had driven them downtown, where a valet had parked his car, and they waited by the river. Lucette thought she had misinterpreted the entire event when a tiny steam-powered boat arrived and they boarded. The maître' d offered them hot, mulled wine, which helped make the four-minute ride extra bearable. They then boarded an enormous ship that smelled delicious, quite the opposite experience Lucette ever had with any other boat. A simple, elegantly lit sign read *The Copper Torlúng*. She'd never seen the svelte river bird in person, and although she knew the name was the result of trendy restaurant-naming conventions, she still hoped to see one cast in copper.

Upon entering, Lucette saw a dimly lit museum where art sat on plates as much as in frames. Polished rock covered the walls from floor to ceiling, framed with dark wood and albino brass fixtures. A massive chandelier sat high in the center of the gilded room, where she counted more staff than customers. She didn't understand how the place didn't sink, or why you'd decorate a boat with giant rocks. The sound of live music came from some other room.

After breathing in the grandeur, Lucette spent a few minutes attempting to decipher the most enigmatic beverage list she had ever seen. "Is this written in my language? And are these free? Because I do not see any prices."

Jin wondered if the usually jovial Lucette had delivered humor he didn't quite comprehend. "If there's any particular wine you have questions about, the sommelier here is quite good."

Lucette doubted how helpful the wine guide would be—assuming that's what a sommelier was—when his name was even harder to pronounce than the wines. She gave up on the beverage list that described its drinks like classical music and shifted over to the food menu. The expected listing of bread, entrees, and desserts had been replaced with a list of numbered courses. "Okay… uhm, I guess I'll take a number two."

"Excellent." Jin looked over to the second-course options. "Which one were you thinking?"

Quite certain she had just indicated which course, Lucette looked at the next table to make sure people did, in fact, eat food here. The room twinkled like a clear night from all the thickly jeweled fingers bobbing around. They had only traveled a few minutes to get there but she found herself in a beguiling, distant universe. "Yes… Jin, Lord Jin. What is it that I'm thinking?"

The ambiguity of their mutual misunderstanding was nearly as loud as the growling of their stomachs, and Jin decided to get things moving. "Well, Lady Lucette, if you are hungry… *are* you hungry?"

"Oh, I am hungry, Lord Jin," she spoke with a slow, exaggerated nod.

"In that case, I suggest we get *every* course."

Lucette opened her mouth but stopped short of actual laughter as the proposal appeared quite sincere. Her eyes went as wide as the fine porcelain plates passing by in servers' hands, all containing delicacies she could neither afford nor pronounce. She finally let out a chuckle.

"Ahh, yes. Nothing quite like ordering the full menu on an empty stomach," Jin said with satisfaction.

Lucette could feel her eyes filling with tears and wasn't sure why.

"Although the chef changes the first-course options a good deal, I always feel pleased starting with the sweet green consommé, red-pepper paste and silver kyupi. Shall we begin there?" Jin hoped she'd like his favorite first course at *The Copper Torlúng.*

The description sounded like novelty art supplies for wealthy children. "I'm so hungry I have no idea what you just said."

Jin felt warm as their faces glowed from the table light. Lucette's golden hair, adorned with prismatic accessories, gleamed charmingly amid the heavy, darkly polished interior. Jin noticed her twinkling eyes trace all over the restaurant and reveled in her apparent delight over his solitary, typical Tuesday night dinner spot.

He knew she had grown up poor, as orphans tend to do, but she seemed unbothered with the difference in their upbringing. In all the years since Jin had left home, Lucette was the first person to accept being his guest. "I appreciate that you trust me to order for both of us."

Lucette's blood sugar level had dropped to a point where she felt loopy. She continued bobbing her head, barely comprehending the food dream she had just drifted into.

"This Hotberry Wine sounds intriguing. Would you like a taster? Perhaps a full glass? Although, I was considering a bottle myself." Jin spoke, picking the wine menu back up. "This sweet wine with Shumé sounds peculiar, though. What do you think?"

"I wouldn't smack either one off the table."

"Bottles, then," Jin agreed.

"Yes, the bottles. Both the bottles. I agree."

"Of course, we can try others if we like."

"Of course, Jin… of course." She rested her chin on her hand, holding up a grin that had nearly grown too heavy for her neck.

When the wine came out, Lucette watched like a child peeking through the window at Michelou's Cold Creamery. The waiter carefully poured glasses with a pressed white towel. He rearranged Lucette's cloth napkin and walked away backwards, bowing as he went.

What followed was a shedding of distant presumptions as Lucette emersed into the true soul of fine dining. A gallery of dishes was presented to her as if she were an exotic monarch. Edible works of art whirled in for her evaluation, only to be replaced by more scintillating scents in a seemingly endless procession.

Jin recounted his recent journey into the mountains, providing a fantastical backdrop to the dance of aromas and appetizing hues. Every plate, some offering no more than a single bite, enchanted Lucette into a fantastical realm. The little child still living within her wondered what magical beings existed beyond the swinging doors, gilded with a copper bird.

After a near-total clearing of the table, the finale descended upon them. A shallow pool of spiced Pats liquor, smelling of sweet summer flowers, lay suspended on a pearlescent plate. An island of chocolate cake sat within, darker than a moonless night. It held a sculpture of meringue buttercream crusted with candied nuts, crowned with a pyramid of mimi berries. With a final stroke of enchantment, the server ignited a blue flame that circled delightedly around the tower.

With her eyes aglow, bewitched by confection, Lucette grabbed a silver spoon and joined Jin in the final act of their edible dream.

○ ○ ○

Suzu scuttled in first, buzzing from the possibility of a new lead. She hurried back to the dining room, which was occupied by only a single child sneaking a snack. Satisfied, she bounded back to the front door.

"Jin's not here. We should probably just go without him." She tried to wedge herself between the doorframe and Gozen's blockade.

"Did you check upstairs? Out back?"

"No, I'm pretty sure he's not here." She grabbed his wrist, leading him back to Neko. "We are short for time, big guy."

The clock was certainly ticking, but he didn't like their odds as only a pair. "I think he has a place down the street. Let's check there first."

As Suzu grunted, a sugar-laced voice bounced in through the front entrance. Suzu's face went sour, watching Lucette and Jin walk in, smiling beatifically as if just returning from their honeymoon. "Where were you guys?"

Lucette rubbed her stuffed belly with both hands, "Oh, we just grabbed a bite."

"*What?*" Suzu exclaimed. "You two had *dinner?*"

Lucette looked up, past the ceiling, and into the heavens. "No, Suzu, *dinner* would hardly describe the experience I just had."

Suzu grimaced. "What does that mean?"

"Only the finest edibles, presented in an endless parade of aromatic bliss." Lucette clasped her fingers to her cheeks as if daydreaming.

"Why are you being so odd?"

Unwilling to allow anyone to spoil her afterglow, Lucette leaned in, her smile not reaching her eyes. "I'm not odd, I'm *content*, because I consumed it all. That's right, Suzu, those edible works of art kept coming, and *I... ate... everything.*"

"I took Lady Lucette to dinner," Jin explained to Gozen.

"Yes, Jin, I see that."

"So, how did your excursion fair? Did you perchance get to see Lady Chichimou?"

Gozen looked at Suzu, still in her standoff with Lucette. "No. We think we know where they're at, but we gotta move fast."

"Oh, have they found themselves in a precarious situation?"

Suzu finally glanced away from Lucette. "Yup, and Gozen thinks you should tag along. Interested? Or would you rather stay and take a nap?"

"Mmm, that's a good idea," Lucette interrupted, leaning against the wall.

"Of course, I would extend any assistance I could for Lady Chichimou. What may I offer?"

"We don't have much time, so let's talk on the way," Gozen said and leaned in. "Do you have any more... flying stuff at your place?"

Everyone turned their attention towards Gozen. Lucette, narrowing her eyes, said, "I'm not sure what that means, but I need to go get a letter signed by Lady Kyoumére. Big guy, fancy guy, little squirt... good luck with your little adventure." She waltzed upstairs, humming a tune to herself.

Jin watched her ascend before turning back to Gozen. "I do not mean to promote redundancy, but do you mean to pursue them... in the air?"

o o o

They had stayed up late volleying a torrent of ideas, questions of procedure, and questions of sanity. Neko rumbled towards downtown with Gozen at her wheel, his face glowing with morning light. Jin, sitting shotgun, calibrated the equipment in his hands. The three had formulated a plan, one that sounded plausible in theory. Imagining the execution, however, nearly gave Gozen hives.

"Okay, I agree that it's *possible*, but..."

Suzu, adrenaline nearly dripping from her pores, teetered back and forth between the front seats. "I can do this, Gozen. I've done harder things, and we know Jin knows how to work a fancy little gadget."

"I don't disagree... because if I did, I wouldn't be driving towards Citadel Station. This just sounds... it sounds mad. I should just notify a Lord Enforcer. I think I still have some pull there."

"To do what? Arrest them for taking a joyride? Besides, there's no time."

"Do you think that would work?" Jin asked. "I recall that you disapproved of Lord Opaji's idle sanctions regarding Daimó's activities. Surely they wouldn't detain Kits for a crime he has yet to commit."

"And Victou would not be safe, locked up. *We* need to get them," Suzu added.

Leather squeaked as Gozen tightened his grip on the wheel. He knew they needed to do something, but every available path looked terrible.

Suzu's voice wavered. "Gozen, little Chichimou could be dead in an hour. You know those two aren't above killing an entire family."

Gozen knew she spoke the truth, but a pang struck him. "I don't want that happening to you, either." They went quiet until Gozen continued, in a voice crooked with frustration, "And why are you so trusting of *Jin* all of a sudden?"

Suzu's face went blank. She heard the heartache in Gozen's voice, buried under years of suppression. Nerves humming with emotion, she felt tears threatening to spill out as she thought of all Gozen had done—and was still doing—for her.

"I won't let anything happen to her... to them," Jin offered with heartfelt propriety.

Suzu swallowed the lump in her throat.

Gozen recognized that he had been outvoted. "You sure about all of this? You positive that thing will work getting down?"

Suzu offered a nod of confidence as Jin looked over his gear, scrutinizing details he had already triple-checked. "I put my life on the line, first and foremost, but I do not plan on losing it today."

Gozen groaned in defeat. The sensation reminded him of moments back with the Enforcers. He'd clean his gun five times, memorize a building's blueprint, then lead a group of young CEs straight into the fire. However, those events never involved exiting a situation by a thousand-foot drop.

"*Nuts and bolts*, are we really doing this?"

16
BREATH

Tailored hats and penciled eyes turned towards Neko's intimidating mass as it docked by Citadel Station's entrance; the passenger hub rarely saw such large vehicles stop here. Some patrons walked past, pausing for a curious glance. Others grimaced at their Tokis while scurrying past the truck, pursuing an imminent departure.

Suzu kneeled in the mid-cabin, tightening her shoes. Jin strapped down his pack and reached for the passenger door, mind locked on the mission. Before he made it out, Gozen blocked him in with a hefty forearm.

"She comes back in the same shape she's leaving." Gozen spoke quietly but Jin felt his full effect.

"Of course."

Gozen kept his arm up. "Don't give her any opportunity to do otherwise."

When Jin had accompanied Nia away from Kora and eventually into Goraka, he'd offered a partnership of mutual support. Gozen would allow no such partnership with Suzu. Jin would be her guardian, even if she refused.

Suzu finally came up from the back, energy radiating off her face. "Alright, time to go up." She slid past Jin, opened the passenger door and jumped down to the mosaic sidewalk entrance. Gozen watched as the chance for any alternate plans disappeared.

"Bring them back, Jin," Gozen demanded and then pushed the young man after her.

Jin took big strides to catch up with Suzu, who had reached the triple set of double doors. Heavy copper frames had oxidized into a rich gradient of colors. A row of glowing spheres, framed in matching metal, created a ladder of light straight to the top. They alternated with the first exterior elevators constructed in Chigou, which offered a final vertigo test for those taking their first flight. Halfway between them and the clouds, giant ships floated in a sight that never ceased to bewilder even those born in the cradle of progress.

Inside, ambient street sounds gave way to expensive shoes tapping on polished stone floors. Eyes and minds were fixated on departure times and boarding gates. The allure of Chigou's most esteemed travel experience absorbed all available attention. Suzu and Jin were dead center in the main lobby but attracted no more attention than potted plants.

Jin had traveled through Citadel Station twice as a youth, but Suzu gaped just as every newcomer did. Her senses were overloaded as towering structures and illuminated information assaulted them from every direction. Enormous glowing boards displayed destinations and times, changing their order and status with soft, mechanical clicks. Bright arrows enthusiastically pointed to the elevators, each going up to their corresponding boarding dock. The interior architecture swept and soared up towards the lobby's forty-meter ceiling. A mechanized mobile of model airships circled above, covered in metal pins to dissuade any intruding bird from using it as a carousel. Advertisements promised an assortment of luxurious, sparkling fantasies, including sugar-crusted hand-cakes and excursions to white-sand beaches.

Suzu's attention then narrowed to a family of three. The father checked their boarding information while mother eyed a new arrival of travel bags designed by someone named *Bolé*. Between them, a young girl mimicked the wonders of air travel with a Buran Class airship model. She floated the toy between her parents' legs as if navigating the towers of downtown Chigou. Suzu thought back to her early childhood, when she, too, couldn't have imagined her parents being gone, no longer there to protect her from the world's endless chaos.

Long accustomed to privileged transit, Jin instead focused on the concentration of CEs. "Civil Enforcers dominate the lower lobby—I'm not sure I noticed quite so many before. Regardless, we need to locate a maintenance worker."

"And remind me why you're not just buying us an escort straight to the top—putting the fortune in your back pocket to some good use," she said, before slipping into a mumble, "unless you blew it all on Lucette."

"That would certainly be efficient, but we will be entirely exposed at the VIP loading deck. We need cover for getting onto the ship, and we agreed a maintenance worker would be our best bet."

"You sure you don't want to try bribing a CE? I'd enjoy watching that."

Before Jin could reply to her irresponsible suggestion, Suzu grabbed his arm and lurched them sideways.

Jin noticed she was pulling him towards a maintenance worker heading for a dimly lit door that half-hid behind a departure sign. He asked her, "How much money do you believe a common labor worker would require in exchange for the clothes he wore?"

"No one is going to strip naked for you because they're poor, Jin."

"But that is the plan we agreed upon."

"I'm sure they have spare suits."

Jin watched the maintenance worker approach the service room as Suzu scurried ahead of him. They easily dodged a few patrons who had only vacation and snacks on their minds. The maintenance worker reached for his loaded keyring, but just before Jin caught up to Suzu, they were cut off by a Civil Enforcer.

"You'll want to head back and find your gate. This is a service area."

Suzu fought an urge to sprint. Jin thought of little Chichimou, awaiting her fateful journey. "Yes, good Lord. My... my sister requires her... doll which is currently packed away in my bag. She wants it for the flight as she is quite fragile and scared of flying, but she was too embarrassed to carry it from the house. I was hoping to discreetly retrieve it over here, out of sight."

Choking on a reply that Lady Kyoumére would have rebuked, Suzu, with an almost painful effort, mustered her most adorable grin.

The Enforcer interpreted her flushed cheeks as quaint embarrassment. "I'm a big brother too. Go ahead—just stay clear of the service path."

They held their breath until the Enforcer walked off, placing his attention elsewhere. Suzu clenched her teeth. "I'll show you something fragile."

"I believe he accepted the performance." Jin hurried towards the service door that the custodian had luckily been slow to open. The pneumatic metal barrier picked up speed as Suzu again leaped in front of Jin, wedging her small foot just inside the door before it shut.

They burst in on the service worker, an older man who jumped as if they'd interrupted him in a bathroom stall. "Can I help you?"

Suzu looked him up and down. "We need your clothes."

"Excuse me?" He covered himself as if already naked.

"My brother thinks it'd be funny showing up on our father's ship, dressed like a service worker," Suzu put the sugar back in her voice.

"Well, go buy one," the man grumbled. "It's not like a Lord Enforcer uniform—I'm pretty sure they'll just let you pay for it."

"But our ship is just about to leave. Please!" Suzu felt her cloyingly sweet voice rotting her teeth. "My brother has a lot of money, so he's fine paying you plenty."

Despite a twisted face, the worker asked, "How much is plenty?"

The maintenance worker watched Jin pull an absurd number of bills from a pocket and his demeanor changed immediately. The man reached out to take what was offered, then looked back to the remaining fortune in Jin's other hand.

Noticing, Suzu stepped in. "If you don't want it, I'm sure there are other service workers here—"

"No, no, no. I got a closet full of these suits."

The man began removing his coveralls down to his street clothes when Suzu asked, "so I can have one too?"

"I meant my home closet, little lady. Time to call off sick." He handed Jin the folded coveralls, flipped through the wad of bills, and left the peculiar pair to their costume.

Suzu looked around for a way up, preferring the seclusion of stairs but doubting they'd reach the ship in time. Jin slid the worker's coveralls over his premium daywear.

"It's like a wedding dress in a cardboard box," Suzu smirked as Jin fought with the zipper. "Any keys in those pockets?"

He checked; they weren't that lucky. "I can likely override..." Jin suddenly halted completely and stared down at his young partner.

"Well, come on." She urged him forward. "What, is your pampered skin having a reaction to those common fabrics?"

"How are *you* getting on board the ship?"

"With you, on the service lift, Jin."

"That'll get us up, but no one will believe you are a Citadel Station service employee. We'll need to go through the primary loading zone; there truly will be no place to hide."

"Don't worry, I'm real sneaky." She pushed his arm.

"I expect no fewer than five Sentinels, and they will question our reason for boarding."

"Well..." She was ready to claw up the side of the building. "... just say it's daddy-daughter day at work."

"Lady Suzu, at that age I would not have been physically capable of impregnating..."

"We don't have time Jin!"

The sound rang loudly enough they both instinctively checked the door. She pushed him again, kicking a large duffle bag out of the way. "We'll figure it out on the way up."

Jin leaned down and picked up the abused duffle bag off the floor. Stretched out to its full length, the bag stood just shy of Suzu's moderate height. Jin's eyes jumped between the comparably sized items.

Suzu caught on. "Jin, seriously, I will punch you."

o o o

Away from the mass of merry families humming with wanderlust, the VIP lobby offered more surveillance than warmth.

Although moderate in size, Victou found the space hollow. With no other passengers present—other than his daughter—the luxury foyer felt more like a holding cell.

Two Citadel Station staff guarded either side of the glass-and-metal door leading outside to the dock where four stone-faced Sentinels patrolled. None of them had acknowledged Victou and Chichi since they had sat down. Kits stood outside in the docking area, watching the Unyo-class ship line up. Chichimou found the entire scene fascinating—impossibly large balloons performing fantastical feats. Since camping in Goraka, the world had bloomed into a realm of wondrous possibilities.

Victou, peering past the station's roof, began to question his plan. He had made a lifelong habit of keeping exits available, and now he was preparing to board a vehicle where an unexpected exit would require wings. He grabbed his daughter's hand and forced a smile.

A docking tech guided the majestic airship onto the mooring anchor with green batons. Massive engines roared, causing the entire lobby to vibrate. Like anyone living in the Naifin Valley, Victou had always dreamed of being on an airship, but those fantasies of wealth and fortune seemed silly at the moment. He looked down at Chichimou, clearly in her own world. Her face glowed, and he wanted to share the wonder with her, an impressive gift beyond what he had ever provided. His heart was beating too quickly. He hid shaking hands under his legs and twitched when the hefty anchor finally clamped down, locking the ship in place.

"Is that the one we get to ride?" Chichi dared to ask.

Victou only managed half a smile and even less of a nod; all he wanted was to get the whole thing over with. Running had worn him out, and even in that moment, Chichimou's face looked pale and sunken. The Red Valley had rejuvenated them some, a gift of nature and wonder. It had also offered a bargaining chip worth more than he could ever earn—or at least that was the plan he'd bet everything on.

Noise and wind flooded the pristine lobby. Victou's head shot up as Kits stood in the doorway, waving them forward. Chichi looked as if someone had just handed her a kitten. They stood, Victou keeping Chichi's hand in his own as if trying to absorb some of her optimism.

"Sure is loud, huh? All the wind and those big engines."

"Yeah," she nodded. "I can feel them shake."

Victou led his daughter to the threshold and felt a sudden impulse to stop, but the air pressure pulled them through the door.

Kits, standing by a Sentinel, stared at Victou and Chichi as they passed. "Go wait on the deck," he ordered.

As the small family complied, a station worker came through the lobby entrance just before it shut, carrying a bulky duffle bag. The worker put his head down and plopped the canvas-covered mass onto the floor, where it made an odd, squeaking sound.

"Think he's ever heard of a cart?" Kits grumbled to the Sentinel as he watched the laborer talk to himself. "If that idiot plans to come aboard, make sure it's not his first day on the job. We don't pay NASF to use this as a training ship." The guard responded with a snappy nod.

As Victou and Chichi walked across the deck, they saw a Danyo-Plus airship rise into sight by the adjacent loading deck. Twice the length of a standard Danyo passenger ship, the Plus variation could transport ninety-six travelers. The current customers lined up, looking past each other's heads to view the incredible feat of industry float in place. Having never been so close to one in flight, Victou and Chichi both stood and stared, completely hypnotized.

"You'll go deaf standing out here," Kits warned them as he walked to the deck. Victou watched him board their Unyo-class ship, forced another smile, and took his daughter to the railing where a crewman waved them forward. Chichi looked down and noticed the floor of the ship move ever so slightly against the loading ramp. It reminded her of the small rowboat they had briefly had back in Primichi, bobbing against the dock.

She then looked back to her father, who couldn't get over the tiny world a hundred stories below. Victou jumped when the crewman rammed the gate shut.

"It's okay Dad, I think we'll be safe," Chichimou offered,

confident in the ship's ability to maintain its magic.

Back in the lobby, the service worker continued to fuss with his load. "I had to drop you. Kits was at the door."

"I hit my tailbone, you tool," Suzu's voice filtered through the bag.

"We need to get on board. Stop speaking." Jin lifted the bag and stood, groaning like an old man. He kept his eyes low while approaching the dock. Ready to push through with his oversized parcel, a Sentinel's arm suddenly barred the way.

"What's your business?" the mechanical voice demanded.

Jin's script was ready. "I need to check the railing along the deck, stairs, and walkways."

"I didn't get any notice."

"I am giving you the notice," Jin plainly stated. "A railing failed just south of Primichi, leading to a few deaths. I have been instructed to immediately inspect every rail base manufactured by Aya Avionics."

The Sentinel looked over the cumbersome load on Jin's back, but before he could speak, Jin cut in. "I will have rather limited access to parts once we depart."

"I didn't get notified of your clearance. Why don't you wait until they return to dock?"

The duffle bag made a sound just as Jin bounced the bag on his shoulder to reposition it. "I could, but if any railing fails during this flight, I will be forced to report the hold-up taking place at this juncture, both to NASF and... whoever owns this ship."

The Sentinel's fixed stare held Jin's a few seconds longer before the man finally moved his arm.

Jin promptly took several steps before speaking from the side of his mouth, "We are clear for a minute, just keep—"

"Get me out of this sack!"

"Please stop talking," Jin mumbled like a ventriloquist just before reaching the gate operator. "This burden isn't getting any lighter." He huffed, shifting the bag up higher on his shoulder.

A crewman started to open the gate. "You going in the cabin?"

"Just on deck," Jin said as he passed forward, helping to push open the gate. The crewman shut the gate behind them and released the mooring anchor. Jin stumbled as the airship shifted.

"That was rather ill-mannered," Jin criticized as he dropped Suzu on the front deck. The ship began to drift back as the duffle's zipper slid down an inch. A shifting eyeball appeared, squinting from the light, awkwardly trying to assess the situation. She half-caught the sight of Citadel Station's central tower drifting away, along with any chance to escape on a solid structure.

"Can I get out of this sweat sack now?" Suzu whispered vigorously through her teeth.

Jin slid the zipper open a few more inches. "Stay patient."

Suzu's nose escaped the prison of recycled air. "I can smell my own feet in here. Don't tell me to be patient."

Suzu's voice grew muffled again as Jin zipped up the bag and hoisted it back over his shoulder. The station shrunk as its staff turned their attention towards upcoming flights. "We'll be clear in a minute. I'm moving into position."

Suzu's reply was drowned out by the humming engines above. Oscillating his extra weight, Jin lumbered down the stairs to the side walkway. He set Suzu down and looked over the edge. He identified the emergency cargo-ballast pods, as well as an anchor point for the rappelling wire, which they had planned to hang Suzu from. Four hundred meters straight down, Chigou scurried like an insect mound.

A finger poked again through the zipper, but Jin grabbed it just as he caught sight of a figure exiting the central cabin. His peripheral vision deciphered a dark outfit, unlike the uniforms of the ship's crew.

The individual leaned on the railing. Jin slipped on a chunky pair of goggles from a pocket and mimed inspecting bolts and base plates. The figure shifted and Jin barely heard footsteps through the engine noise—expensive, hard-soled shoes, the kind Kits always wore. Jin thought of the retracted Masu tucked behind his pack, and then the pistol Kits likely kept in his jacket—the same pistol that had nearly taken his head off.

Jin prayed the steps would continue right past him, but they stopped. He felt the body hovering over him.

"What are you doing?"

Jin prayed again, hoping the engine would mask his voice. "Checking the railing. Another ship had a failure yesterday."

"I didn't hear anything. This railing is above grade. I think you may be on the wrong ship." The voice got closer.

Jin kept his goggle-covered face hidden with the brim of his hat. "After we dock, you can confer with my superior."

"Why all the gear?"

Jin silently persisted in his fraudulent inspection.

The voice seemed to drop by his ear. "I said, what's in that fat bag you brought onto my ship?"

Desperate, Jin grabbed a pocket tool and began hitting the base plate. "The shear strength of these alloy bolts, while rated at 90,000 KSI, fails considerably lower when fitted with these decorative dark-brass heads holding this life support—"

A Sentinel then came out and said something ending with the name *Daimó*. Kits paused before saying, "If this guy drops even one bolt, send him over to chase it." A few seconds later, both men left him alone.

Jin whistled in relief as the flaps of the duffle bag flew open. Suzu squinted and huffed air like a crazed subterranean predator breaching the surface. "Was that Kits?" Too disoriented to run after her mortal enemy, she looked around, acclimating to the noise and altitude. Her fingers pressed hard onto the walkway, seeking solid ground while floating by the clouds. She looked through the railing as the entirety of her world presented itself. Chigou looked like a toy. She gazed north and saw Kora Farm impossibly occupying the same view as the street she'd grown up on, with the dam and reservoir sitting between them. The entire valley sat before her in a scene that stole her breath. Suzu had dreamed of traveling on an airship countless times, of having a soaring adventure with her courageous parents. She wanted to look over at her dad's face and say, *It's just like how I always drew it.*

Jin pulled out a cluster of gear and asked, "Are you ready? It is time."

17
VANISH

With no explanation, Jin started attaching pulleys and hoist rings to Suzu, who had forgotten she had put a harness on before being stuffed in the bag.

"Wait, we're doing this now?"

The airship shifted from a sudden downdraft and Suzu clutched the railing.

"We need to get you over the railing immediately," Jin said while his fingers danced with clips and gadgets. "Please monitor the walkway."

Suzu sat like a doll being built. She looked up at the turbine sucking air in an unrelenting roar. The late sun reflected off a million polished corners below, making Chigou sparkle like an unpolluted night sky. Still waiting for Jin to finish, she turned south and looked down on Goraka, the land of legend. Pockets of heavy fog floated across a thick garden of trees as the Red Valley displayed itself from end to end. She saw everything and she saw nothing. Somewhere inside, Nia's body lay alone where she had fallen to her death, the place where Jin had left her.

A sharp, metal click made her jump.

"You're ready. Hop over."

Her hand shot out and immediately grabbed his wrist. "Wait, wait."

Jin looked perplexed. "Suzu, this walkway will not stay vacant."

An unexpected battering of doubt hit Suzu. Jin had explained—*over*explained—the contraption that dangled off her, but it gave little comfort at the moment her life depended on it.

"I just..." Her throbbing brain tried to remember the plan.

"How does this thing work again?"

Jin pointed through the railing, just below the deck. "Twist the silver lever one half rotation, then pull up. The device adjusts itself as you move." With Suzu's hand still latched onto his wrist, he stood up, pulling her along.

"Okay, okay," she said, leaning on the railing, with a cloud suddenly blocking her view of the ground. She drew deep breaths, readying herself for a leap of faith. Jin was performing a final inspection when she noticed him holding another wire—not the moderately thin alloy cable he'd claimed could hold the weight of his car, but an emaciated filament that nearly looked invisible. "Wait a minute..."

Jin heard a door latch click. Without hesitation, he grabbed Suzu's legs and flipped her over the railing. Too shocked to scream, she swung out of sight as Jin twisted to block any possible view. Someone in a blue jumpsuit walked past, probably a technician. Jin attempted a black-hand greeting, offering a stern, unnatural nod. Down below, Suzu swung back out, flailing like a hooked fish. Jin discretely monitored the technician, who kept on walking.

Suzu began to stabilize and scowled, offering a salvo of curses back up to the railing. Unable to hear her, Jin responded to her moving lips with a reassuring thumbs-up. He commenced with his part of the plan and marched along the walkway towards the front deck. Heading up the stairs, he hung his left arm casually along the railing, dropping the faint filament down below the deck. He continued up and around, allowing the fine wire to unspool and stretch below to the opposite side.

In the navigation cabin, the First Pilot squinted as a razor-thin glare floated across the outer cockpit window. Leaning forward, he tried to spot what looked like a daring spider's attempt to catch insects in the stratosphere. He turned to tell the First Mate just as it disappeared.

The crewman noticed. "What is it?"

Blinking, the First Pilot failed to reacquire the single thread. "Nothing," he replied, and focused on his compass heading: a southern path taking them directly over Goraka.

Jin descended the outer starboard stairs, keeping his head down and eyes active. He hummed at the execution of a well-designed plan. He eyed the next anchor spot, staying ready for any unexpected obstruction.

Kneeling down, Jin fastened another anchor clip just below the walkway and began looping the filament through. Dangling under the port side hull, Suzu saw the other half of her support rig tighten up. She began to rotate like a bloated gyroscope. Her back strained as she tried to right herself, seeing how the contraption stretched out. A firm tug pulled her laterally towards starboard, and she finally understood Jin's convoluted trapeze in the sky.

With multiple, complementary support lines, in conjunction with the haul's array of attach-points, she could suddenly move freely underneath the ship. Leaning back, she started to crawl, inverted like an insect. Her athletic figure quickly acclimated to the bizarre travel method. Looking up towards the bow, she saw a latch sticking out. She climbed towards the floor hatch that Gozen had told her about, the one that Nia had seen moments after Kits threw a man to his death. Suzu remembered Soultai training with Nia, who had her climb up to the silo's rafters at Kora and promised she wouldn't let Suzu fall—or at least wouldn't let her hit the floor.

"I wish you were here," Suzu whispered as she shut her eyes from a blast of freezing air. Her teeth began to chatter. Jin and Gozen had their tasks elsewhere while she waited for the hatch to open—*if* it opened. Kits could have been standing a meter above and not had a clue that she was there, clinging alone below the hull of his ship. "Nia, I *really* wish you were here."

Her eyes popped open. She reached into a pocket and remembered how a loving friend could send a gift even from beyond death. Suzu pulled out a Toki and triggered it. A loud *reeee* bounced across the ship's metal underbelly. "Come on, little friend, I know you're out there somewhere."

Inside the central lobby, Victou and Chichimou looked at each other, confused by the sudden, muffled screech. Chichi's fingers touched the seat, which was covered with a fancy fabric that she couldn't stop rubbing. The entire cabin sparkled with brass and wood so polished it looked fake. A Sentinel stood silent.

How did we end up like this? Victou asked himself. They floated, trapped in a den of luxury that he had asked for. He played the upcoming conversation in his mind a hundred different ways, hoping Kits and his boss would value the incredible discovery he had made. Victou repeated words like *unprecedented, powerful, advanced,* and *exclusive.* He had never planned to be a schemer, yet that had become his and his daughter's life. Tired from their long day, she rested against his arm and sighed.

The soft gesture nudged his self-pity aside and replaced it with the motivation to survive. His back straightened and he breathed deeply just as Kits materialized from the stairwell, lacking his usually smug demeanor.

"He's ready. Come on." Kits gestured down below before looking at the Sentinel. "Go check on that repairman from Citadel. Make sure he's not breaking anything." With a snappy nod, the guard exited to the walkway.

Victou squeezed Chichi's shoulder then followed Kits downstairs; Chichi thought he had squeezed a bit hard. Kits went down the narrow stairwell without looking back. Victou made eye contact with his daughter, mustering as much reassurance as he could.

The stairs ended in the middle of a split room. Victou tried to peek off to the right before following Kits to the left. Elegant seating lined the outer edge while the inner wall had a bar and glasses that looked like they'd never been used.

"In here," Kits commanded, looking solely at Victou. The father bent down and eased his daughter over to a polished leather chair.

"I'll be just inside that door." Victou finally said.

She sat down agreeably, slipping back as the shiny seat gave a refined squeak. She looked like a figurine—undersized and painfully precious. Victou wondered how he could have helped make something so perfect.

Outside light flooded in from the VIP cabin as Kits opened the door. Victou offered Chichi one last smile before squinting at the blinding unknown. She watched as he disappeared into the light.

As the door shut, her suddenly private room went silent. Chichi looked around, her eyes dancing between assorted shiny edges. It all looked neat but a bit lonely, like the big guard who had stood over her in the lobby. As her fingers began to fidget, a face appeared around the corner of the stairwell. She felt a faint familiarity... then every muscle in her body locked in place.

○ ○ ○

Victou's eyes flitted around, adjusting to the luminous cabin. Kits stood off to the side, waiting on the revered figure looking out the curved bay window which made up the entire rear wall of the room. Through the glass, Victou saw Goraka approach from the south, a perfect accompaniment to the story his life depended on.

Victou looked at Kits for guidance, but Kits stood perfectly still and staring straight ahead as if watching a predator that could spring at any moment. Both men held their breath as the figure finally turned.

The man's face, as if cast in iron, gave nothing away. His aged but steady figure looked reanimated, a body living past the point of death. Victou felt his skin prickle. He clenched his toes, trying to keep any remaining confidence from spilling out. His mind held the image of his daughter, demanding that his body stand strong.

"Describe them to me," the nameless man ordered.

To his horror, Victou's voice cracked, barely getting half a word out. Trying to suppress panic, the father reminded himself how many times he'd successfully flimflammed his way through a situation, and this time he only needed to recite the truth. He cleared his throat and made a second attempt. "Well... first, my name is Victou; and how may I address you?"

"Lord Daimó," Kits interjected.

Victou bounced his focus between them. "Yes... Lord Daimó, right, okay. So, I'm assuming you're asking about the creatures, the... *beings*... from... well, from down there." He gestured past Daimó down into Goraka.

The aged man stood with catatonic patience. Kits, who had yet to develop any ease around Daimó, pushed his guest along. "You have a more interesting story?"

"Right, no, I was just... for clarity." Victou tried to find a comfortable pose. Thoughts shuffled down, and once his mind-dive hit bottom, memory took over. "They were unlike anything I've ever seen before. Like everyone else, I'd heard stories as a child about the creatures from Goraka. They always sounded like a sensational fantasy, so it was shocking to discover how right they were."

Subtly, Daimó mumbled a grunt, as if opposing the proclaimed magnificence. Victou glanced at Kits, who was void of any tell. Victou continued.

"I stayed near the edge of the forest. Seemed good enough for hiding and those stories probably kept me from going farther. It was fairly uneventful, but then one day, my daughter wandered off for just a minute. I looked for her, and then... then I found her."

"What were you hiding from that would bring you to Goraka?" Daimó asked.

Victou thought about the truth: he reported to men who reported to Kits, who in turn reported to a frightening man who lived in the sky. He then left with Chichimou on the advice of an unknown teenager with a big stick. "There was a... situation and I felt it best to get my daughter out of the city."

"Directly to the valley of death."

Victou stalled, rubbing his neck. "Nobody followed us, so... it worked, at least. I actually didn't experience any threats in the forest until my daughter found them... or, rather, they found her."

"And they let you go?" Daimó's expression intensified, in interest or disbelief.

"They... I don't think they ever saw me. I'm not sure if those dark... things were indeed eyes." He gestured curving lines down across his face.

"You let them be near your daughter. You didn't intercede at all?" Daimó asked. Victou wondered if the old man was questioning his valor or prodding for something else.

"I was hiding but things seemed calm. I wanted it to stay calm so I just... waited."

"While the creature and your daughter just... chatted?" Daimó's flat voice took another bend. Victou needed to convince him, and not just of the truth.

"There was a device—they stood around it. My daughter stood quietly but the creature seemed to mind the machine."

"The machine?" Daimó's head tilted. "What was it?"

Victou glanced again at Kits, whose face now struggled to hide surprise—not at what Victou was saying, but rather at his boss's reaction to the tale. Victou knew he had hit on something. "It was long, like a pole sticking out of the ground, with this mechanism on top."

In a rare moment, Daimó's expression revealed something from within, and both younger men saw it. Kits had never seen his superior let slip even a faint emotion; it was as if his face had early-onset rigor mortis. The mention of red ghosts had spurred little reaction; those stories were widespread and cheap, but they had never involved any machines. Most would scoff at the notion of forest ghosts utilizing technology, the magic and sole provenance of men. Victou and Kits, however, read no such skepticism from Daimó.

"If I had to guess," Victou continued, "which I do, I'd say it appeared to be some kind of probe. Occasionally the top would glow, and steam would start to pour out. It was mechanical for sure, but something about it still looked organic, like technology made out of rocks and trees. Once I calmed down and my head cleared, I remembered a drawing I found in Pirou's office."

"The eternal power hidden within the mountain." The Lord wasn't only listening—he appeared completely captivated. Kits could barely believe what he was seeing.

"Yes," Victou answered. "I remember a drawing by an engineer named Carmin Komou. It was of a device that looked similar to this... in a way, but it mentioned probing for ground heat—core-thermic energy, endless energy. A note mentioned Goraka, but who would ever test there?"

"Only those unwavering in their pursuit of progress, all the way to the end." Daimó's eyes dropped along with his voice and Kits's disbelief deepened.

For the first time, he was witnessing his master apparently overtaken by sorrow, slipping into a bitter memory. Nothing had ever affected Daimó so strongly—so seemingly personally—and yet it came from a stranger's mention of arcane technology.

Anxious to keep up the speed of his tale, Victou suddenly remembered the photo he had taken. He reached into a pocket and pulled it out. The image looked grainy and soft, evidence mostly of his novice photography skills, but the proof stood right there, center frame. His final play. "Here. I almost forgot, but I took a photograph." He held it up towards Daimó.

Intensely curious to see it himself, Kits was surprised by his superior's sudden indifference. Daimó glanced for only a moment—a minor act of recognition more than an examination.

Kits suddenly felt like a child, isolated by his ignorance. Victou, however, found his back straight and chin up. His pulse galloped. The story had more worth than he realized, but he still had no idea what it would buy him. "So yeah, we got right next to it."

"And it *let* her?" Daimó cut in quickly, suspicious.

"Well... yes. We left completely unharmed, not even followed. It showed us no aggression at all. I'm positive I could find that probe again and bring it back." Victou projected confidence—at least half of it sincere. He waited for an offer, or a request: something to bargain with. Instead, Daimó clarified a point.

"Showed *her* no aggression."

The short response confused him. "Yes... it didn't show hostility towards either of us."

"But you said you were hiding. The creature let *her* go, not you."

Victou's anticipation stumbled into a quiet panic. Daimó had detected a truth that Victou himself had foolishly failed to consider. He'd presented himself and his daughter as a whole—a single unit with a single shared experience. Daimó apparently felt otherwise.

"True," Victou continued, "but she had no idea where we went. I'd be able to tell you the exact location of the device and where we encountered..."

"They are always there. No guide is needed, for they are seen when they choose to reveal themselves. But to be with one and then walk away, *that* is exceptional." Daimó's hollow, floating gaze snapped back onto Victou. "Your daughter, as it turns out, is quite valuable."

Victou had wanted to hear *almost* those exact words. He had never considered himself a model father, but to hear Chichi described as some object to exploit, disconnected from him, felt wretched. His hope began mutating into something like despair. He struggled to imagine how they could escape their glistening prison in the sky. Every idea immediately vaporized as it dropped into the crucible of reality.

Daimó, glancing at Kits, gestured down and walked over to the bay window. Kits looked at Victou, falsely apologetic, the way someone does when they're about to do something horrible. He knelt to the floor, next to a large brass relief modeled after the skyline of Chigou. Kits lifted an alloy circle with the word *PROGRESS* written on it. The word revealed a handle, and when he lifted it, a whirlwind burst into the cabin.

Victou stepped back, gut knotting up as he watched the seal turn into a death hatch. They had reached the edge of the Red Valley; emerald greens and scattered clouds passed below. The wind swirled around, tugging him, as if pulling him down towards a drain. His hands were ready to claw at Kits if he took two steps closer. Instead, the young man patiently stood at attention.

"It is a dark, mysterious place, even for those who have been there. Its lure is undeniable, and it never truly lets one go." Daimó's voice, bouncing off the glass, was still audible through the hellish wind. "If you escape with your body intact, it will forever keep a hold on your mind."

"But I made it back. I offered you information," Victou pleaded, desperate but trying to sound otherwise.

"You dipped your toe into that forest, but your daughter truly swam through its depths. She has experienced the place where life overflows... and is taken." Daimó turned to Kits, his expression almost nostalgic. "You have done well in rectifying past failures."

Kits nodded in shock.

The old Lord's posture relaxed, gazing through the window into the depths of creation below. "Have you ever seen the valley of life?"

"Not the valley of death?" Kits wondered aloud.

The old master looked deeper into the darkness between the swaying trees. He placed his hand on the glass like a child and leaned in as if the few extra inches would give him better insight.

Kits inched forward, wanting to see what those old eyes saw. Daimó had taken Kits in as a youth but never before had the young man seen him so exposed. He sensed an invitation, something intimate and privileged—trust and love, offered at a father's side.

Victou watched the moment unfold. Curiosity gave way to planning and to taking advantage of their temporary shift in focus. He thought of his daughter, alone in the other room, and the giant vacuum at his feet offering a quick trip to eternal darkness. The bewitching sight below then offered something so unexpected his mind froze.

Moving just past the hatch, Kits stepped up to his mentor. The old, hollow eyes appeared to reminisce, pulling some memory from the mysterious canopy of trees. Kits had long ago noticed Daimó's fascination with Goraka but had never understood it.

Kits nervously cleared his throat. "How long were you there? You *have* been there, haven't you?" He had only ever asked questions for clarity, fearing misunderstanding a task; never had he pried for personal information. Kits readied himself for a disappointed scowl, but Daimó nodded benevolently.

Looking out through the clouds, Kits recalled his last conversation with Nia. She had offered him transparency and vulnerability—virtues of the weak, or so he had always thought. In such intimate proximity, they made him uncomfortable, but when Kits had feared he could lose her, he realized those qualities were part of what had attracted him to her. Her natural sincerity—stripped of perpetual defenses that expected the worst of the world—tasted pure and sweet. He felt a need to hide his fascination, but the fruit, impossible to forget, had already been consumed.

Unlike most orphans he had grown up with, Kits had openly dismissed any pathetic longing for mother's baking and father's pats on the back. Time with Nia, however, had changed him. She had infected him with ideas of grace, care, and intimacy. He wanted to be more than *useful*. He wanted to be *valued*.

Despite Daimó's eternally frigid demeanor, Kits was sure he'd just seen something spark in those dead eyes. Kits readied himself for a breakthrough. Daimó then gave what Kits could only describe as a smile—a guess, as he had never seen it before.

As the peaceful moment settled, Daimó glanced back towards Victou, and his gentle veneer hardened in an instant. Kits tensed up, so entranced by Daimó's changing expressions he could not look away. He again felt like a child, being scolded but not understanding why. "What is it?"

Daimó cocked his head to the side. "Your *responsibility* has vanished."

18
TERMINAL

The empty room behind Kits immediately explained Daimó's flip into disappointment: Victou had disappeared. His attention funneled towards the floor hatch, still vomiting cabin air. Kits ran up and knelt by the opening. He half expected to see Victou's flailing body, descending along a trail of screams. Kits saw no figure, but a voice floated in as if right outside the hatch. He leaned forward and heard another voice, arguing with the first.

He darted to the cabin door, leaving his stone-faced patron behind. The lounge offered neither answers nor the little girl who had suddenly become so valuable. *Dammit.* He ran up the stairs, looking for the Sentinel he had tasked with finding the odd crewman.

Seeing the Sentinel just ahead, Kits ran up, head whipping side to side as he searched the passage beyond. "Where are they?"

"What do you mean *they?*"

"The man and the kid!"

"The crewman from the Citadel is the only one…"

Kits pushed the Sentinel aside and ran out to the port side walkway. Recalling Nia—who had successfully hidden above the turbines—Kits made for the engine room. The moment he stepped outside, however, the answer stood in plain sight.

Kneeling at the railing, the Citadel crewman wrangled wire and carabiners as Victou's daughter stood watching with her feet in a duffle bag. The crewman looked up as Kits reached for his gun, but the man's face held his draw. For a moment, he scrambled to figure out whether he knew the man—then it came to him like a gunshot. Jin Aya was stealing his prize.

Reflexively, Kits drew his firearm. In the same instant, Jin turned to cover Chichi, shielding them with his thick backpack. The gun fired. Jin's speed proved too slow, as he felt the round smash into his body. He collapsed onto little Chichimou.

Still struggling to make sense of the scene, Kits leaned over the railing to find another dose of absurdity. Victou dangled on a harness below an emergency drop-pod, with none other than the daughter of Carmin Komou hanging between them.

"What the hell?" His voice squeaked. Kits loaded another round into his single-shot, magazine-fed pistol. He raised the weapon and pointed it at the girl who had demonstrated a magnificent and inexhaustible ability to cause him problems. Her face looked older but she was still recognizable as the girl he had failed to kill along with her parents. With all he had done—all that numbed his soul—that memory still burned. This distracted thought caused him to miss the arm slipping back over the edge. Before he could react, Jin, who still slumped over Chichi on the deck, triggered the pod's release, sending it away towards the earth.

Victou's and Suzu's screams stretched back as the strange cluster plummeted to the ground. A few seconds later, the red and white chute opened, slowing the descent of the empty drop pod and the people attached to it. Kits braced on the railing and steadied his aim, lining up the pair that had escaped the ship, but who had not *yet* escaped his reach.

They rode on a steady air current back towards the city, an easy trajectory for the skilled shooter to track. Iron sights targeted the bodies swaying below the chute. Kits held his breath and began to squeeze the trigger. A cold wind stirred up tears and he blinked to clear his eyes. Upon opening them again, he found something was obstructing his vision—black eyes and claws were hurtling towards his face. With no time to react, he fired.

Kits flung himself backward as pain shot across his temple. He saw the owl arc upward before diving behind the airship. He jumped back to the railing to find Suzu and Victou begin to drift below the airship.

"Demon bird," Kits yelled, wiping blood from the wound that

had just missed his eye. He saw Jin stumble up the stairs, taking the precious girl away with him. Kits stepped forward as he pulled the slide on the gun back, cycling in the next round. He raised the pistol, which unexpectedly collided with a metal cabin door. An alarmed navigator followed right after, ducking at the sight of a gun barrel.

"What's happening?" he asked Kits.

The careless Sentinel from the central lobby joined them, and Kits suddenly felt trapped by incompetence. He looked back over the railing just as the parachute disappeared below the ship. Slamming the navigation door shut, Kits saw Jin crawl up onto the front deck and out of sight.

o o o

Hundreds of meters below, Gozen slowed as he approached the only man-made structure between Chigou and Goraka: a security booth sitting alone in a field along Long Frost Road. Ready to ram the gate if needed, Gozen instead discovered an empty stall. A large sign read *TURN BACK, UNSAFE WILDS*. Gozen had assumed, like everyone else, that someone guarded Goraka, but the government had left that duty solely to Goraka's infamy.

Gozen looked up into the sky and spotted the airship he had tailed from Citadel Station—a nearly impossible task in the dense metropolis. Darting through downtown, he had almost hit three separate cars, probably had hit a fourth, and had narrowly avoided murdering an entire class on a field trip. High above, the ship looked like it had just passed over Goraka. He briefly considered— for the first time—that he might need to drive into the cursed forest. While contemplating that idea, his eye caught what looked like a peppermint candy floating in the sky.

"Uh oh… it's happening."

He prayed Suzu had made her escape without being shot. He noticed the floating package hustle back towards Chigou at an alarming rate, despite almost no wind. In less than ten seconds it had shot past him.

Dammit, they're in the jet stream!

A blast of steam screamed out as he torqued the steering wheel.

The trailer hinge creaked as Neko twisted back towards the city. His heart raced as he readied himself for a mad, acrobatic pickup. He shoved his head out the window, his face slapped by the wind, keeping his eyes skyward.

Up in the clouds, Kits finally pushed through the narrow walkway and ran up the stairs. He saw Jin backed up against the front railing, holding the young girl tight to his body. With his gun raised, Kits saw Jin's eyes struggle to focus. The usually prim heir stood crooked, wincing from the bleeding hole hiding behind cheap, borrowed clothes.

"I guess you realized how valuable that little girl is just before I did," Kits shouted over the spinning engines, finger firmly pressed on the trigger. "Your absurd kidnapping scheme nearly worked, but little Lady Headache made off with the wrong family member."

Chichi looked up at Jin's face, seeming more worried by what she saw there than at the situation they were in. Jin's eyes met hers and his nerves calmed.

"Don't worry, young Lady," Jin reassured her.

Kits straightened his arm another few degrees, poised to fire. "Although I just shot you a minute ago—certainly reasonable at the time—I'd be willing to discuss the situation." He grinned. "The alternative… well, you probably won't prefer that."

Confident the Aya heir would either comply or just collapse, Kits merely watched as Jin, clutching Chichimou, simply leaned back, plunging them both straight over the railing. Kits ran up to the brass bar and saw the pair disappear, plummeting into a cloud.

○ ○ ○

Gozen watched the parachute drift away from the road. Checking to his left, he gauged the wild terrain. "Alright, here we go," he announced, as if diving into ice water.

He activated a lever. Gears and pistons grunted as the entire vehicle raised nearly a foot, steam hissing from the undercarriage. With the extra clearance, he veered into the tall grass and followed the girl he refused to abandon.

The cabin began to rattle as Neko plowed through the field. He struggled with the wheel, fighting to align the truck with the

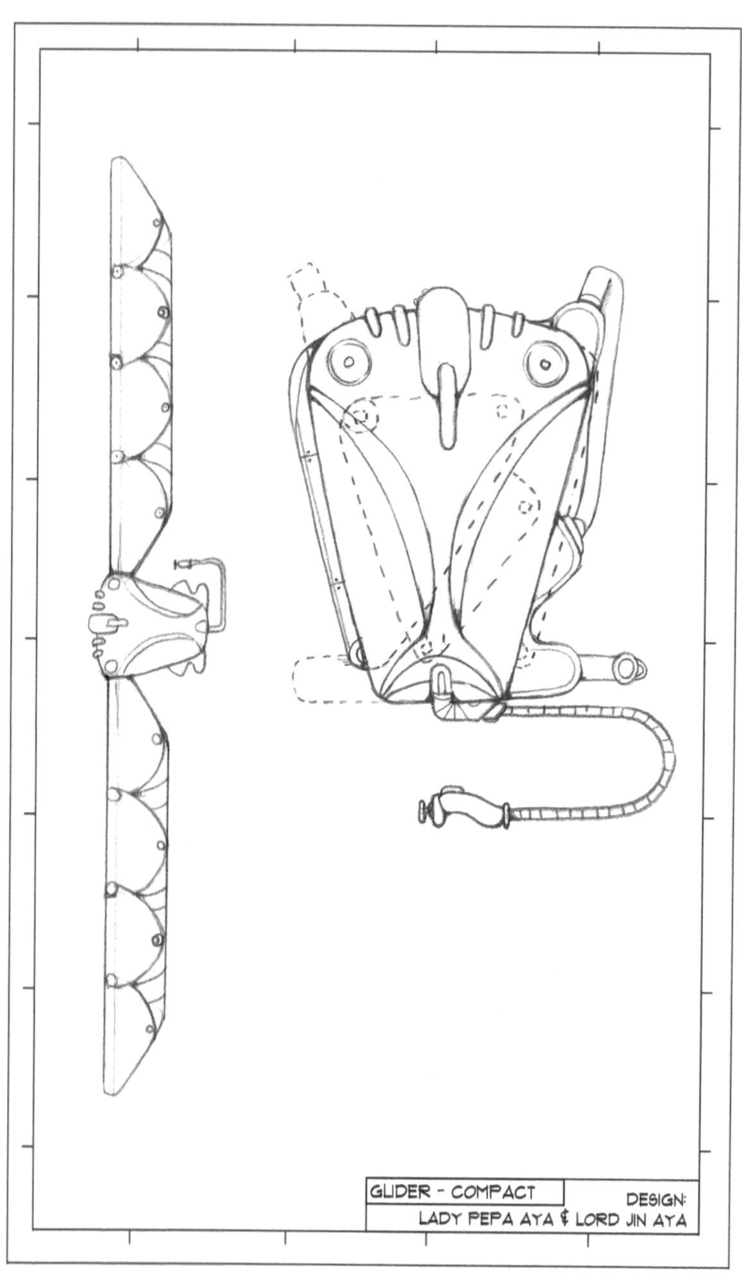

GLIDER - COMPACT
DESIGN:
LADY PEPA AYA & LORD JIN AYA

parachute's path. His neck strained as everything shook, but even as the world vibrated, he finally spotted Suzu, dangling below the pod. A wave of relief hit when he saw her limbs flailing, trying to stabilize: she was alive. He pressed harder on the throttle, anticipating their landing trajectory.

Coming in hot, the pair finally hit the ground and rolled out. Gozen smashed the brakes and Neko plowed a set of ruts as Suzu disappeared out of view below the hood.

Gozen jumped down from the cab but saw Suzu already upright, disengaging the harness. Victou looked drunk. A gust of wind inflated the chute and yanked his body off the ground. His scream was cut off as Gozen jumped in and grabbed the rope. With a single tug, he anchored the entire assembly. Victou plopped on the ground and wobbled like a newborn calf.

"You good?" Suzu asked.

Victou squinted at the two silhouetted shapes. He thought he must have hit his head because the man looked hysterically big. The lopsided pair stared at Victou intently, as if they'd been expecting the last few minutes of insanity. He tried to swallow but his mouth was dry. "Who are you people?"

"We're the reason you and your daughter aren't *dead*," Suzu blurted.

Free of roaring engines and high-altitude descents, Victou's senses finally normalized. It allowed a single question to fill his head.

"*Where* is my daughter?"

o o o

The torrential wind tried to smother Chichi's piercing screams. "Jin!" she cried, inches from his bobbing, lifeless face. Tiny fingers dug into anything they could as she tried to cling to his chest.

The world spun around in a deafening onslaught. Chichi's sore throat managed another scream before feeling an arm tighten around her. Consciousness, followed by adrenaline bursting through Jin's body, lit up his face.

"We're falling," he observed calmly.

"Do something!" Chichimou demanded.

Jin noted how doing something, *anything*, in a free fall seemed futile. Then, a spark ignited in his mind as he remembered conversations with his more aeronautically inclined sister, on topics such as air resistance and flight control. Keeping one arm tight around Chichi, Jin shifted his limbs, trying to stabilize their fall. Chichi felt him struggle as they continued to tumble, but a few seconds later, the horizon managed to level. Without hesitation, Jin reached for the wing-release and pulled. He felt the mechanics kick, but immediately knew something wasn't right.

The two began to spin again. Chichi's fingers cramped, desperately hanging on as their spiraling descent became violent. Air and dizziness assaulted her. The corner of her eye caught Jin failing to reach across with his free arm. He realized the bullet that had passed through his shoulder had damaged the left wing—it was stuck only a third of the way out.

On the ground, Gozen searched for his partner's flying contraption. The others joined just as he saw a twisted shape spiraling too quickly to the ground.

"No, no, no!" Gozen sprinted for the truck. Without hesitation, Suzu grabbed Victou and they managed to jump into Neko just as Gozen turned it around.

Chichi felt Jin's grip loosen and she started to slip out. Centrifugal force began to pull her away to the open sky, but she grabbed onto Jin's sleeve. The ground charged at them, filling her field of vision. With pain surging through her tiny hands, Chichi looked at her protector for some kind of hope, but she saw his eyes flutter shut. A thin line of blood streamed skyward from the back of his shoulder, draining his life. She saw the limp wing stuck, like a toy car refusing to move. Her tinkering mentor had slipped into unconsciousness. So, she tried the only thing she could.

Simple, desperate pragmatism curled up her legs and she kicked at the wing with all her remaining energy. With a snap, the wing flew out and she felt the air suddenly push back from their deadly descent. Fearing being ripped away from Jin, she instead felt something bring her in.

The violent shift of inertia woke Jin back into a half-conscious state. He instinctively wrapped an arm around Chichi and, with his free hand, grabbed the control stick and aligned for a landing. He fought through turbulence to stabilize their flight and his mind cleared, finally recognizing their unfortunate proximity to the ground.

"We're going too fast."

Chichi could only hang on. Jin tried to force them into level flight as a trail of dust appeared ahead of them. Through wind and tears, the shape of Neko emerged below them.

Gozen finally realized the flying pair's speed and anticipated a horrible collision. He slammed on the brakes, causing Victou to fly from the central cabin and slam into the dash. With one second to react, Jin held his breath and banked just to the right. Avoiding a head-on collision, he managed to kick off the trailer and spin around, turning the wings into air brakes. He wrapped up Chichi in his arms as he anticipated the ground. At last, they collided.

In the side mirror, Gozen saw the pair somersault backward into a spray of grass and broken wing parts. They flipped more times than he could count before disappearing underneath the field top. Immediately all three ran out of the truck towards the crash.

Flashes of broken limbs and dead eyes ran through Gozen's mind, cursed sights that had already chased him through most of his adult life. His breath stuck as he approached the mangled pile. Suzu ran up to the grotesque sight of body parts mashed together, covered in dirt and metal. Afraid to even touch them, she looked up to Gozen for a sign of what to do. The old enforcer could only stare in distress.

As she looked back down, the mass of parts began to breathe. As if hatching from a pile of sleeping farm cats, tiny fingers emerged, making way for Chichimou's face. Shocked eyes looked around as her frail body slid its way out. The two observers hesitated, afraid to hurt her, as Victou finally caught up to the group.

"Chichi," he exclaimed with relief. Stepping between Suzu and Gozen, he bent down and picked her up. Training urged Gozen to stop Victou from worsening any hidden injury, but Chichi immediately wrapped her tiny limbs around her father. Victou walked her back to the truck, speaking softly.

With the child looked after, the pair turned their attention back down to Jin. His body remained still, twisted in unnatural ways. Suzu stayed back as Gozen walked up. His mangled partner looked like a used crash-cage. He knelt down and moved a twisted mess of metal that covered half the young man's face.

"Jin," Gozen said, carefully prodding the exposed shoulder, testing for any life. "Jin, can you hear me?"

Hanging on to every second that went by, Gozen waited... prayed for a reaction. A breeze came in and started to push the grass over his fallen comrade.

"Is he dead?" Suzu asked, filled with concern but short on sympathy.

It occurred to Gozen that Jin had likely made the ultimate sacrifice. Sorrow and guilt began to build in his chest, causing his hand to shake.

His bitter tears were then halted by a quiet, "No."

"Jin, just stay still," Gozen gently demanded.

"Sure, that's fine."

"Are you okay?"

"No."

"Alright, what hurts?" Gozen asked, hovering his hands over Jin's twisted body as if magically detecting internal injuries.

"Most."

"What?" Gozen leaned in, trying to decipher Jin's faint voice.

"Most things hurt."

"Gozen," Suzu said in a low voice, "he might be broken. You know, *really* broken, from-the-neck-down kind of broken."

Suddenly feeling even more hesitant to touch him, Gozen plotted how to move Jin; they couldn't stay there forever. He was about to look for something to stabilize the young man's neck when Jin answered. "If my spinal cord had been severed, I would be incapable of having my current engagement with body-length pain."

"So, you're alright?" Suzu asked. "Because you look... oddly bent."

To everyone's surprise, Jin tensed his face and began to straighten out his limbs like skinny balloons filling with air. Suzu cringed at the malformed pose until it finally rested into a more reasonable, prone position.

"Gozen?" Jin muttered.

Having pulled back while Jin un-writhed himself, Gozen carefully leaned back in. "Yes?"

"Is there a bed anywhere perchance? That would be preferable to whatever I am currently laying on."

Swiftly and steadily, Gozen lifted the industrial prince off a wad of twisted machinery. Jin cordially apologized for his weight, although Gozen could have easily carried three Jins. Suzu followed them back to Neko, where Jin was promptly placed onto the central cabin bed. With Chichi resting in the back with her dad, Gozen fired Neko back up and they headed towards Chigou.

o o o

A thin cloud of dust kicked up, mimicking the smokestacks ahead. Kits watched through a small scope, leaning over the airship's railing as the impossible escape concluded. The airship would follow the truck's path back to the city but couldn't match its speed. Before long, Neko would disappear into the forest of metal and glass. Kits had nothing left to do but go back to his superior and explain a defeat he couldn't have even imagined minutes before.

Ignoring a majestic view many could only dream of seeing, Kits walked away with an aching stomach. The air felt cold back in the VIP cabin as he lumbered to the final door and then paused, thinking of the man who had adopted him but had never once acted like a father.

Kits wondered if he had any idea of what a proper father even did. He'd never trusted the posturing ads plastered all over Chigou, selling cars, cold cream, family values, a square-jawed father who didn't exist in reality. With a long breath, Kits straightened his back and walked in.

Inside, his focus skipped right off Daimó and onto the other man in the room. "Where did *you* come from?"

Kits recognized the stranger from Daimó's office back in Chigou, weeks earlier. The man stood with a malaise that nobody else seemed capable of around Daimó. Kits then noticed how much the man looked like Daimó—different ages, but those same terrible eyes.

Daimó spoke only to the stranger. "Tell the pilot to dock at Telekai. That girl might have granted us unique access to Goraka, but it appears she is no longer *available*." Kits felt the reprimand like a knife stabbing straight into his gut.

"We'll move forward with the dam," Daimó continued. "Initiate our contact when we get back."

The stranger finally spoke. "So soon? Doesn't the dam need more time?"

"Despite the setback at the west mine, the exhaust is still going and working better than we estimated. Combined with what has been coming down from Primichi, it should suffice."

Kits had no idea what any of it meant. He recognized the pieces, but they added up to something Daimó had never explained to him. The unnamed trespasser, however, seemed like a kindred spirit. Kits waited for instructions or punishment—anything other than total disregard. He had trouble remembering a time when he hadn't lived for Daimó's validation.

"What should I do next?" Kits finally asked.

Daimó waited to respond, long enough that Kits took it as a silent lashing. When the answer finally came, Kits wished he hadn't waited for it. Daimó, his voice cold, looked the young man in the eyes and asked, "What can *you* do?"

19
GUEST

Dirt splattered into wings on Neko's sides, painted by wild fields and panic. The typically handsome vehicle had declined into a pitiful sight, crawling through the sparkle of downtown. Pedestrians offered condescending stares, as if looking at an abandoned mule. Inside Neko, its passengers looked no better.

"Does Jin need a hospital?" Gozen asked, seeing Jastoú South appear as they pulled up to a red light.

Jastoú South was a hospital in downtown Chigou boasting dramatic architecture. Unusually tall for a medical building, the tower swept skyward in one long, tapering form. Boring through the building's wide base, a cavernous arch allowed visitors to drive directly under the building. A brass hand reached down from the arch's zenith, a colossal symbol of offering aid to those passing underneath. Black-hands often joked it would crush anyone unable to pay for their medical care.

Suzu looked at the thick, saturated bandage on Jin's shoulder that dripped onto the bed. It wasn't bleeding fast, but she didn't know why it hadn't stopped. "I think he might." She leaned closer to Gozen and dropped her voice. "Do we have time?"

Gozen knew they had maybe thirty minutes before Kits was back on the ground. A crowded hospital offered as much protection as it did risk, and that balance would unsettle the longer they stayed; he wanted them in a more controlled environment.

"Just drop me off," Jin coughed as everyone turned to see his face, eyes still closed. "My uncle is the capital surgeon at Jastoú South. I'll just tell the front desk… *cough*… I need him immediately."

"Sounds good to me." Suzu readily approved.

It felt cowardly to Gozen—abandoning someone who had just risked their life to save a child and her father—but they didn't have a better option. Gozen drove into the drop-off area and an emergency crew took Jin away. When asked for more information, Suzu jumped back in the truck, which promptly drove off. Guilt built up as Gozen watched the hospital shrink in the rear-view mirror.

When they arrived at Kora farm, Gozen killed the engine, waking up Victou and his daughter. Suzu sprung out of the passenger seat but felt Gozen grab her shoulder. "Go up to the roof deck, let me know if anyone—*anyone*—approaches this farm."

"Way ahead of you. Bring me some mimis… and coffee."

"Good idea," Gozen said through an exhausted sigh. He turned back and spoke to the small, groggy family. "We're going to be here for a bit. You need any help with her?"

Victou pulled his daughter in tighter. "Is there any food here… wherever we are?"

"It's a farm. There are good people here."

The term meant little to Victou but getting out of large moving vehicles and getting some food was motivation enough. He carried Chichimou to the house as Gozen followed. Having received a stunted briefing from Suzu, Clora met Victou and Chichi at the door. "You look like you could use a place to rest, and something good to eat. Lucky for you, this is a farm."

Victou felt she looked unthreatening enough and offered a half-volume, "So I heard."

"Why don't you go relax in there and I'll get you something to eat." Clora gestured over to the warmly lit dining room, where the smell of a freshly baked bollo tart pulled Victou forward. Gozen followed after and leaned against the doorframe. "One smoked coffee and I'll explain all of this."

"I started brewing the moment I heard Neko coming down the road." Clora offered a tempered grin, sensing the weight on everyone's shoulders.

Gozen found a spot to park himself in the kitchen while watching Clora get her unexpected guests something good to eat.

Once she had rejoined Gozen, he explained the entire situation to her, processing how sensational it sounded as he spoke. He apologized for any danger their presence brought to the farm. Clora assured him that such dangers existed regardless of where they hid, that she and Kojo had built that farm to make the world a little better, not hide from it.

"How is Kojo? I was worried his grieving period might not ever end—not that it ever really does."

"Oh, he's still working hard all day long. I think it's his way to just make it through the day until he can risk letting Nia's death really sink in." Clora took a moment, feeling where she let it live deep in her chest. "I miss his salty humor. It always let us laugh out a long day of work. Maybe that'll come back… I still like to hope," she said, struggling to get her words out. "Come on, that little one looks exhausted."

Gozen walked in on the family of two and sat across the table, carrying two coffees. Victou appeared to hide behind the daughter who sat on his lap, swaying with exhaustion. Clora followed from the kitchen, reaching out her arms. Victou clenched his daughter a bit tighter as Clora said, "I think this one could use a bed. I'll let you men talk."

Powerless against her sweet, well-aged will, Victou felt soft hands effortlessly lift Chichimou from his arms. The cool air of the room chilled his suddenly vacant front. Clora cradled the young girl and walked out into a hallway, leaving Victou alone with a giant. He felt intimidated, like a child unsure of why the adult in the room is suddenly giving him so much attention.

Gozen slid Victou the second mug of smoke coffee. The two sat there quietly and small sounds echoed through the house. The near silence squeezed Victou's anxiety. Gozen began to shut his eyes and take heavy, settling breaths between long sips of coffee. Time went by and Victou nearly found himself beginning to relax on the old wood table, when Suzu suddenly ran down from the roof tower. "Someone is coming."

"Who?" Gozen's head snapped to. "It can't be Jin."

"Not unless they did surgery in the car, which is moving quick."

"Stay with him." Gozen ordered as he ran into another room. Victou sat, afraid to move while contemplating a sprint upstairs and grabbing his daughter for an escape into the bollo orchard. Suzu had her back to the kitchen as she peeked out through the front door.

Victou jumped as Gozen stomped back through the kitchen, loading an old hunting rifle that had been enjoying its retirement over the fireplace. "Stay with him," Gozen repeated as he made it to the front door, swung it open and turned off the center hall light. He identified a hum matching a large, luxury car that began to slow down. Sitting in shadow, Gozen raised the rifle sights up as the vehicle stopped just outside of the spotlight hitting the loop drive.

His heart raced as he felt his years of handling firearms emerge from hibernation. The passenger door opened and he saw a young man appear, along with something mechanical up by the shoulder. Gozen put pressure on the trigger as another man appeared from the driver's door.

Stepping into the light, Jin's face appeared as he said something softly to the other man, but Gozen clearly heard the word *uncle* in there. He lowered the rifle as Jin hobbled up, assisted with an alloy cane.

"I'll be quite alright. Blood loss will keep me weak for a day but thankfully no transfusion was necessary. I might take some tea." Gozen stepped aside as Jin limped inside and turned on the hall light.

Suzu watched Jin move to the dining room, looking like an elderly man past his bedtime. "What is that thing on your shoulder?"

Jin pointed to what looked like a Toki oddly made into a shoulder pad. "It keeps the wound clean and monitors my blood pressure. If it goes off tonight, please make sure I wake up." With that, he found a soft old chair in the corner of the dining room and sat down with a long groan.

Suzu shook her head at Jin's obnoxious ability to glide through all hardships on a carpet of inherited opportunity. Having had enough of the distraction, she grabbed a coffee from the kitchen and returned to the dining room, adjusting a wall lamp towards the table, or arguably, Victou's face. Gozen came in as well and mentioned two farm hands who had just come in from the fields, so he put them on watch. He then leaned the rifle against the dining room table as he sat down. The room quieted to creaking floorboards, and Victou found that his cozy nook had been converted first into a bunker and then an interrogation room in under three minutes.

"Wait, she said I could eat and relax." Victou pointed up to where the kind old woman had vanished with his child.

Suzu took an emphatically loud sip of coffee. "Are you not relaxed?"

Gozen intervened with a resounding cough. Victou saw his face reflected in the large man's eyes. The biggest hands he had ever seen dwarfed the steaming cup of coffee, appearing capable of crushing it into porcelain dust.

Gozen coated his throat in caffeine, sharpening his voice. "I'm sure you have some questions, and we'll get to those, but there are some troubling matters we need to clear up first."

"Yeah, like why are you so stupid?" Suzu succinctly asked. Gozen groaned while rubbing his face.

"Wait... you're the girl from the alley. You broke into my house," Victou murmured.

"And I told you to stay away from Kits and his cronies. Are you trying to get your daughter killed?"

"What?" Victou's tempered voice found some life. "I'd never hurt my daughter. And *you*," Victou's eyes widened towards Jin in the corner. "You're the one who brought my daughter back from that orphanage and then cut that guy's arm off." His eyes bounced amongst the baffling trio. "Who… what are you?"

"Just the people who saved you and your daughter from the death ship." Suzu said.

"Unyo Mark I airships actually maintain an above-average safety…"

"Nobody cares, Jin."

"Regardless, that is not a ship you can just buy a ticket for,"

Gozen interjected, "and I'm greatly concerned with how you managed to get yourself and your daughter invited onboard."

Closed in by silhouettes and accusatory voices, Victou further imagined the vast, open fields outside the house. Anything familiar lay miles away. "I worked for him—them—and we were just having a work meeting."

"Hah!" Suzu barked, a vein swelling in her forehead. "A work meeting? Don't you realize who those people are yet?"

"Yes, they invited me there to discuss… a special work project. And I don't know why you think *they* are so dangerous. *They* didn't pull me down a hatch, dangle me a thousand meters above the ground, then ride a cargo drop to the ground."

"Ugh, you are so dumb."

"I'm dumb because I had a meeting?"

"You're only alive *because* we pulled you off that airship!"

Victou huffed, hiding the fear he had felt. "I think you have very wild ideas about what goes on in a business meeting."

"My parents decided to have a meeting with those people one night." The table kept Suzu from lunging right up to his face. "And by morning they were dead."

"What?" Victou asked, taken aback.

"It's very cost inefficient."

Stunned heads snapped towards Jin who winced from a broken rib. "Airships are an irresponsibly expensive location to conduct a meeting, unless perhaps you are courting an exceptionally lucrative prospect."

"Right?" Victou partially followed.

"But you are poor," Jin clarified.

Gozen jumped in, "More importantly, I'd like to know how you got a meeting with someone who has proven nearly impossible to find."

"Who, Kits?"

"Not that punk. Daimó, his boss," Suzu corrected.

"Oh, is *that* his name?" Victou asked.

"You don't even know his name?" Suzu threw up her arms. "What miracle got you on that ship?"

Victou looked back to where his daughter had been taken and breathed heavily.

"We're not here to criticize your parenting." Gozen raised his finger, anticipating Suzu's rebuttal. "We know you covertly fed Kits—and ultimately Daimó—information about Pirou's fuel project at Kasic."

Victou kept quiet, assessing the extent of their knowledge. They had yet to show any explicit malice, but he knew better than to share more than he had to.

"Now, you very well may not know much about Daimó—frankly, none of us do—but what I *do* know about him makes your association gravely important. That man is responsible for the deaths of hundreds of civilians, and I assume he has yet to reveal all he is capable of. So, I think the least painful path for you, and for everyone in this house, is to tell us exactly why he decided to meet with you on that airship, because I am convinced you have *that* answer, at least."

Light cut around Gozen's imposing silhouette, making him appear as a stone guardian watching under the moonlight. Victou felt painfully tired, and with no energy to be clever, he gave in to the inevitable.

Victou began by describing his simple need to find work and provide his daughter with stability—for once. The process had absorbed all of his focus, which is how he had foolishly allowed Chichimou to end up at the dark Jinsper mine before Jin returned her. Out of desperation, he'd embellished his resume for a solid job and Kits had caught him. Eager to escape punishment and therefore ripe for exploitation, the desperate father had agreed to embezzle information.

Kits had given the research to Daimó, who then set up the necessary patents. The scheme eventually revealed itself in the paper, stabbing Pirou in the heart.

"So, why'd you run?" Gozen asked.

"*She* told me to," Victou replied, nodding at Suzu.

"That's it? You felt no danger on your own, you simply took the word of this little girl you'd never met before?"

"Hey!" Suzu took offense.

"Well... I had information... ya know..." Victou searched his tired mind.

"Incriminating," Jin offered from the corner.

"Yeah, incriminating information, on some really powerful people. I was suddenly more of a risk than an asset. So yeah, I took my daughter and ran."

"But something convinced you to come out of hiding," Gozen demanded.

"Right," Victou sheepishly answered.

"Something so significant you felt Kits's boss, a man you had never met, would look past all the risk you represented and bless you—and your daughter—with a new opportunity, no strings attached."

Victou hated the way it sounded coming out of Gozen's mouth.

"Or he's really just *that* dumb," Suzu suggested. "I mean, that's possible."

"Maybe I'm dumb," Victou countered. "But if I tell you what I found, you'll just think I'm insane."

The group merely waited, as if insanity presented no worry.

Victou submitted with a sigh. Beginning at the moment he left Suzu's sight in the alley, he explained the plan to buy camping gear and head south. He waited for the group to stop him while he explained just how far they went, but they remained unphased. When he finally mentioned the Red Valley, Gozen glanced back at Jin but said nothing. Only when Victou mentioned the red phantoms of Goraka did he finally get the reaction he expected.

Jin shot up in the creaking chair, fighting through pain to speak. Victou, anticipating the group's disbelief, muttered, "See, now you just think I'm crazy. I know it sounds crazy, but at the time..."

"Did you see it simply hover in place, or did it pursue you?" Jin asked, his voice tense.

"It never saw me, but..." Victou had no better way to describe it. "Yes, hovered."

"Did you see its *eyes?*" Jin asked, attempting to confirm his nightmare.

"Sloping down like thick lines."

Gozen and Suzu looked between the two men reciting their shared ghost story. Jin finally slipped back into the warmth of his seat when Gozen asked, "Is that why you went back to Daimó? To tell him you saw the creatures from Goraka?"

"That reason?" Suzu scoffed. "'Hey, I saw a ghost in the forest. Impressed, huh? So, you're not going to kill me now, right?'"

"Well, if you'd let me finish, it wasn't them, it was their machine," Victou declared.

Suzu and the old Enforcer's eyes bulged. "What do you mean, *their machine?*"

"There was this device it operated with these skinny black... arms that poked out of its body."

Gozen looked back again for confirmation at Jin, who was searching through traumatic memories, but nothing corroborated the story's sudden turn.

"Was the machine something it found?" Jin's curiosity flared.

"I don't know... I don't think so."

"A thing someone might have left behind? Did you recognize it?" Gozen added.

"Well, it was definitely nothing I've ever seen before. I'm not exactly sure what it did and it had this... organic look to it, but it was obviously a machine."

Suzu folded her arms. "That clears it all right up."

"Can you describe its form?" Jin asked.

"It was tall like a staff, but had this... thing on the top." Victou's hands attempted to sculpt it out of air.

Impatience crawled over Suzu as her foot tapped below. Jin continued. "Was it kinetic? Did you see it perform any kind of function?"

"Not really..." Victou struggled to explain anything explicitly. Then, his eyes sparked. "Oh, and steam came out of it."

Suzu laughed.

"That's not helping," Gozen murmured.

"Are you kidding me? This guy sees a weird stick in the woods— oh, excuse me, a weird stick that *smokes*—and he comes running back to the man who was ready to kill him, convinced this grand discovery will make Daimó just... fall in love and *not* kill him and his daughter."

Victou opened his mouth, but his momentary pause burst Suzu's impatience. "This is pointless. He is crazy and we should be planning our next move. Or we should be figuring out theirs!" Suzu cast her finger out towards the darkness between them and the city.

"Look, I obviously can't say for sure, but I think it was some kind of... I don't know... energy probe," Victou pleaded.

Suzu exited with a humorless laugh. As muffled sounds of fumbling glassware echoed from the kitchen, the two men turned back to Victou. The bright light bleached the skin around his tired eyes.

"What did you mean? What makes you think the machine probed for energy?" Gozen continued.

"Well, there was this glow on the top of the device and when the red creature touched it, steam shot out like a pressure release valve. Then these panels came crawling up the hillside to the device and connected at the base."

Gozen raised his hand, but Victou had found his momentum. "It... it was like this conduit that assembled itself, plugging in by the ground and snaking the steam down to... I don't know, somewhere."

"Ghost plumber?" Suzu appeared back through the doorway. "Are you two done yet? This is nonsense."

"This does contain some facets of the core-thermic design your father proposed," Jin stated from the corner.

"What?" Suzu snapped.

"Your father, Lord Carmin, proposed harnessing sub-surface heat. His hypothesis, that Goraka offered the greatest yield, would seem to support such a device."

Suzu's impulse to dispute unwarranted comments on her father fueled her burning rancor towards Jin. Although she'd been young when she witnessed it, Suzu knew the project. She remembered her father's dream from recited theories and drawings spread around his office. She had taken that dream to protect it, and in her mind, few had proven worthy to touch it.

"You never met my father," she growled.

"Wait... Lord Carmin... from Kasic? I saw some of his drawings…" Victou pondered.

"And *you* definitely didn't know him," Suzu snarled. "He was the best engineer they had, not a *fake* like you."

The words would have stung once, but that part of Victou's soul had long since become calloused.

"And since you're not an engineering genius like Suzu's father," Gozen gave her a nod before turning back to Victou, "you took that knowledge of the machine and brought it back, hoping Daimó would find it—you—valuable?"

Victou nodded. "Right."

"That was it?" Suzu repeated with double the force. "You don't even know what *it* is."

"It was some way to harness power," Victou replied with burgeoning confidence. "Using a device I've never seen—I'm pretty sure *no one* has ever seen before."

"And that guess was worth risking your daughter's life?" she shouted back, with the authority of one who knew the cost of such risk.

Victou's chair creaked loudly as he leaned back, escaping the accusation's heat. "Hey, look, I'm still not convinced my or my daughter's lives were at risk. And yes, I think he does care that much about what I found."

"You're insane." Her hands shaking, Suzu turned to Gozen. "He's just lucky we found him when we did."

"Insane? Do you even know where you are?" Victou's voice rang out strong. The sudden burst in confidence silenced the panel, except for Suzu who merely muttered, "What?"

"You live in a monument to futurism. This whole damn valley was built on an obsession to be bigger, faster, stronger. Didn't you ever study Valley History? Don't you remember why... what was that guy's name?" Victou paused, tripping over his thoughts. "Batsu! Why the great Lord Batsu and his caravan of crazies climbed up into this ridiculous location?"

"Careful," Suzu warned. "I think Jin back there is related to a lot of those old crazies."

Her interruption failed to stop Victou's rant. "They wanted to build a city that literally looked down at every other society on the planet. If there is one thing people in this place obsess over, especially industrialists cruising around on airships, it's having some new power or technology that nobody else has. So, yes, I figured if I could help that Daimó guy get this amazing, exotic new source of power, he'd find me a lot less expendable."

Nobody argued. Many of the Naifin Valley's citizens joked that Chigou only came about so the greatest city in the world would have the other greatest city in the world to perpetually race against. But despite the indisputable logic, Gozen still doubted the man's ability to sway Daimó in any way. "And since you had never met Diamo before, I have to assume you had some kind of proof."

"I did, but I never needed it."

"He just took your word?" Gozen said doubtfully.

"Hey, it surprised me too. I'd describe one detail then he'd cut me off and describe another. If you really want to know what that thing does, you should ask him."

Suzu's eyebrows went crooked. "You buying this, big guy?"

"What did he offer you?" Gozen asked, ignoring Suzu.

The moment in the airship had been so brief, Victou had nearly forgotten it. Daimó had believed him and wanted what was offered, but Victou had failed to foresee how easily he could be deleted from the equation. In a matter of seconds, Chichimou had gone from normal child to valuable asset—even bargaining chip. He refused to shortsightedly convince anyone else to exploit his daughter.

"I never got to find out." Nodding towards Suzu, he continued, "That one pulled me through a hatch, my daughter almost fell to her death…" Speaking it aloud, the reality pressed heavily on his chest. "And now we're here."

Suzu's next retort was halted at the unexpected sight of tears swelling in Victou's eyes.

"I've… I've dragged my daughter around more places than I can count. I can barely remember a time when she had a home and a…" The father thought of what he had promised his daughter when she was born and how thoroughly he had broken that vow.

"I know…" His voice wavered, his words so simple and honest now that they hurt. "…I know my daughter deserves a better father than I am, but I'm what she has. And you're right, I lied and conned my way into that job at Kasic. I didn't do it for any other reason than to have a home, so my little girl could have a room… her room. But no, I didn't think I was going to make her life bright and shiny. I'm just trying to make it better than what it is."

The room remained quiet as the man's raw sincerity broke through. Victou wiped his face with a sleeve still dirty from the fields south of the city. Memories of the day tried to cycle back through his mind, but he could feel everything shutting down. He had no answers left to give.

"Can I see my daughter now?"

As if waiting for her cue, Clora walked in from the kitchen. She held in her hands two cups of mulled blashu tea. As she sat down, she slid one over to Victou, gently placing it in his hand. Steam danced in lazy swirls up to the ceiling.

"My name is Clora. My husband Kojo and I started this farm together and it has never been a prison to anyone. You can see your daughter anytime you like. At the moment, however, I believe the day has gotten the best of her." She gestured upstairs.

Victou looked up at the ceiling, as if he could see through it to where Chichimou had fallen asleep. He knew any proper bed would feel luxurious compared to what he had ever offered her. The tea in his hands felt warm and smelled of spices, and he felt like crying into it.

"If you want some food, there are some Onipan in the kitchen, and a fresh tart if one of these three didn't steal it first. You're welcome to eat there, or take them up to the room next to where I put your daughter. It's nothing fancy, but it's clean and cozy." Clora spoke with a soft, sincere smile.

The others remained quiet as Clora took Victou's hand and guided him into the kitchen. The father shuffled along, not looking back as he went through the door.

"You buying all of that?" Suzu asked Gozen, wasting no time.

A long breath came out of the former LE, as if he had been holding it through the entire interrogation. He raised the mug of coffee up to his face and basked in the tiny sauna before finally taking a sip.

Suzu began to pace around. "So, what is our next move? Try to get this guy to lure Kits back out? What do you think?"

"I think we all need some sleep." Gozen's knees cracked as he got up. "I'm sure some farmhands would help us keep watch."

"Yeah, but what do you think?" Suzu repeated.

He turned to Jin, still cradled by the chair. "Do you want a bed to lay in?"

"I believe this chair is adequate," Jin said, still wincing slightly from his injuries.

"Alright. Well, I'm going to sleep in my truck. Goodnight everyone." Not waiting for a response, Gozen sauntered towards the front exit.

Suzu stood still, buzzing with energy. Her mind raced, formed plans, and sorted through theories she needed to process. Her collaborators had checked out, but she had no issue working alone.

From the dark corner, Jin faintly spoke up. "May I trouble you for a blanket?"

Unwilling to take more than a step, she begrudgingly snatched a decorative patchwork off the wall and threw it at Jin.

He grunted as the bulky fabric landed on his midsection. "I appreciate that. Would you be willing to locate a small pillow as well?"

She didn't think long. "You wouldn't like the way I'd give it to you."

20
EXECUTION

Clouds of steam puffed out of copper ribs surrounding the aged leader. Water poured down like rain from a thousand spouts, precisely machined to emulate the natural world so intently kept out. Drops fell onto pearlescent tiles shaped into an intricate Po'Kin mosaic, the countless bursts eroding porcelain and grout more slowly than even his old eyes could see.

An internal timer went off, one set by decades of routine. Opaji reached down and turned an array of polished dials. His hands acted almost independently of his mind. One by one, a decrescendo of each instrument fell to a drip. Hissing steam hushed, then lateral, high-pressure jets by his feet bowed out. Rippling cascades dried up along the wall while the central eye closed.

Stepping out into his personal spa, Opaji's feet settled on a floor warmed to just below his body temperature. He opened the vapor-sealed closet and pulled out a dry robe. The change in weight off the hanger automatically pushed bath slippers out from a heated compartment. Opaji docked his feet and walked to a mirror framed with sixty-four diffused bulbs.

The soft lighting graciously illuminated wrinkles that had been setting in since before recollection. Fingers rubbed stubble softened by the warm shower. For a moment, he appreciated his private barber's ability to shave such exaggerated contours. Opaji wondered if he had ever shaved himself as a young man, for he had no memory of it.

Over by a closet, separated by dehumidifying jets of air, he kicked off the slippers that had served their ninety seconds of purpose. An increment slower each day, he sat down on a bench of white wood. The weight triggered a disc player that poured out from surrounding speakers. Opaji disliked the flat, intimate sound of dressing himself and intentionally drowned it out.

Finally clothed in his self-imposed uniform, the grand leader slid his feet over to the north-facing bay window. He ignored the gallery of priceless art that lined his walls, instead noticing a worn track in the carpet. It ran the entire length of the room and faded near the corners. He rubbed the evidence with his custom leather shoe and questioned what had developed from perpetually repeating such a short journey.

He looked across the city he had created and saw a horizon hiding the place of his birth. He had built his city with incredible inertia which he hoped would carry on long after his death, but the carpet suggested he had found a way to keep moving and yet go nowhere.

Unlike past generations of Batsus, Opaji had no son to carry the torch of progress. Always brimming with confidence and content with time, he had never bothered to produce an heir. There was no youthful set of eyes to obey or even to turn away in a declaration of superior ambition. Time had become his most precious commodity, and legacy weighed heavily on his mind. A glistening airship cast its shadow over his office just as a voice entered into his private world.

"Your afternoon recipient is docking now. How long shall I have him hold?"

The voice came from a pair of hidden speakers. Opaji pressed on a crystal button etched with a quote from himself—he'd requested the work but had never bothered reading it. "There is no need to wait."

Daimó transitioned from open sky to luxurious industry. The stairwell down had immaculate walls, likely cleaned more often than seen. Daimó ignored the countless, ornamental details he passed along the way to Opaji's office. The meeting was merely a scheduled ceremony, where he tithed updates and promises. Two Sentinels led him into a waiting room, where two more blocked

Opaji's door.

Mali Opree checked the schedule book that contained not a single erasure. She easily recognized the visitor's face, one that had always emitted the warmth of an industrial freezer. "Lord Opaji will see you now." Her fingers busied themselves with the keys of a wire-type.

Daimó found decreasing worth in his monthly meetings with Chigou's founder. He played the role of an underling, eager to embrace all of Opaji's wisdom and direction. The time their palavers cost still gave a favorable return, providing access and insight to the overlord's operations. Daimó planned to cut them off eventually, and he had far more patience than Lord Opaji could comprehend.

Opaji glanced at Daimó. "Pirou did not take the results of his meddling very well—unless *you* arranged his rather pitiful conclusion. Regardless, the results are satisfactory."

"His final action was his only thoughtful one."

Opaji grunted and with that, the subject was finished. "The plant activating the new patents is already breaking ground, yes?"

"Active and ahead of schedule."

The report led Opaji's aged body to slump even more. "I don't want you to strong-arm Kasic. Let them partner in a way that's… reasonable."

Daimó raised an eyebrow.

"I feel their stability has become their purpose, and that is… that is good."

In all the conversations they shared, Daimó had never heard the patriarch of Chigou compliment mere maintenance. He suspected an imposter standing before him, worn and dubiously content.

"And I don't want anything else like that Etecid business. It's an efficient but ugly way to move forward, burning buildings down in the city. I don't like my city walking around half-dressed."

Opaji went on a stroll of superficial virtues and Daimó let him. He listened to a tired soul stripped of its youthful veneer. He understood the pitfalls of maimed ambition that came with old age. Locked into a perspective just above his creation, Opaji continued to bestow seasoned wisdom on his deputy, ignorant of just how many seasons Daimó had endured.

"…what do you see?" Opaji waited for his answer while facing the outstretching city.

"The same thing I've seen every time you have asked."

"Hmm," Opaji checked his guest. "No, I mean *that*."

A painting hung right beside the bay window, hidden by Chigou's luminous glow. "The world's second-greatest city." Daimó said what he assumed the man wanted to hear about Primichi, the city that had birthed Opaji before he'd abandoned it.

"I had this commissioned for my father, Gaimen. He received it and then promptly sent it back. I felt compelled to hang it here but never explicitly explored why—a tool for comparison, I suppose. As my city has continued to grow, however, this painting has remained in stasis, but certainly the place of my birth has not."

"Has your first home been on your mind as of late?" Daimó feigned concern.

Opaji slumped his hands into pockets and made more throat sounds. Daimó checked his Toki. "I can leave you to your thoughts if…"

"My father was not an ambitious man, and I always faulted him for that. His contentment with life certainly accelerated my drive to create something more—this place. I now ponder over the life of my father. Was there more value in it than what I gave him credit for?"

Daimó took a step towards the door.

"Perhaps my father knew he was less of a man than *his* father and decided to protect what had been set before him. Not an inspiring life, certainly, but I can now respect that he chose to preserve another's greatness."

The temperate words jerked Daimó's head around. It seemed that old Opaji was willingly bestowing upon himself and his revered forefathers a legacy of mediocrity.

"I should see my grandfather's city and how it has been maintained," Opaji concluded. "My sister is still there, I believe.

Perhaps I will have her brief me on the state of things. She always keeps up with the best cuisine as well... something nostalgic for my palate. I'd like that. And it will be good to see how the momentum of Lord Jean Batsu has carried forward past his death. I would find that useful, comparing to see if what I've already done is sufficient."

Opaji was done.

"I'll take the airship you arrived on, if you don't mind. My Mark III is undergoing a cabin upgrade. You'll be alright getting to... wherever you need to go next, I trust." Opaji grabbed his hat.

Daimó made room for the aged leader to leave. "You need not worry about disrupting any of my plans."

o o o

The Plow, The Fuel, and The Blood - Conquering Responsibly.
Alone in the office, Kits reread the title three times, scouring for a way to halt his freewheeling descent into irrelevance. Starting with the directly titled *Longevity is Revenge,* a row of books stretched across the entire back of Daimó's office—an impressive number written by the same Lord Heirité. Although he found each individual volume rather arcane, their collective impression matched how he felt about their owner.

Kits had never grasped the totality of Daimó's mission but contentedly operated under specific tasks. His most recent failure had resulted in an ambiguity which felt more like abandonment. Daimó's last words rang around his head like a disease-carrying insect. Kits yearned to prove his worth and needed a task with essential objectives; he merely lacked a conclusive understanding of what his adoptive guardian found meaningful.

His fingers moved quickly but feebly across titles, as he feared being caught digging around in his overseer's lair. The library of books contained more material than he could digest in a decade, so he moved to Daimó's desk. Although a more obvious choice to search from the beginning, the desk had a foreboding aura that warned Kits to look away. Holding his breath, the young man dared to place his fingers on the first drawer.

Sliding it open revealed an unexpectedly precious revelation.

A single stone medallion sat on a well-oiled Bokai-wood plate. Kits recognized the item, as he had caught Daimó palming it like a lucky charm. An unidentifiable noise from outside prompted Kits to check his Toki. He mentally calculated the time of Daimó's meeting and the time it would take him to travel back. Finding only more anxiety, he shut the drawer and moved on.

The next one squealed as it opened, and Kits winced. Inside revealed the first promising find: labeled folders neatly stacked on top of one another. He thumbed through the first few name tags. They listed the two cities of the Naifin Valley: Chigou and Primichi, and a third for Goraka. Kits had seen these folders before but had never been invited to look inside.

Considering the longevity of Daimó's scheme, whatever it was, the folders appeared surprisingly thin. Starting with Chigou, pages referenced events that had already taken place, such as the great Roukot fire. Kits had never explicitly connected that event with Daimó but it certainly fit. The remaining pages spoke of events he had either participated in or at least heard Daimó discuss. A sloppy footnote suggested investigating Nia from Kora farm as a potential associate; Kits found it a frivolous consideration of an extraordinary person. He hated the gap Daimó had forced between them, but sulking wouldn't solve his current problem.

Nearly all of Primichi's folder concerned the Aya dynasty and its related corporations. The folder also listed other members of the Aya family: Lord Bajuté, Lady Lóname, and even Jin's sister, Lady Pepa. Kits had long ago been assigned to make a connection with the young heir, Jin Aya, but it took little time to grow weary of that spoiled wanderer. The thought of an entire family of Jins made Kits grimace; however, the focus required no explanation. The Aya family—likely the second most powerful name in Primichi—controlled a proper empire of industrial institutions.

Goraka came last. Kits hesitated, as if the arcane forest itself was hiding inside the manilla folder. An illustration sat on top, ink and watercolor depicting a cabin set inside a dense wood. He wondered if the scene came from an early developer of Chigou who had ignored warnings and naively planted his life in Goraka.

Probably didn't go well, as Kits had never heard of anyone permanently residing in the Valley of Death. Although intriguing, the picture offered little information and he moved on.

The next page looked like a mistake. Names descended down like precious, ancestral branches. Kits knew such family trees were precious, sentimental heirlooms or archeological datasheets for those digging in the past. The thought became unsettling when Kits attempted to imagine Daimó as a child and having a mother. Not a single name sounded familiar. He rummaged for a pattern when a timed alarm rang on his Toki.

He jumped. *Dammit.* The lord of the desk would be back soon.

Kits flipped through the remaining pages, frantic to find something—*anything*—that could inform his next action. His thumb slipped and the packet paused on an illustration. Kits picked up the technical drawing and felt something clipped behind it. He pulled on the edge of a photograph and noticed the mysterious man who had come out of nowhere and attached himself to Daimó. Pulling the entire photo out, Kits gasped. Past places and events began to reveal the connective tissue between them. So many events that had seemed isolated, even that dinner where Daimó asked him to murder a family, suddenly pointed to a long-gestating plot, aimed at Goraka and the technology to harvest the energy hidden within. A mission coalesced in Kits's mind and he felt the rebirth of purpose, just as the door latch clicked.

Kits flung all the material into the drawer and snatched the last book he put back. The door opened wider, its creak melding with a second set of footsteps. Kits looked out the window in the dismissive way he'd experienced from Daimó innumerable times, but his bravado was met with utter indifference as Daimó chose to speak only to his guest. If Daimó had noticed Kits snooping through his desk, he appeared wholly unthreatened by the act.

Kits held the book to his chest like a security blanket as he walked around the desk unnoticed. He heard Daimó mention the dam and the name *Mouba*. Kits remembered the bumbling Soran whose disgusting beard failed to hide a doltish face. He then stopped in the middle of the room as he recalled two of Mouba's associates: the designer of the dam and his wife, the protestor. Daimó had tasked Kits with their deaths, and he had carried it out almost completely as instructed.

Daimó continued to ignore his existence. Kits felt like all the pathetic children he had grown up with at the orphanage. He wanted someone older, more experienced, to look down at him with acknowledgment and approval. The insecurity mutated into a hot mass as the conversation ended. Daimó sat at a coffee table as his new confidant walked to the kitchen. The arena of mugs, steam wands, and steak knives seemed a suitable place for Kits to demand answers from this parasite.

After announcing his arrival with heavy steps, Kits crossed his arms and leaned against the counter as if posing for a smoking ad. The stranger put fuel blocks into the coffee smoker and clicked the ignition switch. Kits maintained his brooding indifference for a full three minutes until his opponent drizzled in the hot coffee with the torturous pace of a sand timer. Each gurgle against the porcelain cup stabbed Kits in the eardrum like a rusty needle. *How much coffee could that damn mug hold?*

"Okay, you want to stop being a tease and tell me who you are?" Kits strained to appear calm.

As the carafe finally released its final drip, the stranger leaned against the counter across from Kits. Steady hands lifted the steaming cup and he drew in a confident sip of coffee before sucking the remaining liquid off his teeth. "Caton."

"Not *Lord* Caton?" Kits retorted.

"If you'd prefer, you may think of me as Lord."

Kits wished he had his own coffee to disrupt the tempo. "I'm going to assume you already know about me. How is it that you came to be here in this office?"

Lord Caton looked around the kitchen and smirked. Kits readied himself to defend against a petty correction, but it never left his opponent's crooked smile. "I've known Daimó for what I'm sure you'd consider quite a long time."

"And yet, over the course of a decade, he's never mentioned you," Kits countered.

More coffee was sucked into Caton's mouth. "And in that decade, how many times has Daimó divulged *anything* of his personal life?"

"I don't think any of us have any sentimental interest in the past. So, in the name of almighty progress, what path has Daimó set you on?" Kits asked.

The patronizing grin came back, as if Caton heard thoughts more than words spoken aloud. "Over time, you've done fine, Lord Kits—compared to most," he said, looking out the kitchen passthrough to Daimó. "You really shouldn't compare yourself."

"Compare myself to whom, exactly?" Kits felt like a child attacking an adult, full of effort yet posing no significant threat.

"Initiative, dynamism, perseverance, dominance..." Caton spoke in a slow, steady cadence. "These are the elements of progress—the actions of the progressive. Obedience... *that* is the action of the follower. Or, if it makes you feel better, the actions of a son towards his father."

A tremor ran through him, emanating from his most vulnerable place. Kit clenched his neck muscles, fighting to hide a fragile voice. "As if anyone could understand Lord Daimó as a father."

For the first time, Lord Caton gave Kits a wholly focused stare, one that pierced straight through him. "Well, *I* certainly could."

With that, his eyes dropped onto a book which he had pulled from the office, indicating he was finished with Kits. Caton rejoined Daimó, who had yet to acknowledge the third person in the room, and they sat at the coffee table, reading in a shared, comfortable silence. Kits remained still, an insect, insignificant and afraid to draw attention to himself.

Alone, he fought with every cell to keep those last words from sinking in, replacing what little hope he had spent years fighting for. Kits knew there would be no place among those two if he asked what it would require. Goraka, with its red guardians, remained in possession of a covetable and unreachable technology, somehow discovered by a mere child. The few pieces settled into a plan; they required no consultation or oversight.

All that remained was execution.

21
EDUCATION

She set the case down on fine-grade concrete with decorative inlays. Covered in leather and copper rivets that had oxidized, creating an alluring patina, the piece had been keenly spotted in a Doulan Comeback shop. After cringing at the school's official field cases, Lucette had promptly decided to find something worth looking at. She set the bag on a bench by the Long Frost Reservoir and took a snap with the camera she had found in the bag— sometimes you just got lucky in a Comeback shop.

She sat on the bench and opened the case, revealing color-coded specimen glasses nested into one another. She pulled out a floral length of fabric and unfolded it on the ground. Beneath her feet hummed a torrent of electricity and water feeding Chigou's insatiable appetite. No matter how many times she visited, the dam seemed impossibly big for people to have created. She had seen concrete poured from massive trucks to form sidewalks before, but a hundred fleets could easily fit inside the manufactured mountain. Breaking off an alpine peak and plugging the river seemed more plausible.

On the cloth, Lucette arranged the glass and gadgets for siphoning and labeling. She sat still, gazing at the field tools laid out like sacraments —her own set, compiled after years of dreaming and studying and fighting to climb beyond the expectations for a city orphan. Lady Lucette had been accepted as a student into Upper Academy West and was an intern with Noutess—she had started work. Real, grown-up work. Celebratory energy built up inside of her and she wanted to announce her excitement—and her worth—to the world. An assemblage of aqua-leisure hobbyists floated by, paying her no attention.

"You did it," she finally squeaked out. She pumped a half-formed fist before licking the tear that had run to the corner of her mouth. "Okay Lucette, time to stop imitating an insane person and start *doing* the grown-up stuff."

Glass and alloy chimed as she assembled the components to her Drop-siphon. After a full three minutes of checking and rechecking the device's few connections, she hooked it up to a spool of filament. It felt sturdy enough but the thought of losing her only Drop-siphon into the abyss made her hands shake.

She referenced her depth guide: she needed to take samples at the surface, one meter, ten meters, and the bottom. She bit her lip while lowering the delicate glass vacuum down to the water sloshing against the dam wall. As the device approached the surface—her first act of real science—a scream shot from across the water's surface.

Her shoulders tensed up like a frightened cat, jerking the glass siphon towards the poured rock wall. "No no no no," she squeezed out through clenched teeth. Afraid to even breathe, she could only watch as the sparkling bob swung towards its delicate destruction. She anticipated the devastating crunch of broken glass but heard only a ping. The precious glass vial then bounced back from the concrete barrier.

She watched it oscillate to a standstill before allowing herself to look up and locate the culprit. "You better be drowning or fighting a sea monster."

Across the still water, a young girl sat in a fancy boat with a middle-aged man, probably her father. The girl seemed surprised that a fish would actually end up on the end of her fishing line. The man leaned over and helped net the critter before throwing it in a basket. Lucette assumed they had one of those expensive refrigerated baskets only used by those who certainly never fished out of necessity.

The girl's panic eventually melted into laughter, concluding a lovely moment with her father. On the edge of maturity, Lucette looked back in her mind across the childhood she'd just left behind. So many times she had dreamed of parents. They were like dolls she'd seen in stores, frozen behind a pane of glass. She'd imagine dressing them up, giving them jobs and personalities that would explain where she came from—a fantasy she had never told anyone.

A small steam engine propelled the tiny craft and its passengers back towards the northern dock. Walking hand in hand, they crested the horizon and disappeared, like her dream of belonging to a family. She looked down at the siphon sparkling against the water. Her fingers loosened slightly and she lowered the instrument down, dipping into a new dream.

Lucette's neck tingled as she developed a rhythm of gathering samples, labeling them, and logging it all in her sky-blue field-book. Each glass disk held a city of tiny organisms that she would spend hours spying on back at the Academy's lab.

While logging the final water sample—her pen's silver airship charm bobbing on the end—she noticed a large magnet in the back of her case. The attachment could swap out with the siphon and gobble up sunken treasures on the reservoir floor. The main mission had proven successful, and she felt tempted to sidetrack and explore. It seemed her duty as a citizen in the Valley of Progress.

Visions of giant bolts, pocket change, and dropped Tokis danced through her mind. Lucette carefully stowed all of her labeled specimens and swapped in the high-density magnet. Far heavier than the delicate glass bulb, the magnet shot down with a satisfying *plunk*.

She tried to move the weight around, but the depth made it hard to tell exactly what was happening down below. She chewed her lip while trying to sense through the line, like an extended limb. A flock of yellow Vites flew down and skimmed the water with their talons, swirling the reflected late afternoon sun. Wanting to return to the lab before it closed, Lucette decided to pack up.

She yanked on the spool and grunted as it refused to budge. Perhaps the magnet was stuck to an anchor bolt or one of the generator intakes. Widening her stance, she gave another pull that finally jerked the magnet free. The line came up carrying a concerning amount of extra weight. After breaking a proper sweat, her discovery finally surfaced.

A perfectly spherical clot of metal dangled below the magnet. She strained to lift it, unwilling to abandon her official Academy equipment. She hauled it up as it scraped against the length of the dam wall. "Come *on*, you fat little monster."

With a final heave, the back-breaking ball thumped onto the edge. After a good wipe, the sphere revealed a smooth, machined surface. Although certainly made of metal, the odd color didn't resemble any iron or alloy she recognized. "Curious little guy... and the first passenger on my new scooter."

She made a little towel hammock and picked up her mysterious find. Once slung over her shoulder, its weight proved manageable, although she walked crooked. On the way to her little industrial chariot, she passed two painters followed by a scruffy, middle-aged fisherman with mismatching gear. In a rather content state, Lucette gave a friendly smirk that she immediately regretted as the man's eyes widened at her unusual burden.

"What's in there?" he demanded.

"Uhm, excuse me, Lord whoever-you-are," *and I don't care*, she finished in her head.

"What's in your towel?" he repeated, trying to peek through the fabric.

Paranoid and defensive nerves sparked as she felt the weight of the unidentified object she may have just stolen. "Science stuff," she declared.

"Science stuff?"

"I am here as a member of Upper Academy West on official business."

The man looked her over. "What, a junior academy trainee on a field trip?"

She deflected the patronizing remark with a flick of her hair. "No. I am a student of the biological and chemical sciences and a rather serious one at that."

He remained confused.

"I'm collecting water samples. I'm going to analyze them for purity with a professional microscope. This item is not my main focus, but I found it and will probably do some analysis of it when I find the time," Lucette explained, maintaining a steady voice.

"Oh." Apparently, the man found the explanation moderately satisfying. He leaned back to a more appropriate distance, although Lucette detected a flurry of thoughts behind his eyes, which were still locked on the metal ball. "So, what are going to do? Work for one of the big smoke machines like Kasic? Or are you truly trying to keep this water from being polluted?"

She countered his aggressive tone. "Do you know anyone with braids *this* fabulous who *doesn't* like the beauty of nature?" Her hairstyle was popular among Sorans, whereas bobs, waves, and updos marked a more metropolitan crowd.

"Well, I… suppose…"

"And I'll work for whoever is hiring, because a Lady needs to make a little cold-cream, if you know what I mean." Lucette hoped her delivery was winning.

Surprisingly, the curmudgeon lightened up. "Hey, no problem with getting paid so that you can do what you gotta do."

"Right." Lucette felt the interaction had run its course. "Now, I really do need to return to the lab, so if you'll excuse me, stranger."

She began to exit as the man cast out one more comment. "Is the Lady with the Soran hairstyle going to be celebrating Raka Nusan?"

Lucette wanted to leave, but Lady Kyoumére's etiquette lessons proved inescapable. "I'm sorry, Lord Inquisitor. What is that?"

"Raka Nusan, a day every Soran needs to know."

"Well, it certainly sounds very special. I tend to focus more on my birthday though, so…"

"It's a day to celebrate the sacrifices made for what truly matters."

Lucette gave the most convincing look of engrossment that she could physically produce. The man smirked, giving her a condescending glance-over. "You'll understand soon enough."

The man checked his fishing pole, which was all Lucette needed

This thing can
scoot
AYA MOTORS
PUCHI

to hightail it out of there.

o o o

Since getting the Aya Puchi scooter, Lucette had contrived numerous reasons to drive it through the city. Pen running dry? Better head over to Inky Wells. Ate an overly salted cracker? No choice but to make a run down to Michelou's Cold Creamery—her favorite necessary excursion. Whenever she was sitting alone in a booth with her matching crimson helmet, hand-knitted scarf, and Sweet Treasure Bowl loaded with hot berries, Lucette always felt content. She imagined little girls seeing her as a hard-edged sugar fairy who could get cold cream whenever she wanted. She didn't quite have that in her budget, but the fantasy proved entertaining while she sat there.

Confectionary diversions had to wait that day as the lab was about to close. Finding a rare open parking spot at the school, she grabbed her bag, took off her racing goggles, and shut down her scooter. Removing the key triggered a unique function of the Aya Motors Puchi: clamps dropped over the hubs, securing them firmly in place. Lucette appreciated the feature, as she found security chains difficult to blend into her personal style.

The halls of UAW's Bio-Chem Chamber still delighted Lucette's senses every time she entered. It all felt so fancy and prominent. Every wood or brass surface glistened as if it repelled dirt. Getting lost had dropped from certainty to possibility and she hadn't been late to class in two weeks, a fact she had no shame in announcing despite the teacher's ebbing interest.

A monitor station sat in the front of the Bio-Lab. Three rows of populated lab units occupied the center, and special equipment lined the periphery. Copper, glass, and bubbling liquids sparkled from the bright vapor lights; it all looked serious. After signing out her station key from the timid young man who took Lucette's perpetual spunk as flirtation, she set down her specimen case. Lucette wanted to meet new people—study after dark at Izzy Kai while getting high on pastries, awkwardly navigate love as a not-quite-there adult—but new access to the world of sumptuous academia proved fully captivating. Making friends could wait until next semester.

Holding out the station key with the grace of Lady Kyoumére, Lucette slowly lifted the safety latch and slotted it in. Just as it turned, the station top folded back with the sound of steam and finely machined gears. A set of burners, flasks, tubing and various instruments steadily ascended from its sanitizing chamber as exhaust vapor lightly billowed out. Although she had done this a few times already, Lucette clapped like a proud parent.

The process of identifying unknown biochemical compounds flowed like a dance from her fingertips. Elegant pipettes floated between her choir of glass dishes and crystal slides that had emerged for their solos. She timed activating the steam-cleaning wand to the tempo of her improvised vocal accompaniment, which generated dubious stares from her Academy peers.

Her mind pranced through the rather lengthy and systematic conclusion about the water's compounds. Surprises proved rare until she got to the deepest samples. A circus of substances appeared, many of which she had little to no understanding of. She logged them all just as the lab monitor played exit music through the lab's sound system. Startled by the advance of chimes, Lucette's elbow thoughtlessly swung out and hit the large metal ball she had rested on the counter.

"*Mother Murdes,*" she growled out as she grabbed her throbbing arm. Lucette helplessly watched as the hefty mass rolled to the edge of her station and headed to the floor. It dropped like a miniature airship filled with iron. She felt the cracking thud through the floor and imagined being reprimanded for bringing a cannonball into the delicate lab.

The lab monitor ran up with gaping eyes and a bouncing red coiffure. He looked down at the mysterious gray sphere as if it were a severed head. Lucette continued to nurse her funny bone. He bent down to grab the dense object but dropped it immediately, underestimating its weight.

With cheeks flush from embarrassment, he wiggled down into a more substantial squat and heaved it up a few inches. The monitor evaluated the floor for damage, but Lucette dared not look.

"The floor, is it angry with me? Tell me the truth," she asked.

"Uhm, it just looks scuffed to me. Mobi will buff it out."

"Yes, Mobi is a superb custodian."

The monitor appreciated her compliment of a man whom few students acknowledged. He smiled as he ungracefully returned the dense sphere back to the desk, examining its stark exterior. "What is this thing for?"

"That, Lord of the lab, is precisely what I intend to find out next." She began to collect her things. "Do you happen to know where the..." She searched for the technical term.

"Metallurgy lab? It's down the hall. Take a right and then go down one floor on the elevator, then turn left. It connects with Preservation Hall next door, so don't be surprised if you come out a different building." The young man spoke with military flair.

"Then I am headed there now." She promptly packed everything up. "And what shall I call you?"

"I'm a... Stouman," he stumbled out.

"Nice to meet you, Lord Stouman. I'm a Lucette." She continued her exit.

The majority of elevators in Chigou, like most utilitarian construction in the city, made emphatic attempts to hide the mechanics that provided their functionality. Opaji had mandated that utility lines, pipes, hinges, and any internal working were as hidden as possible, frequently citing the grotesque analogy of creatures with bones and veins poking out of their skin. By contrast, all the elevators in the Science and Engineering buildings at Upper Academy West used tempered glass panels to reveal their steam-powered secrets. The display suggested to budding professionals that their field understood mysteries of industrial power which escaped the laymen. Lucette, like many young technical students, was captivated by the display during every trip. Steam valves, worm drive gears, and pulley systems danced as they carried their passengers on demand.

The display proved so captivating that Lucette forgot the remaining directions when she reached the floor. The hall was quiet, amplifying her sensation of being lost. She hoped whichever professor ran the lab had an insatiable lust for work and only left campus to execute biological functions. After a few minutes of wandering through empty corridors as the sphere began to cramp her shoulder, timed lights suddenly clicked, leaving the hallway in darkness.

Lucette yelped, fumbling the burdensome specimen before heaving it back up. "This is helpful. Thank you, autonomous machine, for so conveniently trapping me on this abandoned floor. I'm certain it's not haunted by the ghosts of dead scientists."

She reached out to feel for the wall, which her adjusting eyes could just barely make out from the red exit light. After tripping once, Lucette discovered something that had been hidden by the vapor lamps. Light leaked out from beneath a door at the far end of the hallway. She initially thought of vengeful spirits luring her to a horrendous end, but the ball was heavy and she was tired of carrying it.

The strike of her boots seemed amplified in the darkness; whoever or whatever hid down there certainly knew she approached. When she arrived, Lucette noticed no window or sign she could see, so she placed her ear on the door. Quiet grunts and scratching sounds seeped through the heavy wood door. Deciding to go with surprise instead of permission, she grabbed the cold brass knob and eased the door open.

Chilled air escaped around her neck and she felt the size of the room more than she saw it. A few lamps provided the only light, illuminating tables and piles of academic miscellany. The room looked more underused than abandoned, as if a single person kept it from fading into complete obscurity. Facing a dead end, she turned just as an obscure shadow across the room turned and looked at her. Only overwhelming shock prevented her from uttering a profanity-laced yelp.

With backlit silver hair and thick-framed glasses, an older Lord spoke up with a calm, inquisitive tone. "Young Lady, are you meaning to be on the subfloor this late in the day? Or perhaps you are looking for me."

A small "oh" escaped from Lucette with barely a breath

before she relaxed her shoulders. "No. Well, unless you are in a supervisory role in metallurgical sciences, in which case I am most certainly looking for you."

"I may disappoint you then, as I am not. You are, however, on the right floor." His voice was refreshingly void of the condescending tone Lucette had noticed in many UAW staff. "Are you looking for Lord Koul? His office is in the next hall, and he shares my stubborn refusal to quit working at a reasonable hour."

"Can he decipher a metal for me?" Lucette took another step into the room.

"If he can't, I'm not sure who else I'd recommend." The old Lord put down the stack of paper he had clearly been working on. "If you don't mind discussing it, what are you hoping to get assessed? And I failed to introduce myself. My name is Rouk KaDela."

"Lord Rouk KaDela—it is a pleasure. I take it this is your... office, Professor?"

"I do have a G.A. in History from Meijune Academy, but I'm more transient with my employment." He spoke of his impressive credentials with pleasing humility.

"Meijune? I'd like to visit there one day. Oh, and I'm Lucette by the way. I also failed to introduce myself."

Lord KaDela glanced up in thought. "That sounds like a name from Meijune, actually."

"Really? I think my parents might have been from there, or maybe one of them. Of course, how would I know?" Lucette silently bemoaned her unusual ease in discussing awkward personal matters, but Rouk KaDela nodded with a faint smile, offering neither rejection nor questions. She continued. "So, what brought one with Grand Approbation in History all the way up here into the mountains of eternal momentum?"

"You mean, what is a History G.A. doing in a city so young its founder is still alive?" He smiled.

"Yes, our big baby of a city."

Lord KaDela smiled. "Well, the valley itself is quite old. It's not a popular field, but I'm currently focused on this place before all of *this* was here." His eyes skimmed across all the metal and brick they stood beneath.

"Oh, so like… Goraka?" Lucette stopped bouncing.

He hesitated just a moment. "Yes. The source of so many fascinating stories for us to excite each other with."

"Have you been there?"

Lord KaDela opened his mouth and then stopped.

"That question always seems to be a real quagmire for anyone who doesn't answer *no*," Lucette observed.

"Interesting… I believe you are right." He raised his finger, offering the young Lady one point. "I have passed the tree line of the southern forest, but I have not experienced any dramatic tales to recall, as most seem to expect."

"Oh." Lucette pulled her heavy case in tight to her chest. "A friend of mine went there. *Two*, actually." Lucette paused, and the next words came as if her subconscious took over. "My friend died, though."

"Oh, I see." His voice was gentle.

Lucette gripped onto her case, trying to find some stability in the precarious situation she'd just put herself in. "I… yeah."

The mention of death hung in the stale air between them. "Well, I certainly have no desire to pry into any such matter. If you'd like to discuss it, however, I'd appreciate your trust in doing so."

"You know, good Lord, I'd be perfectly fine telling you, but now that I'm running it through my mind, I'm pretty sure you'd think I'm as crazy as I look."

Rouk KaDela smiled, and even in the soft light of the table lamp, Lucette could see a twinkle in his eye. "You look a bit like my niece. Or, shall I say, your *look* reminds me of her quite a bit. I've witnessed many people dismiss her as a silly girl who shouldn't be taken too seriously. However, that—as I will strongly suggest—is their mistake."

"Aww… shucks." Lucette wiped the lingering tear from her eye.

"I know it is a bit late, but you are more than welcome to rest a bit and set that on a desk." He pointed to a number of the underused surfaces in the room.

The offer reminded Lucette again of her growing fatigue. She plopped down on a stool and set her fully loaded specimen case on the desk; her arms nearly floated to the ceiling.

"I have some Blashu tea just about ready. You are welcome to some if you'd like." He pointed to a steaming contraption just as its timer ran down. Hot water began to drain out of a small copper kettle and run through a set of glass tubes, filling a carafe fitted with a strainer.

The gentle old Lord got up and fixed two cups of tea onto saucers, which he had to brush off. A single sip coursed straight through her body and began to melt the built-up stress away. She had woken up that day with no intention of telling anyone the story of her dead friend Nia and haunted forests, but an offer to be heard and even believed by a gentle, esteemed professor gave her an unexpected feeling of peace.

"Okay... okay. So, I grew up in the Tree House—er, the North River Orphanage—which is not so bad as orphanages go. Well, one day, this little girl with jet black hair and big, sad eyes shows up with our giant, part-time handyman who used to be a Lord Enforcer... for real. Her parents had suddenly died—not itself shocking, being an orphanage—but as it turns out..."

Lucette recalled personal memories and stories she had overheard. Placing it all in context, even she became amazed at how the incredible events thickened with connectivity. The Red Valley finally made its extraordinary appearance, leading up to Nia's tragic end and eventually reaching the present. "And now I'm getting my science degree right here at Upper Academy West, the craziest thing of all."

"Quite an interesting sequence, indeed, but you did warn me." Lord KaDela, to Lucette's surprise, did not sound dismissive. He then raised his hand, as if releasing a thought he had been hanging onto. "That sad little girl you mentioned in the beginning..."

"Who?"

"The young Lady, whose mother was an art teacher and father an engineer."

"Oh, Suzu." She had thought to keep her friends in the story anonymous, but Lord KaDela seemed more like a mentor than a threat. "Yes, she *was* a sad little girl, but that's all gone. She's bursting full of teenage angst these days. Glad *that* phase is over, am I right, Professor?"

"O… okay. But yes, her. You mentioned her father worked on a special kind of energy project, utilizing core-thermic energy."

"Uhm… did I say that?" she wondered. "Obviously, I did. Yes, he worked on stuff like that."

"Do you happen to know her last name—their last name?"

"Komou. Lord Carmin Komou and Lady Kiara Komou. Sadly, I never met them. Suzu talks about them like they were superheroes as much as parents. Poor little brooding-birdie, she deserves to think of them that way."

Lucette then noticed Lord KaDela rather struck by her explanation. "Wait, did you know her parents... her dad?"

"I remember a Carmin Komou." Although masked in humility, Rouk KaDela possessed a superlative memory. "He was a younger man, but this was many years ago. He could have a daughter that age today. Because of my research, I occasionally get requests for those wanting to understand one aspect or another of this land— even the southern forest. I remember the conversation quite well; he had unique reasoning for his questions."

A sudden noise from the hall cut off Lord KaDela's explanation. Lucette glanced over before looking back at the professor, who checked his Toki. "That would be Lord Koul going out for smoked coffee and chocolate pots. Those blashu cookie bowls filled with chocolate liquors are his favorite vice, so you better go intercept him if you want to get that sphere looked at tonight."

Lucette scrambled to find a clear spot on the desk for her teacup. "Oh, yes! I don't think I have the arm strength to bring it back again." She hopped off the stool and picked up her case with a grunt. "Lord *Batsu*, that got heavier."

"You need any help?" Lord KaDela graciously asked, half leaning out of his chair.

"No, thank you. I need to be a big Lady and carry my own

giant-metal-pond-ball." She went for the door before a final word. "Lord Rouk KaDela, it has been a delightful surprise."

"And one I wouldn't mind repeating it one day if you cared to brighten up this old office again someday. *Matalá.*"

Lucette's face became bright pink. She had taken it upon herself to learn the old Meijune phrase, an example of a formal farewell. The elegantly simple term hadn't survived the efficiently percussive evolution of Chigouan speech. Easily her favorite way to say goodbye, Lucette had never before heard it spoken to her. She then heard hasty footsteps passing outside the door, heading for a nightly indulgence, and raced to catch up.

22

REFLECTION

"Want me to tell you what it's called? Because you're looking at it like you've never seen one before."

"I know it's a tree. It *is* a tree, isn't it?"

"Can't say you're off to a strong start, but it's a start," Kojo said, having discovered Victou wandering in the west Bollo orchard. Silver hair fluttered under the edges of a sun-bleached hat that looked a thousand years old. "Those are Southern Bollo Trees. You know what Bollos are, right?"

"Yeah, they're delicious," Victou replied, feigning confidence. "I just assumed they grew on… bigger trees. I'm almost tempted to call this a substantial bush. Am I an idiot?"

"It's a fair statement," Kojo responded. "These are shorter than what you'd see wild along the edges of the valley."

"Oh, so you prune them down so they'll grow wider instead of taller."

"Close. We grafted good fruit producers with dwarf trees so they'd be easier to harvest but maintain yield."

"Oh, right, grafting... grafting." Victou squinted wisely.

"Fruit trees are sexual, young man. You can plant a seed, sure, but to ensure things work out on a farm, you need to play matchmaker."

"That, I did not assume." Victou subconsciously took a step back, having never enjoyed a sex talk.

"You're not wrong about pruning height to promote girth. Not generally what we do with our crops, but that's a good practice for, say, an herb gardener. You ever try any of that?"

"Me? No," Victou said, easily dismissing the idea. "My wife

loved it—could grow anything. More than capable for the two of us."

Lord Kojo looked back towards the house. "So, the young one, her mother isn't…"

"No. No, she passed away a few years ago—back in Primichi. That's part of why we ended up here, but it's been hard to settle down so far."

Kojo continued a stare that Victou found increasingly difficult to meet. "I saw that Gozen brought you two here. I know he had that little sit-down with you, but I want you to know that anyone invited here is welcome to stay as long—or as short—as they wish."

"Right. And thanks for the bed, and food and everything. I'd be happy to…"

Kojo cut him off. "While you're here, you up for making that time useful?"

Victou had never even stepped foot on a farm before. "I, uhm… sure, I… yeah, that…"

"You drive?"

"I'm generally more of a public-transit, Hotrail kind of guy."

"Alright, I think we'll skip giving you a go on one of the ten-ton harvesters." Kojo gave Victou a look over. "I think we'll get you a nice basket. Royo!"

A young farmhand drove up on a Quick Wagon with spools of twine on the back. Victou took a step back, still traumatized from being yanked out of an airship by a teenager.

"You mind taking a few minutes to show…" Kojo turned to Victou, "…this fella how to harvest Bollo?"

Young Royo looked over towards a Tulúki silo. "Yeah… I was getting binding for Legou and Joushi. They wanted to get the bundles together for the pickup tomorrow."

"Certainly can't halt a moment when those two are actually doing work. Alright, I'll get this." Kojo waved the farmhand off. He plucked a few bollos with deep red flesh. "If it looks like this, just pluck it and tuck it. Anything this light," he grabbed a smaller fruit still swirled with soft pink, "isn't ready yet."

Victou nodded. "Okay."

"There's baskets at the ends of the row. Grab one, fill it up, and then leave it back on the alley. Royo or one of the other farmhands will swing by on a Q'y and load 'em up."

"Cue-wee?"

"Quick Wagon. Sound easy enough?"

The direct task seemed foreign following years of convoluted scheming. "I think so."

"Now, if you get hungry while you're out here staring at all this delicious fruit…"

"I'll try not to eat up your profits," Victou offered quickly.

"No, boy, grab one and eat it. I don't want you passing out in my orchard." Kojo nearly smiled. "Now, if you do well, I'll pay you for your effort. We like to compensate people for their work around here."

So simple, and so much trust. *Who are these people?* "I don't think my daughter and I were planning on staying that long…"

Kojo just bobbed his head.

With no good reason to leave, Victou diverted his attention to the hanging fruit. He'd never touched fruit still on a tree before; it felt healthy and clean.

Kojo saw the young father's exhausted eyes meander across the red orb. "This orchard is the first one we planted here. The source came from wild trees we found just south of here, and from a farm in the central valley. They took real well, got fruit quicker than Clora or I thought they would."

"Clora…" Victou interjected. "…down at the house. That's your wife then."

"I'm the lucky man."

"So…" Victou thought back to their arrival. "…the sign, Kora Farm. Kojo… Clora… is that a play on your names?"

Kojo winked. "Seemed appropriate, as we each gave up half our lives to make the farm work. I think we made out in the end though. But stop interrupting me, I'm old and lose track of what I say. Things went so well, so fast, we decided to spread into a second orchard. We made cuts and planted on the other side of the house. Thought it'd be nice to have one closer to the kitchen."

"Oh, I didn't notice an orchard over there."

"That's cause there isn't one. None of the transfers made it. Died, every one of 'em. Even a couple of the parents here died from the cutting, which is unusual."

Victou felt surprising sympathy for the plants, showing that his wife's spirit was still with him. "I'll be careful with these…"

"So, my wife, Clora, who you met earlier…" Kojo stated.

This guy changes the subject a lot. "Yes. Kind Lady."

"That's the one," Kojo smiled. "I had this farm started a little while before I met her, but it was nothing like this. Still, I ran it nearly alone and it took up most of my time. Whatever energy I had left went to her. Didn't take long to convince me of that."

I know the feeling, Victou reflected.

"When we got married, she liked the idea of being at the farm and growing it into…" Kojo paused, looking out over decades of life. "…I'm not sure exactly what we were aiming for back then. It was beautiful but a lot of work, like a place where the sun never sets. After a few weeks, I started breaking down, getting sick all the time, I figured it'd go away… until one day I passed out cold in the field. Woke up in bed with my wife at my side. Said I'd been out three days."

"Good Lord." Victou winced. "What'd you have? The red plague?"

"Nope. Clora warned me I wasn't resting enough and was wearing myself out. I didn't see any reason I couldn't give all myself to farming—which I'd been doing—and all to my wife, which was new. She didn't let me out of bed other than to go to the window and see what the farmhands were doing."

"How long did you have to stay in bed?"

"Eh, couple days of fever dreams—a few days after that. It helped me see what we had, what we'd already done. I figured I'd just keep running and running but turns out what I needed was to stop for a bit." Kojo looked out over their home, an oasis of life. "A machine you can run and run until it breaks down, then you can replace a part or the whole thing. Us… we gotta take care of who we are, because it's all we are."

"Yeah," Victou let the branch of the Bollo sway back into place. "Did you tell me that because that's how the trees died? You moved them around too much, too fast."

Kojo walked down the row of trees, reaching in his back pocket for a Spark Pipe. He turned it open, clicked the igniter, and puffed a soft billow up towards the sky. As he got to the row's end, he lifted a basket and emphatically laid it down. With a quick nod, he disappeared into the normal operations of the farm.

Victou looked across the estate that stretched halfway to the horizon in all directions. "Farming," he thought out loud. After feeling so absent for so long, his wife seemed to have finally shown up from the other-life. How else could he and Chichi have ended up there? How easily Meilu would have fallen in love with Kora Farm.

But with so many years trapped as an urban nomad, Victou had no idea how to manage such an expanse of life. He had offered his daughter one tiny world after another, each tucked away, providing no more than a few minutes of proper exploration. The current environment stretched forever and hid nothing.

After gazing deep into the sky, beyond where any airship could travel, he finally walked towards his designated basket.

o o o

"That was the longest conversation I've seen that man have in a year," Clora announced with a note of hope. "Your reluctant guest must think this is an interrogation camp."

Gozen finished pouring a cup of smoked coffee and cream before joining Clora at the kitchen window. They stood there squinting as steam crept up between them.

"I'm sure he still thinks we're nice people." Gozen winked. "What do you think they talked about?"

"If my Kojo can open up about anything, it's how to pluck fruit."

From above, Gozen saw the edges of Clora's lips curl up into a smile. She watched the two fathers, old and young, inching back to life.

"I was getting worried there. That kind of darkness can be

hard to escape."

"Oh… I think he buried some of that pain so deep he's forgotten where he put it." She turned from the window and sat on a chair that Kojo had made for her just after their wedding, feeling its soft, worn edges with her fingers. "To be honest, I was worried when Jin showed up. It's the last memory we all have of her—leaving with him. It's hard to look at Jin and not think about it. I'm sure Kojo won't speak to him; he's afraid of what he'd say."

"This just became such a complicated…" Gozen paused, almost at a loss, then continued. "I guess it's all kind of complicated these days. I can take him somewhere else though…"

"No, we've made a habit of keeping troubled youngsters around when they need a place to recover. Just because he's worth more than the farm—and he wears a tie to do car work…" They both snuck out a laugh. "…it doesn't mean he's not hurting too. I remember that day he returned alone—wearing fancy clothes, beat to hell and back, crying at my feet." Clora raised her hand to her mouth, holding in the pain she didn't want to spill out.

"I remember how angry he made my Nia and of course she let him know it. But she had that giant, restless heart. Even that strange prince from the north—who never showed any emotion, whom nobody could understand—he knew what the world lost that day, and he couldn't bear it either."

Gozen recalled the day an angel of death hovered over the farm. "How are *you* doing?"

"Someone needs to keep the spirit going here. Can't just put a farm on hold."

"You are that woman, Clora, but you can still take time to grieve your girl."

Not much able to speak, Clora reached up and squeezed the gentle giant's hand, thanking him. She accepted the invitation, and they grieved for a moment together. The farmer then cleared her throat and stood up. "Let's take a little trip upstairs."

Gozen collected their warm drinks, as Clora had started using the handrail out of necessity. He followed her up to the long hall of bedrooms that had embraced its share of lost youngsters. They stopped at Nia's old room, which Gozen recognized from the green and orange door.

"I remember when a little redhead painted this all by herself," Gozen recalled before looking down at the floor, scraping a few dried paint-spills with his shoe.

"She sure didn't stay that clumsy," Clora joked before holding a breath and stepping in. Gozen followed and they stood there as if occupying a small art gallery. With arms to their side, they looked over the room with reverence.

"We've needed to let a few farmhands sleep here, but..." She looked up to Gozen like a youngster confessing, with watering eyes too big to condemn.

Gozen didn't need to ask. The room still contained all of Nia's things but was as spotless as a memory. Scarves hung on a Bokai-wood peg-board, a poster of the Primichi Soultai school remained over the headboard; even an array of athletic shoes and work boots sat by the door, used but clean.

"I know sooner or later someone is going to tell me it's time to put this all away..." Clora's gaze continued around the room until landing on Gozen. "Is it that time?"

"I don't think it needs to be... not yet."

Clora ran her hand across the cold quilt before sitting on the bed. She grabbed a framed photo off the bed stand and got lost in it.

The room pulsed as Gozen looked at it, flaring with the intensity of the loss he still held inside. He had never thought of Nia as sentimental or concerned with bric-a-brac, but without the room's occupant there, he found himself noticing little details that had always escaped his attention. There were a few figurines she must have kept from childhood, art supplies that she fancied and kept around in the hopes of using one day. Her elbow had rubbed a faded spot on the desk. Two grooves sat in the floor from when she'd leaned back in her chair—faint ghosts of what Nia had done in that room over her short lifetime. He then sat next to his friend, who was still wading in memories triggered by the photo.

"Looking at this, it's hard to remember how hard she fought

against going." Clora ran her finger over the lightly dusted glass. A young Nia stood between two Soultai instructors—one a direct descendant of the famed Chomi and Misko—at the entrance to the school. Although more modern and accommodating inside, the exterior strikingly resembled the first performance tent constructed by textile master Lady Tiké, the largest structure in Primichi at the time. Nia's face radiated happiness, like she'd discovered the birthplace of joy.

"Kojo couldn't wait. He had long since needed a break from mentoring a female adolescent; he figured she'd come back a better worker, too. I didn't really want her to go, but I hid that pretty well. I knew I'd miss her… my little girl… but it'd be good for her." She held the frame up, properly put on display. "Clearly, it was."

"How long was that? Six months?" Gozen thought back.

"It seemed like three years—seeing her when she got back. The Lady inside really broke loose. You knew then she'd be a force in life." Clora set the photo down. "In time, *you* need to find peace with it too, friend."

Gozen grunted as if it hurt to breathe. "You took care of her, she was your little Lady. I was just the guy… I'll be okay…"

"You looked after her before Kojo or I did; we wouldn't have found her without you." Clora rested her cheek on his wide shoulder.

The thought had streamed through his mind for years, forever raging against how it came to be. On orders, Gozen had reluctantly demanded families leave their home, and he ended up blowing a hole through the top three floors of their building. The disaster had destroyed one family—the death of Nia's parents, which had allowed for the growth of another. The two parallel truths ran thick with pain and beauty, forever unreconciled.

"She'd want you to have peace, that I know for certain." Clora patted his heavy forearm.

"I told Nia how her parents died. I… I'm not sure how I became capable of sharing it, but I finally did just before I dropped her off for that… that airship ride." Gozen had only told the story of Nia's origins one other time, to Clora, many years before. He didn't want to burden them with the story—the cost of their child, but he somehow knew she'd prefer to have the truth. "Seven years as a Lord Enforcer… it was about the scariest thing I'd ever done, confessing that." I knew what would happen. I even warned that man… Daimó… I should have killed him right there."

Guilt pulled Gozen's voice into a mumble before he fought his way out of the dark, improbable fantasy. "It wasn't official for months, but I quit the Enforcers that day. And here I am, doing the same things—the only difference is I'm not an Enforcer anymore. It's like I'm afraid of *not* helping people and at the same time afraid of what will happen if I *do*."

Clora stood up. "You put yourself in a position to make those hard decisions—decisions our world faces with or without you. I don't know how you decide, but I know your heart is good and you are willing. Nia knew that, too."

Gozen fought to agree as Clora saw a battle of attrition behind his eyes.

"How did Nia react when you told her… about how her parents died?" Clora asked with tenderness.

His shoulders loosened up. He rocked back and forth, allowing the truth to take hold. "She…" He paused, choked up. It hurt to push the impossible words out. "She forgave me. With a grace I can't comprehend, she understood what I did to her parents and she just… forgave me. She wrapped her arms around me… and *she* comforted *me*."

Clora gave him a hardy grin and he managed a slight one in return.

"I'm just not sure what to do now," he continued. "This evil man is still out there—so much power, so much destruction." He danced between explanation and contemplation. "Does he want more or… I just feel there's something I need to understand about him, but I still can't perceive what he's ultimately chasing. So, I don't know if I can stop him… maybe I'll just cause more harm along the way."

"Did I ever tell you about the dog I found in the Tulúki fields?"

Clora asked, offering a sudden detour.

"No, I don't think so," Gozen said, puzzled.

"This was many years ago, just after we got married and the farm was small. A proper farm—don't let Kojo hear otherwise—but nothing like it is today." Clora's mind pulled the deep memories out. "It had been a tough week, nothing unusual for the farm but I needed a day to just walk through the fields. The day started out warm, but clouds came in, really cooled it down. I thought of walking back when I saw this gap in the field. I thought maybe it was a big rock Kojo must have planted around, but he wouldn't have left that alone. Curiosity got me and I walked up… I walked up and saw a dog—I mean, I realized it was a dog, but it didn't look like a dog.

"It was dead. I knew that before I even figured out what it was." Decades later, she still grimaced at the memory. "The poor creature was there but it was all spread out in pieces. It was the most grotesque thing I'd ever seen, but it had all this perfect symmetry to it that made me feel even less comfortable. And all around, the crop had been pressed out from the center in this perfect circle that gradually went back to normal."

"Wow." Gozen's inner detective couldn't help but come out. "Did you find out what had happened? Was there anything else there?"

"I thought it must have been some kind of demented ritual. Certainly nothing I had ever heard of, but it all looked so specific and brutal. I could barely handle it and ran back looking for Kojo. He had just bought his first A-class harvester and was driving it in the field closer to the house. I ran up—at that point, I still found that machine terrifying with steam and metal churning all over—and yelled for him to come. He was a little annoyed to be pulled off his new tool, but he finally came over.

"Poor man, I'm sure I must have looked terrorized. I wouldn't even go inside the circle, but Kojo stayed calm and went in. He tried to make sense of it and started finding these splinters of wood. I kept circling outside, refusing to go in, but I managed to stumble on a flat piece of metal. I called him over and we figured it out."

Gozen's mind pieced things together as she spoke, cross-referencing a stream of possibilities. "It didn't drop from an airship, did it?"

She nodded. "It was a shipping plaque for a live animal."

"Hmm, but how…"

"Well, you have to remember this was early in the days of air travel, when they could still strap cargo to the outside—before everything had to be in a bay. Now, when we realized what had happened, Kojo looked up, mumbled some curse against airships, and then said he'd clean it all up in the morning. I could see he was too exhausted for a debate, but that sight traumatized me. It shook me so much I turned into Queen Soran of the South. I swore off technology, which poor Kojo endured just as he'd spent so much money on that fancy new harvester. I drove into the city and complained to Air-Co., brought some of the shattered crate and the shipping plaque with me. They offered to clean it up, but I said my husband already had. Then they offered me some compensation for our inconvenience, but I wouldn't have it. I demanded they find out who had worked in cargo that day, that they stop storing things—especially living creatures—on the outsides of ships. Oh, Gozen, for weeks I was blazing a real path of justice."

"I guess that's where Nia picked up her red-hot determination," Gozen added. It felt good to think of her and smile.

"Kojo made his peace about that day, but I couldn't stop thinking about it… it haunted me. I thought of that poor creature falling all that way, scared out of its senses. I'd obsess over how it happened, asking how someone could be so careless, how stupid it was to even ship an animal like that… I had to reconcile it somehow." She finally noticed her racing pulse and took a deep breath to calm herself.

"So, what came of it all?"

"Oh…" she said dismissively, "of course flight regulations changed… maybe I played little part in that. I realized I tormented myself with trying to make sense of it, somehow feeling responsible or that it had *become* my responsibility to make good of it. I felt like I owed that dog." She threw up her hands. "We did bury that little fella, by the way, or Kojo did. But I eventually realized I had made it personal when it wasn't; I couldn't have prevented it from happening. We just live in a world where awful things can happen. We could have hidden a hundred miles north of here, but we choose to keep a connection to the city, to the people. We like our role as a refuge, but to be a refuge you have to let people in who come from tough places. It's hard, but we can do that..." She looked intently at her friend. "*That* gives me peace."

A muffled yelp floated up through the floorboards—Suzu, downstairs. The outburst was followed by muted cursing of all the sharp corners which infest the world, waiting for an unsuspecting elbow or knee to innocently pass by.

"I still have no idea what I'm doing with *that* one," Gozen confessed.

o o o

Down in the kitchen, Suzu reached into the cold-cabinet. She grabbed a small wedge of smoked cheese while still rubbing her elbow. Ticklish pain further cemented the sour face she had sported most of the day. She chomped the artisanal delight and chewed it listlessly.

The interrogation of Victou left Suzu feeling anxious. She had cornered Kits and his master—literally trapped in the sky—but the opportunity had vanished even faster than it had begun. Instead, she'd ended up idling at the farm with a little kid and her clunker of a father who seemed plagued with delusion. Her shoulders felt tight. Food had little taste. She had to *do* something.

Suzu looked out of the window towards the silo where Nia had trained her—had loved her like a real sister. Jin likely occupied it to hone his survival skills as a hobby, too ignorant to recognize his desecration—training in *their* space. Suzu wanted to launch herself through the door and kick him out, but she hadn't entered the silo since last seeing Nia. She had stolen Nia's DaiLansu and lost it in a failed attempt to get her revenge. Thinking of Kits with Nia's precious Soultai staff nearly made Suzu puke. *How could she be dead while Kits still did whatever he wanted?*

A burning throat reminded Suzu that she needed water. She grabbed an old glass·and held it under the pressure spout. Cold water from a private spring filled the glass; Kora had long since abandoned the Long Frost River as a drinking source. Even after Chigou had negotiated measures to limit dumping from Primichi, its water still required massive filtration to drink. She chugged the water so fast her throat cramped. Wiping her mouth, she moved to the dining table.

Paper and brightly colored pencils sat in a haphazard pile at the center of the table. Clora had let her use the big table to draw on when she first arrived, but that seemed a lifetime ago. Suzu figured the art supplies had come out for little Chichimou to occupy her time, as Victou seemed like a real paint flake. A true dad would be at the table with her explaining how airships worked—celebrating the drawing while offering advice on how to make it better. Suzu dropped down into a chair and hunched over the table. Slowly, her fingers slid across the well-worn surface and grabbed a red pencil.

Colour, etc
every color
every possibility
Colour, etc
COLORED PENCILS
9 set

23

RECOLLECTION

Jin pushed and poked at the bandage on his shoulder as if trying to divine the recovery date. The pragmatic focus distracted him from imagining alternate scenarios, such as one in which he had bent a few inches this way or another, resulting in a pierced heart or ruptured eyeball. The headache from being struck in the temple during the rescue on the mountain had finally vanished weeks later, leaving him with one eye colorblind and the notion that he was alive due to mere luck.

Jin pushed a canvas bag filled with grain. It swung away from him on a rope he had tied to a wood beam. He allowed the rustic pendulum to sway past him and gripped his wooden Masu, a practice weapon often found in Maiishi academies. He kept his back to the hefty mass as he heard the rope crunch on the rafter. Sensing the return, he spun around and struck with his unbandaged arm.

Jin's late strike landed clumsily, collapsing his hands into his chest and transferring the inertia through his bones. After an instant of flight, he felt the compacted earth slam into his back. Groans echoed through the silo as Jin's grain-filled opponent oscillated above him with patronizing ease. Jin then sat up, emitting sounds not dissimilar to a dying farm animal.

Throughout his time in Kuitsu, Jin had felt his expectations sanded down and rebuilt. "You're *too slow*" had rung out of Lord Shirér's mouth frequently. What Jin had taken as a dig against his physical abilities, the old man had explained as a lack of empathy... or something. How does one empathize with a sack of grain? Did Jin have an empathetic understanding of the ground—is that how he'd survived the crash from the airship? Would his luck ultimately run out as he continued to misunderstand Kits?

The one thing Jin had lacked in his abundant upbringing was an ability to navigate inadequacy. Growing up, problems in his family had centered around the preservation of their legacy. Jin had never faced a day preoccupied with need. Even in the realm of Goraka he could have walked out, left Nia behind, and bought an elite-class ticket on the first airship to Primichi. Instead, he had stayed, and she had sacrificed her life for him. Born with everything, Jin knew he could never repay that debt.

"Are you okay, Lord Jin?" Chichimou asked from atop a Blashu bail just beyond the light's reach.

"Have you been there long?" Jin forced his bruised body to turn.

"Yeah. That last one looked like it hurt," Chichi sympathized.

How dull must one be to meditate and train for over an hour in an open space and fail to detect a young Lady who sat and watched the entire time? "I have been in a reasonable amount of pain since procuring you from the airship."

"Yeah," she agreed. "Are you done now?"

Jin looked at his dirt-stained clothing. "I suppose I am done."

Chichimou jumped off the bail and walked over to Jin, whose slumped posture was illuminated by the room's single light. He watched her sit down, indifferent to the dirt getting on her pants. "Lady Chichimou, how has your stay at Kora Farm been so far?"

She nodded. "The farm is so big it's almost scary, but I like it."

"I hope not as scary as when I briefly fell unconscious on our descent off the airship. The wing's failure to deploy proved to be a rather hair-raising moment."

Chichimou offered Jin no clear response.

"I myself have unreconciled emotions from the night I severed that man's arm..." Jin second-guessed his impulsive attempt at empathy as Chichi's fingers traced and retraced a circle in the dirt.

"The food here is quite satisfying, I must say. It lacks the refinement of what I grew up with, but it truly exemplifies the potential of simple excellence."

More circles.

Jin thought young Chichimou might be too tired for deeper etiquette. "Do *you* like the food here?"

Her eyes reappeared. "Yeah, it's good, especially the Blashu rolls. Lady Clora makes them better than anyone."

"Even better than your..." Jin stopped just short of mentioning a mother whom he suddenly recalled was deceased. "...father?"

"He doesn't know how to make those."

"Well, how does your father feel about the vastness of the farm?" Jin waved his arm like a show-floor model.

She didn't understand the word but thought she knew what he meant. "He likes it, I think. He doesn't seem so jumpy here."

Jin acknowledged this with a deep sigh. "The serenity of Kora farm does reveal itself quite readily."

"Lord Jin," Chichimou peered over. "Do you practice fighting because of what happened at our old apartment?"

Jin backed up to a few thoughts earlier: a bloody engagement between strangers, a limb flopping in a pool of its own blood, the screaming voice of a traumatized child. "I should consider that. Thank you for asking."

"You're welcome." Chichi sat for a second. "But is that when you started?"

Jin sat straighter, less aware of his pain. "I have trained in Maiishi as far back as I can recall. I believe I was two years old when I had my introduction—a picture book gifted to me by my uncle, Lord Matrou, titled, *Power and the Art of Focus: Children's Edition*. Have you ever read that book?"

"Nope."

"Well, I'd be happy to lend you my copy." Jin's mind filled with pleasant and violent memories: his first training suit, a dismembered man yelling, the trophy he received for his first Maiishi competition, being shot in the face. "Yes, so, as I mentioned, I have always trained... just training. I feel that now I must train because if I don't..."

... someone will attempt to kill me and I won't be able to stop them, he completed the thought in his head.

Chichi waited for the conclusion. "If you don't what?"

She looked so petite, emanating an innocence that made his spirit ache. "Chichi, do you feel safe?"

Healthy in body and experienced in traumatic events, Chichi had a far more complex answer than Jin would have had at the same age. She leaned over and grabbed his hand like it was a plush toy. "I feel safe with you, Lord Jin."

He gently held her hand, unsure of how firmly one should squeeze such small fingers. Jin thought of his mother, when his own hand was as small by comparison, and the value of protection as a child.

"Lady Chichimou, I have something for you."

She looked at him with a suddenly luminous face. "You do?"

"Yes, pardon me." Wincing from the noises speaking from his knees, Jin managed his way to a pack resting on a large table. Chichimou sat up and saw him dig around before returning with an odd, palm-sized device.

"I will confess, I did not create this with the intentions of gifting it, but I currently perceive it as appropriate." He extended his arm and revealed something that Chichimou had never seen before. A beautiful clock face sat in mysterious, intricate machinery.

"Is that a Toki?"

"It is. Very astute, as it is one of a kind," Jin revealed. "I made this sometime after my return from Goraka. I did not have any specific intention for it, but I felt compelled to make it all the same. I believe, now, it is something you should possess."

She reached for it, but Jin retracted his hand. "It is imperative I educate you on its special, however, before I allow you to wield it yourself."

Chichimou didn't know what *wielding* was, but it sounded exciting.

"I have managed to take a flare cannon and give it a weatherproof, compact design. I inlaid a Po'kin-style framing as well so a young Lady could feel confident pairing it with any outfit."

"It's pretty." Specular highlights reflected around Chichimou's eyes.

"To avoid accidental discharge, I have a latched panel over the trigger which you can activate with two deliberate actions of the thumb. At your scale, I'd advise using two hands." Jin explained to a face that remained wholly lost within the sparkles. "Do you know what a flare is?"

Chichimou shook her head.

"I see. It is a pyrotechnic of sorts, this one being composed of potassium nitrate and polymeric resin. Instead of combustible propellant, I constructed a chamber for compressed gas as a launching medium," Jin explained.

"What?" Chichimou asked, again reaching for the shimmering device that begged to be held.

"Perhaps a demonstration is in order. I designed it to take replacement cartridges, so this would be an excellent opportunity to do a field test." Jin always enjoyed field tests.

o o o

Warm sun outlined the western Murde Mountains, teaming with the moon to bring twilight into the valley. Farmwork hushed, allowing the chatter of animals to surface. A few stars twinkled and a refreshing coolness floated across the fields. Independently, everyone stopped and took notice, if just for a moment, until an intense explosion echoed across the farm.

Every soul within hearing distance snapped their attention to a burning red flame soaring into the air, casting its scarlet glow across all of Kora. Victou froze, his white knuckles strangling a fruit basket.

Kojo marched straight towards the launch area while preparing a stern examination.

Clora noticed Gozen instinctively grab for a sidearm that had been locked in a box for years. Their eyes met and he shook his head with embarrassment before hustling towards the front door.

Suzu had beat them to the young man and little girl, captivated by the fiery pixie floating back to the ground. She stopped with her hands already out in protest. "Are you mad?"

"Lord Jin is showing me this Toki's special," Chichimou

happily explained.

"What?" Suzu found their tranquility confounding.

"He's giving it to me as a gift," Chichi clarified.

"Why would you give an explosive to a little girl?" Suzu demanded. "And why would you ever put an explosive in a Toki? *Hot bolts,* Jin, do you also leave that insane sword of yours with the cutlery?"

"I find that to be an irresponsible suggestion."

Suzu maneuvered between him and the little girl. "I can't believe Lady K *ever* let you stay at the Tree House surrounded by children."

"I assure you the device is well machined and designed with multiple fail-safes. I thought it'd be prudent to demonstrate its proper usage to young Lady Chichimou before I gave…"

"And you would need to be mad to even consider any of… *this,*" she pointed to the 2,500-degree incendiary device floating towards them, "…appropriate. Chichi, it's bedtime." Suzu grabbed her hand and headed for the house.

Unable to hear him approach over her rant, Suzu nearly ran into Gozen, who had just arrived. "Who shot the flare?"

"Who do ya think?" Suzu said without stopping. "And, oh yeah… He made the *small child* do it!" She hauled Chichi towards the house.

"Okay," Gozen continued. "Jin, what is this all about?"

"Yes, well, you see, I remember young Lady Chichimou had gone down into the Red Valley with her father, Lord Victou. It is a vast and confusing landscape. I calculated that gifting her a location device could prove advantageous in an emergency."

"Okay." Gozen rubbed his face. "I don't disagree with you in principle, but I'm not so sure she's old enough to handle a flare gun, or that this is a great place to try it out."

"Oh," Jin paused. "I thought anything more urban would increase needless variables and a more rural setting would take her too far away from her father."

"Yeah, right but… I…" A rebuttal failed to form in Gozen's mind, but in an act of reprieve, Legou and Joushi joined from the farmhouse.

"When do *we* get one of those?"

"I thought you two were keeping watch in the house tower?" Gozen pointed to the round deck that sat on top of the farmhouse roof.

"We were," Legou responded. "That's how we noticed that spicy item and ran over here to investigate."

"Yeah, Gozen," Joushi generously added, "we're not just watchers, we're *doers*."

"That's very comforting," Gozen muttered. "But how about you go back up there and return to the watching. I'll make some coffee if you need it."

"Smoked, please, if you don't mind," Legou suggested.

"Oh, shall I bake you some Blashu rolls as well?" Gozen snapped.

"Mmm. Gozen, you're truly like a mother to me," Joushi replied as the two young men waltzed to the house. "See, I keep telling you his gears are all soft and warm on the inside."

As Gozen looked back, he saw Kojo in surprising proximity to Jin as their eyes locked together. A promise lay between them, shattered into a thousand shards. Kojo finally looked up to the flare that began sputtering.

"It's fine," Gozen assured him. "We already talked about it, it's fine."

Kojo shook his head before looking back at Jin. His eyes twinged from the amount of pain and sorrow they held in. It burned, but Jin couldn't look away—the bitter face flickering in red light. The flare sizzled into death and Kojo's black silhouette stood in a thin outline of moonlight. Jin put down his head and walked away.

o o o

Chichimou tried to smile as her head emitted a high-frequency hum. White foam squeezed from the corners of her mouth, visible in the mirror as she tiptoed. Suzu glared at the battery-operated sonic tooth conditioner, silently cursing yet another gadget Jin had bewitched this child with. She spit out a laugh anyway, unable to handle Chichi's efforts to wrangle the buzzing brass wand in her mouth.

"Okay, I think you have achieved maximum polish."

Chichimou turned and let loose with her smile, letting paste drizzle down her chin.

"Another minute and that thing will disintegrate your teeth."

With a clumsy sputter, Chichi managed to rinse out her mouth before setting the tooth conditioner back on its charging base. She wiped her face off with a towel, waiting for the tiny green light to turn on. "Now it'll be ready for tomorrow."

"Fabulous." Suzu gestured to the empty hall. "Let's go, little one."

Chichimou jumped up and grabbed Suzu's hand, pulling her into the hall. Suzu smiled as she was led away in a bouncy, impromptu dance. A warm fragrance followed little Chichi, like what Suzu remembered from early mornings when her mother did laundry. Her life had lost nearly all of those routines.

Chichimou released Suzu's hand and pounced onto her bed. "What story do you want to read me?"

"What?" Suzu didn't feel old enough to be reading bedtime stories to kids, but the age of asking someone to do likewise seemed even farther away. "I guess I can do that. I can read, after all."

"I like scary ones—sometimes adventures, or Lady Fantasias," Chichi recollected.

Suzu turned over to see a humble little library loaded with an assortment of colorful book jackets, and a faint memory resonated within her. They looked well-kept but had a cozy dullness to them. Most scary books would be of shipwrecks—air or sea—and the ensuing dilemma with spirits or being stranded. They had been a favorite in the old port city of Meijune, with some adapted for life up in the valley.

Lady Fantasias, a relatively new genre, involved a young female protagonist having her life abruptly upended by some wondrous happening. They described such adventures as befriending magical animals, traveling to exotic lands, inheriting some power, creating a brilliant invention, or any combination thereof. Romantic flirtations were a popular side story but always played second-chair to whatever adolescent power fantasy stood at the center.

Suzu thumbed across the spines, investigating any peculiar or familiar titles. *Ramosa and the Talking Cat* was a classic for very young kids; Suzu marked it a maybe. *Red Eyes Red Valley* certainly looked scary from the cover; another maybe. Her fingers then stopped as they came across a book that looked untouched. The title, even the spine's color, immediately collided with old memories. Her father had read *Maki Makes an Airship* to her at least thirty times. In the end, Suzu would always ask if they could build their own airship one day. Carmin had always refused to promise, but said if the opportunity ever came about, they'd certainly make the most polished little airship the Naifin Valley had ever seen. She wanted to hear his voice again.

"Oh, hello, little lady," Victou's voice chimed in. "I see you're ready for bed."

"Suzu was picking out a book," Chichimou said.

"Oh, hello to you. Sorry... didn't see you there."

"It's fine, I'm a tricky Lady," Suzu said, her attention still turned towards the shelf of dusty dreams.

"Yes, and deceptively strong." Victou still felt sore from that strap she had hung him from. "I can read her a story. You don't have to watch her anymore." He stepped between the young ladies.

Suzu reluctantly held *Maki Makes an Airship* out. "Whatever, it's fine."

Victou bent down and reached for the book. Suzu tried to pull it back at the last second, but the jumpy father snagged it. "Is this what you wanted to read? Let's see… airships, this looks fun…" his voice tapered off at the sudden recollection of their only time on an airship. "…maybe we should both sit down for this one."

He patted the bed down to make a flat spot and then uncomfortably held the book as if he had forgotten how to read. He started to murmur through the first few pages, but Suzu had no interest in hearing this man speak that story. She practically fled through the doorway, chased by Chichimou's soft *goodnight.*

Suzu descended stairs that seemed to creak louder going down than up, announcing her to the empty dining room. Paper and pencils were spread out on the table where she'd left them. An airship's outline sat alone on a piece of soft, off-white paper, looking frail and incomplete. She considered leaving it, but any earnest design deserved a chance before being crumpled up and discarded.

She sat down and fumbled through the glossy pencils, her fingers attempting to decipher the right one to use so the shape could be rescued from its emptiness. She then looked at the vacant kitchen that seemed to stare back. *It was just a drawing,* she thought. *How can it be so hard to grab a color and start filling it in? Do I know how to complete anything?*

Every color seemed wrong, so she went back to black. After a few absentminded taps, she pressed the pencil to the paper. Since an airship without an engine is just an overpriced balloon, that should be first. Suzu drew a hull, then the intake cone and finally the exhaust. An ache pulsed in her wrist and she rubbed it. *Guess I don't draw anymore.* She looked over the rendering so far and assessed that her dad had been right—too big, always too big with the engines.

A tight hum then bounced into the dining room from outside. Suzu recognized the annoying little engine before it shut off, followed by footsteps in the hall. The shimmer of bouncing charms and jacket lapels confirmed the late-night intruder.

Lucette walked in to find Suzu as she had first seen her. Hopeless posture, hunched over scattered art supplies. Suzu didn't bother to look up. Dark bangs hid her eyes. Lucette saw her dig a black pencil into the defenseless paper as if trying to carve through the table. The absence of a greeting tempted Lucette to cut in with a real stinger, but the long day had already cost her a full ration of wit.

"I hate to interrupt, but is there any food available for a hungry traveler?"

"This is a farm," Suzu grumbled into the table. "You're surrounded by hundreds of acres of food. You may have noticed some driving up."

"Correct. I could go dive—mouth open—into a grain silo, but

maybe I'll just check the kitchen." Lucette maneuvered around the table.

Suzu felt Lucette's energy contaminate the room. She didn't understand how anyone could maintain such perk. She'd never admit it, but she had grown to find it intimidating. She figured that Lucette, with no memory of things lost, had simply developed a superpower against remorse. *How fortunate*, Suzu thought, *to have all the resistance to death with no ghosts to haunt you.*

She heard Lucette *ooh* and *ahh* over the assorted pastries and fruit always occupying the Kora farmhouse kitchen. Growing up, Suzu and her dad would do the same when her mom would bake, a memory whose details had nearly faded away.

A cup rattled on porcelain. Suzu could smell the smoked coffee and spiced pastries piled up on the overwhelmed saucer. The edge of her vision caught the blonde-braided figure settling down at the other end of her bench seat. Chewing and slurping soon displaced the sound of silence.

Lucette noticed Suzu's fingers press even harder into the paper. Dark lead began to splinter at the end, crumbling as it left a heavy, dark trail. Suzu looked stressed from trying so hard to ignore her.

"That looks like what you drew when you first came to the Tree House."

Suzu didn't reply.

"You drew stuff like that with your dad, right? I think I remember you saying that, if my academy-fried brain is recalling correctly."

Suzu's shoulders gave a bare minimum of response.

"I think it's sweet you still do it."

"I don't... not really. These were just here... it's nothing, it's dumb," Suzu finally answered.

"I don't think it's dumb."

"No, it is. I mean, I'm not a kid anymore. I'm just being stupid." Suzu kept her head down. "I don't know why I'm even doing it."

Lucette stopped her chewing and slurping. "It's okay." She nodded, just enough for Suzu to see between the gaps in her bangs.

"I just..." Suzu mustered up the willingness to continue. "I just feel like if I do stuff like this, then it's like they're still here. But I know they're not… like I said, it's stupid."

The words sounded like pain parading as something else. Lucette had felt for Suzu from the moment she had first appeared at the orphanage. She looked so different now from that little black-haired girl who had gone from *daughter* to *orphan* overnight. The sharp exterior, Lucette thought, protected whatever remained of the life she refused to let die.

The pencil began to tremble, going back and forth over the same stroke. A faint urge to laugh faded in Lucette as she became uncomfortable watching the display. She noticed the scattered pencils and thought of offering an alternate color, something not named *Eternal Night*. She spotted a yellow, *Soft Recollection*, just as a tiny drop landed on the paper.

Lucette leaned in to see Suzu hiding the other half of her face in her hand. The pencil slowed to a stop. Lucette heard them both breathing and softly asked, "You really miss them, don't you?"

As if she had waited years for permission, Suzu nodded before another tear fell onto the drawing. She dropped the pencil and put pressed her sleeve to her face. "I do," she wept, muffled by the black fabric.

Lucette sat still, hurting for her friend. She thought to offer some of her snacks as Suzu's inhales became heavy, like it pained her to breathe.

"*I miss them so much.*" The words barely crawled out of Suzu, like a confession she couldn't bear to keep inside one second longer. Lucette pushed her plate back and slid over. Suzu's warm back shook as Lucette gently put an arm around her.

Suzu escaped into her friend's embrace. Hiding from the world, she opened up and let her heart spill out onto bright, floral fabric. Suzu cried so hard she felt like vomiting. Lucette kept her safe, combing her hair with brightly painted fingernails.

"I still miss them, but I keep *forgetting* things about them," Suzu pleaded. Lucette continued to stroke her hair, giving her space for honesty, space to release whatever stuck inside. "My mom used to call me a name when I'd hop on the counter to help her bake."

Suzu's voice settled then broke again as the pain again became too much. "But I can't remember what it was. It's gone. It's *all* gone."

Without either of them noticing, Lucette began to rock Suzu back and forth. She would hold Suzu as long as she needed. The smaller Lady accepted the offer, crying it out until the burden settled down into her stomach, ending in some sniffles and a snot bubble. "Oh geeze," she mumbled, wiping her wet face off with her wet sleeve. A modest smile then crept into the corner of her mouth as she looked up.

"I love you, little Lady," Lucette reminded her.

Suzu's shoulders dropped. "Even though I'm mean to you half the time?"

"I'd say it's more like ninety-percent of the time. But yes, I do. I'm very gracious." Lucette smirked.

"Are you mad you never got to have a family? Or do you think having one and then losing them is worse?" Suzu asked, her voice calming down.

"Oh, who can say?" Lucette replied, like a grandmother offering aged wisdom by a fire. "But I like my family. You…" she emphatically said, eyes drilling down into Suzu's, "…Gozen, Nia…" She got heavy and hunched down, "… yeah, I really miss Nia… gaw, now me too." Lucette wiped her own tear. "Oh, and Lady Kyoumére, whom we'd be lost without."

"Oh yeah, I barely see her anymore," Suzu confessed. "Have you? How is she?"

"Still drowning in an ocean of brats—I mean, little angels. You should go see her," Lucette pressed. "I just saw her for a minute before I came over. I kinda felt bad leaving her there alone... so, *so* many kids. But I'm not about to accuse Lady K of weakness."

"Why *did* you come here?" Suzu asked. Despite being a friend to Kora, Lucette's visitations came at lengthy intervals.

"Excellent transition. It's because of school—in a way. I'm actually here to see Gozen."

"Oh yeah," Suzu slouched with embarrassment. "How is the Academy?

"Exquisite. I feel like I might even know what I'm doing once in a while."

"And what's with Gozen?"

Lucette bobbed her head back and forth. "Oh, there's this project I'm doing where I take water samples, test them for mineral content, impurities, blah blah blah. I found this weird metal ball, some reservoir goblin asked me all about it, went back to Upper Academy West, met a lovely old man—who I need to tell you more about, by the way—found out the mystery ball was made of some currently-inert-but-possibly-highly-explosive compound. Then I said, *I know this big Civil Enforcer guy who would probably know what to do with it.* I figured he'd be canoodling with Lady K, but she said it'd been a while since she'd seen him and that I should try here. It was late, my stomach was caving in, and I know they always have tasty treats and spare bedrooms in this cozy wanderer's paradise."

Suzu never realized her roommate's effervescent lifestyle contained so much actual work. "You did all that *today?*"

"Yes. I'm attempting to be an obnoxiously productive student."

"And you still have that bomb with you?" Suzu interrogated.

"Well, I don't think it's a bomb… now. I don't know, that's why I'm looking for Gozen. Is he here?"

"And you found it at the dam? Who was this reservoir goblin?" Suzu leaned up a few degrees.

"Dismal Suzu is gone now, I see. Hello again, Detective Suzu."

"Did you know him?"

"So young, so serious," Lucette grinned. "Definitely a *no*, as I certainly would never forget someone so passionately scraggy. He certainly wanted to know *my* business, though. Then, he gave me this little Soran identity test. That gave me boredom cramps, so I left."

Lucette looked down expecting a giggle or at least confusion, but Suzu appeared engrossed with the information. Her eyes shifted, pushed around by a torrent of thoughts. Her expression gave little insight into any conclusion.

"You are finding this way more significant than I thought you—or anyone—would."

Suzu's mind focused, clawing into old memories that hid like a pesky, nameless song you can't stop singing. Lucette felt her squirm until black-lined eyes finally flew wide open. Accidentally hitting Lucette's chin with her head, Suzu exploded up in her chair, her fingers clenched into fists. *"That stupid mongrel!"*

24
MOMENTUM

Suzu bounced between walls and tables with fiery eyes and a mouth mumbling in tongues.

"Did you recently become possessed?" Lucette asked.

"*Mouba*," Suzu finally spoke aloud, her gears whirling.

"Is… is the demon inside you named Mouba?"

"What?" Suzu shook her head clear. "No, this guy… he was tall?"

"Yes," Lucette recalled.

"Scruffy… *gross* scruffy."

"Mm-hm."

"Creepy and cringes at any mention of industry."

"He did question the quality of my Soran sensibilities more than once."

Convinced, Suzu paced swiftly around the room. "And this metal ball is explosive?"

"It *can* be. I think a lot of them together would be quite bad. Is Gozen here? I saw his apartment-on-wheels outside—"

"Wait… I saw Mouba at the dam months ago. He could have been dumping these things in the water the entire time. Gah, I sensed him scheming *something*, I just didn't think it'd be so…" her hands spread out defining something big and awful. "And he just let you take that thing?"

"I had the ball fully swaddled in a towel, and he did seem suspicious, but then he got distracted and lectured me about some Soran holiday."

"Holiday?" Suzu couldn't imagine Mouba being festive.

"Gosh, what was it called?" Lucette rubbed her temples.

"Raka… I don't know, Raka Nu-Nu?"

"Raka Nusan!" Suzu blurted out.

"Oh, you too, I see."

"Oh no." Suzu's face drained of color.

"Not a good holiday?"

Suzu began to vibrate, her mind and hands bouncing around. "What's today?"

"It is…" Lucette thought hard. "…the sixth. I know this because I checked out my water sample kit…"

"Oh no oh no oh no…" Suzu oozed panic and Lucette felt it.

"Okay, what is this Raka-Nu…"

"Nusan. It's not a festive holiday." Suzu's mouth had trouble keeping up with her brain. "A long time ago in Meijune, before the Naifin Valley, a bunch of people—angry black-hands, angry Sorans—got fed up with this massive factory that was trashing their water supply and working people to death. They tried to negotiate with the higher-ups but they wouldn't give an inch, so the workers and Sorans torched the entire plant."

"Yowza. Did anyone die?" Lucette leaned back.

"Oh yeah," Suzu sneered for a second, "but fewer than those the factory killed with their horrendous working practices."

"Okay, okay." Lucette felt pulled along with Suzu's dive into paranoia.

"The day is like this… this… *revenge* celebration against industrialists and gilded navel-gazers. My parents didn't really celebrate it. My mom was pretty combustible, but they both hated violence. They just talked about it as this byproduct of injustice. And once, when I was really young, on Raka Nusan, some people in Primichi tried to sabotage a bunch of mining equipment, but it went bad. They all died."

"Oh, so you think this Mouba guy is… oh no… the dam. You don't think…" Lucette covered her mouth.

"This guy? Absolutely, and Raka Nusan is tomorrow… dammit!" Suzu was already up and moving. "Did you drive here?"

"Yeah, of course, I… hey, wait!"

"You drive," Suzu said as she began to drag Lucette through

the door. "We have to get to the reservoir *now!*"

"Uhm, certainly you don't mean the reservoir *set to explode?*"

"Lucette, I'm serious. That dam blocks a mountain of toxic waste and Mouba is going to blow it to hell. The city is right in the path of that poisonous tidal wave. *Lord of insanity*, Lucette, the *Tree House* sits on a bend of that river!"

"Okay." Lucette began to move. "But shouldn't we tell Gozen? The hulking Civil Enforcer?"

Suzu half considered it. "He's… retired and who-knows-where out there on the farm." Suzu pulled harder on Lucette's arm.

"But what are we going to…"

"I'm going to stop him. You can drop me off, then find a CE, a Lord Enforcer—I don't care but it's…" she checked her Toki, "… going to be tomorrow in an hour."

Lucette finally pulled her keys out of her pocket. "Argh, am I really this insane?"

o o o

"I'm going to smash that clown's *face* in!" Suzu screamed over the torrent of wind and engine steam.

Even through her blood-red helmet, Lucette could hear the violent proclamation. "I wouldn't touch him, but you go right ahead."

"This guy always gave my mom problems. My dad hated him. I'm just surprised he managed to have enough patience to do this."

Lucette normally talked a tad loud but found screaming rather unpleasant. "I really think we should have told Gozen."

"Too late." Suzu pointed forward as the lights of the dam appeared. A row of warm, glowing dots lined the walkway across the concrete mountain. They shimmered off the water like stars in endless darkness. A parking lot came into view, leading to the guard station that blocked the dam's top.

Lucette eased up on the throttle, finally noticing her aching hand. "Don't they lock it up at night?"

"Yeah." Squinting from the rush of wind, Suzu looked deadly serious.

"And I'm guessing you plan on sneaking in instead of asking."

"If Mouba is there, I need to find him fast, and there's no way a guard is going to take us seriously."

"Because we're young ladies and my skirt matches my scooter?"

Suzu tensed up like a bow string, pointing her nose to the edge of darkness. "Park at the end of the lot where the lights don't reach."

A few cars remained by the entrance—late-nighters taking their time by the water—plus two in the adjacent employee lot. A long walkway sat between the lots and the dam, giving the ladies an entry route. "Turn your light off," Suzu ordered as they got near the driveway.

Lucette felt her quickening pulse against the helmet's chinstrap. The massive reservoir—held back by tons of concrete—somehow seemed even bigger in the dark. She drove away from the light along the lot's darkest edge.

The tiny motor revved down while the guard window glowed far in the distance; nothing seemed to move. Suzu hopped off with eyes like a hungry cat. Lucette turned off the scooter, put the keys in her backpack, and then dropped her runners to the pavement.

Suzu was already walking. "Come on."

"Where?" Lucette asked, trying to keep up.

"Where do you think?" Suzu's reply was punctuated with impatience.

"To where the *bombs* are?" Lucette asked, dumbfounded.

"And Mouba!" Suzu strained to keep her voice down.

With clenched teeth, Lucette followed in tow. They ran a few meters before Suzu noticed Lucette's gratuitous attire. "Hey," Suzu pointed to Lucette's skull, "you still have your helmet on."

"And it's staying on if we're running *towards* the explosives."

"That's not going to help if it goes off."

"It's either this or I'm sucking my thumb," Lucette retorted.

Running half bent over, Suzu took them just inside a symmetrical row of trees that curved up to the guard station. Lucette followed, trusting her friend's experience with trespassing. Their path led towards a towering steel-rod gate, open during the day but currently closed and blocking the walkway across the dam.

Metal sculptures of airships and boats were sandwiched in a fist holding the word *PROGRESS*. The side transitioned into a link fence that eventually curved down across the artificial beach. It terminated ten meters into the water.

"It's either climb or swim," Suzu explained.

Lucette fought for air. "I am *not* in good shape."

"We can climb over there." Suzu pointed to where the chain link fence angled down near a small mound; a good place to jump off. "Less risk of drowning."

"Oh gosh," Lucette wheezed. "Okay, let's just…"

Suzu scurried over to the fence as if a starter pistol had gone off. She climbed over the fence without breaking stride. Lucette dropped her shoulders and jogged over, eyeballing her aggressive guide through the barrier.

"Come on," Suzu pressed.

Lucette threw up her hands. "As if I've done this before."

"Grip tightly, but push up with your legs."

"Maybe I should stay back," she deflected, still sucking in air.

"You know where they are." Suzu pointed to the stretch of water hiding its deadly secret. "And *you're* the one in upper academy."

"I'm only getting a minor in Environmental Terrorism, I'm not sure…"

"Do you want to get caught?" Suzu snarled through her teeth. "Get your butt over here."

Lucette hated getting in trouble. She reached up and grabbed the thin links of metal. The fence rattled as she tried to dig her narrow feet into the holes. Suzu shushed her. Lucette growled. A sharp pain rang up her arm as the thin metal links dug into her fingers. Wanting to just get it over with, Lucette clenched her jaw and clawed her way up to the top. Straining her groin and scraping her thigh, she crossed over and promptly plopped to the ground.

"That's a bruise," Lucette grunted.

"We'll stay by the water and cut up just between those lights by the first bench." Suzu traced the path with her finger.

"Oh, no, don't worry about me. I'm fine. Mission first."

Suzu crouched again and scurried up towards the walkway

stretching across the entire dam. Benches and lights were staggered on either side, forming offset rows. They illuminated the edges, but a narrow path of darkness snaked down the middle of the path.

"Stay behind me, out of the light." Suzu called softly.

Lucette lumbered up the hill and stopped, coveting the bench's restful offering. Suzu didn't wait but zigzagged down the middle, avoiding the warm lights' reach. Lucette grabbed her side stitch, following along and oscillating back and forth like a child. "I'm having trouble taking myself seriously right now."

"You wear rainbow-dotted socks."

"I'm *especially* having trouble taking myself seriously right now."

"Where did you find that metal ball?"

"Umm..." It looked much different at night, but Lucette remembered the bright yellow access grate as it passed by. "Here."

Suspicious, Suzu slowed down. "You're not just tired?"

"I am *also* tired, but this is the spot." Lucette rested, hands on her knees.

Reaching back for her Lansu—just in case—Suzu scampered to the edge. She searched for Mouba hiding behind a bench or down by the water. The world consisted of concrete, gently lapping water, and a single boat on the opposite side of the reservoir. Between Lucette's strained breaths, Suzu couldn't hear a single anomaly.

"Do you see anything?" Lucette asked Suzu. "Do you see him?"

The tall walkway lamps created a soft haze, prohibiting her eyes from adjusting. Suzu leaned over the railing and squinted but saw nothing more than a dark gray mass holding back a pool of solid black, speckled with cosmic reflections. "No."

Lucette looked back at the sentry station. She barely made out the guard, who at that distance simply looked bored. "Do we just wait out here all night?"

"If we need to. Or maybe he already made his final visit."

"But you don't see anything."

"I *can't* see anything," Suzu emphasized, motioning to the haze from the high lamps. "Not with all this damn light."

"Right..."

"I can't tell if there's a wire or some kind of device down by the water or what."

Lucette looked around at the mountains silhouetted in darkness, the city glowing south in the distance. She felt small. "Maybe it's time to tell a proper adult."

Suzu leaned back up and nodded to the guard station. "If we tell them, we'll be out of options."

"But maybe they'll add more security or search around. Isn't the point to keep this thing from blowing up and drowning the Tree House and every other place along the river?" Lucette thought she could sense the pile of volatile metal just below their feet. Her stomach felt sour.

"Or he won't believe the word of two girls showing up in the night telling stories of bombs and crazy people. Then we spend the night locked in an enforcer's office while Mouba shows up to an empty guard station."

Lucette's voice swelled with energy. "Well, I'm certainly not standing here all night. I don't want to be standing on it right now!"

"Quiet," Suzu scolded her and checked the guard station. However, she knew Lucette was right. "Okay, we still have twenty minutes before midnight. I know he wouldn't do anything before then."

"You think that walking squirrel's nest is that punctual?"

"I know he's that fanatic," Suzu declared. "Does your Toki have a spotlight?"

Lucette dropped her already sagging posture. "The one back at my scooter does," she confessed reluctantly.

"Alright," Suzu's mind raced. "Go get the light and I'll stay here, out of sight, in case he shows up. When you get back, we'll look along the water. If we don't see anything we'll stake out by the shore."

It still hurt Lucette to breathe. "Well don't be offended when I come back smelling like vomit." Lucette ran off the way they came, knowing she wouldn't convince Suzu to leave any more than she could convince a cat to do anything. She just wanted them both off the dam as fast as possible.

Suzu eyed the guard station, seething at the listless dolts who may have let a Soran degenerate plant explosives for weeks on end. While Lucette made her way back down the hill, Suzu was focused on the water. The ink-black pool refused to let her see even an inch into its depths.

She got down on her stomach and put her head below the railing, trying to get as far from the light as she could; it barely helped. She looked down the wall and noticed a concrete shelf near the water, hidden from the buzzing walkway lights, a place her eyes could adjust if she could manage to get there.

She figured the drop to be about five meters. The wall's surface had a grid of thin construction ridges, maybe deep enough to climb. Her hand slid'over the edge and searched for a seam. A chill crept into her fingers from the smooth, manufactured stone until they scraped against a sharp crease. Suzu crawled forward on her belly, trying to get a better read on the grip until her torso hung over the edge. Her tiny, calloused fingers pressed hard into the carved concrete. "Pft, I can climb that."

Suzu looked down the walkway and saw a shadow that may have been Lucette plop over the fence, towards the lot. Suzu looked again for Mouba, checking the opposite side for any shadow drifting towards her. Only the water seemed to move, tapping at the stone down below for attention.

Uninterested in idly laying on her belly, Suzu swung a leg over the edge and dug a pair of fingers into the narrow crack while clutching onto the top. The slight angle of the wall gave her foot just enough to grip. Establishing her anchor points, she pulled the other leg over until her entire body hung along the cold, flat barrier.

Just as her head dipped below the reach of the lights, the world turned black. She held herself in place, feeling the concrete gnaw into her fingertips while her feet slipped a millimeter every second. Finally, her pupils swelled open and she could see the thin construction lines defining her path. Her toes found a thin edge and settled in, allowing a reprieve for her death grip.

Suzu gauged the spacing between cracks, about half of her height. She slid her upper hand down and jammed her fingers into the next crack, beginning her descent towards the water. She found a rhythm, alternating hands and letting the rubber of her shoes slide down. Her strength held up, but her calloused fingers weren't quite conditioned for proper rock climbing. Pain began to needle in between toes finding their next horizontal cut—just one quick break.

As her eyes adjusted, they focused on crisp edges and textures. She searched for an anomaly, some element that didn't harmonize with the stretch of industrial stonework. Nothing stood out against the expanse of water and stone; she needed to get closer.

Ready for another maneuver, she then noticed light faintly pulse in the water. A hundred lights—stars and electric bulbs—all reflected off the water, but something stood out: a single luminous red point. She strained her neck for a better look as if a few inches would help. Her patience had almost given out when the crimson light appeared again below the dark surface.

The small light revealed no further feature—it was a hidden blur within the man-made lake. It could have been some standard feature of the dam, or something intending to cleave it in half. As her chances of remaining in one piece shrank every second, Suzu descended. One foot lowered as sharp edges pressed into splitting finger skin. The next foot swung around, searching for the next edge but finding a clump of wet moss instead.

Lucette had just arrived at the scooter when she heard a distant splash against the dam wall. Her head snapped around. The trees obscured her view of the water, but only one possibility emerged. She ran straight to the shore, dodging dark trees and darker thoughts. *Did Mouba push her in? Can she climb out? Does she even know* how *to swim?*

Just as she thought to go back and get her light, she saw a figure dash out of the guard station. A tall man adorned in a blue uniform ran up the edge of the dam and shone his spotlight down to the water.

"No, no, no," Lucette begged as she watched a beam of light

scurry out across the waterline. It doubled back at the halfway point, focusing on lingering ripples by the wall. The guard immediately pursued the watery trail, weaving between benches while trying to keep his light on the impact zone.

A buffet of problems arranged themselves in front of Lucette as two more lights came from the opposite side. They moved faster than the guard—probably a steam-powered cart. Lucette stood on the shore, her fingernails digging into her palms. Her friend remained underwater, maybe drowning, and she was too far away to help. Would the guards save Suzu? Would they believe her or arrest her? Did she find something and just dive in? Lucette hoped the guards would only see a witless teenager hyped up on nine cups of smoked coffee, going for a night swim.

Lucette watched with relief as her friend finally emerged like a caught fish. Lights from both sides lit Suzu up as she treaded water. Voices skipped across the dam—authoritative men trying to speak over an authoritative young Lady. The guards repeated orders as Suzu lifted something out of the water. A small red light blinked as her voice screamed above every other sound, but Lucette couldn't make out what she was saying.

Lucette saw the guards scramble, bouncing between the cart and the crazed girl below. One of them brought out a rope and lowered it down to the water. It looked like a rescue, but the distorted voices sounded like a back-alley brawl.

Okay, Lucette, you should probably do something. Nothing reasonable came to mind.

With one arm holding the blinking thing—maybe a detonator— Suzu scampered up the wall while guards pulled on the line. Even with drenched shoes, she managed to vault onto the walkway. Security collapsed on her like boys trying to catch a loose dog. They separated Suzu from the flashing object and promptly forced them both to the cart. It took two guards to handle the Suzu as the third guard carried the object away from his body like a parent carrying a carsick infant.

Lucette's original idea to calmly tell the authorities vanished along with the cart, which left in a flood of obscenities to the far side of the dam. Lucette frantically debated options to explain the situation or attempt some kind of rescue. The boys' club certainly wouldn't be convinced by someone as young, female, and prismatically outfitted as her. She couldn't imagine breaking Suzu out of a professionally guarded holding cell either, but she also had no desire to stand on the beach and stargaze.

She sprinted back to her scooter, still hiding in shadow. The walkway gate remained locked, so she needed another way. Lucette recalled a bridge and access road well over a mile downriver, probably just as heavily guarded. The only other way, assuming her scooter couldn't float, was a narrow trail that wrapped around the reservoir. Dim lights dotted its path all around the shore, just inside the tree line. Luckily for her and the citizens of Chigou, it closed at dark.

She reached for her helmet, remembered she never took it off, and throttled up the chariot. Tires ground into the pavement before launching her through a bed of mulch and orange flowers. "Sorry," she muttered while carving a rut towards the trail entrance. She manually switched off the automatic headlight, wanting no attention towards her trail of fury. As soon as she entered the path, a dark hallway of trees closed her in.

Leaves and branches rattled off her helmet. The path faintly emerged under dim lights spaced out just above the ground. Her teeth chattered as small tires chewed through dirt and gravel. She silently thanked the grounds crew for keeping roots and rocks off the trail, as even one could fling her off the single-terrain vehicle.

Lifting herself off the vibrating seat, Lucette acclimated to the rough ground. Unlike traversing paved streets with clearly visible curbs and lawns, off-roading left no space for sightseeing. She dared to dart her eyes over for a second and managed to see a flash of headlights spinning at the far end of the dam. Her tire then slipped, and she forced her eyes back to the path. Trees continued to fly past while somewhere, uniformed men were likely forcing Suzu into a cage. She risked another glance: a small convoy turned, disappearing behind a bulky structure two stories tall.

The road, you idiot, her mind screamed. Her focus returned just in time watch her tire smash into a rogue root.

Everything jerked left, thrusting her center of gravity into dangerous space. She clutched the brake and flailed, fighting to turn straight. In defiance, the scooter lurched forward. Her own protective instincts took over as she tried to jump off the side and run to a stop. Her feet hit the trail, and she instantly fell victim to unforgiving physics. Her knees smashed against the ground as the scooter fell in turn, grating her against the gravel path. Pain shot through her wrists, and she prayed those luscious red riding gloves were doing their job.

The motor quaked against her leg, its heat seeping through her thick leather boots. She coughed out a lung full of dust and forced the scooter back up. Her hands throbbed as she raised them, hidden behind a shredded mess of glossy red and fibrous gray. *Better than my baby digits.*

Lucette felt too many aches to focus on one and not enough time to give any her attention. *Back up, back up. Don't even look at the paint job.* Her knees and back reluctantly obeyed. Moans and unintelligible swears were drowned out by the grinding of metal against gravel as she pulled the scooter upright, its engine still humming.

Back in the saddle, she lowered her head and torqued the throttle. A sudden torrent of wind cooled off her flushed face. Adrenaline pumped through her shaking limbs. She felt like a daredevil as she raced around the pedestrians-only track. The headlights across the reservoir had vanished, and she had no plan for when she reached the other side. If the guards believed her at all, they'd probably wire-type CEs. If they didn't, one or all of them could get blown into bits. The plan would come, thoughtfully or otherwise; she just needed to avoid being murdered by a tree in the next few minutes.

Lucette's eyes strained to avoid the relentless succession of murky obstacles. The path lights glowed just brightly enough for her to avoid disaster as long as she didn't look away. Every second felt critical as fatigue poisoned her muscles. At the north bridge, she dodged a young couple canoodling against the rail after hours.

"Park's closed!" she scolded them in a shrieking flash of red wind.

Lucette made it to the western turnaround just as her throttle hand seized with a cramp. She switched off the engine, pulled the clutch and let the scooter silently roll just shy of the gate. Luckily for her, it was blocking her way with only a single horizontal beam. Looking past the gate, she saw three structures, but only one with lights on.

Knowing her pathetic arm strength, Lucette begrudgingly conceded to sliding her scooter below the barrier. She grimaced at the sounds of gravel gnawing into cherry-red paint, adding to the evening's battle scars.

Suzu certainly sat somewhere in the second building, but Lucette had no intention of knocking on the front door. She walked her scooter around the building's lights and slipped up to the side. The windows were up high—too high to look in—so she leaned her scooter against the wall. Light poured out, along with muffled sounds. She climbed up to stand on the seat as the precariously parked vehicle wobbled against industrial siding. Her eyes peeked into the window as the front door slammed open.

Startled, Lucette's feet slid off the seat and she hung on the window frame. "No, no, no," hissed through clamped teeth. Her fingers began slipping as boots scrambled for the scooter. Foreseeing a disaster of Lady and scooter crashing together, Lucette kicked off the wall, let go of the window sill, and—to her surprise—managed to roll out and land in a squat.

With her head spinning, Lucette heard Suzu's voice cut through a guard squabble. Two male voices argued over the alleged detonator and the girl who had bubbled up from the reservoir. A panicked voice decided to cast the device into an industrial refuse container. A second person insisted Suzu be taken to the nearest Civil Enforcer depot. Neither gave Suzu's interjections any consideration.

She's getting locked up? Lucette wondered, her head clearing while still on the ground.

Before she could move, a guard ran around the corner. Lucette froze like an injured rabbit. Lungs and fingers clenched as the man sprinted past her and then away just as quickly. She rolled her head to see a frantic young man scurry in a straight line, awkwardly carrying something towards the rear of the building.

Lucette sat up on the open ground and watched. *Is that guy throwing a bomb away like a dirty diaper?*

Resting in the relief of her surprising evasion, Lucette turned as Suzu's snarling voice rang out a moment before being abruptly cut off by a vehicle's door slamming shut.

Lucette fought her way back onto two feet and towards the scooter. She managed to push it to the corner and peeked out. Truck lights popped on as an ignition boiler fired up. A few seconds later, the guard vehicle hauled her friend away down the eastern access road.

With aches still pulsing through her body, Lucette pushed herself forward on the scooter in a wide arc to stay in shadow. She thrust forward to gain speed as the vehicle zipped away. Nearing the building's end, she saw someone in an upper window looking down at the commotion. She throttled low and prayed the darkness hid her flashy sprint. The silhouette remained as she continued to glide. The guard vehicle shrank in front of her. She looked back up and saw the figure finally retreat. With a quick hop, she squatted down and punched the engine.

Cool air rushed through her sweat-drenched clothes. Keeping the headlamp off along the scarcely lit road, she followed the pair of red lights ahead. The terrain gradually angled down to an illuminated bridge about a mile away. Afraid to go any faster in such darkness, Lucette then saw the truck pick up speed.

"*Screws and sockets!*" Lucette growled as she dropped the throttle. She reached up and lowered her racing goggles—not that it mattered, since she couldn't see the accursed road anyways. Two minutes later, the illuminated bridge seemed to jump out at her. The truck had stopped at a gate across the Long Frost River. She squeezed the clutch and coasted across the bridge, swerving around more lights. She timed her stop perfectly as she grabbed onto a rear rail on the passenger side.

Lucette left the motor idle as the truck's large pistons easily drowned it out. She looked around and checked her position relative to any rearview mirror. Suddenly, a pair of eyes appeared in the truck's narrow port window.

Lucette's burst of fear quickly subsided—Suzu peered down at her. Through round goggles and a window, the two young Ladies assured each other that they were not alone. The gate went up and Lucette felt the truck begin to pull her forward. She fought to keep her grip on the rail as the truck's large tire buzzed barely a meter from her face. They cleared the gate and Lucette—desperately hiding into the shape of the truck—watched Suzu watching the guard. A few seconds later she saw Suzu nod; they were clear. The light of the bridge faded, and they watched each other's eyes until they fell into shadow. As the speed picked up, Lucette finally let go, fell back to a safer distance, and revved up her engine.

She kept Suzu in sight all the way to Chigou proper. The time gave her heart a chance to settle. She kept the front lamp off and found a surprising comfort in driving through the darkness. She remembered the guard's declaration and knew they were headed to a CE depot, but Lucette had no idea what she'd do when they got there. She needed someone who could navigate the inside of a Civil Enforcer headquarters. A friendly CE would be great, but Gozen would mean a long round trip—probably too long. Suddenly, someone came to mind.

Even a delinquent was better than nothing.

25
VISITOR

"Is Darou here?" Lucette asked.

Lady Kyoumére squared up to the flushed blonde suddenly standing in the doorway. "That is quite a greeting. I'm certain you didn't learn it from myself."

After a night bursting with espionage, Lucette's exhausted mind couldn't manage the topic of etiquette.

Lady K continued. "And why, may I ask, are you looking for that young man at such an hour?"

Lucette's jaw began to bob as if chewing an invisible pastry. "I... I can't believe I'm not coming up with anything." Lucette thought aloud.

"Such as a lie?"

"Y... ye... yes."

The silence, combined with the unusually quiet orphanage, reinforced just how late the night had become. Lady Kyoumére folded her arms, with one finger tapping like a metronome.

"Okay," Lucette relented. "Suzu is in jail, and I need to get her out."

Lady K stood perfectly still, aside from a pulsing vein on her neck. "I see."

"But don't worry, she's not in trouble. Well, obviously she is—she's in jail—but she stopped something bad from happening and *that's* why they arrested her."

"Arrested for being too good... Lady Suzu *would* be the one to manage something like that." Lady K looked up to the faded ceiling. "And I suppose you were planning on taking Lord Darou with you to advocate for our misunderstood adventurer."

Lucette's shoulders relaxed. "Lady K, you understand everything."

"Yes, well, we must bear our gifts as best we can."

Lucette noticed a thick lock of hair drift down across Lady Kyoumére's forehead, landing on a perfectly manicured eyebrow. Anything cockeyed on Lady K stood out, but to see her leave the flop of hair uncorrected induced alarm.

"Lady K, are…" Lucette considered very seriously the implications in accusing her orphan master of being bested by her orphanage. "…Are you… ya know, hanging in there… okay?" Lucette couldn't help but repeatedly eyeball the rogue bangs.

With uncanny elegance, the Lady finally took notice and threaded the loose hair back into order. She then clasped her hands together, waist high, and stood still in a beautiful posture of intimidation. "I always appreciate a thoughtful observation, but I assure you that if I *had* dropped from whatever it is I'm hanging on to, you would have walked into a swarm of little monsters juggling fiery dining chairs."

The suggestion spurred confusion, horror, and then a chuckle. When Lucette had first discovered Lady K's deft sense of humor, it had felt like uncovering an secret treasure.

"Lady K, after I pop Suzu out of the joint, may I treat you to some sunset tea? I'm studying chemistry now, so I'll be sure not to poison you." Lucette offered a toothy grin.

Lady Kyoumére tilted her head down with hopeful suspicion. Sunset Tea became an early Primichi favorite in parlors and cafés as a richly fragrant drink that was best left to culinary experts. A combination of spices and dried flowers—all unique to the valley—was added to hot water. There were two stages of steeping, and some ingredients were stone ground and stirred directly in. Lastly, mimi syrup was poured over whipped cream, which was then inverted on top of the tea, never homogenizing, forming a beautiful gradient of the same warm colors found in a Naifin Valley sunset. The combination of ingredients bloomed with a floral sweetness that would only last a short time before turning acrid. Although sublime, the requirement to start every serving entirely from scratch resulted in few people bothering with it at home.

"I always keep the necessaries stocked in the pantry," Lady K said with a nod.

Her simple words carried more weight than that which any professor could produce. Lucette felt excitement, as if she were finally crossing the threshold to adulthood. She understood the subtle invitation to join Lady K, not as the orphans' mistress, but as a mentor and a friend.

Darou came through the front door, immediately blanching as if he had walked into a Lady's washroom. "I'm sorry."

"No, no. We were anticipating your presence," Lady Kyoumére stated.

"You were?"

"Our young Lady Suzu has apparently been confined to... what's the term... *the cooler*, I believe," Lady K revealed.

"Suzu got locked up? Which Depot?" Darou asked.

Lady Kyoumére gestured to Lucette.

"Oh geeze..." Lucette's mind crawled with fatigue. "The... uhm... it's up North, just when you get into the city..."

"North Park Depot, in Doulan?"

"Uhm... yes," she chimed with realization.

"Pft, that's nothing. She's fine."

"It's prison, Darou. She's not fine," Lucette retorted.

"Technically it's a district depot, not a prison, and they have a bakery counter in the lobby. Now, if she were south in IQ, even downtown, *then* I'd be worried."

"Yes, well, we appreciate your insights, Lord Darou," Lady K said, "but we really can't be having our little Suzu locked away in any Civil Enforcer Depot, regardless of their pastry options."

"Okay, but what do you want *me* to do about it? I was only good at getting *inside* Depots, not getting someone else *out*."

Lady K replied, "You're a resourceful young man, and Lady Lucette is quite bright and charming. I'm sure you'll manage a reasonable solution."

Lucette and Darou shrugged in unison before heading towards

the door. "Oh," Lucette said to Lady K. "I'll be back for tea. Soon?"

"I'm heading right for the calendar," Lady Kyoumére said before disappearing into another room.

"So, what happened, exactly?" Darou asked as Lucette pulled him along by the sleeve.

"Suzu dove off the North Reservoir dam and found a bomb; details on the way."

○ ○ ○

The Barrel-Phón had become the popular choice of music player for aficionados with heavy bank accounts. Its complex, unified design enshrined Naifin ideals. A barrel of etched polymer transferred its perfect record of an orchestra's performance, smoothly rotating around a central speaker that projected every phonic nuance. Platter-Phóns were cheaper and the discs took up far less space, but their sound and preservation quality proved inferior according to anyone with the ear or hubris to say so.

Opaji recognized the Ósenique's final movement, *Rise of The Naifin Valley, IV - Rest Upon My Dream.* Óseniques were a particular form of high-performing art that had been developed in Primichi and carried into Chigou. A full orchestra accompanied any combination of drama, dance, or even acrobatics. The varied form tantalized audiences, and every performance would surprise with its particular combination of elements, melding into a comprehensive work. *Rest Upon My Dream* followed a triumphant third moment of acrobatic choreography with meandering melodies and a solo actor embracing their glorious creation.

The Barrel-Phón needle floated off its white cylinder which slowed to a standstill. Opaji sat in the immaculate listening room alone, basking in the cathartic afterglow and longing to experience it again. The wear of age filled his joints. He thought of a soaring city that had not existed at his birth. His entire adulthood had pushed and pulled a society into form, one that grew beyond what he could fully observe, both in expanse and detail. Could any man possibly do more?

He then wondered, "Have I ever truly lived in my own creation?"

With a burst of stubborn energy, he got up—bones creaking—and walked out into the central office. Expecting to see Mali Opree at her desk, Opaji instead found the secretary's seat empty. The lobby's restroom sat dark with its door open.

"Where could she possibly be?" Opaji asked himself before noticing the large wall clock; the time was well past midnight.

He sat down at her wire-type and plugged in her home number. "I should catch her before she goes to bed," he said with austere sincerity. He then began to type, *I wish to experience an Ósenique. Is* Rise of The Naifin Valley *currently being performed?*

The question revealed his ignorance, as Rise of The Naifin Valley had been performed for six years straight and showed no decline in popularity. Opaji waited a few minutes before sending the message again. After the fifth attempt, the wire-type printed out, *What day would you like to see a performance?*

His fingers tapped on the keys. *Tomorrow.*

He stared at the machine until its little gears began to spin again. *There is an early show tomorrow (today). I shall reserve you a room at Café Three Cats before the performance if you would like to eat prior. Goodnight, Lord.*

Opaji felt the buzz of youthful activity. In the morning, he would head streetside with no need to manage or maintain, criticize, or critique. His creation awaited, and he need only experience it.

o o o

"So, when exactly did you fly off the airship with a man strapped to your back?" The fresh-faced Civil Enforcer utterly failed to mask his amusement.

"Hrmph," Suzu grunted out. "I didn't *fly*, we descended on an emergency ballast balloon. And he wasn't strapped to my back. We were both... look, that's not important right now." After an adrenaline-drunk evening and then sitting for hours, Suzu's heartrate had finally slumped to a jog.

"Yeah, it's just that it's a rather complicated story you rattled off and I want to make sure I have it right for my report."

Suzu leaned out of her seat, noticing CE Moki's nametag. "And we can discuss it over sweets and smoked coffee later. I think the

café
Three Cats

pressing matter now is to focus on the blasted *bomb*."

"Just settle down… in the seat." Moki motioned her down with his hand. "Now, that explosive—*if* it's real—is quite a thing for a young Lady to stumble upon."

Suzu growled into her hands. "Holy *mountain*, can I just get to a wire-type and message Gozen? We are wasting so much time here."

"Who is that?" CE Moki asked.

"Lord Gozen. Lord Z." Suzu said, waiting for his recognition.

Moki's face remained blank. "I'm sorry… Lord Z?"

Suzu's facial muscles locked up. "Lord Z, only the most feared and respected Lord Enforcer to ever work southern Chigou…"

Nothing.

"*Blown boilers*, child, can I please get a *grownup* in here to talk to?" her inner curmudgeon demanded.

CE Moki—a recent graduate of the academy and barely into his first year of investigation—felt his ego wobble. He hadn't expected a young Lady, one who barely came up to his chest, to entirely dismiss his authority. "Most CEs are too busy taking real cases. You're lucky I even had the time to come in here."

"Yes, feeling so blessed this morning." Suzu rolled her eyes.

"So, is that all?"

"Only a conspiracy to destroy the dam just upriver of this entire city, evidenced by the detonator I discovered. Yeah, I'd say that's the crux of my story."

"Okay…" Moki got out of his chair. "I'm going to finish my report on this. It's probably going to take me a while, too," he complained while flipping through pages of notes. "You're certainly too young to go into a holding cell. I'll contact the local orphanage to send someone."

"An *orphanage* can't contain me," she snapped back as the CE shut the door behind him. The lock sounded like it belonged on a door three times its size. Padded walls sucked the intimidating noise away, surrounding Suzu with stuffy silence that her exhaustion nagged her to embrace. She hadn't eaten for twelve hours, hadn't slept in over twice that, and thwarting terror plots proved to be very tiring.

At least I got Mouba's detonator. Her Lansu was going to have a conversation with that grease-rag next time she saw him.

Captivity irritated Suzu, but her sore muscles begged her to succumb. She crossed her arms on the table and promptly buried her forehead into them. The darkness allowed her to remember Lucette, following by the dam and hanging onto a security vehicle. "I'll be right here, Lucette," she mumbled into the table. "No need to rush."

Out in the lobby of North Park Depot, a young couple wandered aimlessly, as if looking for someone to seat them. The Depot clerk surveyed them but didn't speak.

"Let's discuss our plan again," Lucette suggested, her voice low.

"We have a plan?" Darou muttered as his companion pulled him over to a moderately occupied waiting area.

As they sat down, Lucette noticed the multi-density, high-grade upholstery. She bounced up and down, unaccustomed to such supreme seating. "Wow, did they confiscate these from a bankrupt luxury hotel?"

"You'd think criminals would spend more time in Doulan if they knew how nice it was to get caught," Darou stated sardonically.

Lucette felt something tickle her nose as a sweet warmth floated into her nostrils. Her senses pointed to the far left, where a barista—adorably dressed in a matching striped apron-skirt and hat—stood behind a glass counter. "I thought you were kidding. I don't even have a bakery on my block."

"Well, I assure you it's no Izzy Kai." Darou noticed the Depot clerk finally lose interest. "So, are we just going to wait? I need some coffee. You want some coffee?"

"I want to sleep." Lucette rubbed her eyes. "Darou, how are we going to get her out of here?"

"Honestly? Just talk to the clerk and tell him the truth."

Lucette's sleepy eyes turned sharp. "Bounce this color parade over to that stink-faced Civil Enforcer and confess that I spent the evening trespassing to look for bombs up at the reservoir? Darou, I thought you used to be a *real* criminal."

"Lucette, I stole some useless garbage from a few ratty stores... *and* got caught. I'm not exactly a criminal mastermind. Besides, nothing is going to happen to her in here."

"Well, what if they take her somewhere else?" Lucette felt her fourth wind blow in.

"No. She's too young, and she looks even younger."

"But that mouth of hers," Lucette pointed out.

"Sure, but I bet they just send her back to the Tree House with an ankle bell." Darou looked longingly over to the barista pouring a dark cup of steam. "Hell, she might be back there already... eating breakfast."

Sleep deprivation did not increase Lucette's patience. "If I buy you a *wittle snack-ums,* will you finally get serious and help our friend?"

"Hey, I'm here, aren't I?"

"And ankle bell... did you make that up?"

His stomach growled. "It's this chunky ring they strap to your ankle that needs to be reset every day—or two days, whatever—or it makes this nasty ringing noise and won't turn off, no matter how many times you smack it."

"Painful memory?" Lucette sympathized.

"Are you serious? Because I'm ready to go snack or go home."

"Yes, pardon my delirium. Okay, okay... we should... uhm..." Darou cased the lobby. "How about you go keep the clerk busy and I'll see if I can sneak back and find our Lady?"

"How do I keep a Depot clerk busy?" Lucette asked.

"Well, you're very..." Darou looked Lucette up and down.

"Please, go on," Lucette requested.

"It's hard to ignore you when you're around. Even more so when you're talking."

"Oh," Lucette pondered. "I could take that as a compliment. See, I knew you were the man for the job."

"Great, let's hurry up so I can eat something." Darou got up and left.

Lucette sprung up and walked towards the clerk. She peered over at Darou, who meandered towards the bathroom. Lucette wondered if she should wait, but the Depot clerk had already locked eyes on her.

"What do you need, young Lady?"

"Well, I'm not turning myself in, if that's what you're hoping for," Lucette said, attempting a winning grin. The clerk's glacial expression remained intact. Lucette tried again. "Hello, good Lord. My name is Lucette and I'm looking for my friend."

"Is she missing?" the clerk asked.

"Missing from me? Yes." She set her cherry-red helmet up on the counter. "I am, however, somewhat certain that she is in this building."

"Has she been arrested?"

Lucette's answer hung in an open mouth while noticing Darou going into a custodial closet. "I'm not... what?"

"You're not certain?" The clerk sounded bored.

"I'm..." She saw Darou come back out with a *Wet Floor* warning sign, setting it down by the men's restroom. "...you see, she likes taking pictures in strange areas, not always places she's allowed to go. You know those creative types, right? Anyways, I didn't hear from her last night so I wondered... maybe..."

"If she got caught trespassing," the clerk offered.

Darou, with the ease of a CE who had worked there for years, sauntered behind an unmarked door. "I'm not sure what... no... yes, I do wonder if that very thing has happened."

The clerk, following her gaze, looked back briefly before grabbing a notepad. "Okay, what does she look like?"

"Angsty, all of the time," Lucette responded eagerly.

Suzu, face still pressed into her arms, tried to hide from the padded walls and sterile lights of the unsettlingly symmetrical room. She wanted to plot—tell Gozen, get some coffee, look for Mouba, find Kits—but sleep strongly seduced her. The depot didn't make her nervous, but she felt trapped, like a bully was pinning her down for a laugh.

With her eyes covered, Suzu's mind drifted to her parents— warm souls turned into cold bodies. She entered a memory where her home—her life—vanished. A giant man took her to a CE

Depot, where other CEs did grownup things more important than fixing her devastated life, a nightmare that was never supposed to be. Suzu wondered if she would ever wake up.

The door creaked open, too slowly for that anxious rookie. Suzu hoped for his superior, maybe someone with a daughter and pity for orphans. She detested playing for sympathy, but she hadn't the energy for a more dignified approach. Suzu raised her face, letting it stay sleepy and sad. Her eyes opened to a blurry assault of light. The door shut and a figure stood alone, someone young but not the rookie. Her eyes blinked the young man into focus. His sickly-sweet musk drifted over to her nose. It slithered up into her head and awoke the nightmare from its rest.

His voice rang out, corrupt and familiar. "You look surprised."

26
RESTRAINT

"Then again, maybe nothing can truly surprise us anymore." Kits's voice accosted Suzu's ears. Her mouth hung open in disbelief.

"We've been hooking into so many veins in this city it's become quite effortless to know when and where anything happens. Plus, I have a special alert on you, my constant assassin," he said.

Suzu hated his attempts to be personal.

"It's all *him* though, actually. He acts like he created this city." Kits's voice trailed off, unsure of his point. "I've been with Daimó half my life, yet the longer I'm with him, the more I realize I'll never understand more than just a fraction of him."

"That's great. I couldn't care less." Suzu felt her blood heating up.

"Mind if I..." Kits waved off his attempt at etiquette and sat down anyways. "You mind my entire existence, I know."

The padded walls suppressed all outside noises, emphasizing the sound of Suzu's lungs straining like old billows. She could lunge at her enemy with claws out, but it felt like a wall of glass separated them. Suzu had convinced herself that she wanted nothing more than revenge—to smash that table into a million pieces with his face—but history teased her with the idea it may never happen.

"I believe that you don't want to care, but you do; it's what you care about the most. It brought you to my apartment that night—fully intent on putting me to an end—and it's why you're locked up here in this room. But I know you're too smart to think I alone killed your parents—that I was anything more than Daimó's instrument. You only want me to get to him... because *he* is the root of your pain."

"Are you here to kill yourself and save me a step?"

Kits laughed. "I thought it was guilt—maybe it was, at first—but I realized I *can't* kill you, because I like you."

"You want me to puke on this table?"

His laughter drifted away. He went on, as if speaking to himself. "So then, why am I here? What motivation could I possibly have other than to torture you by flaunting my stubborn existence?"

"I won't remember a word you say, but I'm locked in here, and since I don't have my Lansu or a key, I guess I'm..."

"Oh, I'm quite certain you'll remember. Your single-minded fury makes you a bit foggy, so I'll gift you this one. I had... some... understanding of why Daimó asked me to kill your parents—to kill *all* of you, actually. It always seemed rather hasty to me though, especially for a man who seems to have an endless supply of patience—like he's living his third life." The usual smugness of his voice faded into an odd sincerity.

"As each sentence finishes, I can't even remember the beginning," Suzu said tauntingly.

Kits's sharpened gaze struck Suzu like a lance, but his voice sank at an oppressive thought of Lord Caton. "Not too long ago I discovered a photo of someone—a man who has recently come into my life—but I'm certain he's known Daimó for a very long time. He makes my existence feel obsolete to Daimó. This is a man who wouldn't hesitate to kill a little girl any more than he would a grown man."

"I assume everyone in your circle is a disgusting—"

"He was standing next to your father in that photo," Kits stated bluntly.

Suzu halted.

"And from what I could tell, this would have been quite a few years before you were made."

"You're lying," Suzu denied desperately.

"They stood right at the edge of Goraka, along with two other men who are likely dead, knowing that place. It's a simple image, one any layman would assume to be a few guys just leisurely camping. I looked at it for only a few seconds, but the connections emerged like a storm."

"My father only met Daimó the same night you killed them."

"And I've known Daimó half my life, but I hadn't even heard of this Caton until he showed up like a parasite, long after I met you. So don't feel bad. The photo would have utterly confused me if not for that moment I witnessed—Daimó, captivated by the words of that imbecile Victou, describing this thing he barely understood. The idiot didn't even find it himself—his *daughter* did." Kits leaned in as his eyes narrowed. "The first time I saw your father, he proposed a probe that could unlock limitless energy hidden beneath the Red Valley. All of those smug industrialists laughed it off—fools. Your father wasn't theorizing or working from nothing. He had seen a probe with his own eyes when he went into Goraka with Daimó's..." Kits stopped himself, stunned as the word *son* almost left his lips.

"That probe was my *father's design*. He didn't lie and steal, unlike all of you," Suzu snapped, letting her anger override her other emotions. She refused to cry in front of him.

"I don't disagree. I'm no engineer, but I could see that your father was brilliant. Even so, that idea didn't just drop from the heavens. He saw it and *then* designed one of his own. I can see now why he pushed so hard for it, but it must have been quite frustrating. He had seen the technology working, but who would believe the story? Forest phantoms... with cutting-edge technology."

The logic fought its way into Suzu's resistant mind.

"I possess no motivation to lie to you." His voice was calm. "I don't say this to give you solace—I know it won't—but I didn't *want* to kill your parents. I had no reason to, other than doing what Daimó told me, and only now do I understand *why* it happened. Daimó wanted that technology for himself, and your father wanted to share it with everyone."

"So, he's a monster and you're a coward," Suzu said flatly.

Kits sat still, appearing to allow the words to seep in. "You can't respect someone if they do every single thing you ask, never questioning, never needing a reason why."

"*I* don't respect you," Suzu added.

His smirk came back, but less cocksure and more that of a desperate man accepting his fate. "I thought being chosen by Daimó and sitting in his exclusive little circle gave me value, but I've been nothing more than a valet. He doesn't see me like he sees Caton."

The sudden silence made Suzu antsy. "I don't care, but who *is* this Caton?"

"Unfortunately for you, someone I'm sure you'll meet one day."

"You want to give me an address?"

Kits laughed dismissively. "I have my theories, but *I* don't even know who he really is."

"If he's in your little baking circle, I probably know enough."

"Hmm, tempting... truly." Kits envisioned Suzu gouging out one of Caton's eyes. "But you and I, we've endured too much to live for fantasy."

"Are you trying to be friends? Because I'm still going to rip your throat out."

Kits looked around at the industry-grade sound suppression and impact-absorbent wall panels. "Not much point getting violent in this room. We'd get exhausted before either of us managed to cause any real harm."

"I'd be willing to try."

Kits sat back, smiling. "I knew we could get along."

"I hate you more than I thought I could hate anyone."

"I believe in that hate, but you don't hate *me*. Your hatred is from your fear, and I'm realizing that you and I fear the same thing."

Rage buzzed through Suzu. "I have *nothing* in common with you."

"We're just orphans," Kits confessed, "our lives controlled by a man neither of us truly understands."

"I'll rip your tongue out!" Suzu's scream soaked into the thick walls. "You *made* me an orphan!"

"The only real time I had something I would describe as joy... peaceful joy... it got taken away. What truly aches now is admitting that even after he explained it, I still don't know why he forced Nia into that situation."

Suzu shoved the solid wood table, sending it into his chest. Kits's voice shifted awkwardly, clearly untrained in the art of honestly expressing emotion. "Tell me, Suzu, do you *really* know what Daimó is doing? Because... I don't."

Suzu sat stunned by the sadness in his voice. He looked as though he were about to cry.

"I assume you're here," he pointed to the interrogation table, "because you figured something out about Mouba and the dam... clever. I only found out the other day because I eavesdropped on a conversation. You know, Daimó *wanted* that dam built, just as your parents fought against it, and now he wants it destroyed." Kits looked up thoughtfully into the buzzing lights.

"I just need to stop him; I don't need to understand his dreams," Suzu said, putting his musing to an end.

"Hmm, yeah... maybe you don't," Kits said with an exhausted sigh, "but I do, and I need to enter the Valley of Death and prove it."

She was done. "Feel better? You can go now."

To her surprise, Kits stood up at her command. He straightened his shirt and took one step towards the door before shooting back one last question. "Little Chichimou—she's up at Kora, isn't she?"

Too exhausted to hide it, the answer was laid bare on Suzu's shocked face.

"I thought so," Kits sighed as he left, shutting the door behind him—with the heavy lock announcing she couldn't follow.

° ° °

In another part of the building, Darou lowered his head as a taller young man bumped his shoulder. A waft of cologne stung his nostrils. Darou felt the man pause and look back, but he had a mission to deal with. Projecting confidence and boredom—Darou figured—was the best way to avoid suspicion. He began scratching his temple and watched the curious man on the fringe of his vision. As a final tactic, Darou dug around his ear with a finger, and the young man finally left.

Although he had only been back there twice, Darou more or less remembered the Depot offices. Being arrested as a minor had involved a lot of time sitting in a chair, memorizing wall signs and desk knick-knacks. Continuing to soothe a nonexistent ear itch, he looked for a brooding young Lady dressed athletically in black. The array of cubicles only offered uniformed Civil Enforcers. One sharp-looking Lord Enforcer stood behind glass in an office at the opposite end. *Avoid that guy,* Darou warned himself.

With the entirety of the Depot's law enforcement ignoring him and Suzu nowhere to be found, Darou began to move. Although he had never had the pleasure, he remembered the interrogation rooms being down a back hall. Leaning to get a better look, he spotted a polished brass restroom sign gleaming down the hall.

As casually as he could, Darou moved to the reasonable target—the restroom, in case anyone asked. CE hands clicked on Wire-types, masking his maneuver. He made it safely past the outer row and reached the hall, which thankfully stood empty. Expecting some civic theater playing out in an interrogation room, Darou instead heard only the office noises behind him.

The first door stood unmarked; he reached down and cracked it open. Revealing only darkness, the door creaked open more until Darou saw an assortment of custodial tools—*idiot.* The next room had a small label reading *IR-1.* Ready to fake a full bladder if needed, he bobbed the door open and immediately caught a pair of eyes. An apology jumped to his lips but was blocked as he recognized Suzu.

"Hey, what are you doing?" a voice shouted from down the hall.

His eyes firmly locked with Suzu's. Darou wanted to reach out but broke away instead, turning towards the accusatory voice. "The restroom is being worked on, so they said to use the one back here."

The young CE scowled. "They what?"

Darou stood, legs clenched together, letting the inquisitor work it out.

"Why are they sending you back here?"

Darou couldn't say.

"It's behind you. Geesh, don't wet yourself. And go straight back to the lobby when you're done."

Darou promptly followed the instructions while leaving the door ajar. He took one step before the voice again reached out attempting an authoritative tone. "Hey. Shut that door."

Darou silently looked in, unable to acknowledge his companion or offer anything more. Suzu opened her mouth as her friend shut the door, no slower than he opened it. The door again landed its hefty weight. She clenched her shoulders anticipating the sound of the antagonizing lock. Instead of an industrial bolt ramming into place, however, she heard the unmistakable creak of a door that had failed to latch. She then felt cooler air seeping in.

Suzu pranced nimbly across the floor with practiced silence. Temple pressed against the door, she peered through the opening. Authoritative figures occupied themselves with piles of paper. Whoever had scolded Darou appeared to have been satisfied with his obedient performance.

Wasting no time, Suzu slipped out and glided straight to the bathroom, where she assumed Darou faked relief. She primed herself for a fifteen-second meeting to devise a plan to ditch the Depot and head straight for Kora. Instead, she entered and saw a towering Lord Enforcer washing his hands, standing right between her and accomplice Darou. Spotting his neck muscles tighten, ready to turn, Suzu spun behind a stall door, shutting it suspiciously fast. She then straddled the toilet, finding herself trapped in a cell a quarter the size of the one she had just escaped.

Two meters away, Darou became suspicious of the Lord Enforcer having a compulsive hand cleaning disorder. Their respective faucets flushed a volume of water that would make any Soran environmentalist cringe. Darou adopted a sudden concern for deep-cleaning the ridge of every fingernail, keeping at it until he stung a nerve. The Lord Enforcer finally stopped, activated the in-sink hand dryer, and gave the young man his direct attention.

With the obedience of a guilty child, Darou looked up to face authority.

The Lord Enforcer turned his head back to the stall where Suzu hid. His foot then came off the hand-dryer pedal as he looked down to his excessively clean hands. "Lord Jastou," he said, just loudly enough to be conversational.

Confused, Darou also looked down at his pinkish digits, waiting for the Lord Enforcer to permit his next move.

"They don't call him the Father of Modern Medicine for nothing. I wash my hands thoroughly at least seven times a day; I never get sick."

"Thank you, Lord," plopped out of Darou's mouth, passing any filter for authenticity. The Lord Enforcer easily accepted the reverence and left the young man to ponder his new gift of hygiene wisdom. The solid wood restroom door shut, signaling Suzu to step out and breathe.

"Another minute and my fingernails would've fallen off," Darou said.

Suzu had already turned her attention to finding an unconventional exit. "No windows. Looks like standard vent sizes, which I know I can fit through."

"You're going to crawl through the climate shaft?" Darou said doubtfully.

"Go to the corner... is Lucette with you?" Suzu pressed.

"She's probably still out in..."

"She has her scooter?"

"Sitting out front. You're not actually going to..." Darou gestured to the bolted-down vent cover, just as Suzu revealed a Toki he'd never seen before.

Suzu sprung up onto a sink. The Toki popped out a tool head and she began to remove the vent's retention bolts. "Meet me out on the corner. We need to move, fast."

Continuing his day of obeying perplexing orders, Darou promptly turned for the exit. "Whatever gets me peace and breakfast faster," he mumbled as Suzu's feet disappeared into the darkness of climate control.

Thirty seconds later, an anxious Lucette saw Darou emerge from the Depot's inner realm.

"Sorry to keep you waiting."

"No prob—"

He answered by grabbing her arm, giving the clerk a farewell grin, and promptly leaving the Civil Enforcers' den. Outside, Darou explained what little he could and moved them to the street corner. Lucette requested a better explanation, but Darou simply stared towards the Depot's rear until Suzu emerged and jogged straight to them. "Where's your scooter?"

"In a parking space, of course." Lucette gestured. "Which vent did you just squeeze out of?"

Darou and Suzu both swiped their hands across their throats, signaling a sharp suggestion to not use such language on the edge of Depot property. Suzu then leaned past them, looking for the scooter. "I need to get back to Kora. You two need to go to the Tree House and wire-type Gozen."

"I don't think that's possible," Darou said.

"What? Why?"

"I think it's broken."

"You have to go and try anyways."

"How are you getting to Kora?" Lucette asked.

"On your scooter," Suzu replied.

"Excuse me?"

"Take the Hotrail or a Bairide. If the wire-type is broken, go break into Jin's apartment... building, whatever it is."

"That won't be necessary. He gave me a key," Lucette said, blushing to the tip of her nose.

"What?"

Darou cut in. "Do we know *why* are we are doing all of this? Has that been said yet?"

Suzu looked ready to shoot off like a loose piston. "Kits is going to Kora to grab Chichimou."

"How would you..." Darou asked.

"He just told me," Suzu barked.

"In there?" Their eyes bulged.

"Yes, now give me your key."

"Oh, is that who I passed in there..." Darou said, thinking back.

Lucette, processing it all, raised her key in what felt to Suzu like slow motion. Suzu's body began to shake. "He's going to *kidnap* her and use her to find something in *Goraka*. Come on!"

Feeling little certainty, Lucette still obeyed. Suzu snatched the keys and sprinted to the blood-red scooter parked directly in front of the Civil Enforcer Depot. Two CEs gave her stern looks as she launched away.

Lucette turned her surprised face to her equally dumfounded friend. "I just let her take my scooter."

"You just had me break someone out of a Depot... with three Lord Enforcers," Darou added.

Lucette looked down the street as her frantic little friend disappeared around a corner. "Darou, I don't want anything to happen to her... or to little Chichimou."

"At least she's going to where Gozen is. I'm sure he can save us from… whatever it is we're doing."

27
FRACTURE

In a time of conflict, peace is a priceless commodity.

Gozen had heard those words when his first commanding Lord Enforcer had taken him out for a drink. Fresh out of CE Academy, he had clung to every sparse word his superior would offer. Gozen—still years from becoming the infamous Lord Z—had just witnessed his first death as a CE. A petty thief, fleeing Gozen, had carelessly darted across a street and met a six-wheeled carrier late with its delivery. Gozen had needed to guard the dismembered body until a clean-team arrived.

When two men had landed in full-body suits with hazard bags and an industrial steam scrubbers, Gozen had simply watched. He'd questioned his actions, rewriting the event a hundred different ways, imagining how he could have caught the man instead of chasing him to his death. His commander had seen it on his face the next day and met him at Long Frost Bar.

Peace—Gozen had confessed—*feels infinitely far away.* The commander had then suggested it was, in fact, the greatest—and rarest—commodity of all.

The morning sun still sat low in the sky, placing a warm halo around the entire valley while the mountains pulled back their long shadows. Gozen emerged from Neko, parked at Kora Farm, after a restless night. Suzu had scurried off with Lucette the night before for any one of a million possible reasons, and his mind couldn't stop sifting through them. He slid his hands in his pockets and let the sun's glow warm his face.

Gozen cherished morning's moment as the world around awoke slowly. Crops swayed in the breeze while Kojo prepped harvesters near a silo. Even after a full night of silence, morning solace so often felt needed. Birds chirped from the fields and trees, lifting his sleepy mind with their precious song.

A "thank you" floated from his lips.

Gozen meandered to the front door, hearing only muffled sounds from the kitchen. He walked through the empty dining room and saw Clora perform the dance of the provider, with floured hands and utensils lying in wait. Signaled by floorboards creaking under her generously sized friend, she turned to him and pushed a spare smoked coffee to the counter's edge.

He took the coffee with a nod and a grin, making it up the stairs and continuing down the hallway. The end held another set of stairs that led up to the tower. Squeezing through the ceiling door, he found himself above the house on a large circular perch. Kojo had helped build it to keep an eye on the farm—and beyond—as it offered a spectacular view of the countryside.

The platform had a modest perimeter wall that offered some security without obscuring the vista. Kojo had put a chair up there for a time until he had fallen asleep once and nearly tumbled over the side. Gozen stood, relaxed, holding up the mug with copper trim that glowed from the peeking sun. Steam enveloped his first, slow sip. Distant cars and freight vehicles carried out their commute across Long Frost Road. A few airships drifted through the clouds.

He saw a small cloud puff into existence by the farm's entrance and grabbed a collapsible monoscope set on the ledge. A smaller vehicle stopped by the entrance near the river. They had been keeping the small drawbridge closed in a cautious decision that felt in opposition to Kora Farm's identity. A mechanical geo-code box offered either side a means to activate the drawbridge.

Gozen expected to see Suzu, Lucette, and a scooter emerge from the dust cloud, but as he focused, a black pedestrian-vehicle came into view. A sun-flare gently bounced off the roof, obscuring the scene until a cloud rolled in and flagged the light. A tiny flash then appeared.

Recognition fired through his senses in a jazzy, broken beat.

The impact stung his chest, followed by the devilishly sharp whisper. Gozen felt his torso thrust backwards as the crackling sound finally echoed past. His back hit the wood platform as sensation seeped from his body. The signs were all clear and he knew what had happened—and who had done it. He wanted to yell: *Clora, Kojo, Kits, here, gun.* It all came an instant too late. Cool morning air strained through his lungs as glowing clouds passed overhead until fading into still darkness.

"Thought it'd take more than that," Kits mused in relief, dropping the drawbridge with his telephoto capture of the geo-code. He rapidly detached modifiers from his pistol as he reentered the Móstique. Kits looked across the width of the farm as the drawbridge landed. The car shot off in a burst of dirt and gravel. He cut through the quiet farm and went straight for the house, hoping his key to Goraka slept calmly in a room upstairs.

The main threat lay motionless atop the house, but a list of potential hazards remained. Kojo was old but leathery tough; he absolutely owned a gun or two. Kits saw no elitist vehicle, but Jin could have gotten a ride or parked in a silo—a pest more than a threat. Farmhands could trickle in, but Kits doubted their commitment or, at least, relied on their hesitation. He didn't plan on staying long.

Spewing gravel, the Móstique spun around to park for a quick getaway. Kits ran to the front door and swung it open. He stepped in with practiced caution, checking corners with senses primed. Sounds brought him into the kitchen where he found Clora wielding a recently sharpened paring knife.

"I know you're brave enough to scream out and warn the others..." he said behind the barrel of his gun, "...but I don't think your husband would survive long if I had to shoot you here. The good news is, I'm not going to kill anyone that I don't *have* to." Kits allowed the words to settle in for a second. "Where is little Chichimou?"

Clora was as still as a stone pillar. He promptly backed towards the stairs and saw her protective flinch to stop him. Spotting the only tell he needed, Kits reached behind his back. With no desire to kill an old woman, he lunged a stun baton straight at her. Clora winced and fell back as she took a full charge of the wand. She rolled down and collapsed to her side. Designed for incapacitation, the CE-issue stun baton offered little injury while keeping its target incapacitated for a few minutes.

Kits progressed straight up the stairs, gun and baton ready. He checked the first door on the left—empty and perfectly in order. The next room hit his eyes with bright colors, framing a young girl standing by the far wall. Kits checked the entire room before lowering his weapons. "Good morning, Lady Chichimou. Is your father around?"

She stood with a silence that Kits couldn't interpret. He wanted to ask more but knew Victou to be a capricious, albeit lucky, fool. She probably didn't know her father's location any more than Kits did.

He walked up, careful to project as little aggression as possible—time permitting. Kits kneeled down, meeting her at eye level. "I know this is very sudden, but we need to go somewhere you've been bef—" Sounds from downstairs stole their collective attention.

Kojo had burst past the door, firmly holding a hunting rifle he hadn't fired in over a year. His eyes jumped around, but his heart pulled him straight to his wife, moaning from the kitchen. He ran in as fast as his weathered knees would allow. His lovely rolled onto her back, her arms shaking. Kojo went to brace her, carefully letting the rifle lay on the floor. "Clora," he murmured, pained, while he checked her for any more signs of injury.

"Ch... Chi..." stumbled out of her mouth.

Kojo ran his hands down the sides of her face. "What happened to you?"

"I'm... okay," Clora forced out, embracing her husband's care while trying to push him onward. "He's here..." It hurt to breathe. Her body cramped as she forced it to comply. "...upstairs... for Chichi."

Kojo felt dread flood through his gut. His glance shot back towards the stairs as his shaky hand grabbed the rifle. Aching legs pushed his body up. He checked his gun, raised it, and maneuvered towards the stairs.

"Please... careful," Clora pleaded from the floor.

Kojo worked up each step with rattled caution until the second floor appeared over the gunsight. He didn't hear anything suspicious, not a single sound except his creaking steps. The rifle shook, bouncing between doors. Kojo headed for Chichimou's room and forced open the door, sliding his trembling finger just off the trigger. Ready for the nightmarish sight of an innocent girl taken hostage, he instead saw her sitting in the corner. She looked startled but nothing more.

"Where is he, darling?" Kojo forced calm into his voice while taking a step into the room.

Chichimou released one of the hands wrapped around her knees. Anxious eyes followed her fingertip as she pointed straight up. Kojo looked to the ceiling before realizing what she meant. "Up the stairs, on the roof?"

The young girl acknowledged this with a bob of her tiny chin. Kojo stepped back to the empty hall and looked down to the end. The tower perch door sat open, letting sunlight spill in. He never kept that door open and wondered, *Where's Gozen?*

o o o

His body felt fine, but not quite right. Jin had dodged the training bag six consecutive times—the last two just barely, but he worried his success came from routine more than reaction. His mind was crowded with thoughts, like a naive boy in his first month of Maiishi training. More and more, he felt that Lord Shirér was right—he was too slow. Jin tried to *think* his reflexes faster, but that idea seemed increasingly idiotic.

His neck cracked as it whipped around. *Was that a firearm?* The sound certainly matched, although his heightened paranoia towards firearms also presented a likely culprit. He remembered reading about the ability of a traumatic event to affect one's psyche, comprehensively explored in *The Lingering Experience* by Lord Jastou. He got up too fast, became lightheaded, then walked to the door.

His silvery eyes squinted as the sun found a hole in the cloud cover. Jin listened for hunters or a frantic flock of birds across the river, but only hazy blips of traffic seemed to move. He stepped to a patch of grass and felt a sudden cramp from lingering injury. His lungs ached as he attempted a long, controlled breath.

Jin glanced at the back of an Aya Motors C23, mostly covered and sitting in the vehicle silo. His father—or more likely, his father's secretary—had finally shipped it over. Jin had contributed impressions towards the sporty coupe based on his modifications of the C22 that he had abandoned in the Red Valley. "Did I actually hear a gunshot?" Jin felt confused by the farm's continuing stillness.

He then saw a particular sedan parked at the house like an out-of-place shadow and his heart nearly stopped. Jin's feet snared into gravel as every sound was amplified in his head. Suddenly he felt very exposed. His eyes searched again for a hunter, one disinterested in any wild animal. A shape emerged above the house. Jin took a step forward, squinted, and a sickening sight resolved. Kits pulled Kojo up on the tower floor and held him to the edge. Without thinking, Jin began to run.

Every other sound vanished. Jin's vision funneled onto Kojo being pushed against the shallow wall, nine meters above the stone patio. The old farmer fought with his usual grit, but the young assassin proved too capable. The red sun flared off Kits's glossy pistol. Kojo was spun around, holding his hands out like a hostage, wedged between two quick deaths.

"*KITS*," Jin boomed.

The two grappling men diverted their attention to a blur of fine apparel sprinting towards the house below. Kojo felt the pressure of the gun release from his back. His mouth opened to warn Jin as a black barrel slid over his shoulder like a cold, metal snake. "He has a..." he started to shout as a deafening storm burst into his right ear.

Jin felt the familiar little demon smash into his ribs, stealing his breath. His legs buckled. His hands plowed into the gravel drive.

Above, Kits gripped the back of Kojo's jacket. The old farmer could barely stand from the pain of his ruptured eardrum. Expecting Jin to collapse, he instead saw the persistent prince stand and, hand to his side, stumble into a run.

"How many times do I need to *shoot* you?" Kits snarled.

Jin felt a fire spreading from his chest. Pain vanished into numbness, however, as he saw Kits shove his hostage off the tower. The old farmer descended headfirst towards dirt and stone.

Jin's legs raged forward, fueled by caustic adrenaline. In the second before impact, he dove into Kojo's shoulder, forcing the dense body to pitch. The two tumbled down in a violent collision of limbs and dirt. Kojo screamed out in pain. Jin still fought for air as the weight of a career farmer pinned him against the ground. The world faded away at the edge of his vision.

Then Kojo rolled over, allowing a searing burst of oxygen to fill Jin's lungs. Jin squirmed loose and rolled onto his knees. Kojo's stout body writhed on the ground.

Oxygen and adrenaline pumped through Jin, who wanted nothing of civilized doors and stairways. He scaled the ledges and gutters like a wild animal. Kits stood above, calmly loading another round. The gun clicked in the same instant the demon-eyed Jin vaulted the railing and clutched Kits's wrist.

Kits flung a fist, then an elbow, but landed neither. He struggled to free his weapon hand but immediately discovered a critical error. He had assumed that Jin's luxurious childhood had given him a backbone of cream-soaked brioche. Every attempt to gain an advantage found Jin's obnoxiously perfect counter. Kits funneled all his focus on the gun, leaving himself open for a takedown. Jin centered his mass and began to flip Kits over but anchored his foot on Gozen's thick, lifeless leg. His ankle instantly twisted. Grunts heaved out and the two men crashed down.

Counting on his leverage to finally break the gun loose, Jin instead found himself pinned awkwardly over Gozen's knee. He maintained his grip on Kits's wrist, but fatigue and a sharp reminder of his growing assemblage of wounds began to burn off his strength. Jin struggled to get some kind of position but failed to even squirm in the vice of limbs. Kits leaned towards him, hard.

The gun's barrel crept around like encroaching magma, ready to burn and destroy. Jin continued to push back but felt the chilling reality: he couldn't stop it.

○ ○ ○

Suzu failed to notice that the overheating engine had cooked her legs pink. The small drawbridge lay flat across the river, as it typically had done every day before Nia had been chased down into Goraka. The once-welcoming display had been abandoned in favor of caution—Gozen had refused to let it stay down. She knew Kits had beaten her to Kora Farm.

The crimson scooter rattled across the bridge. Suzu strained her eyes and gripped the throttle as if it were Kits's throat. The silos came into view, then the farmhouse. A harvester drove a typical route at the northern edge of the farm—not that the driver would hear anything over that raucous machine. Neko's trailer appeared next over the slope, and finally the villainous black car.

She released her death-grip on the throttle and killed the engine. The soundscape collapsed and she sharpened her hearing as the scooter rolled to a stop. She ran up to the soot-colored car— empty. A horrible grunt then yanked her attention towards the farmhouse tower. Even twisted in desperation, the unmistakable voice still carried its ceaselessly posh tone. She almost pushed off to attack, but a flash from something in the car grabbed her eye.

In the Móstique's back seat, the symbol of Suzu's deepest guilt and failure sat alone. So many seasons had passed since she had lost Nia's precious DaiLansu, but the image was forever burned into her memory. Suzu had stolen it from her mentor—her sister— and the assassin had stolen it from both of them. Her vision tinted red, funneling in on the idle weapon. She could taste iron on her tongue. Suzu reached in, opened up her hand, and reclaimed it.

○ ○ ○

The gun's tunnel of endless shadow pushed forward, revealing the black eye of inevitability. Jin felt small and scared. He then saw tendons and veins contract on Kits's trigger finger. Silently, Jin called out to his mother. The hazy perimeter of his vision closed in, barely revealing a movement of shadow down the roof. Kits grinned and prepared to finally remove the prince of interference, but he noticed those silvery eyes make one last glance past him.

Suzu's feet charged with sinister silence across the hot tile. She spotted the struggle, and more importantly, the back of Kits's head. She launched up and twisted the handle. Black metal ends jumped out to attention, positioned for a full strike. The early sun cast her shadow across the tangled pile of men.

Kits turned his head and instinct pulled his right hand off the gun. It swung up between his face and the diving metal bar. Suzu struck down like brimstone, her mouth declaring every promise of vengeance and death. Bone cracked against tempered steel. She continued her roar, trying to push that staff straight through Kits's arm and into his skull.

Kits lay sandwiched between his two opponents as Suzu continued to spray him with screams and spit. She reared up, confident in her position, and took a strike that Nia would have called greedy. Kits used the open beat to twist away with the gun, making room for Suzu's gluttonous strike to land squarely on Jin's chest. Suzu ignored his pitiful grunt and maneuvered for a faster follow-up strike, but her eyes caught the lifeless face of her guardian angel.

After her parents died, Gozen had become the beacon for her fragile hope to follow. The sudden image of his body pinned down and inert under a struggle between foolish boys sucker-punched her soul. Shock swelled into rage, fueling another strike, but Kits had the only spare second he needed.

Turning his head and holding his breath, Kits raised the handle of his gun. Jin immediately identified a tiny hatch open on the weapon but had no breath in his lungs to warn Suzu.

An explosion of vapor enveloped the group. The shock caused Suzu to gasp and suck the toxic air into her lungs. Her throat seized, and her eyes flooded with searing tears. She swung wildly at Kits whom she could feel slithering away. His groans of bone-shattered pain disappeared down the stairs, but Suzu couldn't follow; the gas had her nervous system running like a panicked crowd.

"Where is he?" she rampaged out between gags, demanding an answer from whoever remained alive on the roof. Suzu's eyelids rammed up and down like pistons, trying to flush the poison out.

Someone moaned below. She felt around and clutched the expensive fabric that certainly belonged to Jin. "WHERE IS HE?"

"Chi... Chichi" barely escaped his struggling lungs.

Light and shadow began to sharpen, allowing Suzu to find the stairs just as the front door to the farmhouse slammed open. She doubled back to the tower's wall and saw a little person being dragged towards the black car. "Don't you take her, you monster!" Her demand carried all the way to the mountains, but Kits ignored every word. Before she could even manage to stand, captor and captive had vanished in a roaring cloud of dust.

Leaning over the wall, Suzu finally saw Kojo's blurry body on the ground. Her heart cracked to the verge of critical failure. After years of struggling to revive her life, she had watched the same killer decimate it again in mere minutes. She cursed all the hope she had allowed herself to feel, the hope that made her pain now unbearable.

The DaiLansu slipped from her hand, followed by tears and everything else that mattered to her. Her family had taught her to care for the world, but she didn't understand what the world wanted from little girls, nor what it gained from offering them so much pain.

"Chichi" again wheezed out of Jin's mouth. He labored to sit up, feeling as if every other rib had snapped, fighting demands from his body to lay still. Suzu looked broken and defeated—just like him. Their eyes met as he crawled to the stairs. "Chichi," he repeated, as if his mind couldn't manage a second word.

Jin looked across the horizon and saw a fading trail of dust. Victou came out from the southern Bollo orchard, walking with ignorant curiosity. *I need to tell her father.* His thoughts halted in the pile of trauma that surrounded him. He wondered how many times one could be shot and survive—a number he had plausibly just surpassed.

Suzu failed to reconcile what lay before her. Gozen couldn't look so weak, not him. She had seen it back in that alley behind Kits's apartment. Even with a knife in his side, Gozen had managed more strength than any two men combined. Suzu knew the forgotten children of the city still needed him. She still needed him.

"I think he's dead," Jin whispered.

"One bullet can't kill Gozen," Suzu said. "Don't be so stupid."

Jin accepted her denial and wished they had time to grieve.

Suzu stepped over Gozen's chest, which nearly came up to her knees. Blood soaked a small hole just below his shoulder. It looked tiny and insignificant compared to the mass of the man. Suzu knelt next to his head. Her small pale hands reached down and held his face.

"Just wake up." She spoke too softly for Jin to hear. Down below, Victou unloaded his confusion towards Clora, who had managed to get outside and was frantically struggling to explain what Kits had done to Kojo and Chichimou.

Jin was dumbfounded, unable to prioritize their next steps. "Suzu…"

She ignored him, still watching Gozen. "You just need to *wake up*," Suzu's voice flared. She remembered her parents' cold hands in the soft glow of the morning sun. She just needed them to wake them up.

Jin inched forward as Suzu's hand swung down and struck Gozen hard on his chest.

"*Wake up!*"

"Suzu…"

"I know you're not dead!" She hit Gozen again. "You wouldn't abandon us. You wouldn't abandon *me*!"

Seeing Gozen's lifeless body tore at Jin's gut, but Suzu's stubborn denial felt worse. She hit Gozen again, and Jin, feeling the pain of every strike, had an impulse to pull her away.

"Stop lying there and *wake up!*" Her hand swung down and smacked Gozen hard across his lifeless face.

Another hand reached out and grabbed her wrist. She tried to tug it away, but her arm felt like it had been buried in cement.

She looked down at the still-closed eyes of her caretaker, just as his mouth moved. "Why are you slapping me?"

"Because we have serious business and you're taking a *nap*," she snapped with relief. Prying her arm loose, she stood and squared up to Jin. "And *you*, are you just going to let that *snake* take Chichi?"

Jin's mouth hung open as Suzu stormed straight past him and down into the house. He looked back at the retired Lord Enforcer's return to the living. Gozen looked at the small hole in his chest as if examining a missing button. "This one stings a bit."

"*This* one?" Jin's eyebrows raised. "How many times have you been shot?"

Gozen finished pressing around his entry wound before fixating on Jin's torso. His eyes narrowed as he leaned forward. Jin stood still, suddenly self-conscious about the state of his attire and flashing back to his mother examining him before guests arrived. A particularly unfeminine finger then prodded Jin's vest before plucking out a small bit of metal.

"How many times have *you* been shot?" Gozen countered.

"Three." Jin rubbed the deep indent in his side with a twisted expression. "I thought to incorporate an experimental industrial fabric into a day vest. My family's company is developing it with Tiké Textiles to mitigate the number of laceration and puncture wounds our employees receive."

Gozen rubbed the curious fabric. "You didn't want to give *me* one of these?"

"It's a prototype. I haven't properly completed testing."

"Field test passed," Gozen said, flicking the spent round over the rail to the ground below.

Suzu rejoined them atop the tower. "Are you two coming or what? Kojo's hurt and Victou's freaking out."

"Jin made a vest that stopped a bullet," Gozen explained.

"What?" Suzu squeaked out. "Where's mine?"

"It's a prototype. Also, I may have a broken rib." Jin took in an exploratory breath.

Suzu grabbed Gozen's hand to yank him up, leaning back as if pulling a fence post out of the ground. Horrendous grunts escaped the giant as Jin jumped in to keep the hulking body from tipping over the short wall.

Gozen sucked in air still laced with noxious gas. "I'm good, I'm good," he coughed. "But where's Kits? What happened?"

"He took Lady Chichimou," Jin informed him.

"And pushed Kojo off the tower," Suzu added. "Gozen, I think he's really hurt."

Gozen thought of the last time he had encountered Kits, a hand squeezing around Kits's throat. The memory sickened him—regret at his restraint—but he'd had more than enough practice dealing with those kinds of choices. "Do we know where he's taking her?"

Jin shook his head, but Suzu nodded. "He's going to use her to steal one of those probes the creatures use to find thermal pockets in Goraka."

Jin and Gozen were stunned at Suzu's certainty.

"Victou was actually right," she continued. "Kits confessed as much about an hour ago at the North Park Depot."

"He talked to you?" Jin asked.

"The North Park Depot… Were you *arrested?*" Gozen wondered at the same time.

"Yes," she replied, "and we're running out of time. I'll explain in the truck."

The battered group went down to meet the others. Twice Jin and Suzu had to brace Gozen, who phased into dizziness; it felt like propping up an industrial boiler.

Outside, Clora fought back the tears falling onto her husband. He was contorted in pain and barely able to speak. Suzu ran up as Jin and Gozen ordered in unison, "Don't touch him."

"He needs help," Clora pleaded, confused at their sudden agreement.

"His legs aren't moving," Gozen observed.

"He likely has a spinal injury. Moving him could cause more damage," Jin warned.

"But we can't just leave him..." Clora argued.

"You must brace his entire back and neck before moving him.

We can use slats from the workshop. I'll wire-type Doctor Moutsu from North Chigou Medical Academy of..." Jin's voice faded as he ran off to apply things he had absorbed from his mother's dynasty of medical celebrities.

Clora's face quivered, revealing a strong spirit on the verge of fracture.

"Jin will get the best doctor in the city," Gozen reassured her as her shaking fingers clinched onto his sturdy arm.

She accepted the faint hope before her grip tightened, filled with fear and heartbreak. "He took her."

"We'll get her back," Suzu promised with grit, still rubbing her eyes. She then confronted Victou, watching helplessly nearby. "Where were *you?*"

"Helping with the farm," Victou explained with panicked grief. "How did he get in the house?"

"Doesn't matter now," Suzu said, and squeezed Kojo's hand before springing back to her feet. She looked ready to sprint straight to Goraka. "Can you drive?" she asked Gozen.

Only then did Clora notice the bleeding hole in Gozen's shirt. "Gozen, you need a doctor."

"Soon," he said. "I can drive... as long as someone stays in the cab with me."

Jin ran back out of the house, carrying an expensive but otherwise nondescript case. "I corresponded with Doctor Moutsu's receptionist. He'll depart promptly." Without waiting for any confirmation, he ran straight to the vehicle silo.

"Where is he going?" Gozen asked.

Legou and Joushi, who had been harvesting in the west orchard, emerged from the trees with stupefied expressions. They slowed as their path crossed Jin's.

"Gozen and I got shot. Kojo fell off the roof," Jin said quickly as he jogged past them, as if the information warranted no further discussion.

The two young men ran up to the house as Suzu hopped out of the misshapen huddle. "Stay with them," she ordered, pointing at Clora and Kojo.

"Are we being invaded by mountain pirates?" Joushi asked with shock across his face.

"Who did this? Legou wondered, his head clearly spinning. "And are they still here?"

"Just *stay* with them. A doctor is coming," Gozen grunted as he stood back up and followed Suzu to his truck.

Victou hesitantly followed behind. He felt fear for his daughter and ignorance towards whatever plan already seemed to be underway.

Suzu saw Jin pull out of the silo in the newly delivered convertible C23. "We can't all fit in that, Jin," she shouted towards the open window of the vehicle. "We're taking Neko—" She paused as she watched Jin pull up to the open trailer of Gozen's hefty freight vehicle. The car backed up onto the loading ramp and slotted into the back, missing either side by a foot.

Jin killed the engine and crawled to the back. Suzu jumped onto the trailer, now clogged with a waxed coupe. "How much are you planning to take? Are you going to put a bike in the trunk next?"

Jin suddenly froze, as if he had become stuck in time. The stasis lasted until he casually broke free and dug into a pocket. A palm-sized object came out and he handed it straight to Suzu. "Here, this is yours."

A memory fired like a bullet in Suzu's mind. Jin's pale hand cradled the last gift Suzu's father had ever made for her. "Why… *how* do you have this?"

"I received it from Lady Chichimou."

"What? Why would *she* have it? And how long have *you* had it?"

Jin wanted to get back to his preparations. "She gave it to me at the Northern Orphanage… the Tree House."

"Yes, I know what it's called. So, why do you have it?"

Deeming the conversation unnecessary, Jin nevertheless continued. "I… she found it, I don't recall where—probably the orphanage or maybe here—I truly do not recall. But I have had it for many months, since for a time our paths remained distant. Certainly, a fragmentary time, but I no longer wish to possess it."

Suzu stared at the Toki as if being dared to pet a Shiroku. Jin had to repeat himself—"I *no longer* wish to possess it"—before she finally snatched the device out of his hand. It looked pristine and well cared for. She remembered the last time she had held it, and then smashed it into a dresser because it could never replace the person who had made it. It rejuvenated the collection of decaying memories she so desperately clung to. The exquisite timepiece still worked, but she recalled her failure to deduce its special. She dug at the precisely machined edges, hoping time would graciously give her insight. The second hand merely clicked away.

Jin's hand then came in and gripped the edges of the device oddly, pausing for her to see where his fingers landed. With a sudden twist, the face opened up and emitted a soft glow. "I now remember how long it took me to decrypt the lock. However, I never deciphered the source of that glow." Jin again went back to work.

Suzu's eyes fixed on the faint light, and she found herself listening, as if the voice of her father spoke through it—something forever lost, somehow returned. The words *thank you* began to build in her throat as Jin cut in with a wincing sigh.

"As we were, then—yes, yes. So, if he is taking her to Goraka as we assume…" Jin placed a large attaché case on the C23's trunk. He clicked the latch open and revealed a silent firework of polished metals and wood reflecting the sun. An impressive array of gadgets sat in precisely carved pockets, like a tiny posh hotel for pretentious Tokis.

"Preparing for the unknown?" Suzu asked.

The look on Jin's face suggested he had little more understanding himself of what they were about to attempt. His gaze seemed to reach far away into another place or time—a setting of darkness. A memory emerged of his previous car, rotting away in the depths of the forest. He imagined Nia and what her body must look like, perhaps still there, alone, cradled by the infinite density of life and death. His dry throat scratched as he tried to swallow.

"If we're going into the Red Valley, it doesn't matter what we take. We won't be prepared."

28
GRAVITATE

Red light bloomed behind the troupe, which was descending in a swirl of limbs. They clung to expansive lengths of fabric that wrapped and unwrapped the acrobats in a vertical ballet woven throughout the entire third act. The orchestra had been building their crescendo in a laboring scale that stepped with such restrained effort that the final note wrung a tear of catharsis from half of the audience.

Like every moderately wealthy patron who filled the auditorium, Opaji applauded with an elated grin and misty eye. His box seat had been discretely arranged by Lady Opree that morning, accompanied by one Sentinel who occupied the back of the private balcony.

The founder of Chigou had long since memorized the music, but experiencing the performance live had offered him a second honeymoon with *Rise of The Naifin Valley*. The crowd's energy washed over him in a joyful wave towards the story they saw and the reality they lived in. Standing above it all, Lord Opaji felt as if he could see the entirety of his creation. Unlike the view from his glassed-in penthouse, he could hear the sounds and smell the aroma of his living creation.

He turned to his private Sentinel. "I'd like to get something to drink..." The guard darted into the hall and summoned a valet, but Opaji raised his finger and spoke with revelatory magnitude, "...in the lobby—the general lobby." The Sentinel raised both eyebrows.

Everyone in Chigou knew the name of its founder. Children read about Lord Opaji throughout school, and adults referenced him in conversations about economy or industry. Few had a clear memory of Opaji's face, and all who did had gotten those memories from a select few photographs, none of which had been taken within the past ten years.

The few looks Lord Opaji got as he stood on the side of a landing came from him having a stone-faced man standing beside him, civilian-dressed but with a bodyguard's posture. A few found Opaji's face familiar, but not a single individual could place it out of context, floating in a lobby filled with commoners. Pressed suits and shimmering gowns drifted between conversations, alcohol dispensaries, and brass closets where an attendant would assist those in need of relief from excessive refreshment.

"That line over there, is that where one may get a drink?" Opaji asked.

A backlit sign notified the entire lobby where to find cocktails. Multicolored neon strips funneled down from the ceiling into an Ósenflute glass. Its shape fit snugly in an armrest's glass holder while still having the temperature barrier and elegance of a stem. A similarly elaborate light fixture showcased the stemless glass used for aged cheeses, smoked meats, small, pickled vegetables, or any other fine snack that generated little noise; Chigoans shared a pride in their ability to eat precious foods in absolute silence. The remaining lobby had elevated Po'Kin architecture, painted landscapes, and lit tubes trimming the space in warm light. An appropriately dramatic chandelier hung from the room's center.

"Yes, let us get a drink," Opaji energetically suggested to his silent companion, who had given a succinct nod.

Heading down the stairs and through the crowd, Opaji found a clear path between those either honoring age or fearing broad shoulders. A few gazes latched onto Opaji, but after a lifetime of running one city or another, he had become numb to celebrity. "Everyone is in fine spirits," he notified his guard, who scanned the room for any potential problem.

The line stretched long as Palace Valley Theatre cocktail crafters upheld their reputation for excellent quality. A tall woman with graying black hair and a junior industrialist with brass glasses exchanged noticeable stares with faintly discreet gossip.

"He's certainly too old, but what a *striking* resemblance."

"I think it's uncanny, minus this old Lord's absurdly naive smile; you'd think he'd never been to a performance before." Neither considered that the actual father of Chigou deigned to walk so close to the ground.

"Could you imagine *the* Lord Opaji down here in the lobby, waiting in line?"

"Not standing next to *you*."

"Oh, stop it."

Conversation matched the bubbling sweet and sour cocktails lofted up towards the ceiling, but it all smeared into a purr for Lord Opaji. He experienced the soaring, ornate space as an academy student might when touring the hulking mysteries of an industrial plant filled with flying sparks, man-sized gears, and soot-covered black-hands. He knew it existed and it benefitted his life as a function of society, but he'd rarely experienced it firsthand.

When he reached the bar, the sharply dressed bartender stood as if being paid for her good posture. She dried a glass with the kind of dish towel people only hung out for looks, but she didn't look down at it once, keeping her attention firmly on the patron. "Good evening, Lord. What shall I make for you?"

Opaji had his preferences for libations but could not recall the last time they hadn't been prepared by either himself or someone he knew. The under-lit rows of glass bottles looked vaguely familiar to him. Some were clear, some glowed with rich colors; all were labeled with precise silk screening or gold stamp labels. He recognized a few logos. "Yes, young Lady. I believe I'm in the mood for Shumé, fifty years, on ice."

The Palace Valley Theatre had a fair quantity of insecure patrons who made pretentious drink orders, but this Lord's casual sincerity while making an impossible request amused the bartender. A faint smirk emerged. "Unfortunately, we don't have any fifty-year. Would twenty-year suffice?" The bar had one bottle of twenty-year Shumé, and it looked no less full than when it first arrived. Its only purpose beyond dramatic effect was to make everything else look more affordable.

It had been decades since Lord Opaji had been denied immediate access to whatever he wanted to drink—typically rare, and always expensive. Looking around, he noticed the crafters spinning all sorts of bottles about. Wands came out of metal devices—tiny boilers, dials, and levers—that Opaji had never seen. They pumped flavored vapors into mixed concoctions that slowly escaped through the surface. Various fruits were carved into intricate shapes and carefully placed onto spears or glass rims. He'd never seen such a performance go towards making a single drink.

"I'll have something like that." Opaji pointed to a woman with striking red-orange lips beam while taking in her bright blue, liquid sculpture.

With only a moment of deliberation, the crafter nodded and got to work. Shumé and Pats went into a shaker along with some shimmering yellow liquid Opaji didn't recognize. The crafter then twirled a copper scoop through her fingers and flung ice into the chrome shaker, topping it with a glass lid. After a brisk shake, she swapped the lid with a strainer, poured into a glass, and then retrieved two wands from the vapor-contraption. She plunged them into the cocktail, followed by gray and amber smoke emerging into swirls above. With a knife, she cut up a baby mimi fruit, which soon spiraled onto the glass's rim. She handed it to Opaji who held up the smoking vessel with glee.

"Why, this is just marvelous."

"Expect nothing less in the great city of Chigou," the artisan proclaimed.

Lord Opaji fought back a tear, proud like a parent.

Her duty completed, the crafter noticed it behind her professional facade. "If you don't mind my saying so, Lord, you share a handsome likeness to the very founder of this enlightened city."

The compliment failed to land immediately, as Opaji noticed a Lord in the adjacent line pay for a pair of cocktails and a small cheese glass. It had been over a decade since the founder of

Chigou had paid for anything in person. He began to dig around his suit like a kid about to spend their first allowance, having not yet assigned any pocket to spending-money. The young Lady's observation finally pierced through his consciousness. "Oh, yes. I *am* Opaji. It had been some time, so I decided to take in an Ósenique."

The statement carried just enough curious energy to make the crafter hesitate to dismiss it entirely. She then noticed the hulking man who looked like a Lord Enforcer in civilian clothes, unconcerned with art but very concerned with being near the man claiming to be *the* Lord Opaji. "Please excuse me for asking, but..." she said, looking discreetly to each side, "...are you being honest?"

He still fumbled through heavily underutilized pockets. "Of course. I'm sorry, can't seem to find any currency. I didn't even consider it when I left the office."

She could not have explicitly explained why, but she was now entirely convinced. "Good Lord, as I see it—*your* city, *your* drinks." Her hands politely waved, as if pushing the drink away in a current of air.

"Oh, that is very fine of you." Opaji had long since considered being given things for free a normal occurrence. "You have enlightened me this afternoon."

He raised the drink to her before turning around. She couldn't help but blush after receiving such a compliment from the man whose name was synonymous with progress.

Opaji's guard fixed his gaze towards the entrance. Two CEs stood by the doors and were promptly joined by a third, forming a deliberate huddle. Their postures lacked the typical calm of Civil Enforcers guarding the lustrous affairs of art lovers. Opaji, there for musical escapism like everyone else, failed to notice the shift in demeanor. He was too busy sipping cocktails and admiring the elaborate decor. The Sentinel, however, read their subtle actions as a warning.

"Lord..." he said vaguely, intentionally avoiding the famous name, "...I recommend enjoying your drink back in the gallery lounge." The theater kept a portrait gallery of their most celebrated artists in a more secluded location which offered one's ears a reprieve from the forceful sounds of brass horns and gossiping socialites. It also, the bodyguard knew, positioned them near a private auxiliary exit that emptied into a rear alley.

"Oh, yes, but in a minute. I'd like to breathe in this space a bit more." Opaji fed off the room's energy, reciprocating his decades-old effort to create the world's most vibrant metropolis. He then felt the Sentinel's suggestion being converted into a more physical mode of persuasion as the guard took his arm firmly.

"I'd rather not rush the moment..." Opaji began to say, before he finally noticed what concerned his guard. Over the pond of well-groomed heads, Opaji saw a CE crack open the front door before dashing outside.

"What is this all about?" the civil leader asked as his personal guardian continued to nudge him away from the simmering situation.

A thud then reverberated through the door, loud enough to grab a third of the room's attention. Socially preoccupied guests suddenly followed the crowd as the door slammed open and a man rolled in. Flushed and sweaty, he sprung up in strikingly plain clothes, sending a collective *gasp* through the audience.

Opaji's Sentinel kept perfect composure while pushing him away from where everyone else fixed their bulging eyes. Civil Enforcers sped towards the man in rough attire, who used his soot-stained hand like a bullhorn. "Enjoying everything we give you?" His other hand shot up, waving towards the thousands of bulbs that illuminated the sumptuous space, devouring a river of electricity.

The Enforcers grabbed the man and promptly forced him out. As the door opened, Opaji saw a frenzy of activity across the long entrance to the theater. Men and women marched down the street, holding signs and shouting indecipherable chants.

The glowing aura of art and performance collapsed. Opaji's heart sank as the Sentinel continued to move him expeditiously through the frozen crowd that offered whispers of "Raka Nusan".

What is happening to my city?

○ ○ ○

"What else can this hellion unleash in a single day?" Suzu snarled as her fingers clenched the air.

"I doubt that even Kits would have the capacity to conjure up a crowd *this* size in such a short amount of..."

"Shut up," Suzu snapped, cutting off Jin's commentary, before stomping back into Neko's trailer.

Gozen grunted as the scene revealed more of its blooming chaos. Picket signs wiggled above a lumbering mass of people who had taken over the entire width of Batsu Avenue. Chants like "black-hands made your city," and "Tasis kill" rang out. Civil Enforcers formed lines, attempting to separate the protesting group from alarmed bystanders who watched while hugging the sides of restaurants and lounges.

"Is this a collective gesture of industrial workers who are unsatisfied with their conditions or compensation?" Jin asked.

Gozen shook his head. Most cars had already detoured down side streets, but he feared his hefty truck would just get trapped in gridlock. "I guess that could have been a conversation your family had over breakfast."

"Occasionally, but I've never been aware of a group this large. What has prompted such a wide gathering?" Jin asked.

Gozen had already turned his focus back on the hundreds—no, *thousands*—of people he needed to drive through somehow. His face, and certainly his reputation, was still well-known enough with CEs that he could possibly acquire assistance. The hordes of fist-pumping black-hands presented the real challenge, and Gozen's days as a Lord Enforcer had taught him that you could sometimes persuade a crowd but never control it.

Suzu rejoined the group. "Do you *not* remember the fuel plant that exploded, sending an entire block up in flames? How many workers died in that?"

"That was quite some time ago," Jin said. "Why would this afternoon draw so many—"

"Raka Nusan, genius. I'm not surprised you can't see what low wages, long hours, volatile and toxic working conditions—oh, and *death*—can motivate a group to do." She turned Gozen. "You got a plan, big guy?"

"Do you see his car or my daughter?" Victou said from inside the trailer.

"Nope," Suzu answered.

"Experience informs me that Kits would have slipped through this," Jin hypothesized. "He's probably south of the city and heading towards Goraka already."

Suzu glared. "*Very* comforting."

"Any ideas before I start bumping into people?" Gozen asked as they approached the rear of the roaring crowd, which had begun to divert its attention towards the encroaching train on wheels.

Suzu had grown up going to protests. She had never enjoyed them but had developed a complicated respect for them, as her parents—especially her mother, Kiara—had valued their ability to make a point. Their size and volume always made her uneasy, but she had understood something about them even as a child. When people drew together into a pulse-racing crowd, they were looking for two things: a feast or a fight.

Squeezing up to the front, Suzu knelt onto the passenger seat and lowered the window, letting the cries of *Injustice!* flood in with the wind. The current of bodies began to form a whirlpool thirty yards away, swirling around a CE. Gozen leaned over, his voice urgent. "Suzu?"

She stuck the top half of her body outside, emerging just above the level of the crowd. Two CEs dragged a black-hand out of the vortex ahead, pinning him to the ground. Half the surrounding advocates stepped away from the takedown while a cluster of others drew in, flinging spit-laced insults.

"I don't want you getting yanked out into that," Gozen said with concern, but Suzu seemed wholly confident. The truck slowed down as it began attracting the hive. Some stepped away from the risk of getting flattened while others inflated their chests with defiant pride. One man went straight in and banged on the front fender as if he could slap the twenty tons away. The air was growing warm and thick. A trio of Civil Enforcers saw the slow-motion collision taking shape and marched over.

"Why don't we go around? He's getting away with Chichimou!" Victou pleaded from the back.

"Side streets are already clogged and half as wide," Gozen explained.

Suzu looked over the bubbling crowd and noticed one particular man who walked straight towards her. Despite being high up in the truck, Suzu was just above eye level with the man, who could have been Gozen's equally large cousin. He easily cut through the thick pool of black-hands, looking displeased with a little girl's joyride disrupting their march of justice. A sign rested on his shoulder like a battle axe.

Gozen tapped the horn, warning the dozens of bodies that pressed against his truck. Suzu kept staring right back at the approaching man, who walked at a slight angle to keep pace with the slowly moving truck. Bulky arms came right up to Neko and raised the sign to Suzu's fluttering bangs. His face was scrunched, ready to blow her back into the cab with his deep, raspy voice. Not interested in his upcoming rant, Suzu reached down and snagged the sign right out of the man's thick fingers. He stood stunned, unprepared for a young Lady to out-muscle him in a heartbeat.

A few more eyes gathered on the scene, suddenly more interested in the asymmetrical conflict taking shape. The crowd pressed harder against the truck on all sides, and Gozen finally had to hit the brake. Victou winced as fists echoed through the trailer wall. Suzu turned around the sign she now held and read its proclamation. The man tried to swipe it back but had no chance against her nimble reflexes. With his pride firmly stuck in his throat, the man watched Suzu thrust the sign skyward.

"Low safety, low pay, low progress!" Her alto voice cut through the first few rows.

The crowd's attention suddenly shifted towards the teenager. Suzu just wanted them to stop staring and get the hell out of her way. She climbed out of the window and onto Neko's hood. When she glanced briefly back through the front windshield, she noticed Gozen had the same stupefied look as everyone else. She stood up and looked down at a thousand individuals on the verge of pandemonium. The volume dropped into a pressure-laden hum.

Suzu stood like the figurehead of a ship. Gozen slowly slid his foot off the brake and laid his hand gently on the horn, ready. Jin began to ask a question and Gozen told him to shut up.

For a second, everyone waited.

Then, with the energy of the entire street pulled taut, Suzu pointed her fist forward and upward. *"No safety, no pay, no progress!"* she screamed.

Her voice soared across the legion. Gozen unleashed the horn and triggered every black-hand to rise in elation. Wasting no momentum, he hit the throttle as the crowd suddenly gave way. Their hands now slapped the trailer instead of punching it, as if propelling it through the crowd. The cathartic roar of an army thousands strong flowed over the young Lady and was carried up into the sky.

Out of nowhere, Suzu felt herself begin to cry. She felt her mother's gaze on a daughter who had stood up for what was important instead of cowering away. The fist stayed high in its salute, leading them forward.

"Are we moving? It feels like we're moving." Victou peeked up to the front, feeling as though he might not lose his daughter forever. The swarm of hands hitting the trailer rattled like an amateur percussion ensemble.

Gozen strained to keep his foot gentle on the pedal, filled with the urgency of pursuing Chichimou while trying not to flatten the crowd. His impatience faded as the crowd fully parted in anticipation. He took the opening and lurched into a higher speed. "Hang on, Suzu."

She gripped a hood vent but as Neko reached second gear, a cluster of Civil Enforcers slid in and filled the gap. A Lord Enforcer then emerged at the front. Gozen eased on the brake, having no intention of precipitating a fatal situation. As the stalemate solidified, black-hands alternated between cheers for Suzu and curses for the CEs.

The Lord Enforcer marched away from the huddle and

approached the truck with its lively passenger on the hood. Although the crowd maintained its fervor, those closest to the Lord Enforcer couldn't dismiss a lifetime of fear and reverence. They let him stride past, straight up to the truck. Even Suzu, a master of defiance, couldn't maintain her battle cry with the striking guardian mounted just below, his gleaming pistol dangling in its holster.

The window slid open and Gozen leaned out. The Lord Enforcer had his hand resting on his service pistol. To the surprise of all but two, the pristinely uniformed Lord Enforcer sported a warm grin. "I don't know what you're up to, but at least you put them in a better mood."

"I'm just passing through, old friend." Gozen said with a matching grin.

And with that, the LE stepped back and waved the truck forward.

The crowd proclaimed their victory, as if every industrialist in the city had just arrived with checkbooks and apologies in hand. Gozen hit the horn again. The crowd increased their volume as Neko crept forward like an ice breaker, desperate to reach open waters. The Lord Enforcer shook his head as he watched his mentor drift onward through the crowd.

Neko gained speed as the density of the crowd finally thinned out. A few black-hands continued to arrive from the south, passing through meandering spectators. Gozen stuck his head out the window as Suzu seemed determined to keep up her zeal. "Hey, I think we're through."

She merely raised the stolen sign and gave another war cry.

"Would you get *in* here?" Gozen ordered, ready to be out of the city.

Suzu threw the sign to a passerby, who dropped her newspaper to catch it. She then crawled around the hood and swung in, feet first, through the passenger window. The seat squeaked as she bobbed back and forth, trying to look back through the mirror.

"Surprising technique, but that was very effective," Jin commented.

She spun around. "*Damn right* it was."

Gozen looked at the buzzing young Lady who could barely focus on anything.

"What," she asked, "drawing a little too much attention for ya? Am I repulsive to your days as an Enforcer?"

"You've never reminded me more of your mother than you do just now," he replied.

The words wove through Suzu's soul, blocking the flood of adrenaline. Tears leaked out and began to mix with the sweat around her cheeks. A subtle but unmistakable moment was shared between guardian and survivor.

Suzu finally settled into her seat and took out the Toki her father had made. It felt so good in her hand. She turned to tell Gozen of its return when she noticed again the dark stain on his shirt, just off his chest; it looked bigger than she remembered. Suzu knew he should be at a clinic, and she also knew that her argument would be a waste of breath.

"That protest appears to be absolutely popular," Jin said.

"Yup," Suzu agreed. "I'd say I got the support of a few hard-working, under-compensated citizens back there."

"It appears you had the entire *district's* attention," Jin said, looking ahead.

The others turned forward as the electricity of central Chigou dissolved into a ghost town. With its population displaced into the city center, the typically bustling Industrial Quarter stood eerily devoid of life. Tired laborers weren't drifting from power plants to side-alley cafés. Children didn't dart out into the street chasing discarded bearings and gears. With no people to mask it, the ever-increasing amount of garbage and debris seemed to be the district's only occupant.

"Are we out of the city yet?" Victou squeezed into the crowded cabin. The void announced what lay far beyond. It felt strange to run back towards that dark forest. Kora Farm had infected him with rare hope for the quiet, peaceful life he had always promised his daughter. He wanted to stop lying and, for once, he felt he could. "I think you can drive faster now."

Gozen agreed and crushed the throttle, driving faster through the city than he ever had before. Buildings and signs raced by in patterns of gray and black. The matrix of deserted streets narrowed into a single road and the city faded away. Unobscured from industrial growth, a thin, dark line of trees appeared between wild-grass fields and distant, alpine peaks.

Voices faded from Neko's cabin, a steam engine's song filling the space between occupants. They each stared at the infamous forest and contemplated their decision to enter—for some, it served as a return to haunted memories. Deep darkness and billowing fog oozed out from between the trees, declaring an endless bounty of life and death.

"I've heard of only a few groups that entered this place. I've personally spoken to far fewer," Gozen stated somberly. He turned to Jin whose nearly gray eyes looked dark with trauma. Gozen leaned in his seat and spoke to Victou, whose face held its own complex gaze. "But I've never heard of a group entering this place and returning completely intact… at least, not until you and your daughter," he finished.

Gozen's words took a good ten seconds to get through to Victou. "What?" he asked, unaware of his delay.

"Every relevant story and fact about Goraka promises that if we enter, not *all* of us will come back out. You and your small child seem to be the only exception. So, before I drive all of us in there, I need to make sure what you've told us is a recollection and not a tale."

Victou finally gave the former Lord Enforcer his attention. "You think I made all of it up?"

"I'm asking you now if your story lacks any critical truth."

Victou had long since forsaken himself as a standard of truth. "Daimó believed me." His voice jumped a level as he gestured forward, towards the forest. "*Kits* obviously believes me."

"Kits is desperate," Suzu said with anger, as if her antagonist sat there with them.

"We are *all* desperate," Jin added. "We wouldn't enter that place otherwise." He then left the conversation and went alone into the back.

Neko approached the small guard station halting the path to Goraka, unmanned like before. Gozen barely slowed down and instead detoured through the service drive. The gate and booth passed by—strong in its warning, but weak on actual authority. Once past it, Gozen sped back up, leaving the known world behind. The engine hummed hard until the forest finally arrived.

Long Frost Road's southern leg still looked new, despite having been constructed during the beginning years of Chigou. It stabbed straight into the sudden wall of trees like a mountain tunnel. A large set of signs stood just before the entrance, well designed and clearly not intended for civilians. Gozen idled Neko to a stop.

Most of the signs gave logistical instruction—backed with coded colors—but the largest shouted a final warning. *Dangerous Wilderness Ahead, Entrance is Discouraged* greeted anyone considering the Red Valley. Shadows appeared to swallow the road as it cut into the endless forest.

"Did you come this way?" Gozen asked Jin who finally rejoined the group.

Jin merely gestured to the far eastern end of the tree line.

"And you?" Gozen asked, turning to Victou, who likewise denied it.

"So, is there a reason we're assuming Kits took Chichimou in here and not somewhere else along the gigantic border of this place?" Suzu asked.

"He's not naive enough to ignore the possibility we'd be chasing right after him. I'd also assume he's sane enough to only be in there as long as absolutely necessary." Gozen looked through the incredible density of vegetation before them. "Unless you have an airship and a very long winch, this is the only quick transit for... wherever they're headed."

"Okay. And even if we see his car conveniently parked on the road..." Suzu's voice trailed off as her thoughts pivoted. "Where does this road *end*, exactly?"

Suzu looked at Gozen, who looked at Jin.

"I'd assume," Jin began, "having grown up much closer to this place than I, that you'd all know more about the ambitious but relatively short-lived Project Red Line and its efforts to pave an access road into the southern valley."

Gozen, Suzu, and Victou shook their heads in unison. The project's existence had never been hidden, although the extent of its progress had been. Most assumed that it had been abruptly terminated decades earlier, although a few theorists argued that the work continued on in secret. Nearly everyone believed that some—perhaps many—had died during the project's brief development. Some cited accidents and treacherous terrain, while tales of red ghosts occupied a hefty percentage of explanations. Regardless of any details, most assumed that the dark forest south of Chigou held rich resources and that Chigou's dominant industrialist had decided to abruptly end his pursuit for reasons never made public.

"I was briefly acquainted with the granddaughter of Project Red Line's head engineer," Jin began. "He held a social gathering at his house to celebrate Kasic's fiftieth anniversary. The granddaughter graciously led me into Lord Joutsu's office to see the project's initial designs and progress charts after development had already ceased. The plan was ambitious, but its designers seemed unable to accurately scout deeper into the lower valley, even with the reconnaissance views provided by an airship. I believe this road descends briefly before turning right and running along the rim of a rather significant cliff."

Suzu hunched her shoulders. "And... does it go down to the bottom? Did they build anything in there? A mine? Did those liars actually try to harness core-thermic energy, fail, and then avoid admitting my dad had a better way of—"

"No," Jin cut her off. "The road just ends."

The momentary silence allowed them all to accept that the infinitely dense jungle held but one clear path, and they would be going in. Victou settled back into the mid-cabin, Jin grabbed a handhold, and Suzu finally squared up in the passenger seat. Steam billowed out the sides, and in just a few seconds, Neko exited the light and drove towards the heart of the unknown.

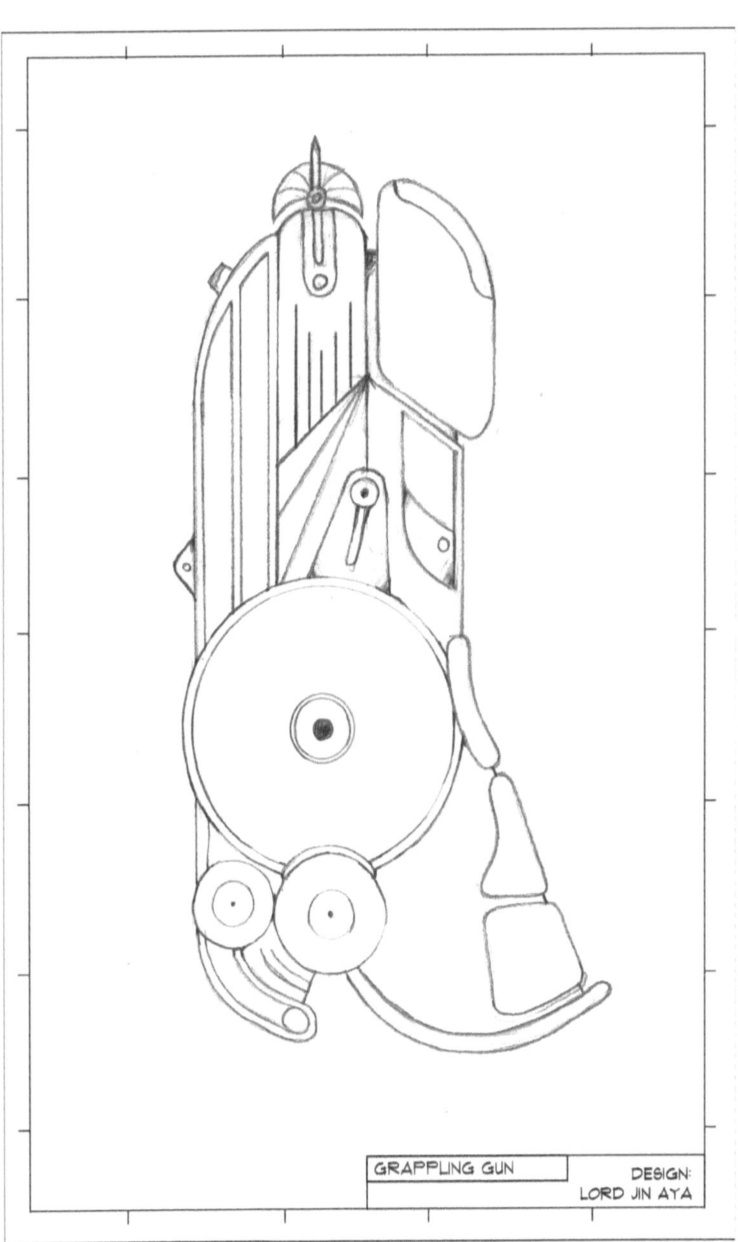

GRAPPLING GUN
DESIGN:
LORD JIN AYA

29
BREAK

The road offered Jin a way into old nightmares. His previous visit to Goraka had begun the same way it had ended: with a desperate escape through brutal terrain. A paved entrance felt incongruous. Although abandoned, the tarmac remained smooth in the center, the only portion not yet reclaimed by persistent organic life.

Light snuck through the treetops in only a fractured hairline despite the generously wide road. The sudden contrast between pavement and plants made the setting appear fabricated more than abandoned. The passengers gazed at the scene from behind glass like vacationers in a theme park full of wild, dangerous creatures.

"Honestly, I expected to feel more threatened," Suzu admitted.

Gozen waited for Jin to reply but heard only the young man's anxious breathing. In the mirror, Jin's eyes raced around like a cat hiding in an alley corner, waiting for some inevitable danger to emerge.

"I guess this fog *is* kind of spooky," Suzu continued.

"Jin," Gozen called. "I know it's not pleasant to think about, but what can you tell us about what we might encounter down here?"

"You sure you don't want Victou's advice back there?" Suzu cut in. "*He* managed to make it out with the person he went in with."

"I'll take any first-hand account," Gozen shot back at Suzu. He felt heat swelling from his gunshot wound, burning off his focus and patience. "Because we've all read the same children's tales."

"They… they're red," Jin muttered.

"Everybody knows that," Suzu claimed.

A frustrated growl emerged from the driver's seat, and a stubborn huff came from the passenger side. Jin stood in the middle, forcing his brain to conduct pragmatic thought processes. "I... I didn't see it first. It entered the edge of camp without making a sound. Nia warned me out loud and it followed her."

Suzu grunted.

"Even when moving fast, it was silent. It kept up with her, but... thinking back, I don't believe it attacked. It did feel threatening, maintaining her pace effortlessly. I do not want to say it properly *flew*, but it moved with such ease and speed... I do not understand what it was."

"That's helpful. Victou, you got anything *useful* to add?" Suzu asked while watching the impenetrable wall of fog and plant life race by. A few sounds pierced through the cabin—probably animals, but nothing she had ever heard before.

"I don't know," Victou finally said. "I avoided them. I don't think they ever saw me."

"But you let your daughter socialize with them?"

"It was already there with Chichi and didn't threaten her or anything, so I chose not to risk making the situation worse."

"Right. So, if I see one of these things, it might try to kill me or it might help me pick flowers. Thanks, you two, I feel *totally* prepared now." Suzu turned back and gestured towards the approaching depths of darkness. "At least our path is unmistakable. A car wouldn't make it ten meters off the road."

The forest suddenly opened up and light flooded the cabin. Gozen slammed on the brakes as the overgrown road veered right along a ridge. The sudden drop provided their first view across the treetops. The end of Goraka—the end of the entire Naifin Valley—still lay far away.

Of the two returning visitors, neither had witnessed such a display of Goraka's incredible expanse. Most citizens of Chigou had seen photographs taken from an airship, but such the perspective of vast darkness increased fear and kept the truth at a harmless distance. Awe swept over the group, along with a vanishing sense of security.

"We are on the ridge now," Jin explained. "The road was clearly designed to switch back as the height tapered off, but I believe development never got that far. This will likely end before long."

"We haven't passed his car yet, have we?" Victou peeked out from the back.

"I don't think we'll miss it," Gozen mumbled.

As they continued, a shelf of treetops passed just below, hiding the steep drop to the forest floor. A yellow bird shot out of the mist like a harpoon, chased by two more with scarlet-lined wings. They glided just above the canopy, scanning the forest below before diving back out of sight.

"Hey," Suzu shouted out, pointing sharply down the road. A smooth, black bump glistened in the middle of their path, only a few hundred meters ahead.

"Careful," Jin warned, reflexively bracing himself against the dash. "His gun might be fixed on us already."

Anticipating that Gozen would slow Neko down, the group instead felt the vehicle veer left. "Gozen?" Jin asked, turning towards the driver.

Instead of answering, Gozen's face hit the window, eyes fully shut. Jin stood, stunned, as the truck rattled over rocks and roots. Suzu leaped across and grabbed the wheel just as they struck a guardrail. Sparks erupted as their momentum tried to push them through the short barrier—the only thing keeping them from a sudden descent. Suzu yanked hard on the wheel, throwing Jin and Victou against the left wall of the cabin. The heavy vehicle overcompensated and rammed against the north embankment.

Dirt flew up in a wave as the jungle drummed against Neko's side. Suzu's forearms tensed as she fought to straighten the vehicle, simultaneously kicking Gozen's unresponsive leg off the accelerator. Jin fought his way back up—vibrations rattling his damaged ribs—and yanked on the pneumatic emergency brake. Victou flew forwards and collided into Jin's back. Suzu reached one hand down and helped with the brake, balancing every limb like a daredevil acrobat. The cacophony of grinding gears swelled with pained groans until the vehicle jerked to a halt.

Pinned up against the dash, Suzu pulled Gozen's face off the window. "Jin, what's wrong with him?"

"Probably blood loss," Jin moaned as he struggled to untangle himself from Victou.

"I thought you bandaged him up on the way down here! Weren't you raised by a coven of doctors or something?"

"It is not called a coven."

"WHY IS HE STILL BLEEDING?"

"Dressing a wound in a moving vehicle is not optimal," Jin said, looking Gozen over. "But I did manage. I suspect internal bleeding."

"Well..." Suzu looked out the windshield and saw Kits's unmistakable car centered in the road. She suddenly felt trapped between the threat of her nemesis and her guardian's fading life. "...how do you fix that?"

Despite a privileged upbringing, Jin's curious mind had developed a fondness for junkdrawers. Estate staff never allowed *actual* junk to be accessible to any Aya family member, but Jin had always collected random bits of forgotten material to inspire designs. He ran straight for the back of Neko's rear cabin, searching for a simple object to spontaneously reveal its brilliant application.

Suzu heard him rumbling through drawers and activating the steam-powered elevator shelves; the clutter of noises pricked her nerves. She reached down for Gozen's hand, which felt unnaturally cold. She turned back to the halted vehicle—dark and lifeless—before hearing a crack on the windshield. She frantically ducked below the dash, waiting for an explosion of glass.

"I think it was a nut or something," Victou peered up from the seat while watching a brown dot bounce off the hood.

"Jin!" Suzu cursed.

Memories of medical chit-chat bounced against an intense visual examination. Jin sorted and evaluated clips, pens, food, hand tools, paper, coffee, hardware; their possibilities were reviewed and discarded. His eyes finally landed on a colorful box illustrated with tiny, brightly colored fruit.

"The med-kit is up here. What are you doing?" Suzu heard the panic in her own voice. *"He's dying!"*

It felt irrational, but Jin believed Suzu somehow knew Gozen's condition better than anyone. He read the fruit dessert's ingredients as quickly as possible before grabbing a small mug, a steel knife, and the steam wand behind the small cabin sink.

He blasted the knife and mug, disinfecting them while simultaneously burning his wrist. He waved off the cloud of steam before half-filling the mug with water and plunging the steam wand in. Pressing the brass handle, vapors and scorching droplets flared around him, one stinging his eye. He ripped open the box and poured the powdery substance into the scalding liquid, stirring briskly with the knife.

Not waiting for the pink particulate to fully dissolve, Jin hurried back to Suzu, whose eyes had filled with tears. They begged him to help, reminding Jin of the last time Nia had looked at him. "Grab a syringe from the medkit." Jin set the assorted items down and bounced again to the back of the cabin. He called over his shoulder, "No needle!"

Suzu's hands fumbled through the medkit for a package labeled *syringe*. Ripping out bandages and cotton balls, she found the glass tube wrapped in sanitized paper. She finally looked to see what Jin had brought from the back. Her face twisted at the absurd sight. "You're pumping *Capi Cake* into him?"

Throughout the Naifin Valley's urban history, citizens had nurtured a fascination with melding its natural bounty of food with technically inventive presentations. Capi—a brand name that had eventually become functionally ubiquitous—had been developed as a way to suspend, persevere, and display food with precision, without the need for containers. A combination of substances derived from connective tissues and plant matter was mixed and then dried, giving it immense shelf life and allowing for reconstitution merely by mixing it with hot water. Food artists loved suspending colorful fruits into immaculately complex displays, the Capi taking shape of whatever mold it had been poured in, forming a sort of futurist-cake. They made incredible centerpieces. Jin hypothesized that the delicious coagulate would work well to artificially clot a wound, especially an internal one.

He came back balancing a bowl of ice water. Suzu held the syringe, mystified by the unfolding sequence of actions. Jin placed the hot mug of Capi Cake into the ice-bath. He then took the syringe from Suzu's tense hand, dipped it in, pulled the plunger, and filled it with room temperature dessert. "Pull off the bandage."

"But... won't he bleed more?"

"Just don't touch the underside."

Gozen already looked dead. Suzu followed Jin's instructions, the only possibility that seemed to exist. She pulled back Gozen's ripped shirt and then the bandage that stuck to his skin. Blood oozed from the hole set in his upper chest. Before Suzu could gasp, Jin shoved the blunt nozzle into the wound. Victou joined Suzu's gulp as the plunger dropped. Jin pressed until the gelatinous treat overflowed back out of the wound.

Gozen remained still. Suzu's eyes bounced between the fallen guardian and his impromptu surgeon. Clear goop continued to expand slowly out of the wound, but she noticed that the flow of blood had already slowed; she didn't even think to put the bandage back on. She looked at Jin, hands shaking.

"I... uhm..." Jin assessed his course of action. "I thought the material would reclaim pressure and help promote clotting. Unfortunately, I based almost all of this on theory." Jin pragmatically checked Gozen's pulse and counted silently. He didn't bother with a Toki, since his internal metronome was impeccable.

"Is he dead?" Suzu asked, watching Jin's pale hand holding Gozen's limp wrist. The sounds of wildlife seeped into the otherwise silent cabin. Suzu looked to Jin for a sign, but his expression was as painfully neutral as ever.

A groan came out of Gozen's mouth, followed by an aggravated, "Good *Lord*."

"No, he is alive," Jin answered, releasing Gozen's arm.

Suzu leaned in, finally remembering to reapply Gozen's bandage. The giant winced, feeling the torn tissue and tepid pudding set into his chest. His mind then reverted to its last memory. "Kits."

The group looked back to the seemingly abandoned car parked at the forest road's abrupt end. Their heads filled with the memory of dreadful sounds: the crack of gunpowder, the whistle of a high-speed round, the thud of metal hitting flesh. "We didn't see him," Suzu answered.

"That doesn't mean he's not there," Gozen warned.

"I know," Suzu and Jin answered in unison. A sudden, indecisive pause filled the cabin.

"Right. So, can I go and get my daughter now?" Victou cut in from just outside the huddle.

Together, they looked out across the ocean of vegetation. The southern mountains stood miles away and the forest offered no clear path between them. Suzu, never having entered Goraka before, finally understood Victou's decision to disappear inside. Even a fool could stay hidden in there for months, if they survived their time.

"Gozen *must* stay here," Jin decreed.

"I think that's *his* decision," Suzu countered.

Springs creaked as the big man struggled to sit upright. "I just passed out driving in an air-conditioned cabin. Today's not my day to mountain climb… or fight."

"Okay, so the three of us," Victou prompted anxiously.

Suzu looked over Victou's thin frame and moderate belly. Even with some time at the farm, he still looked like a malnourished office intern.

"What?" Victou asked, noticing the appraisal.

"I'm just wondering what you're going to offer down there," Suzu answered.

"Hey, I survived in there for weeks."

"You *hid* in there for weeks. We're not here to hide, we're here to *hunt*," Suzu pressed.

"And what if he gets the drop on you two? *Again?*" Victou retorted.

"There is only one place we will almost certainly see Kits and Lady Chichimou," Jin cut in confidently.

"Oh, of course, Lord Hunter. Where would *that* be?" Victou snapped, borrowing some of Suzu's sass.

"Right where you're standing," Gozen spoke, catching his breath. "It's not likely he's going to try and hike back to Chigou."

"Okay, so why are *you* two leaving then?" Victou asked.

"Because having all four of us pinned in here doesn't exactly give us an advantage," Suzu replied, "and I'd rather stop Kits before he does whatever it is he plans on doing." She began to tighten her shoes.

"Perhaps we should block the road with the truck?" Jin offered.

Gozen gave their layout a proper look. The road's width would possibly allow the cab and trailer to make a ten... maybe twelve-point turn, but the bordering landscape offered numerous traps of varying danger. "Might be worth a try, assuming we're not stuck already."

The debate session ended as no one disputed the plan. Gozen squared up in his seat and took another aching breath. Jin reached down for the brake he had yanked back. "You'll need to disengage the alt-brake as I..."

"I know how to drive my truck," Gozen snapped. Neko's boilers fired up as brass dials came alive. The group felt the truck's weight struggle against torque and friction.

Cautiously, Gozen built up force until his precious vehicle began to break free of its earthen snare. Dirt flew as the truck slowly managed to gain momentum. The front tires finally gripped the tarmac and Gozen turned towards a clear path, but something grabbed the vehicle and jolted them all forward.

"Err," ground between Gozen's teeth as the hefty truck sprang back a few meters. "It's got us."

"What?" Victou leapt up with alarm. "What's got us?"

Gozen looked in the rearview mirror. "Probably one of the fifty trees we ran over when I passed out." He tried to stand but his nervous system argued with the motion. "I have a saw in the back. We'll need to cut ourselves out."

"That settles it." Suzu pushed Jin back and moved away from the dash. "Jin and I are looking for Kits and Chichi. Victou, you stay here and deal with our tree situation. Gozen will keep an eye on that devil's car."

Suzu ducked into the rear cabin and grabbed her retractable DaiLansu. Jin checked his chest of gear as Victou peered back. "Why doesn't *he* work on getting the truck loose and I go and look for my daughter? Isn't he a... a car guy?"

Jin pulled out his custom-made, retractable Masu with practiced elegance. He tested the sword's precision action, extending the polished blade out before snapping back in. Victou nervously tucked his poorly fit shirt into his pants, accidentally unhitching his belt.

"I need a decoy that at least *looks* threatening," Suzu said, nodding towards Jin. "Come on, let's go."

They jumped out the back. Victou looked at Gozen, who opened a compartment in the dash and pulled out an impressive-looking firearm, reminiscent of the ones Victou had only ever seen used by Lord Enforcers. It looked odd being pulled out from underneath old tissues and loose pens. Gozen sighed as he looked it over. Maybe he hadn't fired it in a while, maybe he never had; Victou couldn't tell.

Neko's rear door powered shut as Suzu and Jin walked out past the trailer. The black car remained at the end of the road, void of any movement or passengers that they could see.

"You don't think he's just sitting in there, do you?" Suzu asked.

Jin considered this. "I do not think he desires to spend any more time here than he absolutely needs to. We could continue down the road and investigate the car. The drop seems to taper off to something more manageable past the end."

He looked back to Suzu, who had vaulted the overgrown guardrail and stood at the edge. Jin followed her gaze towards the long branches that reached out to them, masking the fifteen-meter descent that eventually slanted out.

"How do you feel about riding a tree down?" Suzu asked.

Jin gave Suzu's proposition some consideration, thinking of his bruised body. He then pulled a device off of his vest, something Suzu had never seen before. The tip looked like a snare or claw, sitting above various cylinders and a trigger. The wider cylinder contained a small slit that revealed a spool of thin, braided wire.

"Gracious, even your *rope* needs to be fancy," she said, shaking her head.

Jin stared at the coil like an old man reminiscing over a toy from his youth.

"Didn't I see you jump off a silo and chase down Darou your first week at Kora? Come on, I can practically grab that branch from here."

Jin looked out to the tree. Although the drop looked properly dangerous, Suzu's point stood firm. They both were more than capable of scaling down the tree, but his confidence had drained away. His body felt like it had only barely recovered from a fever, far worse than the first time he entered Goraka, a journey he had barely survived—and Nia hadn't. "It… it will be difficult to find them."

"No kidding," Suzu dismissed, gesturing to the entirety of the Red Valley. She saw Jin's chest swell more with each breath; a faint panic filled his eyes. "Do you need to stay with the truck? Because I don't want you freaking out down there."

"You'd rather go with Victou?" Jin almost sounded relieved.

"Who, father-of-the-year in there? He can't even keep his belt buckled." Suzu jumped up and down like a sprinter about to race. "So, am I going alone or what?"

Jin finally shook off the haunted whispers of the wood. His pale skin looked more ghostly than usual. "You won't have that confidence when you finally see one of *them*."

His sudden directness and evident fear startled Suzu. "Alright… well, I'm done waiting." She jumped off the high ledge and grabbed the nearest branch. Jin watched as she fluidly swung down, let go, and hopped across a thicker, lower branch. In a seemingly effortless series of maneuvers, she disappeared down the tree's broad trunk.

Watching her graceful descent spiked Jin's anxiety. He imagined failing the first maneuver, falling, hearing his bones crunching against each lower branch. His fingers tested the gadget still in his hand. The anchor dart's spurs retracted and expanded. Spurts of compressed gas whistled out of relief valves. His fingernail plucked the tight, finely spun wire. "Yes, sound enough," he said, attempting to convince himself.

Jin found a thick stump rooted to the edge and aimed the compact grappling tool at it. A burst of compressed gas launched the tiny harpoon into the wood. Jin flinched as bits of timber shot into his face. He tugged on the extracted wire, testing for his weight. Clipping the device to a point on his vest, he took a deep breath and leaned back. The spool buzzed as it released the reservoir's lifeline.

Jin's stomach jumped as he entered a controlled fall. His fingers played with the trigger, trying to control his speed. At the bottom, he kicked out and slipped on a moss-covered rock. His body collapsed into a roll before he stumbled back onto his feet. Suzu stood next to him, arms firmly crossed.

"I'm not carrying you out of here."

"I rolled out to reduce serious joint injury." Jin performed an assessment squat, failing to hide his vanity. "Also, my left eye has yet to recover its color recognition. It seems to be affecting my depth perception."

"Just don't shoot me with your crazy fishing gear," She said while drawing Nia's DaiLansu.

Jin watched her fiddle with a button, then he jumped as an unusual sound shrieked out from above their heads. "That bird sounds familiar."

"Kola," Suzu succinctly explained before walking away.

Jin looked up for the white owl, remembering the call from his last stay in Goraka. He had found Nia's ability to call a specific wild animal to herself incomprehensible. Now, it seemed, the ability had been passed on to Suzu. Curiosity was just getting the better of him when the crack of a gun cut through the forest.

Back in Neko's cabin, Victou sprang up. With his pulse pounding loudly enough to hear, he peered out the window, leaning over Gozen, who hadn't even looked up yet. "He shot at us. Or was it them? Did he shoot at them? Maybe he was waiting for them at the bottom of..."

"That was deeper into the woods."

Far from relieved, Victou continued to peek and crouch. "You sure? How do you know?"

"I'm an expert, that's how." Gozen turned his head towards the forest's unrelenting density. "And I don't know anyone else who carries a Vite Pistol."

"Oh, no... no, no!"

"He wouldn't take the time or risk just to *shoot* her down here."

The grotesque sentence somehow cultivated minor relief. "Well... then... why did he shoot?"

Gozen winced, feeling his wound. "He wouldn't flippantly give his position away either. He's deep into Goraka, and I imagine it has pushed him to desperation."

Victou thought that was a hell of a thing to say, especially to the father of that scoundrel's innocent prisoner. But soft words seemed of little use. Victou couldn't deny his reason to stay. Kits would likely come back to his car. Then they would face off, a pathetic father and his dying companion, against an assassin.

30
HEX

Every legend or fable about the Red Valley had suddenly lost all suspicion of hyperbole. The jungle certainly looked ominous—a foggy woodland created to spook children—but its abruptness shocked Kits even more. Every sense told Kits that he was traveling through a forbidden land. Such a biome seemed more feasible further south or near a coast, but almost impossible at this alpine altitude. Yet here it was. Had pagans hypnotized him and lured him through a burning portal to another realm, he would have been less stunned than he felt now, staring into the wilderness of Goraka.

Chichimou looked almost placid, as if mocking her captor's shock. Kits had explained that her father was in trouble and the only way to help was getting one of those *things* they had seen, deep in the Red Valley. She had asked Kits why he had hurt so many people at the farm. He'd expressed his regret, that time was too short to explain and that far greater devastation would strike them all if the mysterious device could not be retrieved. Once successful, she would go back to her father, and everything would be just as before—*even better*, he had said.

Kits couldn't tell if he had convinced her, but she'd stopped asking questions. For the rest of the drive, little Chichimou had stared out of the window with her knees tucked into her chest. Obtaining the girl had been difficult, as anticipated, but he was rewarded with some luck. Having passed through the downtown protest just as it was forming, he'd reached the valley with little resistance. He thought of Daimó and his own probable fate should he fail in his self-appointed mission. Progress or perish, his destiny lay in this foreboding forest.

"Does this look familiar… like we're going the right way?" he asked as they marched through the endless growth.

Chichi bobbed her head up and down, giving Kits frustratingly vague assurance. The tiny Lady at least managed the terrain well, rarely needing a hoist.

"And you remember what this thing looks like?"

Another nod. *Of course.*

"Alright. So, how are you going to find this thing?" Kits questioned.

"I heard it from far away, like a whistle."

"A whistle?"

"And it's tall, really tall." She put her hand up over her head, pushing just shy of a meter.

"And it sits on a metal rod?"

"Yeah, sort of." Chichi shrugged.

The usefulness of her description seemed to be something like a lie. Many dark tales of Goraka existed, often fantastically violent as if designed to frighten children, but little Chichimou's demeanor argued otherwise. She had allegedly stood right next to one of those red demons, yet she pressed forward as if walking towards Izzy Kai Bakery during an afternoon in Doulan. "So, which is it: *yes* or *sort of?*"

"Uh… it's a stick at first." Her hands gestured low and then swept up. "But it gets bigger at the top with this thingy, and steam comes out of it like…" She pantomimed hot air puffing out of her round cheeks.

"Probing for core-thermic energy?" Kits asked eagerly.

Chichimou continued walking, ignoring the strange mumbling that adults offered so often.

Kits silently assessed his present scheme. His entry into a death-forest, spurred by Daimó's reaction to a con-artist's tale about his fledgling child, illuminated what little control he had over his own life.

"It was a device though, for sure something mechanical? You saw it operate, venting steam?"

Chichimou studied him as they continued their uneven descent. "You don't know what you're doing here." It was not a question.

Even when Kits had lived in an orphanage, he'd found the conversations of children to be painfully simple. He had often kept to himself and would, on occasion, abruptly tell the other kids to stop talking. Chichimou's simplicity seemed to hide a deeper complexity, one he was failing to comprehend. He wondered if her cooperation stemmed from obedience or misdirection; even children can be clever, he knew, especially if they are assumed incapable. "How... how far into the forest were you when you found one of these... things?"

Chichimou looked around herself, as if every new patch of forest didn't look like the last. "It's around here somewhere," she said, with the inflection of an old man musing on a porch.

"Fantastic. Excellent plan," Kits said under his breath. "We'll just keep heading straight down until we find one." He prodded her forward and checked his Toki, counting the time it would take them to get back before the sun dropped. He had no intention of experiencing the Red Valley's witching hour.

The march carried on. Kits tightened the makeshift wrap he had fixed over his forearm. It ached and burned—possibly a small fracture. A small price to pay for preventing Suzu from breaking his face. He winced as he tightened the strap around his arm, which felt damp. Every surface around him looked like it was sweating. The young girl continued to manage herself well, and he found himself lifting her over bulky obstacles with his good arm almost gladly. He wondered if this was what it would have been like to go camping with a younger sibling.

"Do you know what your father does?"

Chichimou looked up blankly. Her father did quite a few things.

"Work. His job. Do you know what he *does?*" Kits smirked.

"He's a farmer now."

"Oh," Kits mocked. "Conned his way into agriculture as well, did he?"

Chichimou wondered if he always sounded so odd. "I help out too, but Dad's done a bunch of jobs in a bunch of places."

"I bet." Kits remembered his days at the orphanage, running schemes whenever he could avoid detection. It seemed pathetic to carry on with that at Victou's age. This girl seemed bright enough—too bad she had *him* for a dad. "No mom? What happened to her?"

Chichimou had clearly heard him but chose not to answer.

"I have one memory of my parents, of them leaving the apartment we lived in. It's my earliest memory, from when I was much younger than you, actually," Kits said, refocusing on the approaching wilderness. "But instead of them coming back, it was a CE with this old man... three days later. Felt like a month. Then it was off to the children's circus. You spent some time in an orphanage, didn't you? The Tree House, as it's called by those who prefer to dress up despair."

Chichimou pulled a branch away from her face, letting it swing back at Kits's. He stopped the branch but caught a few leaves on the nose. "How did *that* one feel, getting sent to an orphanage? I bet you had some words for Daddy when you saw him again."

"Lady Kyoumére told me, *People say harsh things when they're afraid.*"

"Oh?" Kits dismissed. "What about your mom? She ditch you two? Or did Dad ditch her?"

Chichimou didn't trust this guy with her memories of her mother.

"My parents may still be around. Maybe I've seen them standing right by me on the Hotrail. Hell, maybe I've *met* them and didn't even know it." The thought was far too worn out to muster any sort of emotion within him. "Eh, I bet they're dead... might as well be."

A large bird with streaming yellow feathers flew up the slope before disappearing into leaves and branches. It seemed less concerned with them than with whatever was behind it.

"So, wait... did you actually see one of these things? The Red Ghost of Goraka or whatever prattle people call it in stories?"

Chichimou grunted as her foot slipped, nearly failing to climb over a fallen tree.

"Were you scared?" Kits asked, still undecided about the previous question.

She shrugged. Kits couldn't read it as confidence any more than a child confused by her own imagination. "Did it look like a ghost?"

Same answer.

"Did you think it was your mother?"

Kits barely finished his sentence when he clutched Chichimou's shoulder and stopped them dead. Just down the slope, a set of eyes flashed from the darkness, reflecting a moment of light that sneaked through the trees.

"Wha…" she began.

"Don't talk," he said, his voice hard as steel. Chichimou looked at Kits's fist clenching her shirt, his injured arm now holding the gun. He didn't even glance at her. She tried to peer over the tall plants but couldn't see more than two meters ahead.

Kits focused. Black became subtle shades of darkness as the faint stirring of leaves revealed a silhouette in the distance, perched on a small boulder. Sharp ears pointed up and a thick, smooth tail swayed back and forth. Then a large tongue came out and cleaned a set of imposing fangs.

The forest lifted its misty gown and gave Kits a proper peek. Red stripes stretched back around those glowing eyes, cutting into a coat of thick, glossy black fur. Kits had seen large cats in the Chigou zoo before, but those visits had offered no more peril than a painting. He suddenly felt a new kind of fear—being hunted by a creature of the wild.

"Did you encounter one of these before?" Kits whispered. From the corner of his eye, he could see her shake her head. "We'll move sideways until we're clear."

"Okay," Chichi whispered before feeling a tug on her shirt. Kits led them across the shallow slope, allowing her to finally get a clear glimpse of the lurking predator. Kits held his gun in tight, ignoring the pain in his arm, as they began to make some distance. The captivating sight then ruptured as the cat sprang towards them.

Its silent swiftness gave Kits an arresting chill. He raised his shaking hand as the cat suddenly halted. Chichimou felt herself being pulled back, less as protection and more to clear his line of sight. The animal remained motionless, staring. Kits forced his breath to steady and raised the sights of his pistol.

The situation gave his finger pause, not for his ability to aim, but for his lack of experience in facing off with a cat the size of himself. If the first shot didn't kill, it could provoke the animal to charge, and even wounded, the beast would likely cover the distance between them in a heartbeat. Kits decided he had no time to play with the cunning predator. He released Chichimou's shirt and steadied the gun with both hands.

A crack echoed through the trees, an explosion of dark soil exploding between them. The cat lunged backwards as Kits had hoped it would, injured and confused. The two species stared at one another as Kits opened the barrel, sending the spent and smoking casing to the wet soil. Kits blindly pulled another round from his belt and loaded the gun. With his sights back up, Kits saw hesitation seep into the carnivore.

Exposed fangs and glaring eyes disappeared as the animal took one step back, then another. Kits allowed himself to breathe as he watched the threat slip away into fog and foliage. Relief set in for a second, but evaporated as Kits realized that he'd just announced their location to anyone who'd made it into Goraka behind them. "Dammit," he groaned.

He looked back at Chichimou… who wasn't there. *"Dammit!"*

Kits searched for a yellow shirt or shifting leaves. He examined the wet, sloped ground, which wouldn't have allowed any quick retreat. The only other path outside his full range of vision went east across the descent of the ridge. He started to move, confident he'd close the child's lead in under a minute.

He sprinted the first twenty meters, leaping over stone and roots. The jungle continuously smacked his face with its outstretched limbs as he tried to examine the countless possible hiding spots. A flash of yellow then appeared on a tree. He skidded to a halt and reached his hand out to the familiar color. Ready to chastise Chichi, he instead watched a bright yellow lizard jump onto his wrist. Kits yelped and flailed his arm. The blob of yellow sailed away and was swallowed by ubiquitous green.

Sweat trickled down his spine. The thick jungle air seemed to fight against his deep breaths. He wondered if he had somehow already run past the girl as fog crept across his path. Turning back around, he saw that the cloud had swept around, and in one short breath it cut off the remaining world from his sight.

The expansive jungle shrank to arm's reach. He looked down, seeing even his feet half obscured. The sun became an eerie, directionless glow. Sounds made it through—ambient voices growing as his vision was rendered useless. The gentle, clouds he had seen many times from an airship had swallowed him like helpless prey.

Kits checked the compass he'd brought, but it would do precious little when any step could snare his foot, or send him plummeting down into a ravine.

He gripped his gun as he heard the cat—or was the sound in his head? The animal could be standing right above him, licking its chops, that very moment. Perhaps Goraka truly deserved its mythical reputation and this cat had prompted the forest to conjure up a trap. He listened more intently but heard only birds, insects, and his fear-fueled imagination.

Time slipped into a slower speed as he readied himself to react. A whisper in his mind told him to run or he'd be imprisoned here forever. His mouth opened desperately, ready to call out to the little girl.

At that moment, a rare breeze pushed in, thick with the scent of endless nature. It cooled his sweating neck and gently took the thick mist along with it. Light reappeared in thin rays, revealing the brilliant collage of colored birds and speckled flowers in all directions. He felt surrounded by more life than he had ever experienced before; he could taste it on his tongue.

Kits glanced down by his shoe as he heard it collide with something as foreign as himself in that untamed world. It was a tin box, rattling as if full of metal parts and bits of glass. He knelt down and brushed the top clear of soil. A face appeared, once crisply painted and molded but now fading back to its raw materials. Picking it up, Kits shook the remaining dirt off, hearing again that metallic, glassy rattle.

More images and designs adorned the edge, matching the top in an artistic style completely unfamiliar to Kits. Rotted twine slid off as his fingernails dug into the edge, prying at the fused seam until it popped open. He looked inside.

"Hoarder's delight?"

Adults typically used this patronizing term instead of the more polite *memoir reserve*—a small box of detritus, or whatever children considered treasures. The small, private box hid precious items that would mean little to any grownup observer. The small owners of such boxes, having so little control over what they could acquire in life, guarded and cherished the little bits they put inside. Adulthood often relegated the once-precious vaults to tiny coffins of childhood memories, although a sentimental minority would keep them as a private reliquary.

Inside, Kits found an unsurprising collection of random pseudo-treasures. He fingered through a mixture of toys and discarded items whose color and texture would captivate a child. "Now, how did *you* get here?"

He dismissed the long-forgotten crew that had built the stunted road going into Goraka. No black-hand or civic designer would risk bringing it to work, if they had ever even owned one. However unlikely, Kits imagined it had been dropped by some careless child sightseeing on an airship above the infamous Red Valley. Perhaps a sentimental young adult had lobbed it down intentionally, for whatever they felt it would accomplish. As mystifying as it proved, Kits was about to put it back on the ground when the least spectacular item in the box snared his attention.

Absent of the shine and luster of every other object, the matte-gray surface of a small screw stuck out. The corkscrew of metal looked plain and familiar, but his attention gravitated to the head. From the beginning, Lord Jean Batsu had demanded that every fastener type developed in his progressive utopia conform to a single standard. Not one screw in the history of Primichi had ever been produced with a varying head type, and that practice had been wholly maintained in Chigou. The practice became so strict that defying it was deemed a minor illegal act. What should have been a hexagonal star-shaped recess instead had three symmetrical slots. Kits stared at it, small and unassuming and something he had never seen. The strange screw—so simple and yet inexplicable—seemed to be from an alternate reality.

A distinct sound cut through the mystery. Kits jerked his head towards a burning glow pulsing upwards, visible even through the deep thickness of the trees. It flew higher and higher until arcing just above the treetops, blooming into a blinding cloud of light. He stood, stunned, before recognizing what he saw—quite certain that somewhere, others had just done the same.

31
BIRD

"What is *that?*" Suzu exclaimed while gripping Nia's DaiLansu, the flickering hot glow reflecting in her eyes.

Jin immediately recalled what he had given Chichimou back at the farm. "It's *her.*"

"You gave her *another* flare?"

"I did," Jin confessed.

"Well, I guess that worked out… unless we're being lured into a trap."

Regardless, Suzu took off. Jin witnessed her silent sprint through the thicket, straight to where the burning signal pointed. Gripping his bruised and battered core, he did his best to follow.

Suzu's eyes bounced like a drummer's hand between the wild terrain and the fading target she chased. The threat of deadly creatures persisted, but her focus pierced through it. If Chichimou had shot off a flare, she might have slipped away from Kits somehow. He'd be heading to the same spot, and Suzu needed to beat him there. Sweat ran down the curves of her face as leaves slapped it away. She didn't bother looking back at Jin.

As the blinding light above fizzled out, a patch of diffused sunlight peeked through the trees ahead. Just beyond a small cliff, a clearing began to emerge, revealing a single figure. Suzu vaulted to a fallen tree and took cover just before the short drop. She quieted her breath, listening for any movement or voice; a thousand critters distracted her.

Pressing into rotten bark, she peeked up and saw little Chichimou standing alone by something that looked even more out of place than she did. Thin and metallic, it stood just taller than Chichi.

Suzu's eyes squinted, catching finer details. Two panels tilted out of the thing's head—if she had to call it something—and steam began pouring out. A light then pulsed from somewhere around the top, bleeding down a line that glowed cool like electric ice. Another puff of steam and the illumination died out.

So you weren't *lying,* Suzu conceded, seeing exactly what Victou had described—precise technology maintaining organic character.

Suzu recalled her father explaining something again and again in an enthusiastic voice laced with pessimism. The Red Valley held endless amounts of clean energy, and he'd proposed a way to find it. It sounded like a dream that often stalled at the point of inspiration. The thermal probe stood there like a shrine, testifying to the pursuit of a gifted man whom few had appreciated as well as he had deserved. He had been to Gorka—he had seen it.

"Well, Kits, I guess you weren't lying either," Suzu whispered.

The snap of a branch cut through her daydream. She spun around, realizing she hadn't even checked for Kits. With her DaiLansu ready to strike, she spotted a slick-dressed man heading straight for her. Jin trotted like a grandfather while nursing his broken rib. Suzu waved her hand in the air, as if the wind generated would pull him in.

"Saving your energy for a swim later?" she mumbled, struggling to keep her voice down. She gestured from her own eyes towards Chichimou, who now stood next to a homogenous pillar of red.

Air seemed to vanish from her lungs. With panicked effort, she ducked down and waved at Jin to do the same. The afterimage burned in her head like a camera flash, demanding she risk danger and look back. The half-second experience confirmed what had always sat on the threshold of acceptance. Maybe *everyone* in the Naifin Valley believed they existed—they just couldn't cope with admitting it.

Jin slithered up, finally moving as if his life depended on it. He saw Suzu's face awash with more fright than fury. "You saw it?"

"Isn't it obvious?"

Jin peeked up to see Chichimou standing next to the red creature as if meeting a new playmate. The only other time he had seen the phantom, Jin had promptly obeyed Nia's command to retreat, not taking even a second for observation. Undetected, Jin discovered a more delicate quality seeping into his previous impression. The probe stood between the phantom and the girl, acting like glass in a menagerie in which neither knew which side held the specimen.

"What's it doing?" Suzu demanded quietly.

"Observing, perhaps?" His tone wavered between curiosity and terror.

Suzu rolled over and slid up next to Jin. She watched the creature stand... or float, or whatever she was failing to fully understand. It reached the height of an adult, completely red aside from sloping, thick black eyes. Its body resembled suspended liquid, smooth and not quite rigid. "*That's* what attacked you?"

A contemplative hum came from Jin. "I'm not quite sure."

"What does that mean?" Suzu whisper-shouted as quietly as she could. "Is this the thing that killed Nia or not?"

"Nia fell" slid out of his mouth.

At that moment, Suzu realized she had never experienced a full retelling of Nia's final days. Part of her wanted to know, but she had no desire to hear it from Jin's sterile voice. "What do you mean she *fell?* She was like a professional acrobat."

"It did attack us, or it certainly pursued us. We ran from it, but it moves in a way..." the memory drifted like fantasy, "...it was far faster and more agile than either of us, but it did strike. We slid to the edge of a cliff. I... I couldn't hang on."

Suzu's mind pulled away from fantastical creatures and lost children. "You mean you *dropped* her?"

An impulse arose in Jin to clarify Suzu's accusation, but he hadn't the strength. Instead, he tensed up, as if preparing for a gut punch. "Yes."

Aside from Kits, Suzu had always blamed Jin for Nia's death. She didn't burden herself with analyzing hypotheticals, just the singular understanding that he had survived, and Nia hadn't. Suzu wondered if she had made a mistake bringing him along.

"We didn't have time to observe it," Jin said, continuing. "We merely reacted as the moment demanded, but I'm now observing that this creature is not altogether predatory. Highly defensive? Perhaps her size merely does not constitute a threat."

"Maybe you should go down there and find out." Suzu said flatly. "Make amends, clear up your previous misunderstanding."

"I wouldn't recommend provoking it," Jin explained.

"Well, *someone* needs to go grab her so we can..." Suzu felt Jin's fingers go over her lips. She immediately jerked her head away, but his expression halted any rebuke. Jin's focus had latched onto something new. Suzu followed his gaze as it went over her shoulder and down the ridge.

Forty meters away, Kits slinked up to the edge, unknowingly joining Jin and Suzu. With a gun in one hand, his head jutted forward until he paused, taking a cautious look behind. His eyes passed over where they hid, but if he saw them, he gave no hint.

A sharp hiss turned the audience's concern back to the stage. Chichimou stood with her undivided attention on the creature as it positioned itself closer to the densely steaming probe. The observers were transfixed as the fluid being finally gave its first display of limb and structure.

Sliding from the seamless red cloak, a shadow-black appendage crept out. Sharp and thin, it bent like an arm as the end split into what the assembled observers all assumed to be a set of fingers. It reached for the probe's head and interacted with it, demonstrating a dexterity that immediately adjusted everyone's perception of it from *wildlife* to *near-human.*

The onlookers leaned in as the steam shut off and tiles began to flow down from the head of the probe. They descended its thin metal support, sprouting new segments like a molting industrial snake. It continued along the ground with its inexplicable mechanical reproduction. In less than a minute, the magical plumbing channeled vented steam down towards an unknown destination.

"Okay, did you see that last time?" Suzu asked.

Mystified, Jin replied, "No."

Small vents whistled and fluttered, offering a miniature organ concerto. The creature barely moved, like a puddle of blood standing upright. Jin remained entranced by his nightmare. Suzu looked back over at her smug enemy.

"You get the kiddo while I give that one what he's had coming for far too long." She saw Kits rub his injured arm. "There are some bones I still need to break."

Jin saw Suzu, fixated, her attention stuck as if an unprecedented miracle of nature and technology weren't occurring immediately before them. As she positioned herself like a stalking cat, Jin felt the lust of revenge radiating off her. "I think *you* should go after young Lady Chichimou and I should manage Kits."

She turned to Jin as if he had suggested they strip naked and go climb a tree. "No, *steamhead*. You're the only one who's faced that thing and I'm not about to let him go... *or* position myself downrange, even if he doesn't see me."

"I recognize your desire to confront him again, but..."

"Hey, don't trouble yourself with trying to understand me. Also, you got that fancy vest on, so even if he shoots you again, I'm sure you'll survive."

Jin knew it was futile, but he persisted. "We are here for Lady Chichimou."

"*You're* here for the wee one," Suzu insisted. "*I'm* here to make sure that goblin doesn't steal another child ever again."

"Your ability to move incognito is far superior to my own," Jin reasoned.

"Yeah... and?"

"He's far more likely to spot me if I position myself down there. If he shoots me, it will be you contending with Kits, and *both* of you contending with that wraith."

"Yeah, well, it looks preoccupied with the steam stick at the moment. I'll break his face quietly."

He couldn't argue forever. Their time had an end and Jin felt it near. He sat between two antagonists that had bested him, almost to extinction, crouching in a deadly forest next to someone who despised him. Jin wondered what maneuver could possibly get him out of Goraka alive. "You have a better chance of getting to her. We shouldn't risk her life."

"Look around, Jin. I think we're all risking our lives at the moment." She focused again on Kits, ready to approach and pounce. "Some more than others."

"You're overconfident."

"You're irritating."

Jin drew an emphatic breath. "It's foolish to expect a victorious outcome with Kits. We both know that."

"Once, but I managed pretty well last time..."

"*Five people* couldn't stop him from taking Lady Chichimou in clear daylight, including *Gozen*... including *you*."

Suzu's quip lodged tight in her throat.

"Nia distracted that phantom so it wouldn't kill me, and in less than a minute it overcame us both."

Determined rage wound tightly around Suzu's every muscle. She didn't want to give him another second to convince her, but then he spoke.

"If you go straight after Kits, you know it's quite possible that he'll kill you. And if he doesn't, that creature over there will see you, and it will kill you."

"You survived."

"Because of Nia and luck."

Suzu could taste Kits's blood in her mouth, but Jin had a point; she didn't fancy giving her life over to luck. "So, what? You'd rather it be you?" Doubt laced her voice.

"I came to see that Lady Chichimou survives. If I try to make it to her, Kits will see me, and then we'll both die."

Suzu grunted as her blood boiled. Everything was tinted red, blending into Goraka's mystic guardian. Birds trilled all around her. The natural world called out, singing with the spirit of her mother, echoing the wisdom of her father.

"Okay." Suzu swallowed her rage in an aching gulp. "If the forest kills him, so be it."

Without further debate, she moved across the rim, quickly disappearing into the forest. Jin found himself suddenly alone with his promise of pulling the assassin and monster away from the

Ladies. Chichimou and the creature still stood close to each other like old friends.

Jin tightened the vest holding his ribs in place. He had to trap Kits, positioning the unassuming adversary between himself and the forest phantom. Anything but complete silence would be an invitation for a bullet straight into his forehead. Jin plotted his path and dropped down like a prowling fox.

Caution and fatigue cramped his leg with every step back up the slope. Every faint pattering of leaves and shifting of dirt thundered in his ears. He felt the jungle floor pulling at his feet. He paused every few meters, certain that each of his too-clumsy maneuvers was giving his position away. Kits continued to focus ahead, not checking behind him even once. It felt too convenient, and Jin wondered if Kits was merely baiting him.

The heat climbed and his sweat fell, soaking into the underworld. Jin double-checked the presence of his weapon, which seemed to perspire as well. He wanted to be closer, where the sword's advantage would overtake the gun, but he'd never manage the distance incognito. A thick tree gave him cover, just shy of perfectly aligning the other players in their contest. He exhaled dread as a headache began infecting his skull. Everyone stood still, as if waiting for their cue. His companion hopefully lurked further back, playing the black cat.

As if raised by chipmunks, Suzu scurried up the back of a tall tree, just thick enough to hide her frame. Eight meters up, she anchored herself on a branch that bent against her weight. Her eye shifted past the smooth bark and focused through a narrow tunnel of leaves. Just downhill of the small clearing where Chichi and the ghost remained, Suzu's elevated position gave her a view of Kits, still lurking in the same position.

To Kits, any action seemed hazardous with the red sentinel remaining by the exotic device. He thought back to the city, where Daimó was ready to completely forsake him. The seconds tapped on Kits's skull one by one, reminding him of what likely lurked right behind him: a stubborn, black-haired brat who craved his death. The pale-haired aristocrat who had an annoying ability to cheat death. Even the walking fortress had probably managed to flex that bullet out of his chest. He could wait, or he could forge ahead with his own solution.

Jin witnessed Kits's elbow pull in, the trigger finger slide into place, ready to fire. Little Chichimou sat downrange, but what would that gain? The creature stood just as still, but where would you aim, and why would you assume that a bullet would do any more than turn it from docile to enraged? Suzu would be the only logical target, but she remained shrouded, at least from his perspective. Maybe Kits had already found her, and Jin had just sent another young Lady to her death.

He opened his mouth to call out, a reflex of guilt and the memory of Nia doing the same for him. It would take but one sound to turn danger away from the Ladies and onto himself. He had convinced Suzu of his resolve, but fear strangled his voice in place. Jin watched as Kits stood motionless, ready to shoot.

The round shrieked through the trees and Chichimou screamed.

Suzu's nerves spasmed and her foot slipped off the branch, sending fingernails clawing into wet bark. Jin sank behind the rot of an ancient tree.

Chichi watched as thin black tendrils exploded out through a red mist. Ripples ran across the creature as if a pebble had landed in a blood puddle. The movement then ceased, and time seemed to hold still. The being stared at her until its temples began to sink in, stretching its sad eyes down even more. Chichimou covered her mouth with tiny, shaking hands as she watched the creature's body deflate, coiling down into a lumpy pile.

Looks different, dies just the same, Kits thought to himself. He tensed up just as he noticed a single tree nut fall in the distance, cascading between lower branches. A single leaf trailed in a quiet spiral. Growth and decay never ceased in that dense forest as it perpetually recycled itself. Every second something sprouted, something fell... but something had fallen out of order. Kits lowered himself down to the ground and focused his gaze on the shadowy tree.

Nothing else moved. No bird or hoarding little mammal scurried along the branch. Chichi looked like the lost child that she was, standing next to arcane technology and a dead spirit. Maybe gravity had pulled the nut and leaf down, or maybe something had knocked them down and hid. His eyes adjusted to the darker depths. Blackness resolved into finely separated shades of smokey gray. A silhouette of branches appeared, leaves, more branches, and something else—a tail... no, black hair pulled back above the curve of a neck...

Suzu, clinging to the tree as if she'd tried to become a part of it.

"My curse," Kits snarled as he recognized her. He thought back to why he had not been able to kill her before, but those feelings had faded. Nia had convinced him that every life had a chance to aim itself towards whatever it earnestly sought. She had illuminated life in a way he had never seen before. Then she had died, right in that very forest, and he had realized that his faith in any other life, any *better* life, had died along with her.

He broke open the barrel of his pistol, sending the steaming hot metal casing to the ground. He reached into his belt, grabbed another round, and loaded the machine of death. He lifted the barrel, putting the sights between his eye and the silhouette clinging to life high up in the tree. "I'm sorry," he whispered.

Jin finally lifted his face from the ground. A shimmer then swiped across his vision, bright like a ray of sun. He blinked hard but the flash of white continued to streak across the green floor, determined and utterly silent.

Kits squeezed the warm trigger. Another horrible shot cracked through the trees as his head jerked, followed by a wisp of blood. A scream emerged as the echo of gunpowder died. A white owl flew off with a clump of his hair. Kits reached up to the twin slashes exposing his skull. "Damn you, bird!" he blurted out as he watched Kola escape up through the treetops.

The branch broke where the high-velocity round had struck. It knocked Suzu's feet away and her grip failed to re-anchor itself. Arms and fingers flailed as she began falling in a weightless panic. One heel clipped a branch and flipped her backward. The forest spun in a daze before suddenly going black at the sound of her lungs collapsing.

32
INTERSECTION

Victou had heard one gunshot too many and Gozen would not convince him otherwise. He turned away from the window to declare his intentions, only to find the former CE slumped in some state between nap and coma. Although breathing fine, the seasoned investigator had apparently slept through the last ring of artillery.

Seeking to leave a note, Victou found a pistol before locating a pen. He lifted the firearm like a naughty, curious child. It felt heavy and precious, like how he imagined everything in a museum must feel.

He had never fired a gun in his life, but the concept seemed straightforward. At the least, he'd look more threatening with it. Victou looked back outside and noticed a white bird sparkle against the shadowy sea of dark leaves. It circled twice before diving back into the darkness.

Squeezing behind Gozen and opening the door, Victou promised, "I'm coming for you, Chichi."

o o o

A gentle breeze stung his exposed skull like a devil. His sticky red fingers fumbled a new round into the firearm. He pointed the weapon up, never having wanted to kill something more, fantasizing about an explosion of white feathers stained in blood. The forest presented endless shades of earthen tones, void of the ice-colored owl. *Let it go, you child*, Kits thought, reprimanding himself back into focus.

Suzu lay motionless, but odds suggested she hadn't come alone. Kits searched for the others undoubtedly prowling in the living maze. He then turned towards a crunch of footsteps and saw his juvenile guide running laterally across the slope and disappearing behind a curtain of foliage. *No matter,* Kits reassured himself. The probe, his peculiar prize, sat alone in the clearing and he was finally free to claim it.

Just as he got up, the feathered archangel swept back down. Kits raised his weapon too quickly, as if he were being charged by a slaughterous maniac, but the bird ignored him, quietly attending its fallen friend. The girl remained unconscious as the owl hopped around, prodding her face gently. Another shot would practically pinpoint his location, but his advantage was revealed as the owl stopped right by her temple; one shot and he'd be clear. His finger slid onto the trigger. His breaths slowed down. The world carved itself into a point between two steel sights… but Kits hesitated, knowing how that crew always mucked up his plans at the worst times. Kits glanced back one last time just as bits of wood exploded in his face.

He spun his back against rocks and wet moss. A polished, fist-sized claw with fine mechanical barbs had embedded itself into the tree above his head. He aimed his gun defensively, pointing somewhere up the slope. The mechanical talon then retracted its claws and reversed back up the pitch. His stomach strained as he sat up, scanning just above the low-set plants. Leaves danced to a halt where the thing had been sucked back up through the jungle. The barrel shook as he searched for any speck of fabric or flesh.

That was very poorly aimed, Jin reprimanded himself while hiding behind the very tree Kits was pointing his gun at. He looked over his grappling tool, disappointed he had not calibrated the sights properly. The surprise had been spent—wasted.

A few seconds were all Kits needed to guess who his invisible attacker was—who else but the prince of Primichi would own something like *that?* "I'm not impressed by your decorative little harpoon gun, Jin," he called. "Don't they keep any proper rifles in the family cottage?"

Jin recalled the bulky hunting rifle he had taken from the family cabin that currently sat in his car's trunk, encased in a whitewood box—it had never been fired. He packed the failed grappling hook and grabbed his retracted Masu. There would be no sneaking up, and even at a full sprint Kits could manage two shots—maybe three—before the sword could serve its purpose.

"I don't know what you're doing here," Kits called. "You have ten times the life of most people. Just appreciate what you have and go back home."

Jin tested the sword, hitting the trigger and sending the blade up. He imagined blood still hiding in its finely crafted seams. The memory still haunted him, dismembering a man. He didn't want to kill anyone. He didn't want to die.

"Your friend is already down. Your death won't be a sacrifice. You'll just die for *nothing*, Jin," Kits reasoned. "Just run back up the way you came and live your lucky life."

The suggestion had been chasing Jin since the day he left Primichi, but Kits would likely shoot him even if he did try to leave. Only Nia, after months of aggressive opposition, had ever encouraged his decision to explore beyond his privileged life for growth and meaning. He had left home to find true value in life and had found someone who had sacrificed everything for it.

"You're trapped, Jin. You can't get to me now and it's only a matter of time before one of those *things* comes back."

I am not trapped. I choose to be here.

"The only way out is back up the hill. Just go, and we never need to see each other again."

I know you, and you do not let anyone go.

"You know I won't miss."

I know you won't.

"I don't even care if you run after the girl, Jin. I got what I..."

Kits saw Jin's vest jump out from the tree and hastily fired. The bullet hit, but the vest contained no one. "Dammit!"

Jin ran around the other side and rushed towards Kits like a Hotrail train. He held the armored vest loosely in one hand. Kits felt his heart throttle, flushing the pain in his busted arm as he reached for another cartridge. Jin swung the vest and grabbed it with his other hand, stretching it over his torso and head. Kits grunted as his charging target vanished behind the fabric shield, but one part remained exposed. Without hesitation, he raised the loaded weapon and fired again.

Blood sprayed and Jin felt the bones explode in his hand. The vest flopped away like a shot bird. Kits reached for a third round. Jin reached back with his remaining hand and grabbed the retracted Masu. Kits loaded the projectile. Jin saw the barrel raise, watched for where Kits would aim. The muscles in Kits's forearm tightened. Jin triggered the hidden sword and leaned straight towards the still-smoking barrel. Black powder exploded again. Steel hit steel as the bullet diverted off the blade—the final shot, striking Jin's ear.

Kits reached out and grabbed Jin, trying to force his hand. They both felt the sword strike through a mass of flesh. Momentum and weight sent them sprawling to the ground. Small plants and insects were crushed beneath the violent knot of bodies. The impact stunned them, tightening their already strained breaths. Leaves fell from above.

Jin rolled free of the sticky earth and sat up, afraid to see the state of his throbbing left hand. He looked down at his opponent and saw the handle of his Masu low in Kits's chest, handle pointing up to the heavens.

With heavy arms, Kits grabbed the weapon and held on, feeling it pinning him to the ground. Blood seeped out, mixing into the sweat-soaked shirt. He saw the sky through a hazy dome of leaves and branches. More leaves fell, gently spiraling down around him. He remembered looking down at this forest from an airship in the sky, standing next to someone who was unlike any other. "Nia died down here."

"Yes, trying to save her family... and me."

"Of course," Kits smiled as his voice weakened. Color began to drain away from his face. The wrinkles began to smooth out around his eyes. "She had the strength to do that kind of thing." His hands let go off the sword and slid down. Frail fingers held onto the warm moss, feeling the fragile patch of life. "She had the strength to care... about someone like me."

Jin watched as the remaining life slipped out of his eyes, leaving only the reflection of shadow and sky. He reached down for his sword but flinched at the grotesque image of pulling it from a corpse. In his hesitation, Jin noticed a screw that had rolled halfway out of Kits' shirt pocket. He picked it up, grateful for any reason to look away from his Masu buried in Kits. So simple and yet strange. Jin placed the screw in his own pocket.

The lifeless red phantom remained next to the probe, still pumping away. Chichimou had escaped east, and the owl still sat with Suzu.

Amazing… after three gunshots the bird still tends to its friend, Jin thought, admiring the creature's benevolence just as it bit down hard on Suzu's cheek. Her arms flailed about her face and she sat up in a daze.

"Kola, stop," she griped, unsure of her surroundings. She breathed in strange, heavy air. Her fingers pressed into the soggy, foreign ground. Joints and muscles ached as her skull hummed, but nothing felt broken. A silvery blur appeared up the hill, sharpening into a figure. It lacked the irritating posture that Jin insisted on at all times, but who else would wear *those* clothes in a jungle?

"*Kits!*" she remembered aloud with panic, sending a startled Kola up into the trees. Her head spun in a frantic survey until catching the device and creature. She turned to Jin and mouthed *Kits?* in his direction.

"Chichimou," Jin called while pointing east.

Astounded at his careless volume, Suzu waved emphatically with her hand in the shape of a gun—personal sign language for *where is the armed killer, you pampered twit?*

Jin called again, "Chichimou ran—" but suddenly dove down instead of finishing his statement.

Suzu, too, dropped below the ground plants. She listened—heard forest and distant wildlife, but nothing more. Peeking back up, she saw Jin hiding behind a tree while shaking his hand in a frenzied gesture to the west. Suzu finally spotted a second phantom appear into the clearing from that direction.

Digging into decaying leaves and holding her breath, Suzu

saw the creature float towards its fallen peer. It passed between her hiding spot and Jin's before stopping next to the lump of red. Melancholic chords rang out of it, resembling the sound from an instrument rather than a voice. Jin wondered if it was somehow mourning; Suzu wondered if it cried for revenge.

Did Kits and the creature kill each other? Where's his body? Her battered brain finally recalled falling when Kits had shot at her, right after he'd shot the creature from the spot where Jin currently hid. *Did Kits take Chichimou, again?!*

Another creature then emerged from a patch of fog. Suzu pressed herself closer to the ground and watched as the single observer become a pair. Jin still had a clear path up the hill to Neko, and she had no interest in watching the scene turn into a ghost party. Suzu grabbed her DaiLansu and silently made her way east to where Jin had frantically pointed a minute earlier.

Out of the corner of his colorblind eye, Jin saw his companion disappear into the monochromatic jungle, hopefully to retrieve Lady Chichimou. The red pillars remained, their sound morphing into a more complex harmony.

The fog grew behind them. Jin rested, sitting up a bit to ease stress off of his most painful injuries. A bird darted to the trunk above his head, completely inverted. Although wholly black at first glance, Jin soon caught light refracting through iridescent feathers. The bird fluttered as its belly swelled, vibrating the dark crystal pins across its body. It took a few hops down, gripping the bark with gaunt talons.

Ink black pools insisted on watching him. The bird seemed so occupied with him, Jin wondered if he had unintentionally intruded on its nest. The bird was intriguing, but he instead looked back at the creatures that were far more capable of killing him. The cloud shifted and revealed another wraith that had joined the pair. Wind swirled in, bringing more fog, and three soon became ten. Then, like the coast of a blood sea, some forty others emerged in a red tide. They all settled around the deceased in a mourner's huddle, revealing the legendary creature to be an entire clan. Jin swallowed hard, afraid to breathe.

The bird hopped closer to Jin, who saw its sharp beak crack open. Bean-sized lungs filled under its black feathers and Jin prayed for mercy, but the bird seemed to be of a different faith. Merciless chirps rattled out of the tiny creature like notes from a trumpet. Jin looked up to see a single phantom turn towards the sound. Then, in abrupt succession, each ghostly pupil aligned causing Jin to shudder at his sudden audience of demons.

"Time to go home now," Jin mumbled. He quickly stumbled to his feet and finally pulled the sword out from Kits's chest. He turned straight for the truck that hopefully still hid somewhere up the slope—begrudging legs resisting each step—and reached back with his fully intact hand to fumble for the grappling hook. Behind him, the mourner's mass had broken loose and began to flow over the bank. They moved effortlessly, as if gravity had given them a pardon.

Still fighting for his grappling gun, Jin saw the red assembly lift Kits's body. Like a dead animal swallowed by a swamp, in a moment it was gone. The creatures continued slithering towards him. One would creep forward as others shot laterally across the hill, stalking him with the motion of a macabre dance troupe. Pain laced every vein in his body. He briefly wondered why they didn't charge him all at once, but even at that tempered pace, they'd reach him in under a minute.

Jin finally managed to free the gadget from his belt with his good hand and pointed it straight up the hill. He failed to maintain a steady aim, but he figured it would be impossible not to hit at least one tree. The gas cylinder hissed as the grappling hook shot forward, piercing a thick trunk thirty meters away. Without hesitation, Jin triggered the retraction mechanism and felt his arm nearly yanked out of its socket. He stumbled behind like a worn-out fish being reeled in. After skidding his face on a few pads of moss, he managed to struggle back onto his feet before smacking into the anchoring tree.

The grappling hook retracted its blades and Jin's body collapsed against the trunk, begging for any kind of rest. He looked down the hill and saw his clever gadget had managed to make some distance, but his red pursuers seemed to be picking up the pace. Feeling the sting of his test launch, Jin forced his body back up with agonized groans. Barely making any effort to aim, he shot the hook off again and rode the little mechanical devil up another stretch of thick mud and branches.

o o o

Victou finally reached the bottom of the ravine, ignoring the fresh crop of scratches down his arms and legs. Farther east from where the truck had crashed, he found a tree that had grown straight up the cliff's side. Slower and far less daringly than how he assumed the adventure twins had descended, Victou death-gripped the bark and half slid, half climbed down.

The jungle looked as imposing as he remembered, but the flare, owl, and endless slope were triangulated, leading him towards a single location. Sweating fingers gripped the gun, which felt heavy and too big for his hand. He looked at his toes and reminded himself not to blow them off. A bird whistled in the distance. Then, with ears pricked and eyes sharp, Victou began to jog down into the dark mist.

33
PREDATOR

Suzu's limbs automatically decoded the terrain while her dark eyes searched for a kid, a killer, and a ghost. Every square meter had a unique collage of thick roots and slimed rocks, all fighting against her goal. She kept wondering what had happened with Kits and why Jin had just sat there like a dolt.

The question harassed her as a loose rock wrenched her foot. Momentum sent her knee crashing down onto a gnarled root. Her face mimed a scream that she refused to let free, and she rubbed the pain out while cursing the plant.

There's so much crap down here I could run across these stupid trees *faster.* Promptly convinced by her own reasoning, Suzu swallowed the pain and ran straight for the nearest tree.

The trunk was just thin enough to get her hands around it, and she shimmied up faster than she had managed on the ground. Making it to the first branch, she felt as if the forest had finally loosened its grip on her. Lighter air flowed more easily into her lungs, sending a hit of energy. Suzu scurried across the branch and vaulted straight to the next tree.

Her body acclimated more with each step. It felt like bouncing around the silo's rafters back at the farm with Nia. Suzu's heart ached as she thought of Nia's body lying still somewhere in the eternal forest, hopefully swallowed up where nothing else could harm it. Nia would be okay with *that*—back to nature and no fuss—but not with being robbed of so many years. Suzu felt the burden of lives that had been cut far too short. She wouldn't let another girl's life be taken by greedy fools.

As if conjured by Suzu's thought, Chichimou appeared below

beside a thick, old tree. She looked spooked and stood completely still except for her tiny fingers fidgeting up by her chest. Suzu stayed quiet and surveyed the perimeter. Her teeth clenched at the thought of Kits using the child as bait, but she saw no assassin—or floating red phantoms.

Aware that death could be hiding in any of Goraka's countless shadows, Suzu kept quiet as she moved down from trunk to branch. A second before jumping to the ground, a creature materialized out of the forest floor below. Tipping over as she tried to stop herself, Suzu clawed at a passing branch, kicked out her legs for momentum, and swung back up like a child on the first day of Soultai training.

With her cheek pressed into thick, rough bark, Suzu glanced below but saw nothing. She swore her eyes had tricked her until a shape again appeared. It moved steadily but blended in, as if painted to match the ground. As traces of diffused sunlight poked through trees, Suzu finally deciphered the form of a powerful wildcat stalking the unknowing child. It seemed absurd, but the cat's color appeared to shift as it lurked forward.

Suzu gripped her DaiLansu, ready to lunge and defend against the cat that coiled up for a strike on Chichi. The light finally revealed lines of muscle wrapped around the predator's back and limbs. It looked bigger than her and came with an assortment of pointy white fangs and claws. With no desire for a full fight, Suzu settled on one heavy blow to the head—stun and run.

Suzu launched herself downward, but the cat beat her by half a breath. "No!" flew out of her mouth as the cat's lunge put its head out of reach. Her DaiLansu stretched out in desperation, striking the animal's pelvis. She rolled on the ground and prepared for fanged retaliation. Instead, the cat stumbled laterally as needles shot through its nervous system. Suzu had only a moment to react as the apex predator recovered, perfectly distanced between the two humans.

"Run back up to the truck, Chichi," Suzu ordered.

The young girl heard Suzu's command, but her body failed to respond as the cat's meat-rending fangs emerged. Her muscles felt like concrete as the hulking cat compressed its body more, glancing between her and Suzu.

"Run up the hill, Chichi, *now!*" Suzu demanded.

"I… I can't," Chichimou pleaded, seized by fear.

The low growl of the cat pulsed like an engine. Its mouth wrinkled wide open, showcasing a set of teeth that could fit snugly around a human skull. Suzu had fought her share of people— mostly people bigger than her—but struggled to think of any strategy against this born hunter. She dug her worn shoes into the ground and readied herself for force and fangs just as the camouflaged cat started backing up.

Chichimou remained frozen as Suzu slowly closed in towards her, still ready for a lethal encounter. The cat continued its retreat, backing into a bush dotted with blood-red berries. The Ladies watched as its fur changed to a brighter green speckled with red dots, and suddenly it vanished. Leaves then parted like curtains pushed back by a ghost.

Suzu stared wordlessly. "This place is insane."

"Its fur changed colors," Chichimou said faintly.

"Yes, it did."

"How'd it do that?"

"Excellent question," Suzu mumbled while inching towards the berry bush, not looking once at her footing. She gripped her weapon tight, ready to jump back and keep her face from getting clawed off. The leaves settled down as forest noises replaced the hungry, blood-powered growl.

"I think it's gone," Suzu declared while turning around. Behind Chichimou, a rather spectacular flower stole her attention. Alternating red and white petals fanned out around a sphere of orange seeds , and a cluster of green and yellow spines shot out of the center. The vivid arrangement mocked any palm-sized flower she'd seen in the central valley—and with those spines, it would also gouge out the eye of anyone trying to smell it. A fragmented memory then emerged: a photograph of the same flower had sat, framed on her father's desk, for years, often obscured by a coffee mug. She had never seen the plant's image anywhere else.

SPIKED FLOWER | F12
GORAKA
LORD CARMIN KOMOU

"Lady Suzu?" Chichi asked.

"Come on, let's get out of this place," Suzu said as the flower began to move. She realized that she felt no breeze. Then, an entire patch of the forest shifted as if cut out from a picture.

A relieved Chichimou stepped forward just as Suzu recognized the illusion's silhouette. Before she could cry out a warning, the patch of color revealed its menacing teeth—the forest cat had returned. Suzu lunged but the cat's jaws were faster, striking at Chichimou's back. Both ladies screamed out as Chichimou felt fangs scrape her skin before sinking into her shirt, yanking her backwards. Suzu ran forward, pushing the extraordinary plant aside as its vibrant spines lanced her hand. An immense pain stung down her arm, but adrenaline kept her legs charging.

The muscular predator dragged its screaming prey across the jungle floor, its spellbinding fur pulsing with color before perfectly aligning with the forests' texture. Without hesitation, Suzu again went for higher ground. She used a young tree to vault onto a heavier branch, but as she pulled herself up, the pain in her hand struck again. She slipped and swung down with a single hand. She growled as her injured arm twitched. She kicked hard and managed to swing higher up to fewer obstacles and a clear view. Chichimou looked as though the forest itself was dragging her away.

Suzu pushed off into a near sprint across the ancient tree. Too focused for pain, she skipped through the treetops in sober pursuit. With the carnivore nearly invisible, Suzu instead tracked the brightly dressed child. Chichimou stopped, half-floating in the air, so Suzu used the cover of her wailing to dive onto the distracted hunter.

Striking with one hand as best as she could, the DaiLansu managed a fair blow just as she spotted the cat's thick neck. It dropped Chichimou to the ground, but Suzu felt the full force of a massive paw as the cat's perfect reflexes knocked her back. She rolled into a thick, leafy plant and managed to rebalance quickly. Ignoring her own danger, she again ordered Chichi to run.

The word pushed Chichimou to her feet. Half-dazed, she

managed to locate Suzu and the wild cat between them, its chromatic fur spazzing like fireworks.

"I'll catch up, dammit. Run to the truck, *now*." Suzu charged, keeping her eyes locked on the predator.

Too rattled to disobey, Chichimou began to struggle back up the hill. Suzu watched through her peripheral vision as a new pain joined the collection. Looking down, she saw her thick jacket sliced right at the belly. She hoped it had kept her from serious injury, despite her abdomen stinging like a paper cut doused with lemon juice.

The beast's colors wobbled as it tried to focus between the two girls. Suzu pulled its attention back to herself by grunting through a flamboyant twirl of the metal staff. The creature ignored its initial target and focused solely on the immediate threat. Its muscles flexed as prismatic fur settled into a murky red. Murderous, fiery eyes burned through her confidence.

Suzu knew that, despite her training, she was no match for such a perfectly tuned killing machine. However, if the large cat shared any spirit with its domesticated cousins crawling all over the city, she wouldn't need to. Even small cats could be ferocious, but their self-preservation usually outweighed any primal obsession to fight. She didn't need to kill it—she just needed to make her death not worth the effort. The cat crept forward as Suzu established a strong footing, trying to force her throbbing hand into obedience.

Chichimou looked back, trying to see Suzu, but she had already run too far—only an endless jungle greeted her. A scream rang out, rattling her nerves. It sounded frightful, just like Suzu's last order. With her whole body aching, Chichimou continued her climb back up through Goraka.

o o o

Jin wiped the bile from his mouth as his distracting lust for water doubled. He assumed adrenaline or some emergency bio-process kept his muscles moving at all, but it wouldn't last. Resetting his grappling hook for the twenty-third consecutive time, he leaned against a tree and tried to recover, looking back.

Expecting the army of red phantoms to be scurrying up behind him through the plants, Jin instead saw a calm jungle. The gadget had provided an effective boost against gravity and fatigue, but the lack of pursuers still surprised him. He wondered if they were sprinters and had given up, or perhaps they had been satisfied by his retreat. If Suzu had found Lady Chichimou, it would be wise to meet back at Neko. Jin hoped for that but knew Suzu would be just as likely—if not more—to find trouble. He contemplated a return to the darkness as a slithering pain crawled up his left arm.

Jin finally looked at his injured hand, sticky with blood. Technically, all of his fingers were present, but the smallest two looked nothing like proper digits. He tried his best to ignore what would certainly require a series of operations. Amputation seemed more likely, but that thought did little for his growing nausea.

A single red being then appeared, hovering a good forty meters away. It moved so gradually that at first, Jin thought it was standing still. He sensed no panic or aggression and wondered if it had simply tagged along to ensure the foreigner was continuing its withdrawal.

Almost unaware of his actions, Jin's feet began marching backward up the hill. He stumbled but kept watching, his eyes unable to leave the ghost. The grappling gun was cradled in his good hand, and Jin contemplated racing off again, but feared his body might give in.

Jin had decided on a brisk march back to the truck just as the noise from what sounded like a machine reverberated through the forest. Noises cranked and pulsed, coming from somewhere behind the ghost. The industrial mix of rhythms possessed soft tones that felt at odds with anything Jin had ever heard. A faint vibration came up through the ground as leaves and branches began fluttering in the distance. Jin moved his finger to the trigger, ready to abuse his body with another cable ride through raw jungle, but a grotesque curiosity pulled his eyes towards the emerging sight.

A cluster of dark panels pierced through the trees. The collective mass appeared as a giant mongrel of machine and insect. Limbs and torso fluidly exchanged places; the individual segments seemed capable of rearranging at will. An opening formed in the maniacal automaton, allowing the red phantom to disappear as if swallowed. Just as quickly, the hole vanished and the mechanical creature advanced straight towards Jin.

Jin's blood- and sweat-soaked hands fumbled with the gadget as he stared in panic. He witnessed the behemoth smash its way straight up the hill, chanting like a demonic calliope. Once he finally wrangled the grappling gun, Jin aimed for one of the thousand trees ahead. He fired, saw the barb strike a target, and then felt his body vaulted forward into a desperate escape.

o o o

Still worried about exploding toes, Victou ran with the gun angled out like he meant to drop it, but the weight became burdensome. Enough time had gone by that he considered yelling out for his daughter, despite the certainty of attracting some other, hellish creature.

He stopped, rested, and took a deep look around. "Chichi," he called softly. His protective zeal started slipping into doubt. Goraka seemed to have grown, but that might have been an effect of searching rather than hiding. Victou had started in the right direction, but he had no clue how far he had run. Unable to see into the mass of plants, he instead closed his eyes, hoping that would somehow sharpen his other senses.

"Dad!"

Chichi's voice cut through the soft echo of birds and insects. Victou's eyes popped open to see his daughter running straight at him.

"Chichimou!" Victou burst forward with near disbelief. They stumbled over plants, eventually colliding in a silent embrace. Victou squeezed his daughter as if they stood at the edge of an abyss. Chichimou let out a burst of tears, soaking her father's already damp shirt.

After a moment, Victou finally gave his daughter a good look. She had scrapes and bruises, more than he had ever seen on her before. "You're hurt… What happened?"

Chichimou finally had a moment to consider her struggle against death. She tried to explain but hadn't the strength for more than a few fumbled words.

"But you ran here. You're okay?" Victou asked.

She managed a nod and he offered her another minute buried in the safety of his arms. He looked out over the jungle for what had hurt her, wary that it might still be in pursuit. He stroked her tangled hair and prayed thanks for having her again. Gray clouds of fog drifted by them.

"Okay, Chichi, what did this?"

Enough terror had expelled to allow full words. "A cat."

"A little cat did this?" Victou asked in disbelief.

"No, a *big* cat that you couldn't see."

He didn't understand. "And it attacked you?"

"And Lady Suzu attacked it," Chichimou explained, becoming more upset.

"Okay, it's okay." Victou gently cleaned some of the mud off of her face. "Well, she's really brave and really strong, right? Let's go back to the truck and she'll meet us up there," Victou offered.

Chichimou's face twisted; she didn't look convinced.

"Come on. She's so fast, she'll probably beat us up there," he managed with passable conviction. "Let's go." He stood up and led her forward.

After a brief climb, Victou picked up his daughter and placed her on his back. Every two minutes her body would slip and he would feel her thin arms tighten around his throat. He thought to place her on his shoulders but figured that the taller center of gravity would send them falling face-first onto some deadly plant. Instead, he'd boost her up every few minutes—mindful of the pistol he still gripped firmly in his hand.

Victou's pulse eased while he felt Chichimou's breathing gradually settle on his back. He had rarely offered to carry his daughter, and he didn't know why; her weight still presented little burden. He sensed her cheek rest against his shoulder, and it felt warm—like trust.

A wondrously small bird zipped by, causing Victou to flinch before settling into a smile. He knew Chichimou, who loved fanciful little things, must have passed out, as she offered no reaction. The father watched as the bird hovered at a flower and then zipped on to another. The bird seemed to join them as it bounced from one scarlet bloom to the next, ascending the hillside. It paused at one, inspecting it a few times before darting up into the treetops. Victou watched as it disappeared into the fog.

"Did you see that?" he asked in case she still listened.

"Huh?" she mumbled over his wet shoulder.

"Look," Victou said brightly as the bird returned with a mate racing behind. They convened at the same flower and took turns feeding from its multi-colored center. "Neat, huh?"

He heard the sweetest breath of affirmation puff out from an exhausted smile he couldn't see. The small family paused for just a few seconds, appreciating the display, setting it into their memory.

"Wow, what amazing little creatures," Victou whispered as he continued his march back to a cooler, drier world.

Chichimou watched the whisping birds, recalling their name from a book gifted by her mother. Magical energy floated around her as she witnessed the beautiful illustration from her book come alive. Even knowing quite well what dangers existed in this forest, Chichimou decided she liked the woods. She remembered how much her mother had smiled after the only time they had gone camping together, as a family.

The birds disappeared behind thick leaves the size of her face, and Chichimou turned her attention to the ethereal patches of fog and passing vines crawling up trees. The ambiance soothed her, and the steady pace her father found rocked her towards an exhausted nap. Just as her eyelids became blissfully heavy, she felt their steady momentum halt.

She noticed her dad's head cocked rigidly to the side, blocking her view of whatever had seized his attention. With a soft grunt, she pulled her head onto his other shoulder and saw a bright area not unlike where all the scary business had happened before. As her eyes fully regained their focus, another probe with a scarlet keeper became clear.

"We should go," Chichimou suggested.

Victou stood still as stone, staring back at the guardian that had clearly spotted them. He felt stupid for not choosing his path better; the creature had a perfectly unobscured view. Victou turned slowly, putting himself between his daughter on his back and the strange creature before them.

"Dad, can we go?" Chichimou said again, anxious for them to leave.

Ready to take his child's advice—very carefully—Victou only managed a step before the creature began to approach. Although its speed was slow, it moved with an eerie consistency that seemed to ignore the wild, uneven ground below. The pace wasn't anything Victou couldn't beat on flat ground, at least for a short distance, but, even as light as Chichi was, he'd never maintain speed up that hill.

Chichimou felt her father's arm raise, the one that had awkwardly cradled the gun. It shook from nerves, or fatigue. Although shiny and beautifully intricate, the device made Chichimou nervous. She knew it could hurt people. "Dad?" she pleaded softly as she hunched below his shoulder.

With no warning, a deafening crack rang out and they both jumped with surprise. The scarlet phantom shot sideways, a small speckle of red shooting just off its side. Victou's quivering hands struggled to regain control as the creature slithered backward, making a ghastly hissing sound. Panic shot through his veins as Chichimou's arms strangled him. Ready to fire again, intentionally if needed, Victou attempted a defensive stance. The creature rippled down its long shape like vibrating Capi Cake before suddenly wriggling back into shadow.

"Oh my goodness," he said, voice trembling. He'd never fired a gun before and immediately decided he never wanted to again. "It's okay, it's gone," he said while trying to stash the gun, deciding on his back pants pocket. The heavy weapon stuck out like it wanted to escape, but at least his finger wasn't touching the trigger anymore.

Their collective breathing settled as the father resumed their ascent. Victou looked back every three steps, checking to see if the creature would reemerge, claws out. The surrounding plants remained still, and only the steam probe hinted at the presence of a bizarre society of forest demons. He thought of getting back to the truck, then back to the farm with its open fields, orchards... and the farmhouse where his daughter had been kidnapped in the clear light of morning.

Chichimou felt her father's progress stop again.

"Are you too tired? I can walk," she offered sweetly.

Victou had turned back to the probe, half-obscured by plants and idly puffing steam. The device looked odd but more or less simple. It seemed strange to him that so much effort and so many resources had been marshalled to claim this mysterious tool. It seemed to work but he had no idea how. Did Kits's boss know? Did anyone? Victou had no answer, but he knew that the cost of most things was determined only by what people were willing to pay.

Chichimou felt her father's grip ease as he let her slide down his back. "Hey, Chichi, I want you to stay here for a minute, okay?"

"Why?"

Victou saw that she didn't want him to leave. Neither did he, but what leverage did he have to bargain for a peaceful life once they returned to civilization? He'd never had much to protect her with. She deserved peace and safety, not an exhausting life running to nowhere. She deserved to be loved and not be used as a tool for powerful men to achieve progress.

If these people needed her to get this damn thing, I'll just get it for them. If they had what they wanted, why would they even think of us?

"I'll just be right back over there," he said. "See that thing sticking up?"

"Yeah," she replied half-heartedly.

"I'll just be there, then I'll be right back."

She just looked at him.

"Okay," he said, wiping some dirt off her face. "Hey, I love you."

Half of her mouth curled up in a weak smile. Victou flattened some of her tussled hair and marched back to the coveted treasure, the key to their future.

34
RUSH

As a child, Jin had once read of a Shévika that had been ridden to death. The hefty yet swift animal, which had been quite popular as pre-industrial transport, had two thick, swept-back antlers that splintered at the ends like flame. The story had followed a pair of Shévika that carried two hunters deep into the northern Murdes. Minutes into their return journey, one hunter's mount slid off a cliff. His Shévika died while he sported two compound fractures.

The partner carried his crippled companion on the remaining Shévika, running as hard as possible to a doctor. The Shévika got them back to town, although it collapsed and died. The injured hunter had to have both legs amputated, but he lived.

The tale had sounded hyperbolic at the time, like suffocating by holding one's breath, but Jin now understood the Shévika's plight. Mechanical red death chased him from behind while the fatality of exhaustion waited just ahead.

Jin prayed for the eternity of trees to end. The cliff would eventually appear—he knew it must—but the distance back to it seemed to have multiplied five times. Avoiding a complete collapse, he stopped every few minutes just to keep upright, allowing the sound of haunted metal to reemerge.

His eyes ached from a sudden flood of light that burned through the everlasting shadow. It seemed like the end, but instead of being washed in relief, he smacked straight into a wall of rock.

His exhausted groan wheezed through a desperate breath. Jin looked back and saw the machine pushing jungle aside. With his left hand practically useless, he wedged the grappling hook in his armpit and tried to reset it one last time. The barb locked in and aimed up high, his dilated eyes blind to any detail. Jin fired and heard the snare whistle away, striking something solid. Without hesitation, he anchored the gun to his vest and triggered the spool. Jin felt his body snap upwards. A second into the escape, the hook broke free and gravity sent Jin's back slamming into the ground.

Another groan croaked out of his bone-dry throat. The machine closed in, its sound torturing him like a child's nightmare. The falling harpoon continued to coil itself back in until it finally snapped into place, whipping his blood-stained cheek in the process. Jin barely had the energy to flinch as he got up, ignoring the fresh line of blood joining the rest on his face. Standing crooked, Jin reset the grappling gun—surely for the last time. He aimed wildly as the ground beneath him began to shake. Barely able to feel the trigger, he squeezed down with a blistered finger.

The hook shot up again. The metallic monster drowned out any sound of the harpoon. Jin then felt the wire go taut. He whispered *please* through chapped lips and squeezed the return switch. He was launched violently off the ground and raced up into the air. Screeching faded into the thuds of his body as he bounced off the cliffside. More light poured in as he ascended past the treetops. Just shy of flat ground, the small winch stopped and Jin twisted, hanging suspended just below the trunk of a cliffside tree.

Ignoring the fatal drop, he kicked into roots and began to clumsily climb up the cliffside. His burning limbs wailed as he managed to drag his body up inches at a time. He wedged his gnarled left hand between roots, not wasting a single resource. Pulling and clawing, he rounded the lip of the cliff with just enough momentum to keep him from slipping back.

The machine still taunted him below, far enough away that Jin felt safe enough to lay on the ground like a dead fish. He didn't want to move ever again. His lungs drank up air in long, shaky breaths. The encroaching sense of insanity gradually seeped away, and he began to think of his next steps, starting with how to roll over. As he managed to balance upright, a shriek assaulted him from below the cliff.

Vibrations infected the ground as the noise swelled. Jin managed to peek back down the cliff and noticed a spider crawling up. Its body—matching the size of a commercial truck—contorted in strange ways as it ascended.

Jin instinctively labored onto his feet and began to flee the tenacious beast. He managed two steps before being slammed back down to the ground. Jin screamed as he felt the beast reach out and grab him. Panic flooded in until he realized he hadn't yet unhooked the harpoon. Reaching over the edge, he retracted the barbs out of the tree and began hobbling away from the nightmare.

Jin searched for Neko and promptly discovered he had returned right between the truck and Kits's car. Paying the dark coupe no mind, Jin staggered up towards Gozen's cockeyed truck, still stuck over the trunks of murdered trees. He moved slowly but the last few steps over flat ground felt impossibly luxurious. While the frightening howl continued to rise, Jin finally reached the driver's door.

The sudden noise woke Gozen up from his nap. He felt decent, but the bright light stung his eyes. "What time is it?"

Jin stepped up and pushed the heavy man about an inch. "Let me in," he wheezed.

"Just go around," Gozen grunted.

"It's blocked, please..." his throat nearly seized, "...just let me in."

Gozen's recovering eyes finally got a proper look at Jin. Covered in blood and bits of forest, Jin looked as though a demon had successfully wrestled for possession of his body. "Good Lord, what happened to you?"

Without the energy to do both, Jin pushed Gozen and kept his mouth quiet. Shifting his large mass around, Gozen slipped to the passenger seat as Jin stumbled into the central cabin. He dug through Gozen's stuff like a tiny mammal burrowing in for the winter.

"What are you... wait, where's Suzu?" The entirety of the day—their location and their purpose for being there—began to brighten Gozen's foggy mind.

Jin pulled a bottle out of the compact wall fridge, sheared the cap off, and slammed the liquid into his throat. The shock caused him to gag, but Jin fought through it until he managed a steady chug of the fruity tonic Lady Kyoumére had brewed for her dear friend. Gozen could only watch as Jin forced the last of it down.

After coughing up what had dripped into his lungs, Jin asked, "Where's Victou?" Without waiting for an answer, he went straight back and hit the lever for the rear door.

Gozen, starting to shake off the languor, slowly followed Jin. "He's not here? He's not here. What are you doing? Where is Su…"

"Get in the car, we need to go," Jin commanded with his partially reclaimed voice. He then ripped open a first aid kit and performed the most frantic dressing Gozen had ever seen. Catching some of a cabin light, Jin's mangled fingers flashed before being mummified in gauze.

"Your hand looks bad. Is Suzu with Chichi? Is Victou with…"

"We shall pick them up… I hope."

A jarring, heavy racket then echoed into the cabin. Gozen leaned over to look outside. "What the hell was that?" he wondered aloud as he felt Jin pull on his collar.

"You'll prefer not to be introduced," Jin warned. "Trust me."

Jin led the giant man through the tight corridor. As the trailer door stopped fully open, Jin fell into the driver's seat of the Aya Motors C23 and fired up the flash boilers. Gozen squeezed up between the convertible's passenger door and the trailer.

"There's a hunting rifle in the trunk," Jin informed him.

"Okay," Gozen replied, noting the young man's terse tone. "Jin, we shouldn't leave the truck here and I can barely fit in this thing." As Gozen awkwardly attempted to climb over the back and into the passenger seat, a devilish roar from outside stopped him cold.

Jin slammed the throttle. Gozen felt his outside foot start to drag as the car took off. He hurled himself forward, clambering into the passenger seat to avoid being dragged by the car. The C23 shot out and slammed onto the overgrown road.

"Dammit, Jin. Can you just explain…" he paused, seeing Jin's clearly rattled face turned back towards the truck. He glanced back as well, just in time to see a machine straight from hell crawling up the cliff face and onto the road. The mutating hulk barely touched the ground with its few emerging legs, none of which looked capable of supporting such mass. It paused for a moment as if to orient itself. Then, what appeared to be a massive compound eye slid across the machine's body, passing from panel to panel. It finally stopped, pointing right at the two men in the fleeing C23.

"What in all existence?" Gozen breathed in disbelief.

"I think it sees—" Jin's comment was cut off by a dreadful sound, like the growl of a wildcat mimicked by demonic machinery. He fumbled with the accelerator, trying to increase their speed as the shadowy contraption began its pursuit.

"Jin," Gozen warned as he watched the metal giant approach. With a grunt, Jin finally wrangled the accelerator as Gozen stared back. The beast squared up to Neko and smashed into the driver's side, tilting the massive truck nearly two meters off the ground before it balanced on one row of wheels.

The infernal machine carried on after them as Neko dropped back down, bounced hard on the uneven ground and kept rolling. In a breath-stealing moment, Gozen helplessly watched as his traveling home slammed onto its side, the sound of metal and exploding glass rocketing towards them.

Jin continued to drive, struggling to navigate his sporty coupe over the road that had been reclaimed by the forest. He prayed that, somehow, he and Gozen would find the others and manage to escape hell together.

o o o

Suzu's theory about felines had proven true. She had burst into a confusing display of acrobatics once Kola had joined her, circling just beyond the fanged predator's reach. The wildcat quickly found them to be an irritating pair and not worth the effort. Eventually, it gave up and sulked off to lick its wounded pride. With barely time to recover, she heard another gunshot ring out.

Kola followed as Suzu ran straight towards the sound. The pain in her left hand screamed for attention. She clenched her fingers, desperately trying to squeeze out whatever toxin invaded the wound. Although fighting to focus, she found herself repeatedly looking at her fingers, now puffy sausages, swollen to twice their normal size.

"Ghosts... demon cats... and I might lose my hand to a damned flower," Suzu grumbled, imagining what other denizens existed in that circus of biological wonders. She climbed up in an intermittent jog, trying to catch up to the small girl without shooting right past her. "Come on, she couldn't have gotten *that* far."

As time passed, the jungle proved a powerful distraction. Although not as wholly in love with nature as her mother had been, Suzu still held a deep appreciation for the natural world. Beyond the immediacy of her mission, she saw a wonderland that her parents would have treasured, even with all of its dangers. *I could go camping here*, she decided, *but just up at the top.*

A face then appeared to her right, stark against leafy patterns. Suzu grabbed her DaiLansu and crouched low, slipping into silence. She crept along until realizing who she was looking at— Chichimou stood tranquilly, with her face half angled to the ground, looking almost hypnotized. Suzu's eyes probed the wood. *Okay, Kits, where are you?*

A large, winged insect flapped up from the ground. Chichi smiled as she offered her finger to the delicate creature. What first appeared as a single pair of large wings split to reveal six buzzing sets. A long red tendril bounced below its body like a dancing thread. Suzu recalled it from a childhood book and remembered being fascinated by the red tail ten times its body length. Her mother explained how the tail baited would-be predators and would easily snap off for a swift escape, growing back within a day or two. *I could have used one of those a few minutes ago.*

With no sight of the kidnapper, Suzu briskly made her way over to the distracted girl. "Chichi," she said in a low voice.

Chichimou looked up and around as the fairy-like creature flitted away, head snapping to Suzu as she emerged from a thicket of leaves. Her smile disappearing, the youngster looked downhill with a fearful expression.

Suzu likewise turned, ready for bullets or fangs. "Is Kits here, the one who took you?"

Chichi shook her head.

Kola screeched and then shot up into the treetops. "Because I have a friend who'd like to snack on his eyes." Suzu said before pointing uphill. "Come on."

Chichimou didn't budge. "What about my dad?"

"Yeah, I'm sure he's very anxiously waiting for your return." She grabbed the girl's arm.

"Nuh-uh," Chichi argued, pulling away.

"What do you mean?"

"He'll be right back."

Confused, Suzu peered around. "Chichi, did you see your..." The question answered itself as she spotted Victou off in the distance through a narrow gap in the trees, looking as if he was struggling to assemble a pup tent. "What's he doing?"

"He's getting the *thing*," Chichimou said.

Victou finally stepped aside to reveal the steam probe he fussed with. He scratched his head before bending down and reaching for the thin device's base.

For a moment, Suzu imagined her father installing the core-thermic probe he had designed, blessing future generations with energy that didn't poison the land—a family dream. It felt surreal, seeing a man steal what her father had invented but had never gotten to make.

Suzu waved to get Victou's attention. They had to get out of here. She grunted as his obsession with dislodging the device made him oblivious to his surroundings. Her wave became fiercer and, out of the corner of Victou's eye, he finally noticed. Tension faded into a smile of relief as he recognized the zealous young Lady standing guard by his daughter. He waved back.

Suzu's throat seized as red drifted into view. Before she could even begin to scream, the scarlet creature lunged into a blur, straight towards Victou. With no time to warn him, all she could do was cover the eyes of his daughter. Victou's head turned just as his body bent in half. Suzu screamed *"NO"* as the red ghost threw him into darkness. The sickening cry of a terrified man rang out, fading quickly into the depths until it disappeared.

Suzu held the child in shock—another little girl forced to endure her family being taken right in front of her. Something inside her wanted to run, reclaim the life that, no matter how foolish, was owed to this young Lady, but he was gone.

"Dad?" Chichimou's anxious voice asked as she pulled Suzu's hand off her eyes.

"Chichimou…" Suzu's voice faded out, not knowing what else to say. She couldn't speak of her own trauma without crying or screaming. A bomb of suppressed anger and grief felt ready to explode as another red ghost emerged behind the steam probe. Without thinking, Suzu pulled Chichimou back a step.

"Daddy?" The word came out of Chichi's mouth frail and frightened.

"Chichimou, I'm sorry, but we need to go." Her anxiety rose along with the phantom population in the distance as the second one joined the first.

"We can't *leave* him!" Chichi looked up with pleading eyes, but Suzu had nothing to offer.

She swallowed her guilt and pulled on the girl's arm. A third ghost appeared near the probe. "I'm sorry, Chichi, but it's not safe." And as if attached with a winch, all three ghosts began to hover towards them, accelerating every second.

"We need to run," Suzu said firmly. Chichimou had barely managed a step when Suzu shouted, "*Run!*"

Dragged by Suzu as she bolted up the hill, Chichimou ran away from the red creatures and away from her father. She had no choice but to move her feet to keep from falling. The athletic young Lady pulled and lifted her, making her feel as if she ran just above the ground.

Suzu noticed a large Toki bouncing off the young girl's belt, throwing off the young girl's weight. Suzu reached down and snatched it to toss it away until, only then, realizing what she held. They could use the device… but first, they'd have to make it back to the cliff.

○ ○ ○

Gozen twisted in the small convertible sedan, trying to see the metal leviathan emerging from the fog sea. Roots and rocks offered endless speedbumps along the forsaken road. Every obstacle sent needles into the gunshot wound in his shoulder.

"It's getting closer."

The wheels fought back like rabid vermin being put in a cage. "The road contains less debris the closer we get to the exit. We should pull away then."

"Right, but we are missing a few important passengers. What was your plan to get them in this tiny car?"

"I…" Jin's answer blew away in the rushing wind.

"Do you even know where they are?" Gozen looked at Jin, realizing they might be driving *away* from Suzu and company. "They are *alive*, correct?"

"Oh, yes. They should be."

"So, where are we… ?"

Another horrifying scream came from the behemoth. "Lady Chichimou hopefully still has the Toki I gave her. It has two flares and I only saw one discharged, so we should keep an eye on the tree-tops."

"So, you don't know where they are… *at all?*" Gozen's heavy voice pushed through the cacophony of pursuing machinery.

"I don't see why they wouldn't still be in there," Jin said, glancing at Gozen. "We *really* should keep an eye on the tree-tops."

35
HAND

Chichimou didn't run quickly, but she persisted like a little machine. Suzu prepared her general's charge for when the girl inevitably stalled, but Chichi must have been running on a hidden vat of energy. Suzu wondered if Nia had felt the same way when Suzu had first arrived. *With some proper training, this one would make a good accomplice,* Suzu decided.

The energy pulsed heavily through her body, but she knew their muscles had a limit. Suzu wondered if those things ever tired, practically floating above the ground. The relentless slope promised them that they were headed towards Neko, but the rock wall presented an unavoidable challenge. Suzu squeezed the Toki tightly, ready to launch a flare the second they arrived cliffside.

Chichi was finally slowing. "I can't run anymore," she gasped.

"We're almost there," Suzu breathed, feeling Chichi's weight dragging more heavily on her arm. Suzu thought about carrying the child, but she'd need that precious energy for the vertical climb. She looked back, hoping the creatures had perhaps decided to stop their pursuit, but flashes of red destroyed that wishful thought. "Come on… we're almost there... we *gotta* be."

Moss covered everything and felt slicker with every shaky step. Suzu wondered if the forest truly contained a dark spirit that had them trapped in an endless loop. Curses piled up in her strained throat just as the shelf of light bled through, revealing the cliff.

"Yes, please, yes," Suzu wheezed out.

"I can't. I have to stop." Chichimou dragged, a dead weight on Suzu's failing arm.

"Almost… almost there," Suzu spit out as they finally cleared the gauntlet. Taking one second for her brain to steal oxygen back from her legs, Suzu could see the cliff looked higher, meaning their retreat had slanted back towards the entrance, away from Neko. She held up the Toki and looked it over. "Okay, now how does this blasted thing work?"

She rolled it over in her hand, feeling each decorative feature that teased some kind of function. "Dammit, Jin, can't you ever just keep it simple?"

Chichimou, who had collapsed to her knees in a plea for rest, tilted her head up. She raised a feeble arm and tried to speak.

Suzu dug her nails into every seam of the Toki. "Are you *kidding* me?"

Chichi then closed her mouth and regained enough spit to speak. "You have to…" Before she could finish, a flare shot out and ricocheted into the forest.

"*No!*" Suzu screeched as she squeezed the Toki in punishment. "Is that the last one? No, no, no!"

Both of them looked up as they heard a strange noise coming from the cliff's peak. They watched as the top of some massive black thing clawed and twisted its way up the road towards them. It was utterly unlike anything either of them had seen before. Suzu then noticed debris shoot off the cliff ahead of it, along with the echo of a car engine throttling like mad.

"Are they leaving? They're gonna miss us." She looked back down at the Toki, but its weight signaled an empty metal tube, so she chucked it. She stood between Chichi and whatever creature came after them. Her injured hand throbbed, hurting worse than ever. She grabbed the DaiLansu with her good hand as something brilliant emerged from the dark fog. It slotted through the trees before fixing its path straight at the pair of exhausted Ladies.

○ ○ ○

"Do you see it?" Jin asked again.

"I'm not keeping secrets," Gozen answered. "This road won't go on forever."

"Correct."

"And we're *not* leaving without them," Gozen emphasized.

Jin looked in the rearview mirror and wondered how they could possibly stop. The tireless machine spread across the road, capable of flicking their car like a table crumb. If the missing travelers awaited them roadside, they might have just enough time to hop in and outrun the monster.

"Hey," Gozen called out, pointing ahead, just off the cliff, but Jin didn't see anything. The big man leaned forward and squinted. "It's an owl. Nia's owl!"

Jin closed his colorblind eye and squinted until he saw the white bird circling a fixed point. "Suzu must be just below it."

"We can't stop long," Gozen warned, "but we need to get them up that cliff somehow."

The two men silently pondered the situation as the road continued to resist their car.

Jin had only one idea. "I'm going to get them, so you need to drive."

Gozen lunged sideways and took control as Jin released the wheel, then crawled over and across the back seat.

"Good Lord," Gozen mumbled as he forced his thick leg over the center console. Jin waited in the back seat and saw the machine chuck a small boulder clean over the edge. Turbulence rattled Jin's bones and he pulled the grappling gun off his belt.

"This car was made for *children*," Gozen complained after he'd finally managed to wedge his body into the driver's seat. "Whatever you're planning, we're getting close."

Jin looked up and saw they were indeed approaching the point that Kola was still circling. He checked for the machine behind them and saw that they had managed to gain some distance. Just then, the machine's torso began to morph. While still running, the machine shifted its black panels until an opening formed, ejecting a single red devil towards them. It flew just on the edge of the cliff at twice the pace of either machine.. Jin's focus narrowed and he realized it must have spotted Kola and whoever waited below.

"Jin? Plan?" Gozen shouted as the bird approached.

With no time to explain his actions, Jin searched for good footing. Gozen looked in the mirror and saw the red streak screaming towards them. Jin stepped onto the passenger door and leaned forward, looking like a swimmer about to cliff dive.

"Jin?" Gozen asked, sensing Jin's insane intentions.

The red creature flew up beside them before suddenly diving below the cliff. Jin vaulted off the door like a madman. His body disappeared and Gozen yelled after him, "Jin!"

The phantom flew down and Jin fell just as quickly. With only seconds to act, he raised the grappling gun and fired right at the gliding red target. The harpoon whistled but shot right past, disappearing into a cloud of leaves. Jin braced for a miracle branch to break his fall and likely half the bones in his body. Instead, he felt the line begin to straighten out in the opposite direction. With only an instant to brace himself, Jin realized he'd anchored into something he had already flown past. Clicking the grappling to his belt, Jin felt the line choked by the pneumatic brake, overextending every limb on his body like a stretch toy. The phantom raced to the ground as Jin swung into a minefield of branches.

From below, Suzu and Chichi watched the cascading pair. She ignored Jin, who flailed uselessly somewhere in the trees. The phantom that had pursued them up the hill had stopped just shy of the light. Suzu gripped Chichimou tightly as the descending ghost flailed like a flying squirrel before easing into a perfect, upright landing.

"Stay behind me, Chichi."

On the cliff above, Gozen continued to push the C23 along the overgrown road. Ready to draw the monstrosity all the way to Chigou if needed, he watched in the mirror as it suddenly stopped. Gozen likewise hit the brakes but left the engine running hot. The metallic monster bent towards the cliff's edge and shifted its cluster of eyes to look below.

Emergency CE protocols resurrected themselves in Gozen's mind, driving him straight to the trunk to grab the rifle. Expertly crafted and needlessly heavy, it flashed more filigree than an antique tea set for twelve. Gozen pulled a few rounds from an equally extravagant ammunition box and loaded one into the rifle, shoving the rest in his pocket. The anchored beast hummed and, keeping a safe distance, Gozen ran up to the same ledge.

Steadying himself, he lined up the sights.

Blurring in and out of his vision, Gozen saw two young Ladies far below, facing a stark red shape. He blinked quickly, trying to discern shapes within the vivid patch of color that floated towards them. A thousand ghost stories were then validated as he got his first uninterrupted look at a living myth. Gozen's foot shifted, and a few pebbles took the forty-meter drop. He forced steady breaths through his lungs, fighting to keep the scope still.

Suzu glanced up as she heard the small rocks smack boulders on their way down. She spotted Gozen's hefty silhouette at the cliff's edge.

Jin finally freed the snare and grunted as he hit the ground. Suzu heard this, too, but kept all her focus on the ghost that approached, stalking them like the forest cat. She gripped her DaiLaunsu but kept it low as Chichimou stood behind her, clinging onto her shirt.

Gozen settled his aim on the creature that was displaying neither aggression nor any apparent desire to stop. Anxiety flooded his veins as he evaluated the scene. He wouldn't let the creature attack them, but he also knew better than to provoke a violent response. He checked Suzu again; she kept glancing back into the woods. Jin had yet to emerge.

Too many variables, he thought. He'd wait, holding the rifle's ornate grip as it grew slick in his still-sweating hands, until he couldn't wait anymore.

The creature finally slowed to a stop. Suzu prepared herself, ready to defend Chichi and fight, but something told her to stay still. She looked into the long black eye of the creature that stood two meters away, almost close enough to touch.

Gozen's hands shook as the target stood dangerously close to the girls. Images flashed from the last time he had pulled a trigger—fire burning through floors, children screaming. He kept them all in his sights.

Jin's silver hair caught the light, along with a sun-flare coming off the sword he wielded, twenty meters behind the creature. Suzu stared at him, shaking her head for him to stop. He didn't, inching forward instead with delirious, blood-red eyes and blood-caked skin.

The creature stared, and Suzu felt her heart about to beat out of her chest. It stood so close she could hear its sound, like gears in an old organ, humming up and down. The smell followed, bright and rich like a potter's shed. She stood like a child lost in wonder.

Jin continued his silent prowl behind them, his sword ready.

A bump then appeared in the creature's center, followed by a limb—thin and so deeply black it seemed to deny every color in existence. Sharp, gawky extensions unfolded from its wrist while the red surface closed once more around the arm, showing only the faintest line of a seam. It aimed one of its spikes and reached towards Suzu's chest. The girls squeezed each other's hands so hard they went numb. The creature's hum grew louder as the red skin began to pulse, like a speaker was powered on within. The sharp end of its limb then lifted to point right between Suzu's eyes.

Jin moved faster. His sweating hand ached as he gripped his sword.

The creature stayed in Gozen's crosshairs, but now Suzu's head was bobbing too close. His finger rested against the rifle's trigger.

The creature's vibrato dropped off into silence. Its sharp black finger moved down to Suzu's throat. She swallowed hard and watched as its arm shifted off-center, relocating its shoulder behind the red curtain. Unable to resist, she moved her arm aside as it reached down her pocket. A glow appeared as it reached in and pulled something out. In its dark claws lay the Toki her father had made for her. With little effort, it opened the glass face. The surface radiated far more brightly than ever before, taking on a brilliant blue hue that matched the color she'd seen glowing on the steam probe.

Jin and Gozen froze at the light embracing Suzu and the ghost. They both recognized the piece as the creature examined it, tracing its finger around contouring lines. The appraisal ended as it reached out to return the object to its owner. Releasing Chichi, Suzu reached up slowly with both hands to take it back when the creature suddenly grabbed her left wrist.

Gozen's finger tightened on the rifle. Jin lifted his sword and took one more step before finally spotting the other two phantoms that had been pursuing Chichi and Suzu. They crept up closer. Gozen's rifle moved over them as they materialized from the tree's shadow.

The creature prodded Suzu's aching, swollen hand, almost like a doctor ready to lance an infection. Then, like the prick of a pin, she felt it jab the center of her wound. Suzu winced, and Gozen found his mind and body battling to pull the trigger.

The creature then yanked her hand inside of its red shell. Immediately, she felt her hand locked in place by what felt like more fingers. A sensation washed over her trapped hand, like the sweat when a fever broke—somehow both hot and cold. Her hand tingled so intensely it ran up her arm and into her neck. The creature then released her as suddenly as it had grabbed her. She pulled back her suddenly restored hand, its skin glistening and looking reborn. Tingling warmth had replaced pain. She and the creature looked at each other as everyone watched them.

The red creature then backed away. Gozen spun around as the monstrous machine began its strange calliope song. The modular body realigned itself into a long shape—giant eye first—and started crawling down the cliff like a centipede. The humans could only watch. It slithered down the entire wall in one continuous movement and picked up the phantoms as it had before. The machine and its strange cargo disappeared into the forest, their existence fading back into legend.

The bright light of Suzu's Toki faded into a subtle glow. Jin stood dumbfounded. Chichimou's grip on the back of Suzu's jacket eased up as Suzu knelt before her. She looked into the little girl's eyes and saw what Gozen must have seen the first time he had seen her—frightened and alone in her old apartment, unaware of the glass stuck in her foot. She pulled Chichi's head to her chest and held it there, knowing better than anyone what the young girl now had to face.

o o o

Jin ran them back up the cliff on his grappling gun, one by one, as none of them had the energy to climb it or even walk around. Everyone moved as if they hadn't slept in three days. It wasn't until they all reached the car that someone asked about Victou. Suzu shook her head, glancing at Chichimou, but she had fallen asleep in Gozen's arms.

"Are you sure?" Gozen asked, his voice heavy.

Suzu felt little certainty of anything, but she couldn't forget Victou's body being dragged away and disappearing into the jungle. The scream still rang in her head. Gozen looked down at the suddenly orphaned girl—her doleful face half hidden—and his heart split in two. He laid her gently in the backseat and then grabbed the side of the car, fighting to keep it together; they still had to escape the forest.

"It's okay," Suzu said, leaning against her friend. "None of us have the energy to spare." She slid into the backseat next to Chichi.

Jin remained quiet as he slipped into the passenger seat. Gozen, who had insisted he felt well enough to drive, squeezed back into the driver's seat. He started the car, which rattled from the sticks stuck in its undercarriage.

The group headed back to civilization, the breeze brushing between them in the open cabin. The road slowly cleared along the way. Suzu noticed Jin looked like a medical student's book of injuries. His left hand was swaddled in a thick layer of gauze. He still held his retracted sword, which was crusted with even more blood than the rest of his body. The self-assured young man didn't say a word as the towering trees of Goraka passed by, and then, it finally dawned on her.

"You killed him, didn't you?" Suzu asked sharply.

The thought already sat like a stone in his head. He looked back at the young Lady who had obsessed over Kits's death since before they'd met. The words nearly stuck in his throat. "I did."

Suzu looked at his blank gaze as years of injustice, pain, and revenge vaporized into the wind. She had fantasized about killing Kits countless times, but she had never imagined someone else taking her retribution for themselves. She wanted to hate him. She *did* hate him. How could he steal that from her? Didn't he already have enough?

"Why?" she asked.

He understood the question. Jin knew what had happened, and there had even been virtue in his action, but he had killed a person and as grotesque as it was, he had taken something away from her at the same time. The idea of an explanation seemed utterly insignificant. Who would want to place the action of death onto another? The thought came, but he could not speak.

Suzu wanted an answer, but Jin's vacant gaze floated forward, out the window. With Chichimou nuzzled against her, Suzu turned and watched the trees passing by. She wanted to see Goraka as her parents would have: beautiful, powerful, dangerous, lovely, important, life-giving. Instead, she felt only grief during her final retreat from the dark, secretive forest.

Suzu's hand still tingled and her head felt fuzzy. She looked up to see if Kola followed them out and a flash of white appeared in the trees, but it wasn't Nia's owl.

Streaks of red, some of them braided, fell down around a soft face. A young Lady stood high up in the tree, beautiful and strong, the way Suzu had always remembered her.

They watched each other as the car drove off. She didn't turn even as the car finally passed out of the woods and back into the valley's open air. Memories fluttered in and out of Suzu's mind, faster than even the passing wildflowers of the open field. She thought of being saved, someone pulling her out of a dark abyss. She remembered life on a farm, her first laugh in a year, the love of a sister.

36
MEND

"Dila, did you not hear me when I asked you to get the door?"

"No. I mean, yes, I heard you," Dila answered.

"Very good, but tell me, my dear, why is the door still closed and you nowhere near it?" Lady Kyoumére asked from the first-floor hallway, reapplying a bandage to a skinned knee.

"Coming," Dila sang down the stairwell, accompanied by size fours tapping eighth notes. She skipped up to the front door and opened it, backing right up for a full look. "Hi, Lord Gozen."

Lady Kyoumére focused on the injury she was treating, but a smile bloomed on her face. "Thank you, Lady Dila."

"Chichimou!" Dila squeaked out as the small girl was revealed behind Gozen's leg, appearing surprised anyone remembered her name.

"Hi."

"I'm Dila, remember?"

Chichimou nodded.

"Hey, want some cold cream? I saved mine from last night; I ate too many cheesy bread bearings." Similar in size and shape to industrial ball bearings, the bread variety was filled with any assortment of ingredients, sweet or savory.

"Dila, dear?"

"Yes, Lady Kyoumére?"

"This is only because you did save yours from last night, but please eat your confection outside. I don't want half the children seeing you down here and begging me for an afternoon delicacy."

"Great!" Dila stepped up and offered Chichimou her hand. They snuck off towards the icebox like kitten burglars.

Lady Kyoumére raised the boy's bandaged knee as he sat on the stool. "This is why I suggest you mind when and where you decide to run." She set his knee down as he offered a humble nod. "And don't take that bandage off until I say. Not even a peek." Then, with a smile, she sent him away.

Despite the harrowing last few weeks, Gozen beamed as he offered his friend a hand. Lady K floated up with his assistance, then snapped the first aid kit shut.

"Do you think they're smoking some coffee to go with their cold cream?" Gozen asked.

Lady K's eyes narrowed. "I had considered teaching one or two of them, but that was before we had a *new* kitchen."

The smell of smoke and spice hit Gozen's nostrils as they entered, his eyes popping wide at the shimmering display. "You've kept the remodel up very well."

"No number of children could keep me from also maintaining this sanctuary," she smirked. They stayed on the opposite side of the kitchen as Chichi and Dila, working together to get some smoked coffee brewing. Their shoulders managed to bump together more than once.

"Are you still juggling more children than beds?" Gozen asked.

"Oh, yes."

"I was wondering if the Doulan orphanage had opened, as you seem restored to your usual elegant composure." Gozen smiled.

"It has not, but I have adjusted as needed. Also, I'm pleased to say, Lady Lucette has offered to assist at least once a week, even with the Academy taking up so much time—as it should," Lady K said as the water bubbled, then nodded towards Chichimou, who meticulously gathered the tools needed for outdoor cold cream. "How about this one? I heard she and her father were adjusting rather well to Kora Farm."

Although largely recovered, Gozen hadn't the energy to hide his pain at their failure to keep father and daughter together. Pensive eyes watched the young girl in a precious moment of joy. "I'm sorry, I thought I told you at the clinic," he sighed heavily. "They *did* adjust well. I felt hope for them, but in Goraka, I... I just couldn't save them both."

She softly touched the wound on his chest. "You certainly can't do more than risk your life." She waited until he had absorbed her words. "Lady Chichimou is always welcome here, of course. At least she can feed herself." They looked over at the girls just as a scoop of cold cream rolled down Dila's front.

Their shared laugh felt nice. Gozen rubbed the back of his neck as the smoker fired up. "Smells good. Is that a different kind of wood?"

"Yes," Lady K replied, impressed. "A young upper academy Lord—a classmate of Lucette's, I believe—has stopped by a few times. He's studying cross-level social development or something like that. He gifted me some exquisite smoker pellets that were apparently sourced from the actual Red Valley."

Gozen snorted. "Oh… well, that's certainly not true."

"I know, but I had no desire to disrupt the pleasure of delusional enlightenment. Wherever they're actually from, they do smell marvelous." She slowly poured their cups full. "So, I didn't hear you pull up—did you not park in the drive?"

Gozen sighed again. "I guess I didn't tell you about that either, I'm sorry."

"Well, you were on a few medications, if I recall."

"Correct. Unlike these smoker pellets, my precious Neko has been to Goraka. Unfortunately, it will be staying there."

"Oh, my dear, not your precious!" Her hand went over her mouth. "That was your *home!* Oh, I am so sorry."

"Yeah, so anyway, I'm driving a little Aya Motors U17 these days… used, of course." Gozen forced a wink.

"Can you even fit in one of those?"

"At least it's bigger than what Jin drives. I had to pry my body out that sporty little devil when we returned."

"And how is that young Lord? I should visit him. I still don't think I've properly thanked him for this culinary temple."

"I wouldn't worry about it." Gozen looked conflicted. "He'll be… okay. He's related to thirty doctors or something like that. He… uhm, he might lose a few fingers, though."

"That's horrible. And him, he's always designing and building things. That poor soul." Lady Kyoumére held her coffee without sipping.

"So, I think I'm going to be staying at Kora, semi-permanently."

"More semi-permanently than you already were?"

Gozen bobbed his head. "I don't have my truck and I'd like to keep an eye on things for a bit—keep an eye on that little one."

They looked back to Chichimou as she ran out of the kitchen with Dila. "You aren't worried about her being back there, with all that happened?"

"I am, and I think it'll be a little easier there than here."

"Why," Lady K smirked, "do you find ninety wild children *distracting?*"

They shared another much-needed laugh.

"Lady Clora will be pleased to have her there."

"Yes, of course. Oh, and what of poor Lord Kojo?" Lady Kyoumére asked.

"He just got back from the clinic today, I think, so I'll find out."

Lady K shook her head as she stared into the dark mirror of her coffee. "I know this city has never been as perfect as some believe, but attacking an earnest farmer, kidnapping one of these innocent little..." Tears sprung up and settled at the base of her eye.

A small stampede rattled through the hall until one little voice warned, "Shh, Lady Kyoumére is in there."

"I may be outnumbered," Lady Kyoumére said, straightening her back, "but I will give all I can to look after them." She looked lovingly at her friend. "And I am so thankful for you."

Now alone, they took a moment to share in the peace of hope, no matter how frail. As they basked in the warmth of coffee and the trust built over many years, time slipped by them unnoticed.

Chichimou then returned to the kitchen, mouth stained with cold cream. "Can Dila come visit the farm sometime?"

Gozen nodded before turning back to his dear friend. "I probably won't be around quite as much, but I assure you, I will certainly be around."

∘ ∘ ∘

Kora's drawbridge lowered, allowing the small truck access over the chilled, rushing water. Joushi waved before Legou squeezed his fingers close together, an emphatic gesture of smallness. Gozen shrugged his shoulders, snugly tucked into his compact box truck. The boys smiled as he drove young Lady Chichimou up to the farmhouse.

Clouds danced their whimsical marionettes' shadows across the farmland below. Chichi sat on her feet and watched through the passenger window. The farm looked as serene and delightful as she remembered it being while living here with her dad. She wished he could have stayed there. He had never smiled more than he did at the farm. Her eyes followed a utility vehicle bringing in a load of orange fruit piled into wooden crates.

Pulling around the central loop, Gozen stopped just in front of the house. He turned off the steam engine, which sounded weak compared to Neko's roar.

"You know, Chichimou, that man who took you, he isn't around anymore."

Her small hands folded in her lap. "Like my dad?"

It ached to admit, but he nodded. "I'm going to stay here a lot. I'll keep an eye on things—drive you into the city sometimes."

"To see Dila?" Her eyes lit up.

"Yes, and maybe we can bring Dila here sometime, like you mentioned."

Chichi smiled and suggested they could get Michelou's on the way. The idea sounded nice to Gozen, but he didn't have the heart to tell her that Michelou's was very much out of the way. She stared out of the window, smile disappearing like the sun behind a cloud.

Gozen reached to open the door, anxious to stretch, but Chichi stayed put. "Are you sure you're okay? Are you worried about anything? It's okay to ask."

"What about the man?"

Gozen rubbed his chin. "Well, like I said, he's gone for good."

"The other man," Chichimou spoke into the glass. "His dad."

"Uhm… do you mean his boss?"

Chichimou shrugged. "He was on the airship. I didn't like his face. He had spooky eyes."

Gozen offered a simple answer, the way a puzzle looks simple from the picture on the box. "He's never been here, and I don't think he'll ever come."

Chichimou turned, leaving the foggy ghost of her breath on the window. "How do you know?"

She heard a small grunt before he answered. "Because I met him a very long time ago, and this place is much too bright and sunny for him."

"He likes the dark?"

"I think he does."

Chichimou thought about it for a second, then gave Gozen a rather wistful look. She promptly opened her door and jumped down to the gravel drive. Gozen followed her in through the door of the farmhouse and announced their entrance. Clora came in with a cane but kneeled as quickly as she could to give Chichimou a hug.

"I didn't hear you drive up." Clora smiled, thankful that Chichi smiled back.

"Yeah, I had to say goodbye to Neko," Gozen confessed.

"Oh? I didn't imagine you'd ever sell such a great truck. And when did you find the time to…"

"I didn't sell it… I'll explain later." Gozen said quietly.

Clora looked out the front window. "That one's a bit… tight in the seat for you, isn't it?"

Gozen smiled while rubbing his back. "Now, *this* one hasn't eaten anything but cold cream today, so I think she might be needing something farm fresh."

"That's good, because my counter is resembling a mountain range of fruit. Why don't you run in there, Chichi, and grab something to chomp on?"

After checking with Gozen, Chichi immediately ventured into the kitchen for her fruit expedition. Gozen helped Clora up off the floor and placed her cane in her hand.

"Ah, thank you," she said, trying to hide the strain in her voice.

"You seem to be recovering quite well." Gozen guided them over to the dining room to sit.

"I'll be fine. Sore is all, really." They sat down, half watching Chichimou explore the range of berries and tree fruit. "It'll be nice to have you both back here, but I do hate to think of anyone having bad memories of this place."

"She seems to be handling it alright, but I'm afraid it just hasn't sunk in yet."

"Speaking of which, what are you doing out of the clinic so fast? Didn't you get *shot* not that long ago? I don't want you passing out on a tractor."

"Clora, please. I'm the toughest guy in the valley. Haven't you heard?"

"Ha, he finally admits it," Clora snickered.

"I am surprised *you're* not still at the clinic though."

"Hey, just because I'm not clickin' my heels like Lord Iron Chest doesn't mean…"

"Sorry, sorry," Gozen said. "I meant with Kojo. Is he doing okay?"

"Kojo? Okay? I wouldn't say that."

"Oh…" Gozen murmured, not quite sure of Clora's tone.

"He's *better* than he was before he fell."

"Really?"

Clora leaned back in her chair, throwing her voice to the living room and around the corner. "Kojo, my darling, we have a visitor."

After a few moments, the old farmer rolled into view. The sullen face Kojo had worn for over a year had been swapped out with a vivid expression of satisfaction. He sat in a wheelchair that looked more expensive than Gozen's lost truck.

"Well, look at this young man finally getting out of the clinic." Kojo wheeled into the dining room and took a spot by the table.

Gozen turned to Clora, who shrugged.

"Kojo, where did all this energy come from?" Gozen marveled. Turning to Clora, he whispered, "Is he still on some medication?"

"I'll skip the mystery and get right to it." Kojo held Clora's hand. "I woke up in that clinic and saw this young Lady's face and it just hit me, clear as the sky outside. No matter what trials we endure, no matter what condition this old body is in, I have more reasons than I need to appreciate every day I have. I got this farm—one that so many people rely on—and I got this Lady right here. Every morning it's like I get to open a gift, the most beautiful one a man could hope for."

The words sunk in and they all wiped away a sudden tear. Then Gozen cleared his throat. "That… that's one fancy-looking wheelchair for a no-nonsense man like you."

"I hear ya." Kojo tapped on the shining frame and various levers. "But… it was the only chair they offered. I thought it looked downright foolish, but I wasn't about to hop around on my butt, so I plopped down on this convoluted contraption, and I tell you Gozen, if this isn't the comfiest damn chair I've ever sat in, I'll eat my hat."

"Kojo," Clora scolded her husband, gesturing to little Chichimou in the kitchen.

"Oh, she's a city girl, she's heard worse." Nothing could bring his energy down. "But Gozen, this thing is height adjustable, you can tilt it, it's powered with this tiny steam engine…" he trailed off, losing track of the assorted buttons around the chair, then brightened again. "…Oh, and the boiler heats the seat," he finished with a wink.

Clora grinned. "Yeah, I think he's finally accepted retirement."

"Well, I don't know about that. We're hoping this chair isn't permanent but…" Kojo held a sobering breath, "…but you know what, either way, I'm a lucky man."

"Well, it's good to see you smile again," Gozen confessed.

"So, not to spoil the mood, but what about—" Kojo tapped his legs, "—you-know-who."

"You don't need to worry about him. He's gone," Gozen reassured them.

"You sure? You… took care of him?" Kojo asked.

"He's been taken care of," Gozen hedged. "I'll tell you this at least, I'm pretty sure it was the guy who paid for that fancy wheelchair."

Memory jabbed Kojo in the gut. The news felt like bitter justice, offering a little peace but no joy. "Well, I hope… I do hope Jin is okay. Hell of a thing to endure, I'd imagine."

Chichimou came in with the bottom of her shirt turned up like a basket and overflowing with fruit. They all reached in and helped her get the haul onto the dining table. Their mouths filled with the vibrant treats plucked right from the land. They talked and laughed for a long time, sharing the burden of their pain while basking in the joy of one another's company.

○ ○ ○

Jin sat alone on the sterile bed wearing a gown, accessorized with bandages and a few braces. Rubber tubes and steel pins branched out from his cocooned left hand, like a miniature engine running diagnostics. Food sat uneaten on a side table, beautifully plated but cold.

The peculiar tri-head screw he had gotten from Kits in Goraka rolled between the intact fingers of his right hand. He assumed it had belonged to those forest creatures. He understood now that they possessed a mastery of machinery, although the term *machinery* still felt insufficient. They seemed utterly inhuman, and yet he held in his hand an invention that had been independently conceived by both species—or so he theorized. The meandering thought eventually became tiresome and he put the artifact down.

Western mountains stood outside his window, soon to cast their vast shadows across Chigou. He tried to spot Kuitsu, the hidden paradise, seeming more and more like a fairy tale again. It hid behind one cloud or another, and he felt unsure of its precise location.

Music played over a single speaker in the corner of the room, some symphony Jin recognized but couldn't recall by name. It had a familiar, delicate tone that reminded him of the music his mother preferred. In the sky, he spotted a distant airship that made its final approach to Citadel Station—just in view, if he leaned a bit. He remembered taking trips with his mother and his sister, Pepa—and occasionally his father—and wondered if they ever considered visiting him in Chigou. Jin thought of writing his sister back. He had never thought of them as close, but he longed to see her again, more than anyone back home. His mother disliked writing letters and always mentioned so leading up to the valley's biggest holiday, Leimikou. It felt like an excuse wrapped in a complaint.

A family in the hall wheeled an older man past the open door. The four of them had sunny demeanors, especially for being in a place that collected the ill and dying. The old man glanced in Jin's room and gave him a nod—camaraderie amongst paper-gowned Lords. Jin smiled back as his sudden compatriot was rolled away.

He looked out the window again, seeing the vastness of a valley that never failed to remind citizens of their puny size. A cold draft blew in, easily bypassing the garment that was barely sturdier than gift wrap.

He remembered the strange statement Kits had made about Jin's father on the airship, right after he had shot Jin. The relationship between his father and Kits had been a small business arrangement set up by Lord Aya, but that had ended quickly over a year ago. Jin had never imagined Kits and his father sustaining their communication. Perhaps it had been more than a bluff—one more enigma to pack into his overextended brain.

Sitting in that sterile, utilitarian room, Jin realized a metamorphosis had occurred. The place of his childhood no longer seemed like home, but neither did Kora, the Tree House, or his new apartment. Longing and loneliness swelled inside him. He pulled the thin sheet up to his waist to keep his tears from getting on his fragile gown. Jin thought it would pass, but the tears streamed out until footsteps landed by his door.

"I'm…" He wiped his eyes and sniffed a few times. "I am fine and in no need of assistance. I apologize if I appeared otherwise, nurse."

"Well, you *are* in a clinic wearing a paper tablecloth made to look like a cocktail dress." Lucette's joking voice came through the cracked door.

"Oh, Lady Lucette." Jin covered himself more thoroughly with the sheet and straightened up. "I did not expect to see you here."

Lucette slipped into the room. "I didn't mean to make you

uncomfortable. Shall I join you and wrap a notebook around my waist?"

"Certainly not," Jin assured her, looking around his room. He indicated a plate of blashu crackers and nut butter. "May I offer you something?"

"I've been in a clinic before, so that would be a *no*." Lucette's golden hair was styled as intricately as usual, somehow unaffected by the red helmet she held under her arm. Jin spotted a paper envelope in her other hand, and Lucette caught his glance.

"Oh, I stopped by your place on the way and got your mail," she explained. "This was it, actually, but since I heard you were tied up—*tubed* up as it looks like—I thought I'd play dispatch for a day."

Jin took the letter with his good hand, which was adorned by a single bandage. He looked at the outside and simply held the envelope.

"I'm sorry, and here I am with two hands," Lucette offered.

The tears began to well up in his eyes again and he promptly wiped them on his medical bracelet. "No, thank you. It is from my sister. That is good. Thank you. I think I will open this later."

"Okay, okay," Lucette said, bouncing anxiously in place. "Are you sure this is a good time?"

Jin nodded.

"I guess the Red Valley isn't any easier the second time around, huh?" she asked softly.

Trying to answer, Jin held still before he felt a cry coming on, yet again. He almost tried to wipe his eyes with his left hand, briefly forgetting it was still tied to eight different machines.

"Okay, uhm…" Lucette slid a chair across the tile floor. "Hey, how about one of those crackers after all? They really are tempting me over there on that cold, steel tray."

"Of course," Jin managed with a wet nose. He handed the tray over to Lucette who promptly put down her helmet. She pinched a single cracker like a hand model and dipped it ever so daintily into the nut butter.

"Mmm, exquisite. Did we have these on that floating

establishment we visited awhile back?"

Jin's fuzzy mind took a moment to recall. "The Copper Torlúng. We should go there again sometime."

"Unquestionably. I've been saving up so I can treat us to a shared salad."

Jin huffed out a laugh. "Thank you. I enjoyed your joke about the crackers as well. That was finely said."

Lucette smirked. "Wow, a real breakthrough. You know, I think you're gonna be alright."

The sweet silence sobered as they both looked down at Jin's heavily damaged hand.

"Will it live?"

"I will be fine," Jin replied. "Although I am not sure how many fingers I will get to keep."

"*Sweet steamers*... I'm sorry." Lucette cringed with embarrassment. "I shouldn't joke about that."

"I will keep my hand," he reassured her, "or most of it, at least, which was a concern for a while. My uncle, Lord Henri Jastou, specializes in prosthetics and has developed some uncommonly intricate work. So, I should have a full set of fingers in the end, maybe just not all of my *original* fingers."

"You... you mean, magical machine fingers? Like, will they have baby steam engines in them?"

Jin smiled. "I believed he managed to utilize the body's own musculature and connective tissue with fine wires and sculpted finger segments. I read a paper on it—quite remarkable, my uncle."

"Yeah, blows *my* uncle right out of the boiler."

"Oh, what does he do?" Jin asked innocently before interpreting Lucette's sardonic stare. "Yes, you were an orphan. I retract my question."

"Retraction accepted." Lucette bowed her head. "So, does this uncle live here?"

"No, he resides back in Primichi. Most of my mother's side of the family are physicians. A few moved to Chigou, but most of them practice up north."

Lucette nodded. "So, you'd have to go back home to get your fingers of progress?"

Jin thought the question over. "I had already been thinking of returning. It… has been quite some time. I would like to see how my sister has progressed in her study of aviation." He set down the envelope. "But how has your schoolwork been progressing?"

"Great!" She perked up. "I love it, actually. It's cured my laziness and, honestly, I think all that learning is really fun. *And* I can break *three* beakers before I need to pay for one."

"I am glad to hear that. You deserve such a life-changing experience."

She sat back, hardly accustomed to people telling her she deserved anything. "Why, thank you, Lord Aya, and I will agree with you. Although I do need to intern somewhere and I have absolutely no connections whatsoever, so that is a current problem."

Jin spoke with the directness of an academy advisor. "Does it need to be based locally?"

Her first word was stretched out as she considered his question. "I… am not sure. I don't think so."

"You could intern with one of my family's companies. There is a clinical research center as well, which is in downtown Primichi. It offers an excellent view of the river," Jin said as casually as he could.

"A view of the river, you say?" Lucette smirked. "That is prettier than a brick wall."

Jin's gaze held as if waiting for an answer.

"Oh, so you're *seriously* serious?" Lucette asked.

"Yes, of course. You'd be welcome to live at our manor if you'd like."

"Oh?" Her eyebrow lifted. "I bet your family has some fancy couches."

"Yes, they are nice, too," Jin confirmed, unsure of the relevance. "But nearly the entire north wing is guest rooms, so you'd have your choice."

With her lips fused into an odd smile, Lucette rocked back and forth as the thought settled. She thought back to a frilly old dollhouse she had adored at the orphanage, imagining herself tiny and living there alone. "I will think that over, kind Lord. I will absolutely think that over. I might just need to let Suzu know she'll have a little more space for a few months—not that she has more than one outfit."

"Very well. I think that could be… quite congenial." Jin sat up straight again, his eyes brighter.

"I always aim to be congenial." Lucette tucked her hand under her chin. The two sat in their differing attire and felt the moment's spark settle down. Needing more than another cracker, Lucette continued. "I do require a trip home, however."

"How… how is she?"

"Suzu?" Lucette asked. "Oh, it's a daily discovery. But hey, you know me… I love surprises." She grabbed her helmet and walked to the door. "Next time, Lord Jin—crackers, *my* treat."

○ ○ ○

Lucette bounced into her apartment to find her roommate looking down at the street. Suzu welcomed her with a sulking hum that Lucette interpreted as some attempt at *hello*. With her stomach rumbling, Lucette pranced to the cold-storage box, finding it rather empty. "So, my smash noodles seemed to have escaped."

"I ate them," Suzu said, speaking to the window.

"Suzu, I smashed all my favorite leftovers into the greatest sauce of all time."

"Sorry, I was really hungry," Suzu apologized. "It was really good."

"Hmm, well, maybe I'll just run over to the bakery." Lucette jumped onto the efficiency couch by Suzu. "So, Lady Scout, how are *you* doing today?"

Another indecipherable hum.

"Wow, amazing. I just saw Jin at the clinic." Lucette casually offered.

That got Suzu's attention. "Really?"

"Yeah, it turns out he might be getting some metal fingers." She flared hers out.

"What?" Suzu jerked her head. "Like a claw?"

Lucette gestured to her already claw-like hand pose.

"…like he's not odd enough already," Suzu winced.

"Very compassionate. Anyhoo, I might be spending my internship up in Primichi… at his family's *mansion of progress*." She cupped her hands like a megaphone.

"You mean… *living* together?" Suzu looked alarmed.

"Oh," Lucette leaned back. "You know, he'll be in the east wing, I'll be in the north wing, our chefs will have different schedules. Honestly, we'll hardly see each other."

"I'm sure you'll enjoy that."

"You bet your brassy britches I will." She sat up again. "Actually, I have a hunch I'll feel like a squatter at first, then a princess, then a member of a cult... but I'm not even sure I can go."

Suzu turned back to the alley outside the window, hiding in the shadow of a taller building. "He killed Kits, you know."

The statement hung around the suddenly quiet room long enough for Lucette to know she didn't need to doubt it. She then slid over the cheap couch closer to her friend. "I bet that's given your tough little heart an awful lot to deal with."

Suzu quietly agreed.

"How are you feeling about it?" Lucette asked. "Relieved, confused… angry?"

"Yes."

Lucette rested her chin on the back of the couch. "Yeah, that's okay. I'm sure after so long…"

"Kits confessed... in an interrogation room," she said, letting out a humorless snicker. "Before Goraka. He killed my family because he was *ordered* to… by someone who is still breathing… lurking… hiding."

Lucette thought of the insane, fragmented stories she'd heard about what had happened in Goraka. It was hard to know what to think about any of it. "Just be sure to include Gozen *before* you do anything. Like, for example, running across a dam you expect to be blown sky high."

A cloud passed overhead, and the room grew dark. Suzu let out a harsh laugh. "I think those idiots at the dam finally believed me enough to investigate. Security is crazy now. But they'll never publicly admit they failed to notice someone filling up their fake lake with high explosives for months."

"That would damage their family-friendly image."

They sat for a few moments in silence.

"Well, if I do decide to intern up in Primichi, I'll miss you," Lucette said, her suddenly bashful voice directed into the couch cushion.

Suzu slumped down and looked over the room, which would be practically empty without Lucette there. Suzu had long since lost her family's apartment and had outgrown the orphanage. Lucette's apartment felt no less temporary than any other place she had tried to call home. "I'll miss you, too."

Lucette's stomach rumbled quite loudly. "Yes," she said talking to her tummy. "I know she stole your dinner, but the bakery stays open late so stop being rude." She stretched her arms out as she sat up. "Snack ya later, tough girl."

As she hopped over to get her helmet, Lucette's face then froze into a crooked shape. It confused Suzu until the fragmented memory finally sprang up. "Yes!"

"*This* sounds like something." Suzu inquired.

Lucette pursed her lips. "Oh, little lady. You remember a little while ago when I broke you out of prison with Darou? But before that, you got arrested and we were almost blown to bits on the dam? And before *that*, I drove up to Kora and showed you this almost-bomb that I found and had this old history professor look at it?"

Too exhausted to respond, Suzu simply didn't disagree.

"Well, I forgot one potentially important detail that, considering the following events, reasonably slipped my mind... until now."

Suzu waited. "Do you want me to guess?"

"No, I'm too hungry for that." Lucette waved her hand. "This historian, Lord Rouk KaDela—are you ready for this?—seems to have known *your father*. Claimed to remember him quite well."

The information wormed itself into Suzu's mind. "Okay. So, did he have a story or something?"

Lucette checked her memory banks. "I'm pretty sure he had one—a real one. Again, I had the bomb, so I was in a bit of a rush... but I think you should just hear it from him directly." She promptly scrambled for a pen and something to write on. "He's very polite... and he makes tea."

Suzu kept her arms to her side as Lucette walked over with the note. Everything she'd ever known about her father was from her own memories, which were fading a bit every day. She had never considered the possibility of a new experience with him, a glimpse of her father through someone else's eyes. Suzu wondered if she was prepared for what that humble little scrap of paper offered her.

"No rush, but if you left soon... I'm pretty sure he works late," Lucette offered with an encouraging grin.

37
FABLE

In the short time they had been together, Suzu had always cherished her family's Hotrail trips to downtown Chigou. The tunnel artwork from Doulan focused on the play of color more than anything. Vibrant, saturated lights were arranged in curving lines or alternating panels of color that—as her mother had explained—would move by so fast they'd appear as a single mixed color.

She had heard of the famous "living shapes" on the Upper Academy West train but had never seen them before now. She promptly understood their reputation. Sculpted tube lights strobed at the train's speed to produce a dancing image of lines, from one geometric shape to the next. They looked alive, magically floating along the wall to delight each passenger.

Suzu, exiting the station, stepped into a world bustling with creativity, nestled on the western edge of Chigou. A row of quaint cafés and shops stood across from a decorative gate of stone, brick, and metal. Grand buildings and landscaping sprawled out just beyond. Handsome intellectuals in dark pastels traversed the area with stacks of books or expensive cases. They moved freely without the towering structures of downtown forcing their path.

She fantasized about an alternate reality in which she was going to art and engineering classes, meeting friends on the beautiful campus her parents would make excuses to visit all the time. Instead of the black outfit Lucette had once described as "athletic-urban-moody-utilitarian-chic," she'd be wearing sophisticated clothes. She'd have friends. She'd go out late, impressing them with all the cafés she already knew from the gastronomes who had raised her. She'd tell her parents about all of it—well, most of it—and they'd be proud.

The bright sun warmed the courtyard as she walked across. It felt balanced and hopeful—like the life she should have experienced.

The campus's grand majesty intimidated as much as it inspired her. Suzu figured she'd get a similar sensation were she to visit Jin's homestead, whatever *that* opulent monstrosity looked like. She felt lost for the first twenty minutes, exasperated by the confident faces she saw on those barely older than herself; she didn't want to ask for directions.

She finally managed to solve the campus's wayfinding mystery. Looking repeatedly down at the note Lucette had written, she worked her way into the western corner of campus, where the landscaping went neglected around a fortress of knowledge. A half-obscured sign reading *Preservation Hall* poked out from behind a hedge. Lucette's note mentioned a specific room but suggested it could be in either *Bio - Chem Chamber* or *Preservation Hall.* She didn't understand how a room could be in two buildings, so she simply took the first turn she encountered.

Unlike most of the continent, which taught local and expanded history, citizens of the Naifin Valley concerned themselves solely with preserving their more recent accomplishments. A well-known speech by Lord Batsu had sparked the desire to *Remember our work but rely not on the limits set by those before us.* Those words were treated as prophecy, coming as they did from the very founder of the Naifin Valley, although a few rogue archeologists argued that an entire society had existed here before Lord Batsu had ever set foot in the hidden mountain utopia.

Unintentionally stepping on a weight-triggered grate, Suzu watched solid metals doors open, accompanied by the song of a steam engine hidden below. Preservation Hall's lobby sparkled with the accomplishments of Chigou's founders. Suzu squinted from the excessively polished displays and albino brass placards, which were brightly lit in all directions. An airship engine, cut right down the middle, sat in a glass case displaying its infinite formation of moving parts. Models of buildings and industrial machines surrounded anyone who entered, offering no escape as the automatic doors shut.

Suzu wondered if her father had known about this place. She easily imagined him pressing his nose to the glass, examining designs and having imaginary conversations with their creators. Her mom would have enjoyed it for a time before stealing away to look at flower beds and the art gallery. It dawned on Suzu that she couldn't hear another soul in the entire space.

The gallery alone would take half a day to experience fully and she had somewhere to be, so she made her way into a central hallway that appeared overcast by comparison. The air became stale and a few corners looked stained from age. She wondered if the place had been built for an earlier, smaller campus plan, perhaps one that had been buried under grander visions. She checked the note and a cracked sign on the wall, both pointing her below ground.

"*Mother Murdes*," she blurted out as she took her first step and laid a death-grip on the rail. With no warning, the stairs had begun moving her into darker depths. Although Suzu had ridden more than a few Up-rides, an umbrella term for any transit machine meant to be ridden while standing up, this one was activated by an initial step.

Upon swooping down a long curve and reaching the bottom floor, Suzu finally understood Lucette's references to two different buildings. The hallway stretched so far she almost couldn't make out the other end, which likely ended in another basement. The air thickened further, suiting the lack of any noticeable life. She checked the note once more and began to walk, steps echoing, counting down the numbers on each door as she passed.

The steady stream of identical doors nearly hypnotized her until she halted at a placard simply reading *KaDela*. She put her ear to the wood, detecting a hum that gradually revealed the irregular taps of office work. Suzu stood up straight and stared at the door, not quite sure what kept her from just walking in. She knocked before the anxious feeling in her gut could turn her around.

Fidgeting taps were replaced with the approach of footsteps. As the door opened, Suzu realized she was holding her breath. Dimly lit, the old Lord stood only half a head above her. She made out a bushy mustache and the fuzzy halo from his backlit sweater. His eyes hid behind thick-framed glasses, but his voice had a gentle growl. It was the voice she imagined a grandpa would have—not that she'd ever met hers.

"Hello, young Lady. May I help you?"

Suzu looked at her note and the placard again. "You're KaDela, right… Lord Rouk KaDela?"

"You were right the first time." He waited patiently for a moment before continuing. "Did you have a question?"

"Y… yes. Maybe a couple," Suzu explained.

"Oh. Please…" He stepped back, welcoming her with a vague wave of his hand, and led them to a desk. "I wasn't expecting anyone, but I can make some space." Folders and books began to disappear off the corner of a desk. He brushed some crumbs off and threw them into a small, overflowing trash can. "I just brewed some…" He paused and looked her up and down. "You probably don't drink smoked coffee, do you?"

"Black, if you don't mind," Suzu said casually.

"Black it is." KaDela then pulled up another chair and retrieved some mugs, checking to make sure they were clean. "I probably shouldn't be drinking smoked coffee. I'm trying to switch to tea." He moved a few things around. "It being late in the day, I think I'll take mine with a bit of sweet-cream. Are you sure you wouldn't like some?" He held up the same brand of sweet-cream her family always had in their chill-pantry.

"N… uh, yeah sure." Suzu gave in, feeling strangely comfortable as she sat in the well-worn chair.

KaDela stirred the liquids until they had blended into a warm, caramel color. He slid Suzu her drink and sat down, their faces softly lit by a pair of desk lamps. "Are you old enough to be a student, or am I so old now everyone looks younger than they are?"

Suzu swung her feet, dangling just above the ground, while

staring at the mug. It had a deceptively intricate pattern that captivated her more as she watched it. She seemed to remember a similar one growing up. "Oh, I'm just short, so everyone thinks I'm younger than I am."

"My apologies. So, what are you studying here?" KaDela asked.

"I'm not a student either… yet." Suzu had never considered pursuing upper academy until that day.

"Not a prerequisite for conversation in my office either way." He took a sip of his coffee and Suzu followed in turn. She inhaled the savory steam before sipping, just like her mother had always done. As her eyes adjusted to the dim light, she discovered the room was deceptively large, and she also realized that the only reason it appeared small was that it didn't *sound* big. Their voices failed to reach the outer walls because a dense arrangement of labeled items and shelves filled most of the space. It looked thoughtfully cluttered, as if KaDela had more heart than time for his work.

"You have a lot of stuff in your office," Suzu stated bluntly.

He smiled. "I do. They wouldn't give me an office *and* a proper storage room, so I'm doing my best to combine the two. I'm sure eventually I'll be sitting on a stack of paper and writing on top of a flat-file." His voice carried a calm self-assurance that had shed the posturing insecurities of a young academic. "I do find that old thing rather comfortable though. I'm sure it'll outlive me."

Suzu agreed, rocking in the seat and taking another sip; the sweet-cream did taste good. The mug warmed her hands. Questions still zipped around in her head but she ignored them for now, enjoying the slow pace of their conversation.

KaDela watched her for a second. "You're the second young Lady to visit me down here recently—two more than usual."

"Blonde girl, smells like sugar?" Suzu asked.

"Yes," KaDela said slowly, "and I think I know what you mean. Lucette—I believe her name was—was carrying this…" He shaped his hands into a sphere.

"Metal ball. We're roommates."

"Ah, interesting. Did Lord Koul manage to help her decipher its makeup?"

"Something very explosive."

"Interesting." KaDela took a long sip before raising an eyebrow. "And where is this object now?"

"That particular one?" She thought back. "She might still have it, I don't remember."

"I take it there were others?"

"There certainly were, but that's… a complicated story." Suzu began to fidget in her chair.

"Interesting. So, are you curious about studying here? Or did your roommate suggest I may be able to answer some other question for you?"

There were too many ways to ask it, so she just blurted it out. "She said you knew my dad—that you met him before."

"Perhaps, although I haven't even gotten *your* name yet."

"Suzu Komou."

He mouthed the family name to himself, needing little time to connect the dots. "That young Lord Komou, Carmin Komou…"

Suzu threw caution aside. "You *did* meet him."

"I did—a few meetings over a relatively short time. That probably would have been before you were born. Bright young man. I must say, I'm suddenly very curious about what he is working on."

Nausea swelled in her stomach. "He's dead."

The blunt statement pushed him back in his chair. "I am sorry to hear that, for you and your mother."

"She's dead, too."

"That is… truly unfortunate," he said gently. "I can only imagine how difficult that must have been. For what it's worth, I am glad that such a thoughtful and ambitious young Lord can continue on—in a way—through his daughter."

"My mother was great, too," she said, choking back tears.

"I have no doubt." The aged professor let Suzu catch her breath before moving on. "Did your father ever tell you the story of his expedition?"

She wiped her nose on her sleeve. "What expedition?"

"Interesting. I suppose then I may offer you what few memories

I have of your father."

Suzu's fingers tucked under her legs and gripped onto the seat.

KaDela needed only a few seconds to corral the old memories into narrative order. "He requested my discretion upfront, but not in any threatening way. I was younger then, but had already developed a reputation for my archeological work in the Naifin Valley, for the few people concerned with such things. To most people in the Valley, nothing had existed here before Jean Batsu and his band of futurists had set eyes on it. So, your father's request was an unusual one."

"Did he ask about Goraka?" Suzu leaned forward.

"Yes, he most certainly did. On rare occasions I'll have someone ask about the Red Valley at the tail-end of a more serious inquiry—sensational curiosities, nothing more, so I don't waste my time. Your father, however, spoke with much candor, and I never once doubted his intentions. He worked as an energy engineer for Kasic, if I remember."

Suzu nodded briskly, eager to hear more.

"He came with another man, a Lord… Caton, I believe. They were planning an expedition into Goraka, which certainly got my attention, but despite my personal curiosity, I was forced by my professional responsibility to recommend they not go. Legalities settled, we then started the real conversation.

"It revolved around your father's theory that the valley sits on a large bed of thermic energy, with achievable access residing lower in the southern forest. I had come across a few studies of Goraka's dramatic temperature difference, observations of a hot spring, and even one about a boiling lake supposedly sitting at the very bottom. Studies of this kind, however, were always discarded as frivolous grasps for attention, as they had never been accompanied by any evidence. Yet your father soaked in every account I could offer— any information that would help him harness the valley's 'cleanest, most powerful energy source.' I remember him saying those exact words a few times."

"He never quit working on it," Suzu marveled, "even when nobody believed in him… nobody besides us." The images flashed in her head. She saw what he must have seen—the evidence that no one would believe. "So, he went… he *saw* it down there."

KaDela waited for further explanation, eventually asking, "Saw what, exactly?"

"The device… that glowing…" She reached in her pocket and pulled out the Toki that had radiated light not long ago. She looked over to the coffee smoker, smoke and steam still seeping out. Getting out of the old chair, she stepped up to the machine and placed the Toki by the warm vapors. The face of the Toki began to glow softly, a feeble light compared to its shine while near the probe in Goraka.

"That's an interesting one," KaDela observed.

"Not as interesting as who touched it last," she muttered, remembering the black fingers of a phantom.

"Did your father give that to you?"

"He made it." She sat back down, cradling the Toki in her hand as its light faded.

"Impressive. I'm not surprised—he seemed very bright, even in the short time I spent with him."

It felt good to hear but she already knew that. "That other man, the one you remember…"

"Lord Caton? If I were to guess, he probably paid for that expedition. Your father didn't seem overly concerned with him, aside from glancing back to get his approval a few times."

"But why? Who was he?"

KaDela shook his head. "I wish there were more I could tell you. Again, your father did nearly all the talking. He said they planned on being down there just a few days, would search for thermal leaks and then return. We did discuss the potential dangers of Goraka. Your father was a rare individual, eager to enter Goraka, yet full of caution. I avoided a few specifics that most people would laugh off, but he seemed to understand what I hinted at."

"The red ones who live in the forest." Suzu felt no need for vague metaphors.

KaDela smiled, unaccustomed to anyone speaking of the matter so blatantly or so seriously. "Yes, the ghosts of Goraka."

"They're not ghosts," she cut in sharply.

"You seem quite convinced," he replied.

"If I'd had a camera with me, I'd be showing you the photographs."

KaDela didn't look like the type to take such improbable statements at face value, but Suzu noticed that he appeared to mull it over with consideration. "Quite interesting. I think we might need to meet again sometime."

She was fine with saving *that* story for another day. "What else happened? What else did they talk about?"

"Perhaps I could recall some inconsequential details, but that essentially sums up the event."

"My father..." She thought of his face, struggling to read the faded memory. "Did you like him?"

The simplicity of her question seemed to strike him. "I did. I wanted to speak with him again, and not just about the expedition. He seemed like an astute man... a thoughtful man—the kind you hope to work with. It must have been quite a loss you endured, quite a loss indeed."

Suzu didn't want to cry again, but her broken heart was stronger than her resilience today. Her body shook and she hid her eyes. She needed her father back for so many reasons. How would the pain ever go away if he never came back?

"The more we share with someone, the more we feel their loss. That can be a painful part of being loved." He spoke as someone who seemed to know it all too well. Wiping his own eyes, KaDela stood up and grabbed the coffee pot to warm up the mug. "You can take that with you. Your father liked the design."

She looked up in disbelief. "Really?"

"Funny thing to remember, but I tend to remember a great deal. It is a fascinating design, but I've seen it plenty of times in twenty years. Now it's your turn." KaDela turned off the coffee smoker but stopped just short of the light.

"You know, I do remember one more thing that man, Lord Caton, said, an odd little comment I dismissed in the moment." He mused over the recollection. "But it was so odd, maybe it's not worth…"

"What'd he say?" Suzu asked, sniffing her runny nose.

"I remember having had a very difficult time placing that man's age. He seemed plenty bright and fit, but something about him read old… very old, even older than I am now."

"Yeah?" Suzu leaned forward.

"Normally, I don't give such superficialities much more than a moment's concern, but I found it very distracting. Sounds quite silly, saying it aloud."

"No, it doesn't. What did he say?"

He thought harder, wanting to be accurate. "I uncovered a report while in Primichi. Not the original, mind you, but I managed to find a copy. It's not old for an archeological finding, but for this progress-obsessed society, it practically marks the dawn of existence."

She imagined herself sitting next to her father, their ears sharply tuned. "What was it?"

"The report is unsigned, although as a best guess, I would ascribe it to Jean Batsu himself. I am not aware of any other written reference to the events mentioned. It wasn't filed in a manner consistent with his early documents. The report's singularity puts its validity into question, considering how sensational it sounds."

"What?" She wondered why he was talking so slowly.

"It recalls an expedition to the southern end of the valley by a man and two brothers; this would have been soon after they arrived over the mountains. It mentions other expeditions to all cardinal directions, but those reports only mentioned a few material findings. The three men who voyaged into the south were expected back in roughly a week, but only one returned, clearly traumatized."

"I've heard of this. It was one of the last stories my dad told me. He said they ran into something *red*, but that's all anyone knew of what happened."

"Ah, yes. I consider *that* word-of-mouth variation to be the genesis of all Naifin ghost stories, but as more colorful tales have taken its place, it has widely been forgotten."

"But the report—what happened? I mean, I can imagine..."

"The document contains several updates; it seems to have taken quite some time for the returning man—a Lord Martouk—to manage a complete brief. He claimed they found beings living in the southern forest, wholly red, like someone standing under a red blanket."

"Floating on the ground," she recalled.

"Certainly. It read like any number of children's stories now, but this is the earliest written account, by many years, of an actual sighting. One of these forest beings killed an explorer. Lord Martouk didn't see it, but he recalled the young brother being covered with blood. It's the *end* of the account, however, where things veer away from popular folklore. It speaks of machines, black and somewhat organic in appearance, puffing out steam like an engine. It essentially declares the existence of a previously unknown, intelligent species, arguably, more technologically advanced than even Lord Batsu and his pilgrims. So, if it were true, one can imagine why the information was suppressed."

"And you told my dad?" Suzu asked.

"He seemed like someone who would value that particular report, especially considering what he planned on doing."

As if stumbling out of a dark forest, the name suddenly emerged into clarity. "But the other man, the Lord Caton guy." Suzu thought back to the man Kits had mentioned in the interrogation room, a man he feared. "He said something?" She ached for something else, anything else, pointing to the man who had ordered her parents' deaths.

"Yes, very interesting," KaDela recalled. "He smiled. I remember that clearly, as he hadn't yet, up to that point. I expected some condescending dismissal about grown men sharing ghost stories, but no. Lord Caton said, 'Batsu looked so surprised that only one returned, but the real surprise was that *any* of them came back.'"

"Yeah..." Suzu thought hard. "I guess that's kind of odd."

"At first, it felt like a poor attempt at humor, but he mentioned Lord Batsu's reaction as if from personal memory. Like I mentioned earlier, the report gave no mention of Lord Batsu specifically, nor any idiosyncratic critique by the author. Considering the subject, it was a rather dry report."

"Right..." Suzu considered, "but..."

"But he would have been well over a hundred years old at the time I met him, if he had truly been there during the events of the report."

It sounded like pure fiction, but so did many of the events from the past few weeks. "But you don't think he was *really* that old?"

KaDela laughed. "It's utterly improbable, but I had been distracted by the ambiguity of his age long before that comment slipped out."

"So, you *do* think he was that old." Suzu's desperate mind was ready to accept nearly any impossibility.

"I briefly considered it at the time but dismissed it. I felt embarrassed. I didn't mention it to anyone else and certainly not to any colleagues."

Suzu thought of Nia, haunting her so strongly she had even appeared in a tree at the edge of Goraka, watching like a red-haired angel. She hadn't told anyone that story, either. "What about now?"

"Oh, I am often driven by my curiosities, if not by my imagination, but I tend to describe myself as a man of science and reason. I had no reason to believe someone who witnessed the tragic return of Lord Martouk—not to mention the discovery of the valley itself—would be alive to tell me about it. But then..." His voice trailed off, distracted by another thought.

"But then *what?*" Suzu asked, almost falling off her seat.

KaDela shook his head. "Then I met one of the brothers, the one who *didn't* die on that first expedition into the heart of Goraka."

SUNSET TEA

INGREDIENTS

<u>First Steep</u>
10 oz. water
4 gray spice pods (smashed)
1 coin of hot root
A few bitter seeds
1 t. blashu honey

<u>Second Steep</u>
1 T.+ dark tea

<u>Stone Ground</u>
1/2 t. monnican spice
1/2 t. red dried field flowers

<u>Topper</u>
3 T. full cream
2 t. mimi juice reduced (syrup)

Bring water to a simmer.

Add all of the *First Steep* ingredients. Allow ingredients to simmer for at least three minutes, but you may steep longer for a stronger flavor.

Remove the mixture from heat and add *Second Steep* ingredient.

Steep for 3 to 4 minutes.

Strain tea into a porcelain mug.

Gently stir in *Stone Ground* ingredients, forming a gentle swirl, but not fully homogenizing into the tea.

For the *Topper,* whip full cream until puffed. Fill a spoon with a soft pillow and drizzle mimi reduction on top. Allow mimi reduction to seep for a few seconds, then invert the pillow gently on the surface of the tea.

Serve immediately.

Read all of the books in the
Valley Of Progress series written by
Cory Sheldon

· The Murde Mountains ·
· Chigou ·
· The Red Valley ·
· Goraka ·

Cory Sheldon grew up between the Cuyahoga Valley National Park and Akron, Ohio (an industrial curiosity, formerly the nation's fastest growing city). After graduating with an industrial design degree, he spent several years designing tires, directing films, and creating a movie theater. While teaching film and design at a local college, he decided to write his first novel, which turned into his first series: Valley of Progress.

Learn more about Valley of Progress online

MORE BOOKS · BLUEPRINTS · ADVERTISEMENTS
READING MUSIC · ARTWORK · MAPS & MORE

valleyofprogress.com